My Sister's Continent

a novel

by
gina frangello

chiasmus press
PORTLAND

Chiasmus Press

www.chiasmuspress.com
press@chiasmusmedia.net

PRODUCED AND PRINTED IN THE UNITED STATES OF AMERICA
ISBN: 0-9703212-9-5

cover design: Lidia Yuknavitch
cover photography: Robin Hann
layout design: Matthew Warren

"*My Sister's Continent* is a slow burn that slices deep beneath the skin. This book agitated me as I read it; infiltrated my sleep, haunted my dreams; it clings to me still, long after having finished it. With great finesse, Frangello lets her story grow—lusciously, seductively, disturbingly—to a truly unsettling crescendo. In this intimate portrait of a family, of two contentious, enmeshed sisters, we learn what drives their sexuality, morality, self-perceptions. But as is true of the best fiction, that which we feel we are watching from a safe distance grows beyond the bounds of the story and, without our notice, unwraps us with its insights, implicating us and laying bare our own desires."

—Ian Chorão,
Bruiser

"In this brave novel, Gina Frangello's narrative about a Chicago family transcends desires, fears, fantasies and acts that bleed into each other. With mastery and integrity, wit and intelligence, she shows the coil and recoil of extreme pain in body and heart. Frangello exposes mysteries of the human contradiction to the last knot."

—Rose Rappoport Moss,
The Family Reunion (short-listed National Book Award)

"In *My Sister's Continent* Gina Frangello's characters talk postmodern trash, the ids of Kirby and Kendra battling the psychological landscape of sex and siblings and turning Freudian theory on its head. The sharp prose here will sting you like a slap. This is an edgy, compelling, brightly dark first novel that I couldn't put down."

—Lisa Glatt,
A Girl Becomes A Comma Like That and *The Apple's Bruise*

"*My Sister's Continent* is one beautiful kick in the teeth: deftly written, aggressively sharp, compulsively hard-to-resist, this novel limns the shadow world of secret and not-so-secret desire, exposing the dangerous, knotty ends of impulse and longing. Gina Frangello's wonderfully addictive prose radiates with real heat."

—Joe Meno,
How the Hula Girls Sings and *Hairstyles of the Damned*

"In *My Sister's Continent*, Gina Frangello has added unusual and compelling insights into feminist "hot button" topics—bulimia, incest, AIDS—steering them off well-worn tracks and into new, sometimes treacherous territory."

—Cris Mazza,
Is It Sexual Harrassment Yet? and *Disability*

"In this reworking of Freud's famous case study, a modern-day Dora exacts her revenge, plunging the analyst-reader into a phantasmagoria of neurosis, psychosis and hysteria which defies resolution or cure. A chilling post-mortem of the Freudian Century."

—Alex Shakar,
The Savage Girl

Acknowledgments:

In the late 1990s, I created and taught a class called "The Hysterics in Literature" in which we read the infamous Freud case study of "Dora," *Fragment of an Analysis of a Case of Hysteria*, as our introductory text. In reading that study "like a novel," I first recognized the many parallels between the families in the case—the euphemistically labeled "B's" and "K's"—and two families I had been writing about for several years in a series of short stories, the Brauns and the Kelseys. Once this connection was made, I was compelled to explore the parallels more deeply; this novel is the result. In attempting to create a dialogue between classic (patriarchal) psychoanalytic theory versus the "repressed memory" theories that reached a fevered pitch of popularity in the 1990s, I owe as much to the feminist revisionists and theorists who refuted Freud (some of whom had already resuscitated Dora in their work), as to the father of psychoanalysis himself.

This novel also owes much to the encouragement and feedback of many *living* people. They include, in some rough chronological order:

Tom Johnson, former writing mentor turned miners' union activist, and Stacy Bierlein and Amy Davis, editors extraordinaire of the short-lived but luminous literary journal *Fish Stories*, all of whom believed in these characters long before they ever landed in this particular text.

My friends in the Program for Writers at the University of Illinois-Chicago, in particular the excellent writers Charles (C.W.) Cannon, Alex Shakar, Lisa Stolley, Gene Wildman, and especially Cris Mazza, who not only led the workshop where this novel began, but pushed me to get off my butt and finally send it to Chiasmus—thank you Cris!

I would have gone insane without my writing groups—first the inordinately talented and fascinating members of "The Nauman Circle," and more recently the small group of women who sustain my work and continue to impress me with their own: Zoe Zolbrod, Laura Ruby, Cecelia Downs and Karen Schreck.

To the staff of *Other Voices* magazine/OV Books, especially founding editor Lois Hauselman and current Assistant Editor JoAnne Ruvoli, who have many times had to cope with my self-imposed leaves of absence while I was manically working on my own writing, and who always held down the fort with grace and gusto.

My husband David, who has a Ph.D. in space physics, by all rights could claim no interest in contemporary fiction— yet he has read this novel in its various incarnations at least a dozen times, and has been my most tireless and wise critic and advisor, because despite not being a writer, he understands these characters as well as I do. And I would like to thank my twin daughters in advance for their future patience in the face of inevitable questions about whether they were the inspiration for the twins in this novel, which was actually written before they were even born!

As the editor of a nonprofit mag, I have made a career of hitting people up for favors, but no one could surpass the tireless efforts of Allison Parker and Kathryn Kosmeja, copy-editing goddesses who made this project their own grammatical baby.

A huge thanks to the Chiasmus gang for their faith in independent publishing *and* in my work. Every writer should be lucky enough to have an editor like Lidia Yuknavitch, whose uncompromising artistic integrity puts me to shame in a good way.

Finally, last but not at all least, I would like to thank my former literary agent and creative collaborator Bill Clegg, a fiercely intelligent advocate, and the very kind of complicated, interesting human being/reader we all hold in our minds as we write. His insights shaped this novel enormously.

for David

Third Dream

Victims and torturers alike recall their earliest
youth in the same way.

—Sigmund Freud,
Origins of Psychoanalysis

Susan Friedland, M.D.
333 North Michigan Avenue, suite 2900
Chicago, Illinois 60610

SUSAN:

I never expected to be the subject of a case study. Before receiving your manuscript, with a crisp release form on top for me to sign, I'd done my best to forget what a disaster my time in therapy was. But though I told half-truths in our sessions, and you never met Kendra, your years playing shrink to our father apparently gave you enough material (ammunition) to fill "my" chapter with neat diagnostic labels for both my twin and me. Funny, some things never change, huh?

Somewhere, under all the lies and analysis, there is a "true story." It's not the skewed version my father clings to and you wrote down. It's nothing I could have told you either, back when you knew more about my family than I—remember the pathetic way I used to beg for clues? Yeah, *Confidentiality Ruined My Life*, how's that for the title of your book instead of *Hysteria in the New Millennium*? If you'd opened your mouth sooner, chosen ethics over confidentiality, Kendra might still be here. Then again, you always saw her motives in black and white; you hoped to wash her craziness off my thin skin and "cure" me. Well, I will not let you document me without her side being told—not at any cost.

Freud, you said, called female sexuality the "dark continent" of human psychology. Allow me to shed a little light, to tell truths I hid in therapy—and Kendra's truth during those same ten months, before I lost her. The easiest thing would be to copy her journals word for word, but because she'd never consent to your poking around inside her head, I've told her story in my words, not hers, protecting her that much at least.

2

To speak for her is to tread on dangerous ground, confronting secrets that proved too heavy for her, always the braver twin. How can I bear them? What she omitted I have imagined—as I have thousands of times since she disappeared, as I will continue to do—hoping to construct from the rubble of her clues and my own subconscious a version more whole than the divergent realities we each clung to that final year.

Susan, it's in your hands now whether or not to send your book to press. Here is my signed release form—but with it, my rewrite of your case study: *our* version. You choose.

KIRBY

Analysis

There is never any danger of corrupting an inexperienced girl. For where there is no knowledge of sexual processes even in the unconscious, no hysterical symptom will arise; and where hysteria is found there can no longer be any question of "innocence of mind . . ."

—Sigmund Freud,
Fragment of an Analysis of a Case of Hysteria

When Our Lips Speak As Four

PEOPLE ARE ALWAYS trying to work out a way to prove they aren't alone in this world. My junior year of college, I was required to read the works of a certain group of French feminist theorists who, like most French intellectuals, were super-humanly horny and therefore fun in a sexy-librarian kind of way. At least until one of their rank declared—not without a certain irony, yet with the kind of deadly earnestness no one outside the feminist camp has ever been able to muster—that women are basically dual in nature, due to the fact that our vaginal lips (two, *mais oui*) are constantly rubbing together. In communion, if you will. The idea of individual identity, under this two-lips plan, would be outdated; the notion of a unified, singular self, counter-revolutionary. A tool of the patriarchy, meant to keep women down.

Though at the moment I read these words I was an eager French major equipped with unshaven Euro armpits and flowing chiffon scarves of every pattern imaginable, I knew that this vaginal lip communing business could mean nothing but bad news for me. After a lifetime of being an identical twin, I was now expected to swallow that there were not just two of me, but *four*, and that the individuality I'd longed for all my life was nothing more than the passé mythology of a dying "phallocratic order." I promptly changed my major to psychology, where thinking you are more than one person will get you a heavy dose of Thorazine. My sister (for reasons completely unrelated), simultaneously left her dance program at Julliard to join the New York City Ballet, where the applause she would get on stage would be all hers, would have nothing to do with the two (or four) of us. The differences in us were obvious even then: I wanted to be integrated, whole. Kendra wanted to be a star.

Let me be clear: identical twins are mutants. Sure, fraternal twins may be the result of especially Darwinian sperm and egg, but we, on the other hand, are a mistake. A split, an error. Clones by accident. Two sets of experience enacted on the same genetics—a psych experiment in the making. A life lived twice, but *at once*, without what might otherwise be an enviable ability to learn from the other's mistakes. Because in the end, lips and genes aside, isolation prevails. If she got slapped, I did not feel it. If she cried, I came no closer to understanding grief.

Not that she ever cried.

I know, I know: if I'm going to do this, I'm going to have to make my examples more convincing. But how do I tell the story of a life I've shared since inside the womb? How do I tell the story of a life I've never shared, can never share, that is outside my own experience, wrapped in shatterproof glass and secrets that have everything to do with me? Will inaccuracy be held against me? My past remains tangled up in itself like damp sheets after a night of sleepless thrashing, only to greet daylight with hours unaccounted for.

Like most siblings, Kendra and I went to school, took family vacations. We separated when she went away to New York while I remained behind, close to our parents, whose sole attention was finally mine. Had she never moved back to Chicago at all (as was her intent), everything would have turned out differently. She *did* return, and we welcomed her, a prodigal daughter who, as always, would frighten us a bit but make our lives more interesting. My father, mother, and I, who had always formed a tentative union against her impropriety. *Her impropriety*. Mild by most standards: she was neither junkie nor criminal—not even prone to interracial dating or homosexuality. We were a tame family, and her small-scale rebellions, such as they had been, were enough to keep us awed and ill at ease. We worshipped her, and resented one another for it. Or do I misremember everything? You had known us, some of us, for a decade. No doubt there were demons to which you became privy that even now I cannot glean.

6

The storm that had been brewing in my family for that entire decade, though, did not officially hit until the November of my twenty-second year. The world was approaching a millennium. Nuclear weapons were becoming popular again. America had divided along lines of those who believed Bill Clinton the devil, and those who thought the devil to be Kenneth Starr. In a recently gentrified area of Chicago, in a newly constructed loft, I was living with my longtime boyfriend, Aris. Aris and I were getting married. Everyone was happy about the engagement. Everyone likes weddings, particularly when they are expected. My engagement ring was quite big. Aris made a good living considering his age, which was twenty-six, but the ring was a family heirloom, so neither of us was responsible for its grandeur. Since getting the ring, I had taken to polishing my nails. They were short and stubby, but looked reasonably nice if I didn't paint all the way to the sides—just a slash of red to elongate. I'd learned the trick from my mother, who despite her devotion to God, always managed to know such worldly details. Because my sister lived far away, in a universe where the ghost of Balanchine was the only parent a ballerina required, I was often able to receive the full brunt of my mother's considerable wisdom.

Kendra did not approve of my engagement. She found me, I assumed, a pathetic sell-out to some lofty, unspecified goal that marriage at an early age would surely thwart. Luckily, nobody much cared what she thought, since she rarely came home, and the fanatical rigor of her life, with its accompanying dismissal of love as a lower art form, made us squirm. All we required was that, come the following October, she dutifully don a maid of honor's dress that would not outshine my restored, Victorian wedding gown, and give a well-mannered toast before getting sloshed. Then she'd be free to seduce a groomsman or glare at my new husband as she chose.

First, however, before my father would fork over the requisite miniature fortune for my century-old dress, he insisted I make an appointment with his former psychiatrist (that'd be you) about the matter of my diarrhea. Mere vomiting he might have understood: we all have delicate stomachs in my family, and somebody or other was always throwing up in the bathroom, the car, along the side of the road. Even my mother began to suffer from nausea the longer she was exposed to my father's lineage, as if having borne my sister and me was enough to transmit our shortcomings into her purer blood. But diarrhea was another thing entirely. Vomit is bad, but shit transcends all boundaries of good taste.

I was not surprised to find my father had a lady shrink; with few exceptions my father neither liked nor trusted men. I *was* surprised to realize that, in the ten years since he'd been your client, he had always faithfully referred to you as "Dr. Friedland," never "she"—as though to reveal your gender would cheapen everything. Despite my own relief at your chromosomes, I found the likelihood that you could cure my irritable bowel, which three medical specialists had been unable to master, scanty to say the least; the likelihood of your giving me some kind of interesting drug, however, titillatingly high. When planning a wedding, one should employ any distractions available. Clearly a woman psychiatrist would better understand how it produced a great deal of stress being so young and having such a big diamond and a dull temp job and a very nice loft that did not at all match my taste in décor. Yes, *Kirby must make an appointment ASAP*, my father, my mother, and Aris agreed.

On the phone, you had a pleasant voice. Because no one in my family possessed what could be described as a pleasant demeanor, I had never trusted nice people, but I felt reasonably placated by the belief that you were only faking it. I had this talent myself (it was one of my few skills Kendra had not long since usurped). As you spoke, I began to calculate my future polite lies, and those you would tell back, until déjà vu and a certainty of forthcoming Valium caused a warm glow to spread over me. I made the appointment happily because my dress was going to be breathtaking, and my father would pay for it if I consented to speak about my excrements to a total stranger. Unlike my sister, I was good at being dutiful when the occasion called for it.

Unfortunately, the only time slot I could wrangle also happened to be the Friday Kendra was arriving to spend Thanksgiving week with the family. A visit of such length was rare, all the more because NYCB was celebrating a fiftieth anniversary season, and Kendra had been on tour nonstop. Touring exceeded even the usual chaos of winter season, or what our non-balletomane father dubbed "Ball-breaker season," in glib honor of *The Nutcracker*. This time, however,

Kendra informed me exactly two days before her arrival that her ticket to Chicago was one-way; that our parents did not expect her until Monday (and I was to keep my mouth shut); that she had recently undergone back surgery on a herniated disc; and that her life as a ballerina was over.

Or so went the punch line. As was always the case with my sister, the whole story was more hidden and warped. Her surgery had actually taken place in September, when we'd thought her in California performing *Agon*. Since, she'd pursued every path imaginable to get back in form—from the Company's resident physical therapist to chiropractors to Chinese herbs. No use. Though her injury would go undetected in civilian life, less than seventy percent of her former flexibility was restored. She could not perform her solos—certainly she would never make principal. The Company might have kept an innocuous place for her in the corps, but Kendra could not live in a world where the only direction was backward. She quit. In the springtime of her career, her departure sent barely a ripple through the dance world. She had joined the Company late due to her "misguided" stint at Julliard (college had been our father's imperative), and had danced professionally for a mere three years, only a year of which outside the corps. Despite recent, heady comparisons to Gelsey Kirkland (they were exactly the same size) and our childhood idol Darci Kistler, rows of aspiring stars now pushed up behind to take her place. "It's like I never existed," she said, and I couldn't comprehend; I'd always believed her glory preordained, inevitable. "They're rehearsing a new Dewdrop. Suddenly I have nothing in common with anyone I've spent the past three years of my life with. The past *thirteen* years. Every day I wake up and promise myself I'll go on interviews, but this is all I know how to do."

True. Like a 1950's bride moving from her father's home to her husband's, Kendra had progressed from our first dance school in Evanston, Illinois, to Ruth Page in Chicago, then to summers at The School of American Ballet, pre-Julliard. My sister had never held a normal job. Now she owed nine hundred and fifty dollars rent on her tiny studio. Her name was not on the lease. Without the Company, she had no prospect of making the rent that month or any month in the future. As a result of her botched efforts to perform, her back still hurt horribly. No longer under the auspices of Company physicians, she was running dangerously low on Vicodin and Flexiril. No longer dancing ten hours a day in leotards and legwarmers, it had come to her attention that she was despondently lacking a wardrobe. Chicago heralded shiny new options. Our father had money, which he could be quite generous with when things were going his way. Our old friend, Otto, would let her stay with him free—and supply all the painkillers and muscle relaxants she desired—if she would sleep with him, which would be nothing resembling an ordeal. I possessed a convenient plethora of clothing I'd lately grown too thick to wear. Kendra, in the four and a half years since she'd left home, had never so much as joked about moving back. But she was in a great deal of discomfort due to her surgery. Perhaps she was not thinking straight. Pain, you may have discovered for yourself, can do that to people.

My mother called while Kendra was on phone. When I clicked over, she said, "Darling, Kendra is coming back to us." Her wording struck me, if not as pathological, then at least as totally, if inexplicably, false. I muttered, "Yeah, I've got her on the other line," and hung up.

Kendra said, "Was that Mom? I *knew* she would call you," as though it were a crime. I began to suspect some level of foul play. I said, "Are you really staying for good? Or did you just say that so they'd pay for the ticket?" She laughed, and I thought for a moment that we were complicit, that I'd been right not to get too excited (this was why I was not excited, I told myself—I did not believe her). Then she said sullenly, "What do you take me for?" But while I tried to conjure the conviction to swear I did not think her so manipulative, she laughed again. "They always pay for my ticket. Why would I waste effort on such an unnecessary gesture?"

For no reason I could think of—but in the bizarre game of kamikaze chess between my sister and my parents, one could never be sure.

In the breath that followed, Kendra offered kindly, "It's either come home or break out the fishnets and start walking the streets. I know you like it there without me. You choose."

"Oh right," I said. "Then Dad would have to spend all his money bailing you out of prison and hiring some hotshot New York attorney and he'd make me call off the wedding."

"You don't think he'd defend me himself, Bee?"

"Are you kidding?" My throat felt thick with a clog of hairy words fighting to get out. That I was sorry her dream had evaporated into the brutal fumes of the city. "The rest of us will be in Maui until the court date's over."

"Well," she drawled. "Guess I'm a Midwesterner again then. Maybe it'll be quaint."

Chat Room

THE MOMENT YOU opened the door of your office, I thought, *Oh, she's just what I expected.* I had never been to a psychiatrist before. I only knew I could picture my father telling you things: his fear that Kendra hated him, his resentment of my mother's vigilant Christianity and cleanliness. I did not imagine he mentioned me.

You were too polite to ask about the excrement I'd come to discuss. Instead, you made ice-breaking small talk: about Northwestern, which we'd both attended; about the historic Oak Park mansion where my wedding reception would be, which was purportedly haunted by Frank Lloyd Wright's mistress after she'd been hacked to death by a disgruntled butler. About the cause of my ballerina sister's back injury, to which I shrugged, "Oh, I forgot to ask—dancers fall all the time." Then immediately felt deficient, like I wouldn't live up to your assumptions of whatever telepathic-twin-connection singles are not privy to. (Years later, my deficit is certain: I never found out. Kendra had a way of looking away when she said "accident" that made me think she'd been beaten up or jumped out a third-story window. When I asked pointedly, she mentioned being dropped on her ass during a lift—by a surprisingly not-gay dancer with whom she'd cheated on the lover whose name her lease bore. I was unaware she'd been living with a man. To our parents, later, she rendered ballet blameless, claimed a car accident. My father wanted to sue for damages; my mother took Kendra's reluctance to mean drugs were involved.)

"How do you feel about your sister's homecoming?" You spoke like it was necessarily a loaded question. "Are you looking forward to it?"

And I, stubbornly: "Of course."

You smiled. We were both psych majors at Northwestern, and you kept giving me this ironic sort of grin as though you thought I was toying with you and refused to be disappointed or act as though you expected better from me. "So what brings you here then?"

"Other than the fact that I have diarrhea all the time?"

The smile dissipated. Had I been too blatant, leaving the realm of the symbolic by forcing you to conjure images more concrete: me on the toilet sweating, gulping Gatorade to prevent dehydration, with Aris outside the bathroom door pretending not to hear me groan? I glanced above your head at shelves cluttered with books about travel rather than psychology—as if these experiences were your credentials. "My health really *is* my main concern right now," I qualified. "Aris thinks the stress of the wedding is making me sick, and my father agrees. But then I guess you know that. My dad's unleashed loads of theories on you, I'm sure."

"If I'd said, 'Tell me about your daughter, Henry,' what might he have said?"

"That one doesn't send a wedding dress to the cleaners if someone's shit in it. He hates to waste money, it's his upbringing, I'm sure you guys talked that to death when he was in here."

The slight raise of an eyebrow. I was already calculating the frequency of this gesture, anticipating telling you sometime in the future exactly how often you did it per session. "Have you done anything to make him worry about that? Have you ever lost control?"

"My God, I'm in the *Twilight Zone*. I was making a joke. Aren't jokes allowed?"

"Anything's allowed." Too quick to convince. "It's safer, though, never to . . . assume."

"Yeah, well I don't know what my father told you, but I shouldn't even be here. I've already seen a zillion *medical* doctors, but my father thinks everything is mind over matter. Anything that holds him back, he overcomes—poof! I'm an embarrassment, or my sickness is."

13

"You portray your father as larger-than-life and invulnerable. Is that how you see him?"

I knew the tricks. Anything ending in *Is that how you see him?* meant you thought my view deluded, or at least naïve. I backpedaled.

"My dad's one of those self-made men who wanted to give his kids a better life than he had, and ended up shocked by how we turned out. He handed us stuff, and now thinks Kendra doesn't understand what's important, and maybe he thinks I know, but I'm too weak to keep it."

But still: "You believe your father perceives you as weak?"

"Well, that's the real reason I'm here, isn't it?" Irritably now. "I know he told you. He's afraid I'll lose Aris with all my bowel nonsense, right? My engagement is the one thing I've done that he totally approves of—I'm sure he's floored I even managed to snag a guy like Aris. I'm finally higher than Kendra in his esteem, albeit only because she dropped out of college, but since he thinks education and family are life's most valuable commodities, and she's shunned both . . . Now I'm the favored—" My gut gurgled. "Aris is helping me get closer to my dad."

"What's so valuable—and strong—about Aris in your dad's eyes, do you think?"

This made me laugh. "It's funny actually, I always assumed it was that Aris's father is old money, and Aris is really . . . polite and clean cut. But the other day my mom told me my dad was going on and on about how lucky it is that Aris's mom is Greek because Greeks are such hard workers. So I told Aris, and he was all horrified, like, 'My mom is not that kind of Greek!' You know, how she's not some immigrant who owns a Greektown restaurant or dry cleaners or hotdog stand—he was really agitated—we got in a huge fight. My dad just got Aris a job designing the new wing at his law firm. My mom said the senior partners resisted because Aris is inexperienced, but my dad went to bat for him. It kind of made me want to tell my dad not to bother helping Aris, like, *Sorry, Dad, he's not that kind of Greek.* My dad would have just gotten pissed, though, like he used to whenever I tattled on Kendra, so I kept my mouth shut."

You said only: "That doesn't sound very helpful on Aris's part."

"Oh, no . . . I mean, Aris wasn't really mad after a minute. He was just momentarily hurt that my dad would"—I giggled—"perform such an offensive act as calling Aris a hardworking Greek. The stupidest thing is, Aris *is* a hard worker. He loves his job—he loves the whole idea of architecture. He usually looks up to my father . . . he thinks my dad is like Howard Roark."

You did not ask who Howard Roark was, stirring in me a vague disappointment that I would not be supplied an easy lead into a cathartic diatribe about how my relationship was, in effect, a foursome including the late Ayn Rand and her infamous maverick architect creation. Instead you were leaning forward with what appeared to be genuine sympathy.

"It must make you very angry," you said, "to watch your father and your fiancé looking past you and instead posturing to impress one another."

Had I said that? I managed only, "I'm not angry at all. In fact, in just about every sense, I'm the least angry person in my family by a long shot."

You nodded; I realized sickeningly that I enjoyed the gesture despite my utter conviction you had no idea what I meant. The chime of your grandfather clock felt like a loss. But you looked satisfied, sipped some long-grown-cold pinkish tea. "I'm sorry to hear it. Especially since the family member least likely to display rage often has the most to be furious about."

My yearning to remain a moment before had clearly been a rift in my sanity. You did not have to collect your fee from *me*; there was no requisite payment-talk to stall my bolting out of the office. On Michigan Avenue, crisp fall wind rushed into my lungs fast, both too thick and too thin with the sudden illusion of having stayed my execution.

But only for one precious week.

House of Eros

KENDRA WAS WAITING outside "arrivals," smoking a cigarette and doing that smoker's thing of looking around compulsively in whichever direction she blew smoke, yet seeming to see nothing. She did not see me; I had to honk and call her name, and even then she took another drag—then another on top of that without exhaling—before trudging to the car as though she were having trouble carrying her remarkably small bag. She stabbed her cigarette out in my clean ashtray instead of tossing it out the window. Her hair smelled cold like Christmas. I said, "Your hair's so long, wow, I shouldn't have cut mine."

From behind a thick wave shielding one eye, she peered back at me, burgundy mouth pursed and considering beneath the blond curtain. "You have to have long hair in New York," she said finally. "Otherwise your face is like the bow of a ship sticking out too prominently—exposed for any kind of freak."

"We have freaks in Chicago, too," I said.

"We have food in New Jersey, Grandma," she answered, and we both laughed as I pulled away. It was a line from *Are You There God, It's Me, Margaret?*, our favorite Judy Blume novel when we were kids. Now the line served as my standard retort whenever Kendra acted like New York was the only city on earth with character, art or indoor plumbing. The fact that she had caught herself this time struck me as absurdly poignant.

"You're late," she said. "I was about to chew off a limb—being at O'Hare is like waiting in line for Noah's Ark. Everywhere I looked there were two of every animal, kissing and holding hands and clutching at each other like monkeys. All these herds of people with their mates to pick the lice out of their hair and lick their faces when they get sticky." She pulled her long black coat around her as if to hide every inch of potentially touchable skin. "It's gross."

"Sometimes I think it'd be better if we could go through life without ever being touched again," I agreed. "You couldn't last, of course."

She just stared, which I took as an admission that she was guiltier than most of the constant need to be touched, and that her own complicity in the grooming rituals that passed for affection shamed her.

"So what if you were sitting there in your car waiting for me," she began, "and a strange man emerged from the crowd and said you could sign your name to a contract then and there that would bar anyone from ever falling in love with you again, and would keep your own body from feeling that itchy, craving need for sex or any of that. Would you sign?"

I sighed. "Don't try to trap me. I didn't mean Aris. I meant other people."

"Oh, right," she said. "I forgot you're one of Noah's bears now too. You and the Architect bear are right there in line, all set to hibernate for the flood. Look at you, you're even stocked with surplus padding and fur."

"At least I don't look like I escaped Dachau. What, doesn't Peter Martins let you eat?"

"Actually, no."

I didn't believe her for a second, but I shut up.

Kendra was facing her side window. It'd been a year since she'd seen the city, but stuck in traffic on I-94 with a stellar view of the skyline, she didn't even face ahead. We'd grown up in Kenilworth, a North Shore suburb boasting exclusive, pastoral lake views—Chicago's collective view of the John Hancock building lording over the Magnificent Mile on Michigan Avenue never ceased to spark in me that buzz of feeling I was somewhere more important, engulfed by urban splendor that contradicted yet complemented the violent water of Lake Michigan. But from her side window, Kendra would have seen only pink-tinted O'Hare hotels, identical brown Chicago bungalows, and a gigantic likeness of Gary Sinise painted on one side of the Bigsby & Kruthers building flanking the highway. Watching the flatness of her face as I exited onto

North Avenue made my throat tight. As I plodded through street construction, I waited for her to make some crack about how in New York people were smart enough not to own cars. Finally, once I found a parking spot in Bucktown, she sat curled in the bucket seat, holding the shoulder belt weakly like she didn't want to get out.

"I changed my hair this morning," she said quietly. "In New York, I wore a ponytail or bun like all dancers. But I'm not a dancer anymore. Today I threw my hair all over because my features don't even belong to me now. They've been mine for four years, but now they're ours."

I did not know what to say. Any display of empathy would only cause her to pull back.

Despite Kendra's distaste for Aris—or maybe because of it—as soon as she saw him any trace of melancholy vulnerability evaporated, and she was all smiles and witticisms. "There must be twenty-seven copies of *The Fountainhead* in this place," she cried incredulously after casing the loft. "What the hell, Aris, do you peddle them door to door like a Jehovah's Witness? Send them in the mail to some underground list of like-minded architects?" When she tossed her bag in the corner, she made it look light.

"I asked Guitarist to sleep over tomorrow," she announced like she owned the place. "We'll order pizza and have a Monty Python marathon. It'll be nostalgic, like old times."

The comment bordered on the sociopathic. While both my sister and I had indeed spent many pizza-and-movie evenings with Otto "Guitarist" Groebner, these had not been communal events by any means. Aris, too sturdy opposite us at the kitchen counter, as if things like diarrhea or back pain could never touch him, dared snort aloud. I couldn't look at him, for fear if he saw on my face that I knew she was whacked, he'd take it as permission to start a fight.

He said only, "I'm not paying. When Bee's exes come over, they buy their own food."

"He was never my boyfriend," I amended quickly, fearing Kendra might correct him first. "I was only sixteen, it didn't count."

Aris: "You lost your virginity to him."

"Fucking doesn't equal coupledom," my sister explained, as if to someone from another planet. My armpits burned. But then, "He *was* your boyfriend, Bee. Why would you deny it? What, Aris has to be the only relationship you've ever had now, or the marriage won't count?"

"Shut up. I was being polite for your sake, so Aris wouldn't realize what a man-stealing Jezebel you were in real life."

"But Aris likes thinking I'm the evil twin, don't you, Aris?" Kendra leaned against me, tweaked the end of my hair hard. "Never mind that it was an act of mercy. I was rescuing you— you thought the sex was gross and were dying to be rid of—"

"That boy never took a bath! His fingernails would be all long for his guitar, corroded with boy-grime, and he'd poke them around like he was hoping to pawn some of it off on me—"

"You weren't wet enough!" she shrieked. "He had to get a more responsive chick so his cleansing ritual would work!"

We howled. Aris stared at us with something like horror. My body stiffened. Kendra, clutching my sleeve in a fit of giggles, immediately drew away. Drifted soberly across the loft to sift through our CDs, as though hoping to add some noise to the brew since conversation with my fiancé present had proven hopeless. I felt stupidly crushed, disproportionately annoyed with Aris as he took over her stool. Imagining her further disapproval of his music collection egged me on. Aris found classical nerve-wracking or boring (depending on the piece), and was familiar with only the most staple of jazz greats—Coltrane, Miles—whom he played exclusively when we made love. Kendra, to my vague disappointment and befuddlement, chose his Steely Dan over my Messiaen or Jack Teagarden. But when she couldn't work the CD player, and Aris rose to help, she scurried back to me, reclaiming her stool and lighting a cigarette.

"So don't make too much of this little Guitar reunion," she whispered conspiratorily. "I mean, I can't be blunt, he's giving me a place to stay. But we're not getting back together."

"Bull. You always say that."

Aris turned around. "Um, K, can you not smoke in here?"

She glanced at me to check whether he might be joking. I averted my gaze. She chucked her lit cigarette in an empty glass. Smoke hit me in the eye, continued to swirl around the air. "I'm serious." She raised her voice for him to hear too. "I've joined Musicians Anonymous—step one requires that I spit at any long-haired boy who even asks me out. Step two involves repeating the phrase *B.O. is bad* to myself on every new date. I'm almost to step three. Anything *emotional* with Guitarist would definitely be considered backsliding."

Aris ignored the inference. "You mean Otto is actually in a band? I thought you guys just called him Guitarist because he looks . . . like that."

Kendra, dead-pan: "We could call him Pusher if you'd prefer optimal accuracy."

Aris didn't even smile. Scooped up her fuming glass and dispatched it in the sink behind us. With his eyes hooding and nostrils flaring, he struck me as a great stern stallion, if one gone paunchy after settling down to a life that did not provide the most challenging of runs. The first time Kendra met him, home on winter break of our sophomore year, my heart had thumped unevenly with nervous pride that he was mine. He'd let me bring her along on what he called a "building date": driving us around to look at his favorite buildings and talking to us about why they were so great. I thought he was like the guy from *Hannah and Her Sisters*, only not so unpredictable. Even though Kendra laughed when he called *The Fountainhead* a "manifesto," he'd held his own by quoting Nietzsche to justify his devotion to what my sister dismissed as a "romance novel for misogynists." I had not yet read Rand; I was stalling on giving Aris's aesthetic tastes the opportunity to disappoint me. I knew only he didn't care for his father, who'd never taken much of an interest in him, so I assumed Howard Roark to be a sort of surrogate father figure. I found this sentimental fantasy humanizing. When he treated us to dinner and martinis at a restaurant where my father took clients, instead of one of the vegetarian cafés Kendra's boyfriends frequented, I thought she should be jealous, even if she wasn't.

Now, my fiancé and I a combined thirty pounds heavier and wiping excess olive oil and food-processed basil off our T-shirts, I couldn't blame her for being unimpressed. I gulped my wine, waiting for the water to boil for my "famous" pesto pasta and watching Aris watch my sister. Though she'd grown bored with him (and by association, me?), he kept glancing her way with plain confusion. Leaning with one arm on the counter, eyes dreamily unfocused (she was probably worrying about seeing our parents), she appeared transformed by silence into a slice of nostalgic beauty from a generation when things and people seemed frailer, less solid, all hair like wispy clouds and transparent skin on airy bones. Her 1940s dress, though likely under $10, was not one I'd dare wear for everyday: a beige so pale it blended with her skin, blue flowers scattered like tiny pulsing veins. I feared such outward gestures of beauty even more than her bawdiness a moment before—both too conspicuous. She looked incapable of crudeness now. Aris had to be wondering how this ghostly, irreverent chameleon could possibly be my twin.

He murmured, "It never ceases to amaze me how perfectly alike you look."

By midnight we retired to our bedroom to escape her. The loft's makeshift walls lent barely the illusion of privacy. I imagined her out there alone, any inch of bare skin sticking to the cool leather of Aris's couch as she tossed and turned, never able to sleep this early on a weekend. Like an animal in a trap, she would be waiting for us to fall asleep so she could chew off her foot, flee to a nearby bar and call Otto, beg him to come and stage a rescue. Meanwhile, she would listen to our bed creaking through the pseudo walls. She would visualize Aris mounting me like a horse from behind (*Those Greeks!* she would tell Otto later), lips sneering at his low grunts, the sounds of sex always icky to anyone not involved.

In reality, Aris liked to see my face. But though we usually made love in the missionary position, or sometimes with me on top, now I interpreted his failure to live up to what I imagined her imaginings to be as: *I've gotten heavier; our butts wouldn't look the same.* It never occurred to me that he *wasn't* playing a mad scientist who'd cloned us as his personal love slaves. I should have been grateful, I supposed, for this respite from my usual three-times-a-week paranoia that he was secretly acting out the rape of Dominique—Howard Roark, it turned out, was not much of a paternal role model at all. But I was not grateful. I was stiff and unreceptive and utterly silent. If his wanting to have sex when she could hear was predictable in a way that made my lungs feel swollen, my resistance was equally so. We were no doubt a disappointment to her. So like the parents she and I shared, she might have been in a time warp, in the attic bedroom of Henry and Gail Braun's Kenilworth home ten years before. Would she masturbate now as then, fingers fast and furtive in rhythm with Aris's on my cold, dry flesh? Or was that mere child's play, and at any moment she would throw back the plywood door with, *Hey Aris, let's make like you're a casting agent and we're aspiring Doublemint Twins*? Would he turn her away? Would I? Could she, a stand-in under his fingers, find the release that eluded me?

Sharing an attic room at thirteen, we had both lain perfectly silent in bed. Sounds rose from our parents' room beneath: boxsprings squeaking with enough indignity to make our blood freeze. I always pretended to sleep. Let my mouth hang open and even drooled a little, the way Kendra said I did because of my allergies. She had allergies too but took medication. I couldn't because it made me too tired. Or nervous, maybe it was too nervous. No moaning, no screaming then either. But grunts, like the sound of a fist in the stomach, stealing all the air required to holler. Ugly. I couldn't tell if it was my father or mother but elected *him*: the baker pounding dough. I did not want the *ummphs*, the sound of lost air, to be coming from her.

From the bed across the room, I had learned the wetness of my sister's fingers. The slick, clicking noise of slippery flesh rubbed fast so that the rim of the vaginal opening vibrated, creating a suction that was a miniature replica of the sweaty stomach of our father slapping onto our mother's also-moist skin. Kendra's breath moved slow and purposeful—ceased altogether when she came. I felt drool on the pillow against my cheek, imagined a sticky bed of the dried spit I'd expelled that week, collecting bacteria. It would cause my skin to erupt into acne craters, would make me uglier than Kendra, who also took Tetracycline for her skin. I couldn't because it made me puke. It made her puke too; I had seen her, but she denied it to our mother, claiming I was only jealous. Soon she smoked so much pot nothing made her nauseous anymore.

The slight vibrations of my sister's bed always finished before our parents' mattress stilled, before silence from their room below could expose her. But I swore I detected a musky scent wafting from beneath the moist haven of her covers—incongruent with a girl not even menstruating. I slept with my face in wetness, in a pool of spit that merged in my dreams with the clear, sticky substance drying between my sister's thighs, the mucusy cream coating my mother's internal walls. In the morning, my mother shouted because I'd wet the bed again. She threatened to send me to a shrink, make me wear an adult diaper. Nothing like this had ever happened before. I was forbidden to ingest any liquid past 6:00 PM.

In the loft that was his before ours, where no furniture belonged to me, Aris whispered into my unyielding throat, "Relax, Bee, she can't hear, and if she can she doesn't care. Like she's never done this before?" He was right; it was nothing, I knew.

Something like this was bound to have happened before.

I pushed Aris away and said, "Not now." Pushed him away, "She's laughing at us." Pushed, "It's her you'd like to screw, isn't it? Men always want her 'cause she makes them mad." I pushed; I whispered, "I want you." I pulled him inside then muttered, "Not like that."

The remainder of our eighth grade year, our father avoided my eyes, silent for fear of revealing disappointment in his weaker daughter. Night after night, I lay listening to the friction of my sister's fantasies, the suction of my parents' hearts trying to stick. Waiting, inexplicably, for an ascending shadow on the wall.

The Capitalist

ON KENDRA'S SECOND night at the loft, my stomach rebelled. I should never have eaten pizza. I'd avoided dairy for months, but now the combination of cheese and tomatoes scorched my insides like acid, competing for which could cause me greater discomfort. Since the Levsinex, my pain had been insidious—but manageable. I no longer spent hours in the bathrooms of restaurants and movie houses. I could be taken out in public again. Good enough, since I'd already forgotten what it felt like to be normal, to eat what I wanted, to sleep without hurting. To have sex without fearing the pressure on my bowels. I'd been tricked by watching Kendra bite into a slice of pizza, slimy with cheese and grease. Between mouthfuls, she'd subjected us to the intricate differences between standard vegetarianism—which she'd practiced since high school—and being vegan, which she'd flirted with briefly in New York but abandoned as "too fanatical even for me" because of restrictions against dairy. It was genetically impossible that I should be allergic to a food she could tolerate. I wolfed down five slices—more than she but less than Otto, who ate seven—before growing so ill I retired to my room.

Aris was out, taking advantage of Kendra's presence to get together with an old frat buddy he hadn't seen in months. In the main area of the loft, Kendra and Otto made a noble pretense of being quiet in deference to my illness, but drywall is hardly soundproof, and my sister and my first boyfriend were high as kites. I smelled the weed thick in my throat and wanted some, but couldn't face going out there and watching him put his hands all over her. I would never quite get used to it, the fact that he could compare our scents, the way we squirmed when he slipped his fingers inside. I'd learned to climax (alone) six months after Kendra started dating him, and it irked me to no end that I'd never done so with him, that I would forever be labeled the "frigid" twin.

11:43. I might need to go to the bathroom again, and the thought of being stuck there, Otto wondering what was taking me so long, made me sweat and feel faint. I was on my feet before I knew why, pulling Aris's leather coat over my sweatsuit. He would return to cigarettes crushed in glasses, used condoms on the hardwood floor, loose weed he'd be sure to knock over in his fumbling for the bedroom, sending Otto scrambling on his knees buck naked to salvage his stash. I didn't care, couldn't breathe, had to get out of there.

Kendra and Otto jerked when they heard me. He was lying on top of her, his shirt off, a disheveled boy from a Kureishi film: junkie-pale and thin, with an ethereal, almost feminine sexiness. She wound under him, her legs snared in his, their hair falling together like a light-dark curtain over their faces. A slithering, headless *pas de deux*. She peeked out from under his curly locks. Her legs were bare; I glimpsed a flash of fabric where her skirt rode up around her hips.

"Bee, where're you going? Could you get me a carton of Camel Lights? I'll pay you Monday after we see Mom and Dad."

I didn't answer. Went down into the street and walked over to where Damen met North and Milwaukee in a chaotic six-way intersection of gyros stands, dive coffeshops, and the irritatingly trendy restaurants and bars of Bucktown. I had no recollection of where I'd parked. I wandered first up North, then back to Damen, where I spotted my car only half a block north of the loft, in the opposite direction from where I'd originally headed. A tall, Eurotrash boy was leaning against it, the cheeks of his leather-clad ass leaving greasy prints on my window. He looked out of place amid the frat and yuppie types who invaded Bucktown on weekends. I got in the car without meeting his eyes, irrationally horrified that he might speak to me.

I didn't have a premonition, don't think that's what I'm saying. My motives were simpler, far simpler than that. The night was hers and I was an outsider—it's just the way I was back then, that's all. My energy was lowest after sundown; I preferred to make love in the mornings; I wasn't a partier; my own lucid dreams frightened me. Night's black hours were dull and best spent unconscious. Lost time, you see, had never yet meant anything to me.

Naturally, my parents were not home. My father's best friend, Michael Kelsey, had just turned forty-two, and my parents were in the city at his surprise party. It was an odd age to make a fuss over a birthday, but at forty, Mr. Kelsey's divorce had just been finalized, and so a party would have been in bad taste. My mother had told me several times in the past week how she dreaded this event. She was not crazy about Michael Kelsey, who had cheated on his wife with an almost-presidential shamelessness prior to the divorce, and she found the hostess of this particular party even more unnerving: an attorney who rarely smiled and who had once commented that my mother was incorrect in serving chilled brie. (My mother, of course, knew this was incorrect, but had been out all day volunteering at the Presbytery and had forgotten to take the cheese out of the refrigerator in time.) Career women, my mother often told me, enjoyed nothing more than portraying women whose work went unpaid as idiots.

Alone in the foyer, though, pulling my arms out of the coat to feel the warm air (always exactly seventy-two degrees) on my skin, I could still feel traces of them. My mother's perfume lingering, the discarded tie my father must have been wearing earlier before he abandoned his work suit for corduroys and a sweater. And garlic from the kitchen, though my mother did not cook with garlic, besides which, it was unlikely they'd eaten in tonight. It must have been some kind of leftover from the night before, devoured by my father standing up at the counter, certain that the food at the party would not excite him as much as day-old Italian. My mother would have scolded him, not for spoiling his appetite but his smell. Would have winced when she saw him kissing his colleagues' wives hello. By now they were probably bickering about whether or not to come home early, each chiding the other for being old. My mother's lipstick would be growing chalky; my father would be bored of talking business and would be flirting, garlic and all. If I went into my old room,

26

they would not know I was even there until morning had come. Comforting, to think of hearing them in their natural state as the backdrop of my much needed sleep. Nothing but the sounds of home: perhaps an amusing recap of Mr. Kelsey's startled alarm when a room populated mostly by people he didn't care for yelled "Surprise," or a mild reprimand from my mother over my father's behavior. Something constant. Safe.

I climbed the stairs to the attic and flopped on the sofa in what was now my father's study but had once been my room. It had been Kendra's too at times—when we moved to Kenilworth from Cincinnati, we were already twelve and old enough to demand that neither be given the drama of an attic all to herself, so we alternated. And for a while, when we were in eighth grade, we'd even shared. It was my turn, but Kendra threw a fit and moved in with me. I tried to pretend I minded but really I was disappointed when she voluntarily moved out later.

I'd had this space most recently, though. I was the one to leave my things behind, while Kendra took everything and moved within two weeks of our high school graduation, traveling Europe and then moving straight into her Julliard dorm. I waited out the summer before moving only a few breaths away, to Evanston. I'd spent it watching my mother, smelling her, sitting on kitchen stools until my back ached from lack of support just to be near her while she cut flower stems, addressed church mailings, scrubbed things—everything—until her world shined. She was smooth and beautiful as porcelain, still enough of a habit not to feel out of reach. She was only thirty-eight then. And my father. My father was forty and splendid, just elected junior partner. His hair was scarcely gray, and he'd been sober for five years. We'd never discussed it, my mother, my sister, and I. Never gloated over his magnificence, never said we were proud of him for picking himself up off the floor. We acted as if things had never happened. I wished we hadn't now, in the flickery way you wish something when you know in truth you would likely behave in the same manner should the situation present itself again.

How could it be otherwise? You were right; my father remained as larger-than-life to me as during the years I'd lived at home. Self-made, flamboyant, with the romantic vestiges of a Southern drawl, he embodied all-American success, having pulled himself up from a small town in Kentucky. His mother had been a fat, state-aid dependent woman who suffered chronic depression. Her husband abandoned her and her two children. My father was the elder. His sister was also obese and mentally ill. Family rumor was that the sister became a hooker. My father lost contact with her long ago. Being affluent, of finicky appetite, and within the boundaries of what is thought of as sanity, he felt they had little in common. His mother is dead.

Though I loved the stories of my father's exotic trailer-park youth, the time in his life when he seemed most real to me was when he was putting himself through the University of Cincinnati on scholarship. My favorite story was how he tricked my mother, the daughter of a Dayton dentist, into dating the likes of him. He was a waiter at her sorority and thought she seemed sweeter than the other girls, so he dropped spaghetti in her lap to test it, to see if she'd scream at him or try to make him feel less humiliated by downplaying the worth of her skirt and stressing her own clumsiness. Though a near-fanatical Christian of nervous disposition, she was also very beautiful; he was willing to risk his job to find out. Six months later he got her pregnant. Family rumor has it that the Dayton dentist believed he'd done it to get his hands on her money and so offered no financial support. (*Family rumor* is a euphemism for my mother, who always speaks as though things are only possibilities, never facts.) Yet I held that memory closer than if it'd been my own: my father, so devoted to his family he'd put off law school, taken work at an insurance company in Cincinnati without complaint, just to keep us.

The clock read 1:30 when I heard a distant crash of noise on the first floor—had I been asleep? A moment of burglar-panic gripped me, but when I sat, I made the noise out clearly: my father talking, my mother not responding or doing so very quietly. I hesitated. Suddenly I did not want to announce my presence and risk their thinking I'd had some horrible fight with Aris that they would assume was my fault. I wanted to admit Kendra had been on my last nerve, that I was furious at her for hiding from them until Monday. For her irrational need to "get her bearings" before seeing them. As if she didn't know that our father was doing research on the best physical therapists to help with her back; that our mother was making a list of new vegetarian restaurants in the city so Kendra wouldn't feel out of the swing of things; that she was planning a mother-daughter day when we could find Kendra's maid of honor dress then get our hair and nails done. My sudden pity for them propelled me to the stairs.

My mother, stunning in a green, silky dress, wept salty mermaid tears in the foyer. My father moved behind my mother, not touching her. Her profile was twisted in a way I did not understand. Both of their backs were mostly to me; they had apparently not heard me rushing down the carpeted steps. A vase lay broken, the weird one Kendra had sent from a Village art fair when she missed our parents' twentieth wedding anniversary. Expensive too: the proud gift of a nineteen-year-old flaunting her first paycheck. My mother stared at the vase as though she knew she had committed a sin so unforgivable that it would haunt her for the rest of her days. I cleared my throat—my mouth was dry. Moved; no, did not move. A phantom spy on the stairs.

My father spun around, his face already gelled into grief. My mother shrank back a bit at the sight of me: an unexpected intruder. Her tears froze like she'd been injected with a solution of ice water. It is not good to weep before your inferiors. I imagined myself, hair falling so that half of it was hanging jaw-length, the other half still restrained by a scrunchy. The grimace of my mother's mouth stretched into a frightening, artificial smile. My father, though, shrank to a vapor substance; capable, as always in times of trouble, of walking through walls. I wanted him to walk through me, to feel the chill of a ghost passing. The moment felt somehow borrowed. He seemed on lease to us—how was it that I had never seen?

"Bee. What are you doing here?"

My mother's crystal earrings caught the light of the Tiffany lamp so that they appeared kaleidoscopes. Rainbow colors played off the red of her lips, the blue of her eyes, the yellow of her hair. Her dress lay crisp and smooth as if she'd just put it on, cleanliness next to godliness, while I, rumpled beyond all recognition, must've seemed to her analogous to sin.

"I got, um, in an argument with Aris . . ." I too could not take my eyes off the broken vase on the floor, its power oddly magnetic. "I was just planning to go to sleep and cool down."

"Sleep sounds good to me too," my father said, solid once more and dismissing the not-too-subtle hint of trouble in my relationship with an ease that wounded despite my lie. "I'm getting too old for these late-night, aren't-we-fashionable affairs."

My mother kept her face bent, blond hair spilling so I could not see her eyes. A mirror image of Kendra in twenty years, all expression hidden from view. Of me too if I did not wear my emotions like a loud garment wrapped around me tight. She held a jagged piece of the vase, sharp end pointed toward herself; she resembled a child handling a knife. My father took the scrap and set it on the end table next to the sofa. Even empty-handed, though, she did not move.

"Mom?" I lingered now only inches from her. "What's the matter?"

"Nothing, darling. It's nothing. Everything is fine."

My stomach a cauldron, full of bats and eyes of newt: "Um, I guess I should go home."

My father smiled too, his face becoming fluid. "Don't be ridiculous, sweetheart. It's much too late to go alone. Call Aris and tell him if you're worried."

"Okay, I guess I . . ."

He nodded, turned, and ascended the stairs. A churning noise rose from my belly, and I wondered if my mother heard, if she knew that my having ever lived here in this sparkling house was some kind of a farce. My body did not behave right; my hair did not stay put; my lipstick rubbed off on people, wine glasses. But she was looking past me, after his shadow, and I noticed in the moment before she took flight that there was still another piece of the vase in her hand, cutting into her palm so that blood trickled down her ivory arm, turning the diamonds of her tennis bracelet into dangerous rubies. Then she moved up the staircase with a rustle of slippery silk, into the realm of my father, leaving me alone on the hardwood floor below, shoeless among the shards of glass.

Fragment

Hold still, we're going to do your portrait, so
that you can begin looking like it right away.

—Hélène Cixous,
"The Laugh of the Medusa"

March 1994

The key was missing. No, stolen, that much was clear. If Kendra told her mother, her mother would say it was simply misplaced; Kendra was always misplacing things. Never important things, though, never things that were important to her. If her mother were observant, she'd know that. The question wasn't whether the key had been deliberately taken, it was by whom? Kirby had been poking around her things lately. Kendra caught her once, snooping when she thought Kendra was in the shower. She'd probably been looking for love letters from Kendra's boyfriend, Otto, but instead found one Kendra had started to him. The letter stated that if things were up to her, she'd stick her mother's head in a meat grinder — but first have her gang-banged by the football team. Kirby was crying when Kendra came back in the room. She kept demanding, inexplicably, to know whether Otto thought she'd inherited her frigidity from their mother, and if not, why would Kendra say that about the football team? She threatened to tell. It could have been Kirby. Kirby did not believe they should desire any privacy from each other; she would have taken the key to Kendra's bedroom in a minute. Kendra said it over and over to herself. She wished it so many times that there was no longer any possibility it was true.

*   *   *

So maybe it went like this:

Kendra Braun felt four sets of eyes following her as she strode through Gordon, headed for her father's table. The wall behind the table was covered with a mural so that everything appeared static except those eyes: one synchronized movement in an otherwise indistinguishable still-life of colors. She was cold. She'd worn a dress she knew would piss her father off, either because it was too tight or because her body underneath it was too thin—at least from the point of view of a man who'd had his first hard-on when the ideal body belonged to Marilyn Monroe. The other man at the table was just enough younger than her father to have perhaps been weaned on Twiggy. Besides, to him Kendra wasn't susceptible to easy chills or ill health—dangers reserved for his own daughter—she was simply an aesthetic form. Excessively thin, if you wore it right, could be compelling. Something about the idea of hipbones jutting under heavy thrusts. Something jagged that let you know what you were doing was wrong. Kendra felt her back straighten, spine slanting forward to accentuate hipbones—

a dancer's walk. She knew she looked good, always, looked just right from that point of view.

Michael Kelsey rose from the barrage of colors, the angles of his gray suit cutting harsh lines against the mural. The movement seemed automatic, but once he was on his feet, he remained still until her father had a chance to stand as well. It struck Kendra as the sort of deference afforded a senile old king—the incongruity of the gesture disturbed her, made an old, illogical envy rise up in her. Power lay implicit in such magnanimity. Kendra wondered whether Mr. Kelsey's presence was an ordinary occurrence, if the divorce she'd assumed he'd obtained in order to pursue a more glamorous existence had in fact only resulted in a series of dinners in another marriage more boring than his own. Kirby, dateless too, seemed a stand-in for Mrs. Kelsey: an understudy in the wings rehearsing for the middle-age she would inherit.

There was a tightness under Kendra's ribs. It may have been her dress. Her surprise had worked perfectly; apparently Kirby had really stuck to the story that Kendra's flight wasn't arriving until ten. Kendra wanted the opportunity to re-enter her family on an ordinary night. She had not lived at home for a long time, but if she had never left, this might well be what they would be doing. Her mother would still be frazzled from the commute from Kenilworth to Rush Presbyterian Hospital, where she was on the Women's Board and volunteered Mondays. Her father would still have run late to meet his family for Monday-dinner-in-the-city, a ritual for the past decade. Tonight, Mr. Kelsey's presence might explain their choice of the elegant Gordon rather than the sort of chaotic, family-run restaurant her father preferred. Yes, it was an ordinary night. There was no reason not to think it was what all nights from here on out would be. The waiter brought another chair and scooted it next to her father's. An empty space, meant for her.

Kendra's mother was beaming. Her father was beaming. Bee grinned foolishly, feigning surprise. Michael Kelsey's expression, though, had gone preoccupied. His eyes did not leave hers, but they started to darken: a dry stone turned deeper gray from rain. Kendra said, before addressing her parents, not even acknowledging her sister, "It's good to see you again, Mr. Kelsey." He smiled then—lopsided, with only one corner of his mouth—like a joke had been exchanged. Glanced around the table making the eye contact she had foregone.

"Please," he said, "call me Michael."

There would be a dinner. There would be an incident. There would be a savior. It would be as simple as that.

Michael Kelsey, Kendra recalled, had always had a lubricating effect on her father, one which left her father's jawbones loose with smiling, his hands paradoxically worn from pounding tabletops for emphasis during casually heated debate. Kendra could not imagine why a man like Michael had nothing better to do than serve as a libation during her family dinners, but she was grateful nonetheless. Maybe he could be of some assistance tonight. Tension hung over the table like a fog; it never occurred to Kendra that she might not be the cause. Her father's movements were choppy. He ordered a scotch right there in public for the world to see. Next to Kendra, Bee's thigh brushing hers clenched up so tightly Kendra could feel the muscles—still hard from years on the New Trier swim team—bulging beneath Bee's navy skirt. Kendra's own legs did not twitch. If she were interested enough to care, she might have actually been grateful that the moment contained some element of truth. She wanted to kick her sister under the table and tell her to grow up. Why shouldn't their father drink in public if he wanted to? Everybody knew he was only a dry drunk anyway. *Didn't they?* Wasn't that what they all thought-her mother, fiddling with a chip in an otherwise perfectly manicured nail; Kirby, stricken with that deer-in-the headlights expression she took on whenever Aris was absent; even Michael Kelsey, who didn't drink at all to the best of Kendra's knowledge, whom she had never, ever seen with a drink in the ten years since her father first brought him home. But he fucked up his own family anyway without even alcohol to help him along, so who was he to judge? Kendra wanted to lean over and say to her father, *Go ahead, get sloshed— I would if I were you.* She and Kirby were nursing twin, dewy glasses of Pinot Grigio, but Kendra wished for a scotch of her own. Something fiery in her throat that would hurt going down. Ground her.

Her father said things.

He said: "So, K, what are you going to do now that we've got you back in the Midwest? Have you given any thought to going back to school so you can teach?"

He said: "How long are you going to stay with Kirby and Aris? You know, you're welcome to stay with us instead. Those two are young, they need more privacy than we do."

He said: "You should choreograph a musical! There are so many new theaters popping up around the city, I'm sure someone with your skills could make a go of it. You should see some of the half-assed productions I've been subjected to."

(A musical, really. I am not lying. That is what he said.)

Quickly, Kendra demurred that she'd already been hired by her first, appreciative dance school and would need neither tuition nor lodging. She knew her mother could not be happy to hear her father inviting her back to the house, or offering to pay for more schooling which Kendra would be sure to squander. And obviously her mother did not take well to his drinking in public. She did not, Kendra believed, much care what he did in private. It didn't concern her, for example, that he once had an affair with one of her friends, Michael's ex-wife, when the Kelseys were still married. Such indiscretions were not important because no one ever mentioned them, and if things were not articulated they could not be real. Kendra understood this, though she was certain her mother and Michael Kelsey both knew what had occurred, and that her father and Mrs. Kelsey knew they knew. In fact, Kendra had always imagined that Michael and his wife cooked up the idea together: that Mrs. Kelsey should take a lover and Henry Braun should be the one. There was no foundation to her belief, yet she could not shake the image from her mind of her father as helpless pawn in a game between the Kelseys. The thought comforted but angered her at the same time.

The incident occurred at the precise moment when Kendra was wondering how she could possibly escape after dinner without having to go back to her parents' house. It happened as she was staring across the table at a man who had known her since before she had even what little tits she now possessed and thinking how she must be imagining it, the way he was staring at her, because otherwise everyone else here must have noticed too. It happened while Kirby was in the midst of joking that as soon as their mother didn't have a wedding to obsess over, she'd be on the newlyweds to produce grandchildren. It happened on the word "grandchildren." Without warning, Kendra's father rose and gripped the table, knocking over her mother's wine. He did not look down or seem to notice. He headed in the direction of the toilets. An undiscerning mind might have assumed he'd gone to take a piss, but Kendra knew better. Her father never went to the toilet in public. A residue of his trailer-park upbringing, he overcompensated, clung to the dignity of his personal hygiene as though with it, he might gain entry to the world of those whose dignity was implicit in their blood. He walked from the table, and Kendra's mother sat, Merlot oozing onto the lap of her beige skirt. Kirby gasp-squeaked. Michael extended his napkin. Her mother stood. Outside on Clark Street the snow fell lightly, the kind of evening that offered not even a glimmer of the slushy months and frozen pipes ahead. It promised to be a beautiful holiday season. Kendra was home after four years. Her mother turned and walked out of the restaurant without her coat. Kendra could see her past the maître d', under a streetlight illuminating the fat flakes: a figure made small by the narrow frame of the glass door.

Kirby said, "I'd better go after her." But she did not get up to leave.

Kendra looked at Michael—she could not say why. She hoped perhaps that he knew her parents better than she, that maybe he had witnessed this sort of thing before. He was staring in the direction of the restrooms, where presumably Kendra's father lingered, oblivious to his wife's sudden departure. Kendra heard herself say, "I'm sure everything is fine. Dad just ruined her favorite Carlisle suit. It's enough to require air." But she too looked off to the far end of the restaurant, some hidden corner that housed the kitchen and the toilets, hid them and her father from view. She started to stand, but Michael Kelsey reached across Kirby's body and took hold of her wrist. Unexpected. She jerked under contact with his skin.

"Maybe you should leave them alone," he said.

It was on the tip of her tongue to say, *Maybe you should mind your own business*. But she sat, letting his command settle over the table. Kirby sat too. Waiting.

When Kendra's mother returned, her eyes were runny with brown mascara and eyeliner. It was as likely as anything else that the disarray of her makeup was due to the falling snow. She gripped her purse. "I've sent the valet for the car." No explanation of why. Kendra's father had been gone long enough now so there was no chance he might be unaware anything was off. Though Kirby had not stepped outside, her eyes were wet too. Kendra had forgotten how it was like watching yourself bleed without feeling pain. "Mom. What's going *on*?"

"Nothing, darling. Your father must have just had too much to drink."

Kendra's body clutched up—a fight or flight response. That, in case you were wondering, was the moment when she knew. Knew that the drinking tonight was only a camouflage for some other, unspeakable thing. Though she could not imagine what it was, her face burned at her mother's lie—so transparent. Of course they all knew that if alcohol were the problem, nobody would announce it over dinner. Kirby began to cry aloud.

"Come on." It was Michael; he was an intruder; he was not supposed to be there. He turned to her mother and said, "Gail, why don't we get out of your way?" Took Kirby's arm, and for some reason she rose. A tangible barrier of authority that kept her from running back to their mother's arms, he led her right out of the restaurant, her cream-colored coat trailing the floor. Kendra faced her mother, but only for a moment. Then she followed, left her mother standing slit-eyed, with shuddery breath and a thin shield of composure, her father still gone.

Kendra knew Michael Kelsey would call. It was perhaps the first thing in twenty-two years she had ever been certain of, but she was more certain of it than she would have thought possible. She knew that, however discreetly, he would procure Aris's number through the new wing contract and call during the day when no one else was around. She never doubted that he would contact her within twenty-four hours of having unexpectedly run into her at Gordon.

He called at three in the afternoon. Kendra was supposed to move in with Guitarist that day, but had claimed an incapacitating backache. She was lying on the black leather sofa next to the phone. She let it ring three times just in case.

"Kendra," he said, "this is Michael Kelsey."

"Yeah, I had a feeling it might be you."

He laughed. "How could you have known? I didn't realize myself that I'd call until five minutes ago. You must be teasing . . . or was I that obvious at Gordon?"

"I wasn't teasing."

37

"Well. Then I suppose my saying something subtle like that I called to check on your parents is out of the question. Will you have a drink with me tonight?"

"I guess so." She was surprised by how easily the words came out. "I don't have a car, though, so you'll have to pick me up."

"I can go along with that. Where does your sister live?"

Something pricked at her spine, made her sit upright. The thought that he would drive to Kirby's apartment and come to the door like a prom date, for all the world to see. A dangerous lack of shame. Kendra realized she had been testing him. She was not sure what she *hoped* the outcome would be. Though she felt breathless, she groped for a cigarette.

"Not here, for God's sake. There's a bar, just down the street."

He did not ask where she wanted to go. She got into his decade-old, black Porsche, heavy with nostalgia before the evening even began. His daughter's car seat had once been crammed in the passenger's side, and Michael used to have to shove it in the trunk so thirteen-year-old Kendra could ride next to him when he drove her home from babysitting. The memory of him as a brash thirty-two-year-old throwing his money away on a fast car amused her. The realization, though, that the Porsche should have been traded in long ago, betrayed a sentimentality she could not discern from his eyes, and she grew unnerved.

He did not ask if she wanted dinner, if she would be more comfortable staying in her own neighborhood. She recalled that even when she was a teenager, he never tried to make conversation while driving. He did not try now. A CD spun; *Le Sacre du Printemps* filled the car. Too absurd. She could not resist, turned it up, said, "I hope you don't have yourself believing I'm a virgin." He looked at her strangely for only a moment before the light of recognition went on, then said, "Virgins get too much press. They weren't the only creatures ever to be sacrificed, you know." She did not answer. Resolved not to test him again since, when his response was not what she expected, she felt at a loss for what to do.

She realized too, with trepidation, that the boyish agility, the feline grace she had always admired in him, had led her to remember him as smaller than he actually was. This illusion was exacerbated by leanness; he had lost a significant amount of weight since his divorce. At Gordon, his suit hanging loose around his limbs recalled a delinquent kid ill at ease in his father's business clothes—made her feel they could be peers. Now she saw that, like a *danseur noble*, his bones possessed a substance that belied thinness. His body did not hunch in on itself weakly the way non-dancers' usually did. Yet it was a body that functioned in settings foreign to her: he had become among the firm's top earners, would make senior partner before her father, was said *by* her father to never lose at anything, even racquetball. His eyes were blue tonight. As a girl she'd preferred this—water to stone—but that preference now struck her as immaturity on her part. The lack of gray in his hair was a disappointment. Such indicators of age would have been a fitting seal to the old contract between them, the kind that never needed words or promises: that someday she would be grown enough to want him with a woman's authority, that someday he would be middle-aged enough not to care about the consequences of a desire beyond the realm of propriety. Or maybe nothing mattered: his bones, his eyes, his hair. Maybe Michael Kelsey looked to Kendra as he had always looked to her. He looked like an escape.

Above the desperate glow of streetlights, the sky was black and starless. Music filled the car like thunder, and though the Porsche was small, the noise did not make her claustrophobic. She did not care where he took her. There was the simultaneous sense of edginess at being out with a man twice her age, her father's closest friend, and of unexpected comfort. Her thought was only, *This will be easy*. Already she saw herself there, right on the brink, so close she could touch it, of making up for everything she'd done wrong.

He took her to the Gold Star Sardine Bar, an obscure, Lakeshore Drive oasis crammed in amid Northwestern medical buildings. At the front of the too-small, too-crowded room, stood a singer. She was tall and black with green contacts and eyelids painted gold so her eyes appeared elongated, sun-bleached leaves. Michael said she often played here, and Kendra found herself wondering if he fantasized about the singer, if he came here alone or always with a date, if he and the singer had ever spoken. The contemplation was not unpleasant. It was accompanied by Michael's lifting her fingers to his lips and pressing them there lightly. He ran her silver ring along the line of his mouth, as if to study the imprint. Then he let go of her hand.

"I thought you didn't drink." But before he could comment, she amended, "I guess it's just you don't drink in front of my father. That's nice of you. Patronizing, but nice."

He said, "As a matter of fact, I'm not much of a drinker in any setting. Maybe I'm becoming one tonight because you make me nervous."

"No," she said, "that's not it."

Kendra felt dizzy. He had ordered them Dewars on the rocks. She was on her second. Despite a two-drink minimum, Michael said he always drank only one. They stood along the bar; not a table was open. No one looked at her, transfixed as they were by the singer. Kendra envied it: the self-contained power of voice. No stripping dancers hurling tights and headpieces backstage, no mountains of tulle or discarded cotton balls swathed in baby oil and a rainbow of wiped-off makeup. No tendonitis or sprains, no moaning bodies on the floor. After closing, the singer would nurse her vocal chords with a serene cup of lemon tea, still in her evening gown. Kendra may have thought, *She can have lovers and the stage, she does not have to rehearse twelve hours a day, she is nearly twice my age but her life might be just beginning.* She may have thought something like, *If only.*

The second set began. Michael looked startled, as though he had run out of time to speak despite his seeming inability to do so. He took her hand again, against a backdrop of other fingers warming up on the piano. His words came out fast: "Listen, I manipulate and tell half-truths for a living. I choose to be direct in my personal life. When I saw you at Gordon, I got a hard-on for the duration of our meal—by the time I went home, I had blue balls like I haven't had since high school. I don't usually go out with women as young as you, in fact I haven't dated a woman under thirty in five years. This is all pretty embarrassing."

"Five years." Slowly. "You were married then."

"Yes. Look, Kendra, you know all about that. I can't see the point in reinventing myself for you." He smiled. "Not unless you absolutely want me to."

"Don't bother, I don't care if you bedded half of Chicago while you were married. But what do you think can come of this? What do you want from me?"

"Maybe at this point my interest is purely sexual. And friendship—I no longer enjoy sleeping with women I don't like. But I have no inclination to try a relationship with someone your age. It could only make us both miserable."

"So let me get this straight. I should have sex with you, and if you like it maybe you'll want to do it a few more times when you're not too busy, and then we can call it a day. What exactly do I get out of an arrangement like that?"

"Maybe good sex, maybe great sex. You'd have to go to bed with me to find out."

"Does this approach work with many women, have you found?"

"I'm not sure." Without looking away, he lit her cigarette with a silver lighter he extracted from his pocket, though she knew he did not smoke. "I've never tried it before. If it turns out well tonight, I'll use it again and let you know."

She laughed before she could stop it. "You know, I was always attracted to you because you're good looking and my dad's partner and all. But I never had any idea how weird you are."

"You probably still don't have any idea."

"Look, Michael, it's not that I'm not flattered . . ."

"Don't do that. I don't want you to be flattered. A man wanting to take you to bed is no cause for gratitude, you know that. Are you *interested* or not?"

The bar was dark. She was grateful for the darkness; her face burned. There was a heat in her legs that could be described as nothing other than inconvenient. His eyes were on her but she didn't meet them. He leaned in suddenly and touched her throat, a light, searching touch, as though he had been wanting to do so for a long time. The feathery imprint of his fingers on her pulse made something rise up inside her that could be described as nothing other than her soul. How close she was to crying made her laugh aloud.

"Why not? Pay these people for our drinks then, before I change my mind and say no."

He reached into his pocket and put a handful of money on the bar without counting. She held her coat tight around her, but before she reached the door leading to the lobby, she knew nothing she put on could possibly protect her from the teeth of the lakefront wind.

41

Michael Kelsey had moved since the last time she'd babysat in the Old Town, Victorian house inhabited solely now by his wife and daughter. For the past two years he'd lived on Chestnut, in a high-rise with a doorman, only a few blocks from the Gold Star. When Kendra was sixteen, she had dropped acid in this very building, at a party celebrating Otto's band opening for Material Issue. That night she had not been a baby ballerina, merely the up-and-coming guitarist's girl. An impostor who'd stolen her sister's civilian boyfriend, appropriated Bee's normal friends. Here with her father's partner instead of a group of stoned high schoolers, she was again just a date, just a prop, the six years between a dream. She felt suddenly old.

His apartment was smaller than she'd expected, and cluttered as a dorm room. She stood in the foyer studying the photographs on the walls, black-and-whites that looked as though they'd been taken in the Southwest. He took her coat and made her a cup of cinnamon tea. The act seemed out of place amid a seduction, but the warmth of the liquid helped calm her trembling hands. She sat on his couch, taking off her knee-high, black boots and tucking her cold feet beneath her buttocks. He sat down next to her and started to laugh.

"You know, this is ridiculous. I should send you home right now. This is perverse."

She gripped her teacup so tightly it burned her fingers. If he made her leave, then everything would be spoiled. "I thought that was the idea."

"Maybe my idea. But why would you come home with me? What do you think Henry would do if he found out about this?"

"He might kill you," Kendra said. "He wouldn't do anything to me."

"You're probably right. He dotes on you, doesn't he? You can do no wrong."

"That's not exactly it," she said, "but it's as close as you need to get."

He laughed again. "The proverbial performer, aren't you? Unsure which face you want to present, Odette or Odile. You've always been that way, even as a teenager. Except you can't carry off childlike innocence like some ballerinas. The mystery, yes, but you've got the savvy of a stripper, not some sheltered flower. Who's your idol, Kendra, who are you emulating?"

"There's nothing mysterious about me. I'm very open. You don't know me at all."

"There was this time," he said, so close she felt his breath at her throat, tickling hidden veins that wound beneath her skin, "I went with Henry to pick you up from ballet. It was downtown, the middle of rush hour, and you were sitting on the sidewalk barefoot in a flowing skirt, drawing on the concrete with your fingers while business people stepped around you. You didn't even notice us pull up. I wanted you then. You couldn't have been more than fifteen, but I wanted to lift up that big skirt and fuck you on the street. You have no idea how sexy you are."

She lifted her chin. "One moment you say that I'm emulating someone and it's all an act. The next minute you say I have no idea. I think you should make up your mind."

His mouth was at her neck now. It would be fair to say she felt inordinately exposed. She took comfort in the knowledge that it would not last long. Thought, *All love stories begin and end outside the earthy realities of consummation*, both aroused and nauseated by the sudden notion that she was only a romantic after all. Surely only the most hideous of romantics would wait ten years to make a point. Almost, almost time.

"I made my mind up the minute I saw you at Gordon," he said, and she closed her eyes, just for a moment, just to take it in. "I don't care if everything you do is an act or entirely accidental. It doesn't matter to me at all."

And he would kiss her, yes, of course he would kiss her. A fine kiss, a good kiss, but not art. Afterward she would remember: the first time he touched her, his hands reminded her of a ballet master not at all. That split-second, minute, half an hour in which she first moved against him would always later strike her as a memory of another man altogether. What if she had relented then—if she had not piqued in him the curiosity a choreographer has for his muse but had merely yielded, as women, not muses, do? She would never know. Never know as she would never know Balanchine, as she would never dance Odette/Odile—much less share the role with Kirby as they'd dreamed as girls: the first time in history it would not be performed by a single ballerina. No, she would never regain the opportunity to be Michael Kelsey's conquest instead of his collaborator. Oh, how easy it might have been:

43

to surrender to the hands of a lover. Instead of awakening the mind of an artist.

Standing up so fast she almost tripped, it was the first time she realized she had been sitting on his lap. How she got there seemed a mystery. His shirt was off. Hers was unbuttoned in front, and she still felt the heat of his mouth on the bones that stretched across her chest. She backed away as though any closer proximity might cause the heated area to burst into flames.

"You made your mind up at Gordon," she said, "but I didn't make mine up until now."

Or maybe: "I prefer my sex less civilized and urbane than this cigarette-lighting, Noel Coward routine you call being *direct*."

Better still: "You say you don't want me to be flattered, but that's exactly what you were counting on. What else would prompt me to go to bed with someone who's just admitted he's only satisfying a creepy curiosity to fuck a fifteen-year-old sitting on the street?"

Surely she must have said some of these things.

She buttoned up while he sat on the couch surveying her with an expression entirely more pleased than she felt comfortable with. He did not speak as she turned to leave. Not until she paused at the door did he ask, "Are you waiting for me to make my case? It'd be inane to berate you for being a tease when that's exactly what you intended to be. Why don't we say instead that you're good at what you do, and I'm fortunate to have a warped penchant for the unexpected?" He stood, did not put on his shirt. Reached into a pocket of his discarded jacket and held out a ten dollar bill. Said, "Take this. I doubt you brought money for a cab."

Kendra did not feel powerful, did not feel vindicated, did not feel fulfilled. She felt, if anything, disorientingly aware that what she always most *desired* in this man was his air of knowing when to leave a room. His ability to read the signals during those precarious moments when it is best to cut your losses. Kendra had never grasped such things, but could appreciate a man who knew. Then the burden would finally be lifted from her shoulders. Imagining such impossible freedom, she stared briefly at the ten in his hand before opening the door without accepting it. With, "Remember the El, Michael? It's a buck fifty. I think I can swing that."

He put the money down. "Fine. I'll see you around, I'm sure."

But she could not walk through the doorway. Wanted to strike him. If she never had the chance to see the surrender in his eyes when he came, the hateful fantasy would remain forever unwashed from her mind. She said, "A 'penchant for the unexpected.' Well, I'm glad to be of use—I wouldn't think you have the opportunity to revel in rejection very often."

He half-laughed. "Don't indulge yourself with fantasies that you're the first woman to say no to me, Kendra. My wife, my daughter, and a good deal of my money reside only a few miles from here as proof against any theories you have about everything going my way. There's nothing unique in this scenario. Now goodnight." And he went into the kitchen to pour another cup of tea, so she had no choice but to step into the draft of the hallway. No choice but to leave.

*   *   *

March 1994

For days Kendra dressed herself quickly. The lock on her bedroom door offered no protection. She told no one the key was missing, so there was no way the lock could be replaced. Not that replacing the lock would have been her mother's initial impulse anyway. They would look for the key first, and Kendra knew that would be pointless, so why bring it up? By then, the key could have been put to use a hundred times over, and then what would she do? There's no point in telling people things when you know you won't follow through. Kendra put her combat boots in front of the door when she slept, so she could hear them clunking if anybody came in. She lay traps in her diary, but things remained unperturbed. Finally, she started to push it—walked around her room naked, left her diary open on her bed while she was in the bathroom, then while she was at school. Nothing happened. She removed the combat boots; it was not so much a volitional decision as that she just forgot to put them in front of the door one night, and then again the night after that. No one looked at her any particular way around the breakfast table. It was like there had never been a lock at all.

Analysis

The one must kill the other who kills the one
who wants to kill who wants to be killed?

—Hélène Cixous,
Portrait of Dora

First Dream

THE HOUSE IS ON FIRE. My mother is running around upstairs in spiked heels—I hear her from my hiding place in the basement. She is shouting for assistance; her garnet drop-earrings are missing, she put them next to her bed last night— who has taken them, who has seen them? My father ignores her. He is looking for us. I can see him, though I am hiding in the cellar at the time, as he searches under beds, behind doorways, frantic for his missing girls. Beside me Kendra grips my arm in silent conspiracy; it strikes me that the earrings my mother tears the house apart for are in Kendra's ears. We will not come out, however much smoke fills our lungs. Our father is nearly mad by this time. He comes pounding down the basement stairs with his arms outstretched amid the flames. It is a remarkable gesture. Honestly, he could be killed—and if we were not even here, not hiding from him, then the gesture would have been in vain. The smoke has grown heavy, and I know I will never be able to leave now. I am coughing, ashamed of myself because Kendra has simply started holding her breath. She does not cough at all. But *he* is too much for her, our father with his piteous gesture, performed for the darkness and thickening air. She bounds forth before I can stop her, runs into his outstretched arms and leaves with him; he is carrying her up the stairs. A mistake has been made. An error in my calculations. My mother's heels puncture the floor, so loud I cannot hear myself coughing anymore. My throat hurts. I would like to warn her that it is time for her too to run for the door, but my voice has shriveled to smoke. The ceiling is a sheet of flames, so magnificent I cannot force my eyes away. Outside in the garden, my father and my sister are laughing, exclaiming in joy to have gotten out alive. They may be speaking of me with regret, but it is only because they know I can hear them.

"I HAD ANOTHER dream about fire."

"Kirby, I hardly recognized you. That color really brightens up your face."

My hand—how could I have been so stupid?—rose to my hair. I felt my cheeks boiling into a shade some distant relative of the dye. Started to say, *God, you must think I* . . . Stopped. Some things even I refused to call attention to. Never point out your own flaws, that's what my mother always told me in high school. Never point out your own transference.

"Oh, you like it? Aris thinks I look like Lucille Ball. He says I should at least dye my pubic hair too."

"Typical. Not all redheads have red body hair, you know."

I did *not* want to go there. Heard my voice, struck by a sudden epiphany which might or might not have been feigned: "I did it because it makes me and Kendra look less alike. She's terminally attached to blond, so really I had no choice."

"No choice. Hmm. Well."

I tucked my hair behind my ears, a gesture I hoped would magically render me bald. "So, about my dream . . ."

"Yes, right. Another? I wasn't aware there'd been a first fire dream."

"Well it didn't seem important until there was more than one. But now it's a reoccurring dream, right? Or is that *recurring*? Is there such a word as recurring, or do people just pronounce re-occurring that way?"

You were looking at me. You were always looking at me, but now I found that, in my straight-backed chair, conscious of my butt cheeks pushing into the stiff cushion in a futile effort to make their mark, I could not negotiate what to do with my own eyes. I lowered them to my fingers, fidgety around the Christmas mug you'd given me (you're *Jewish*, what's the matter with you?). The hot, indeterminate liquid inside smelled good but tasted like a bath cube.

"Why don't you just tell me about the most recent dream."

"Kendra always tells me my dreams are boring."

An eyebrow rose. "I promise not to nod off." Then, "Is it hard for you to talk about?"

"No. It's an easy dream, really. There's all kinds of smoke in my room." I coughed nervously, to illustrate. "I bolt up in my bed to look for Kendra, and instead my father is sitting there, in a rocking chair next to my bed. He's just sitting there. When I grab his arm, he says, 'Good, you're up. I didn't want to wake you, but now we can go.' We walk down the stairs. I can hardly breathe with all the smoke, but I don't feel hot or see any flames. Outside, Kendra isn't there. My mother is waiting for us. She's hugging me, but when I ask about Kendra, she turns away and starts to water the rose bushes. Then I know that nobody wants to tell me, but Kendra is dead. I'm not sure if it's the fire that killed her, or if she's just gone."

"So it's a calculated act on the part of your parents to keep you from her. Or even to sacrifice her for you?"

I snorted ungracefully. "That's wish fulfillment in action, all right." A tingle up my spine. "But wait, actually when I was telling you just now, it made me remember how in the first dream, my father rescues Kendra from the fire, and I won't go to him, so I'm going to be killed. I'm always thinking she's his favorite . . . well, because she is. But maybe I felt guilty. Maybe I had the second dream to punish myself, like, *Oh, you don't want him to help your sister? Well how would you like it if he didn't and she was dead?*" I smiled—I could feel it—triumphantly.

"That may be one possibility."

"You think it's too easy. Not everything has to be complicated, you know. I've always been jealous of Kendra's relationship with our dad. It's normal that I'd feel guilty for—"

"Hold on, slow down. If my response was tentative, it wasn't because your solution isn't 'complicated' enough, it was because you were doing it again, hyper-analyzing. That's just more intellectual than I personally feel is useful. I'd rather hear how the dream made you feel."

"Maybe it made me feel guilty."

"I'm sure it did. But is it all right if I ask you not to label it and file it away under 'guilt' just yet? That closes off any other possibilities. And even if you're right on target, isn't it more useful to look at how that guilt manifests while you're awake? Dreams are just dreams."

I laughed the way people do when somebody has said something horribly wrong and doesn't know it. Blurted—I could not resist giving you the chance to redeem yourself— "Don't you believe in dream analysis? Don't you believe we create symbols in our dreams?"

"That dreams are symbolic doesn't necessarily lead to their being the keys to how we should live our lives."

"Well, sure, I don't mean it's like some formula. But in high school, Kendra and Otto and I used to go to all these occult bookstores and get books on what different dreams meant. I kept a journal of my dreams my whole senior year. And I was a psych major in college."

"Oh, yes, believe me, I know."

"What is that supposed to mean?" But before you could respond, I was touching my hair, thinking of it again, trying to jam it down but it wouldn't go. The bloom of a new flush scattered from my cheeks to my chest. I did not think I had ever seen my sister blush. The physical conspiracy fate and my body were in against my dignity made me want to howl.

"Maybe I dyed my hair red because I've been dreaming about fire. That would make symbolic sense."

"Kirby." You touched your own head in mimesis. "Are you under the impression that I think you dyed your hair because of me? You seem very skittish, but honestly, I don't think that, and if I did I'd be flattered, not upset."

"Well, let's face it, it looks a little *Single White Female*. One week I meet you for the first time and the next I'm waltzing in like Little Orphan Annie. What else would you think?"

"I think you shouldn't worry so much about my impression of you. I wish you'd stop wondering what your old psychology professors would say or whether you're going to get an A on the test. There is no test here, and if there were, I would be the one being tested. And the first thing I'd do would be to wonder whether anyone else in your life has red hair besides me, not to assume some transference that gratifies my ego. Just relax. Please."

Oh, I did not feel relaxed. Did not think I would ever be able to relax again. I half-yelled: "But I've said it all wrong anyway, this is all—none of this matters! I don't know anyone with red hair and I don't care about my dream, I don't even know why I brought it up. Something's going on with my parents. My father's drinking again, I know for a fact because I've seen him. But I didn't know until the other night that he's on antidepressants. Shit, wait. Okay, the night after Kendra came home, I went to their house. They were acting weird, and my mother was crying. Then they had this scene at dinner the other night, and my mom left in some melodramatic cloud of weeping and mystery. That is not like my mother. My mother is very calm! They're freaking out, and they won't say why."

You took what people less uptight than I might describe as a deep, cleansing breath. "Okay," you exhaled briskly. "You've switched gears here suddenly, and I can't help but wonder why. But what you're bringing up seems important, so we'll go with it for now. What exactly are you afraid your parents are hiding?"

It was not that I had expected you to hug me for my outburst. It was not that I wouldn't have run out of your office screaming had you tried. I was too erratic for affection, too *something*—somehow wrong, I knew. But in that moment I had my first hint of how pleasurable it would be to hurt you. In that moment, a line was drawn with sides, and you were not on mine.

"Why don't you tell me? I know what *you're* hiding! I went to their house the other day when I knew they'd be out. I went to look . . . for bottles of alcohol, I don't know, and I saw the Paxil and Risperdal in the medicine cabinet. You prescribed them! I thought you hadn't seen my father in, like, nine years! Has he been on them all that time, or is this—"

"You know I can't comment on that."

"Yeah, well that's unfair." And tears. No noise, but still another bodily betrayal. "That's failure to protect, that's . . . When I was thirteen and he was drinking . . . it was bad, okay. He was pissed off all the time. My mother stopped talking to or even looking at us. But what do you care, your confidentiality is with him."

"I do care, Kirby. I'll tell you that I thought about you and your sister a lot back then, what the two of you must have gone through before he got into treatment. If you suspect him of drinking again, that brings up a lot of old memories. A lot of old pain."

"No, it makes me furious!" I strained at the edge of the cushion, the muscles of my thighs holding me upright lest I and my chair topple forward. "You don't get it. Everything's a secret from me. Even Kendra acts like I'm ten years younger and have to be kept in a blindfold. She's complicit. I'm the only one who isn't in on what's going on."

"Is that true, Kirby? Slow down and think. Are you sure it doesn't just feel that way?"

"No!" The way you kept saying my name, I couldn't bear it, if you did it again I would claw my leaky eyes out just to disappear. A long time. A long time passed before I could speak with neither panic nor tears. "I have no idea what Kendra knows. We never talk about it. She says we're adults now and have to forget about *them*. But she always stabs me in the back. She's in on whatever skeletons they're hiding—I don't know if they told her, or if she just knows. But she'd sell me out for them. She denies it, that's the worst part. Just like in the first dream, when she told me to hide in the basement to keep safe from the fire, but as soon as our dad came down the stairs, she ditched me and ran into his arms."

"So the dream is less about your parents' betrayal than your sister's? But does it have to be such an either—or choice? Couldn't you just run to him too?"

I shook my head hard in irritable desperation you must have found childish but which I could not control. "Of course not."

"Why?"

My eyes rose to yours: a challenge I didn't understand. "I'm too weak. His arms were full of her, and it'd be easier if I were dead, for everyone concerned. I'd be out of the way. Then I'd never know."

Fragment

For me, this long ago ceased to be primarily a
legal or political issue and became instead a
painful personal one, demanding atonement
and daily work towards reconciliation and
restoration of trust with my family, my
friends, my Administration, and the American
people.

—Bill Clinton,
Response to question posed by the House
Judiciary Committee, November 27, 1998

May 1994

Kirby's head flopped back and forth on her neck like a cartoon punching bag; Kendra sputtered laughter into her Williams-Sonoma napkin. Her mother averted her eyes, but her father glared head on. Kendra knocked her fork to the floor, wove into the kitchen under the pretext of a new one although she couldn't eat with Mr. Kelsey and his glamorous wife at the table, felt like a cow chewing its cud. Kirby swerved around in her chair to stare down the corridor into the kitchen; Kendra willed her to come back, ask ask ask, *but no, of course not, no. She stood at the counter, frustrated by the lack of alcohol—what kind of household did not have a bottle of wine sitting out to breathe for when the (nonexistent in her family) first bottle was drained? Such hypocrisy, when her father, like she, had probably downed every substance he could get his hands on moments before arriving home tonight; already speeding, she'd still sucked the bong so long Otto yanked her shoulder back, "Hey, get off." He made her swear not to touch the acid until Sunday when she had no ballet and they could spend the day tripping—she'd promised, but when his car veered onto Woodstock Avenue, it was too much, she shoved it onto her tongue before he could stop her; he made a big show of getting mad. "Now I'll have to come and break you out later, baby, so it won't be wasted," he said, but she didn't buy it, he'd get distracted jamming with his buddies, forget about her problems like guys always did.*

Mr. Kelsey emerged from the half-bath, glancing in both directions like he was crossing a street. She was the wrong direction, but he headed to the kitchen regardless, said like it was his house, "Can I help?" She said, "Uh, I know where everything is, I live here," and he just looked and looked, then, "If we ask for you to sleep over tonight so you can babysit in the morning, they may not know how to get out of it and let you go. You shouldn't be here, flaunting your high, looking for trouble. Your father is worried about you." She started laughing again, even though his head wasn't flopping, just sort of blurred and multiple and too bright like a neon sign. Said, like she'd say to anyone because really he was just anyone, being hot didn't change that, "Gee, thanks, but I've got it under control." "Then you should go back to your seat instead of behaving like you're lost," he said and turned her by the wing of her shoulder blade. At the table her mother's eyes didn't raise but her father and Bee were watching with opposite expressions that looked exactly the same: concern and fury, which was which? She sat, body like butter, and maybe Mr. Kelsey was right, she should get out of here fast, maybe—

The doorbell rang. Otto stood, a stack of physics books in his arms. "Is Kendra ready to go to the library?" he said. His long hair belied studying on Friday night, but he was a science freak, everybody knew. "She hasn't finished dinner yet," Kendra's mother said, "but you're welcome to sit down." Kendra bolted from her chair, slung her motorcycle jacket on before her mother could maneuver the door shut. Bounced up and down, unable to control the movement a millisecond longer. "Don't worry, Mr. Braun," Otto chimed from the foyer, giving a salute toward the table. "I won't let your daughter fail Physics, you have my word." The last thing she heard was Mr. Kelsey's aborted burst of laughter before she shut the door.

*   *   *

There would be a dinner. There would be an incident. There would be a savior. It would be as simple as that.

Kendra was embarrassed. She was embarrassed by the way her mother sat, hands folded on the kitchen table, preparing to break the news. She was embarrassed by the image of herself and Kirby as vulnerable children about to be dealt a blow. She wanted to say, *Look, do we really have to do this?* She might be expected to cry. Kirby was crying, although this was less a happening than a given. At one time, Kendra had believed her sister's tears a sign of weakness, but had since come to understand them as an indication that Kirby was smarter than she. Tears meant nothing else was required of her, meant she would not be looked upon to speak.

"Your father is depressed. Dr. Friedland had to give him some medication."

Kendra was supposed to do something to indicate at least a mild level of surprise. But she was not surprised. Her father had worn the aroma of grief for as long as she could recall. It had never occurred to her that he was not perfectly justified in his despair. It was the drinking her mother minded most anyway, not the despair. It was that people would say, *Her husband drinks, you know,* and Kendra's mother would be humiliated, as humiliated as Kendra felt now.

"Your father needs you," her mother said. "Remember him in your prayers. And stay for dinner tonight, he'll want to see—"

"Fine." But she'd spoken so quickly her consent sounded rude.

In the year since Kendra had last been to the house, nothing had changed. Ordinarily this might have been reassuring, but since the night at Gordon, Kendra had come to suspect the ordinary as possessing a secret, violent undertow. When her father returned from work, though, his shoulders slumped in a way less familiar than the house. The surprise in his eyes at seeing them there—unfamiliar too—made her sad. It made Kirby happy, even though Bee was worried—Kendra could see it in the way she pursed her mouth. Their father hugged them, each in turn. Kirby looked hungry for the hug. Kendra knew it was only the novelty of her presence that inspired this show of affection; she could not remember being hugged upon his entering rooms when she lived at home.

Aris showed up for dinner too, unexpectedly. Kirby must have called him earlier in secret, while they were on Oak Street shopping for Kendra's maid of honor dress. Kendra imagined her whispering into a payphone during one of her alleged trips to the bathroom: *Please come, I can't handle them alone.* The fantasy made her feel closer to Kirby, even as she felt a sudden hole of loneliness at having no one upon whose mercy to throw herself to save her from her family.

Aris, in a shirt buttoned too high and a leather coat he failed to take off within a reasonable amount of time, would not conform to her vision of a savior. He smelled clean as the house, like he could be part of the furniture, except that her mother's tastes ran to florals and embroideries, not leather. Her father wore a cardigan and corduroys with leather house slippers. He seemed an accessory to Aris, or maybe it was the other way around. The two of them could be a house of their own: clean, coordinated, big.

Over salad, her mother said, "Kendra, darling, you look thin. You're not under Company dictatorship anymore, you know. Men in the real world like a little meat on the bones."

Kendra laughed. She couldn't help it. She was thinking of herself at fourteen, kneeling on her parents' bathroom carpet (hers at the time too), with Kirby's toothbrush crammed so far down her throat she thought it'd disappear. No use, the damned thing was ineffectual; she had no gag reflex to speak of. How convenient: she anticipated a lifetime of compliments due to this gift. In the base antithesis of art that was sex, even big girls could blow a guy, everyone knew. The thought was sickening, so she'd swallowed a mouthful of Scope and left the toothbrush right where she'd found it—who'd guess? They shared the same germs anyway, though Kirby had grown squeamish, was into this thing where she wouldn't use utensils after others and dabbed her cheek with the back of her hand after being kissed, so it was kind of funny, considering. The kind of joke Kendra liked best: one she couldn't tell.

"Mom, you need glasses. I haven't taken class in weeks, I'm too huge for the mirror."

Her father said, "You look lovely. Get off her case, Gail, the girl's been skinny all her life, she's not going to change now."

Aris offered, "Since you can't dance now, K, if only you were taller you could model."

It was an absurd thing to say. Kendra recalled this from her adolescence—how being a twin sometimes created the illusion of beauty simply by virtue of there being twice what, in a single person, would amount only to a mild prettiness. Also the way one twin always got all the credit. Clearly Kirby remembered too, because she snapped, "Oh, that's just great! Maybe I could be her wardrobe assistant, and nobody would even notice we have the same face."

Aris said, "Your looks are different, though. You heard your mom, models have to look half-starved and sick. Heroin chic and all—not that *Kendra* . . ." He glanced at his future father-in-law. Swallowed. "It's a stupid term. You're too normal-looking, Bee, that's all I meant."

"Uh-oh," Kendra said. "Kirby hates nothing more than being accused of being normal. Cool! If she dumps you, I won't be subjected to another day of looking for a dress."

And everybody laughed. Sort of. Probably they all expected Aris to drool a little over her, even Kirby. Families grow attached to patterns. Nobody, Kendra knew, was afraid of a cancelled wedding. Events of such dramatic weight were not common in her family, at least not instigated by Kirby. Everybody exhaled, tension evaporating like the memory of a short, inconvenient trip. So good to be back in America. The salad was fine. Everybody laughed.

The main course was served.

How do fights begin in families? They are contextualized, embedded in the underlined verses of well-worn scripts. Scenes are skipped, and one is suddenly at the climax without knowing how one arrived. Those on the inside understand their cues. Lines are rattled off mechanically—a chain reaction—until the body count accumulates on the floor. If a family dinner were the theater, the director would yell "Cut!" Actors would not be allowed to ad-lib. But between the lines of a family's text, improvisation is allowed. Critics have been encouraged to fill in the blanks. There is no director on the premises, only the multiple interpretations of an ambiguity that confuses and disarms. If a family dinner got reviewed in the *New York Times*, it would be called a *tour de force*. "The emotions," the reviewer would write, "oscillate with a range worthy of *King Lear*—from excitement to despair in a second flat. The characters are convincing allegories of the state of postmodern, suburban decay. The way Mrs. Braun's hands shake when she carries in the dinner rolls, the way her daughter, Kendra, pulls the sleeves of her sweater over her wrists and tucks pieces between her delicate fingers—these are the details that make a memorable performance. Only an unknown, tragically Miss Clairol redhead, in the role of a peripheral daughter with few lines, seemed weak."

But as an extra, my lines were expendable. The star was on a roll.

Kendra was staring down at her untouched chicken breast realizing that her mother's very essence boiled down to an inability to process the fact that poultry was still meat, when her father said, "So I hear you're taking Otto for a ride again. Don't you think you should be a little more considerate? He's not exactly . . ." he groped the air, "successful like Aris, here. The poor kid needs his money."

For a moment Kendra could not remember where she was. She glanced at the bodies around her at the table to gauge their familiarity—to see whether any of them belonged to her.

"Guess you're too busy spending the day in his bed and the nights partying with his grunge band friends to bother coming over to see us," her father railed.

"Guess even though you're not the up-and-coming soloist anymore, you still feel entitled to break men's hearts for fun and neglect your low-culture, bourgeois family," he continued.

"At least when you lived in New York, we could pretend it was the distance that kept you away and not your indifference."

Kendra downed her wine in one long sip, a drop of which ran down her chin. "So, Dad." She tipped her chair back on

59

one leg. "I hear you're popping antidepressants like they're going out of style. Ever try speed? Guitarist deals it if you'd like to give it a try."

"Whoa," Aris muttered. "Kendra, hey—"

"Then we could all party nights together instead of your having to compare notes with his parents on what a selfish, corrupting temptress I am. Gee, Kirb, aren't you glad I came home? Dad has to make up for lost time—you're in for a good year of the target always being me."

"It was never me anyway," Kirby said matter-of-factly. "Nobody cares what I do."

Kendra burst out laughing. Her father rose from the table. Her mother pleaded, a weird urgency in her voice, "Kendra, apologize to your father. His feelings are hurt that you've been in town a month and this is only the second time we've seen you. You're overreacting—please."

"Yeah, I'm sorry." Kendra sneered. "Let's just eat this decapitated body we all said grace over, or God might strike us dead."

"Why must you always be contemptuous of everything?" her mother asked, and Kendra shrugged, stared at her mother's crestfallen face, then averted her gaze. Anyone who did not know her might have taken her expression as one of contrition, but Kendra knew her father *did* know her better. She wondered whether he wanted to slap his wife for begging Kendra to be nice to him, and if her mother had done it only to humiliate him. She tipped her chair back further. Her father watched as though he hoped to see her fall on her ass, but was resigned to his belief that her instincts were steel and gold: she never miscalculated, never got it wrong. He had told her once when she was seventeen that if she jumped from the ledge of a building, she would be sure to break her fall by landing on somebody she knew and didn't care for. She had screamed back that she would aim to land on *him*, but he shook his head sadly and said no, he would not be so lucky, that instead he would be the one left living to foot her hospital bill.

"I will not be insulted in my own home by a spoiled girl who conducts her life like a whore in Amsterdam," he was shouting now. "You have no right to judge me! Look at you!"

"But Dad," Kirby began, feeling her way. "Kendra wasn't judging you, you're the one accusing *her*. You picked a fight for no—"

60

"Don't you get it, Bee?" Kendra laughed. "He lives for these *Poor me, my daughter is the whore of Babylon* encounters. This is fun for him. Tell her, Henry, what a blast you're having—look, before she cries."

That did it. You will be reminded that King Lear—whom I invoked earlier and promise not to mention again—ultimately caused the demise of his entire royal house due to a daughter's failure to declare her boundless love. And maybe then, you will understand how the balance in which my family's entire future hung amounted to simply that moment: my sister's blatant disrespect in addressing our father—there in front of all of us—by his given name.

Kendra's teeth clacked together loudly; she clenched her jaw tight enough to lock. Her mother lowered her head, part revealing not a touch of gray. Her father stared at his wife as if to compare her steadfastness with his daughter's treason. Kendra knew it was she whom her father wanted to see cry; that he wished to replace the tears of his loyal wife with *her* tears. But if he could not hurt Kendra alone (as he never could), he would content himself (as he always did) with their tears flowing simultaneously. Motionless, her father stood at the head of the table. At the opposite end, her mother whispered, "Oh, Kendra. If only you knew what you were doing."

Her father roared, "She wouldn't care!" Gripped the edge of the table, linen crumpling under his fingers. "She'll be happy—no one to interrupt her sense of entitlement by nagging her to go back to college. She'll be free to do whatever she damn well pleases once I'm dead."

Kirby shouted, "What are you talking about?"

Their mother jumped forward to grab onto her husband's arm and restrain him, but he was too far away. Instead she swayed into Aris, who caught her wrist and steadied her, looking befuddled. She tottered around the table like a woman blinded, groping her way to her husband as though her touch might re-ignite reason in his brain. Kirby too was crying, "I'm sick of these code words and spy games! I want to know what's going on, and I want to know right now!" *She's become a woman,* Kendra thought. *First defending me and now this.* Kendra's mother tugged on her husband's sleeve, but he turned to her with the incomprehension of a stranger and shook her off. Kendra had stopped looking at any of them, was staring off at the wall thinking, *Shit, I really did it this time. How the fuck do I*

*get the money for a ticket back to New York before our rollicking
Christmas dinner? What can I sell, what can I do?*

"I'm sorry to break the news at a moment like this, Kirby,"
her father said, and it was all Kendra could do not to press her
hands over her ears, to sing to drown him out. "I'm sick, honey.
Very ill. I've known for a while now, and I just have too much
to deal with to put up with this kind of abuse anymore. I'm
sick, sweetheart. I'm sorry to tell you this way, but I promise I
will be at your wedding—"

Her mother actually screamed, "Henry, no—"

"I've known for three months. Your mother only one. We
never meant to tell you; we never meant to burden—"

"Tell us what?" Fear in her voice where she wanted
defiance. Stinging in her eyes, focused on him now. Was this
what he wanted? Did he feel the devotion he needed in this:
the palpitations of her heart, the gooseflesh of her skin? Was
this love—*manipulative—bastard—storm out—show he can't—
holds no power any—God—*

"Tell us what?" Kendra repeated.

"There's no other way to say this." In the stillness of the
room, he laughed a little. Next to him, her mother was silent.
She had gotten a clue. He reached for her hand and she gripped
it. Aris grasped for Bee's. Kendra's alone remained unheld,
her body ununited.

"AIDS isn't a death sentence anymore, girls. They're
making advances every day. So many new drugs, sometimes
there's not even any trace left of the virus in your blood . . ."

Kendra's fingers groped the air, loose and empty.

And then, right then, the world began to close.

*   *   *

May 1994

*She woke to the feel of eyes on her skin. The darkness, after
several hours of sleep, seemed a gray-blue lens through which she
could see perfectly. Her combat boots were not at the door; it had
been some months since she'd militantly propped them there before
retiring. In the neon illumination of the bedside clock, she saw him,
sitting quietly at the foot of her bed. He seemed almost to support
his own weight, so little of his body rested on the mattress. She
could not feel his weight, or maybe it was just that he had been there
so long that the slope—if there was one—felt natural. She found
strangely that she was not afraid. It was not without relief that she*

gina frangello

sat up to view him head on. Not even, in the hazy fugue of sleep, without pleasure. She stared at him, though he was not looking in her direction. He held something in his hand which she could not see, and his eyes rested on it with a sadness or resignation that also struck her as ordinary—no cause for alarm. What she said, if anything, was, "I knew you would come."

It was not a dream. It was not that, later, she ever suspected she was dreaming. It was simply that he never answered. Only that—just when she thought she had won something, some small measure of predictability if nothing (though there was something) else—he didn't respond, still didn't look at her. She gleaned only a flash of the bag he held tight between his fingers before he stood and—Kendra felt the consequence of his weight after all; the mattress sprang back tight—without a word, left the room.

*   *   *

And then, right then, the world began to close.

Strobe lights. Kendra kept repeating in her mind, *I am at the Artful Dodger dancing with Guitarist, I am at the Artful Dodger dancing with Guitarist.* Nearly a week had passed since her father's announcement, but if she let herself feel too high she would be there again in the dining room, the sound of his fist pounding against the table echoing like the *boom boom boom* of bass in her ears. *Strobelightstrobelights.* She had heard that if you were pregnant or had a heart condition, strobe lighting could bring on a seizure, or maybe it was a stroke. She was pretty sure she was not pregnant, but as to her heart, one could never tell. When it came to the heart, who could ever tell? She might be in danger. Guitarist might have purposely put her in danger. Before they went to the dance floor, she had told him the lighting could harm her, but he'd only laughed and said, "Baby, your heart's made of stone, a little flashing light sure can't break it if I can't." It was possible, though, that he would like to see her hurt, convulsing on the floor. Perhaps she would wake paralyzed, without even the good grace to die, and then he would sure as hell not stick around. Next to her, he convulsed with volition, twitching to the beat of the music. Acid house. Acid. House. He waved his own hands in front of him, turned his face up to the light. Under it, his skin assumed a greenish pallor that alarmed her. His flesh hung loose, peeled off when the light struck it just so. Acid light, burning his face.

63

Kendra did not move. Could not move. Bodies pulsed around her, more dangerous than the light. An elbow hit her in the temple. If the temple was struck from a certain angle, your eye could pop spontaneously out of your head. Everybody knew that since grade school. Children understood that bodies were dangerous. Things sometimes just fell off, fell apart. Kendra felt her feet falling off. Falling off the edge of something that was high and tall and long. Dark. Under the light, Guitarist writhed to protest his peeling skin. He seemed nobody she knew. The light was not flashing anymore. Hands gripped her, tugged her; she crouched at the edge of the ledge to avoid the jagged limbs. A chair there, suddenly, a chair for her; if she sat, she would be easier to push off the ledge. She would have no resistance. Everybody knew it was dangerous to sit, that the body created its own resistance. The stranger who was Guitarist bent over her with his face still full of skin. "Let's go to the bathroom," he said. "Come on, K-hole, let's go." Purple everywhere. Walls of purple; there was nothing to fall off of in here. He promised. Nobody could fall apart in here. Hair spilled over her face to protect her own skin. She dragged deep on a joint hoping it would mellow out the trip. The stranger put his tongue in her mouth and it tasted of the joint she was sucking on, his spit tasted of the sweat she was sweating, he murmured, "Come on," so she might as well suck on the sweat he was sweating. She might as well get on her knees where it was harder to fall off anything because she was closer to the ground. From the ground the stranger with his fly open loomed over her like a balloon. "Baby," he begged. On the other side of the door, somebody was yelling, pounding. There might be a fire. Fellatio in public places had been known to cause accidents, everyone knew. But that was mainly on the road. Kendra was not on the road. Was not on the road was at a bar was tripping on acid with her best friend was in the toilet blowing her best friend was making a fool of herself because everyone knew having no money and a sore back and not being a star was nothing to fall into the ground about. It was possible this herniation in her disc had always been there, waiting to reveal itself. Maybe she just hadn't known. Maybe her father had always been dying, and she just hadn't known. It could take a decade for a flaw in a disc to materialize it could take a decade for a virus to materialize. Guitarist moaned, "You look so hot tonight, K, so pretty, I'm so fucking pathetically in love with you, you won't remember I said it tomorrow, let me inside you, let me in, baby, please." Ten years to finish dying. Bodies were treasonous, everyone knew. Look what treason it took to acquire just one word, that one she'd never mastered, treacherous girl hiding out on a bathroom floor with a boy not a man a boy who never could save her. *No.*

Then: nothing but dryness. Cottony tobacco and oily weed and the synthetic aftertaste of a trip, which meant everything was done. Her body on the futon lay wrapped in what she must have been wearing the night before. Next to her, Guitarist's vulnerable hard-on pulsed under the thin, sweat-dried sheet. She stood. No sun, no way to gauge time. But not night. Possibly she had to get to the Dance Center, possibly she had slept through work and would be fired, but no, they wouldn't fire her this soon, not their token NYCB star—she was fresh cachet. Still, if she didn't get a second job, she'd never have money for rent let alone food. On the futon, Guitarist's arm reached out for her; she watched it slosh around searching the way one watches a dying insect writhe. Even if she *had* let him fuck her, she'd only have bought another week here, maybe two. Unconditional pussy would just piss him off if what he wanted was a girlfriend. With ballet no longer his competitor she knew he expected her to relent, but too late. The slow erosion of whatever elusive quality constituted *otherness* in him had already taken place, year by year, so he seemed less a lover than a sibling—a stand-in for Bee—a surrogate twin. With a real job she could afford to study modern dance. She'd learn fast and go on auditions and work as a waitress like ex-ballerinas did. Other injured girls in their prime whose fathers were not dying. On the toilet she checked to make sure last night had really played like she remembered. *I'll let you come-shot instead*—what if she'd dreamed it? Okay, dry. Her breath slowed down.

Outside, the air was half-heartedly cold, without the snow that would make people happy this time of year. Without the kitsch of a white Christmas to make them believe their problems had dimmed. Wind whipped her hair, shoved a sharp wisp of stale smoke up her nostrils. She could not face the El. Had been down this road before: en route to throw herself on the mercy of the court, for schools, tours, costumes. With her last twenty, she hailed a cab.

On a Thursday afternoon, her father presumably still at work, she and her mother standing in the oak foyer of her parents' house, Kendra's coat still on and feet confident in first position on the damp entrance rug, her mother would say no.

She would say: "After the way you spoke to your father at dinner the other night, after everything he's been through, you have some nerve to come in here and ask for a handout."

She would say: "You are twenty-two years old. You chose to throw away the college education we offered. You chose to pursue a career in which girls are over the hill at thirty even if they don't hurt their backs. You will live with your choices like the rest of us. You can work at McDonald's to save money if you have to, young lady, this cash store is closed."

The weak rain falling from the chilly sky seemed fittingly anticlimactic for her defeat. This was the meaning of irony, surely. This rain and the figure of her father, medicated, infected, heading up the stairs just in time. Just in time to witness her there, where she had stood so many times before, not even begging, having felt both too entitled and too ashamed to beg. His arms were full of packages wrapped by Bloomingdale's, Marshall Field's. He came to her with his arms full of offerings. He came like a lover on the stairs and offered his money and his secrets. He said, "I'm sorry about the other night, princess." He said, "You can imagine the stress I've been under, not to mention these damned meds." He muttered, "That whore of Amsterdam comment. Honestly, that was uncalled for, it was too much, even for me."

He would say: "Here is the key to an apartment I've rented for some time."

He would say: "Here is a check. Fill in whatever you need."

He would say: "Don't tell your mother."

She did as he asked. Struck a bargain like old enemies who, through random chance or the death of previous acquaintances, somehow mistook each other for friends. The rain dripped relentless in a way that could not be good for him, not now. Kendra pocketed his check fast to keep the ink from running, felt it safe in her grasp within the pocket of another man's coat. She knew no comment was ever uncalled for; there was no comment she could not merit. She left him and his virus, abandoned them under the suddenly treacherous rain on the once-again complicit negotiating table of the front stairs.

She knew she was a whore.

There would be a dinner. There would be an incident . . .

Kendra's stomach was growling hard. She thought about calling Guitarist to come and get her, but he had a painting job in Pilsen and needed the money, plus he didn't own a car. Though she had not eaten in twenty-four hours, she was sure she would throw up soon. She walked a few blocks west and went to the bathroom of an Amoco station, but nothing happened. She had been so certain. Her body's lack of predictability alarmed her.

When she got out, the rain was coming down harder. She had next to no cash now and did not know whom to call. Kirby? Aris was off for Christmas Eve, and they would be hanging around doing some quaint bullshit like hanging stockings, or else crying over her father. In either case, she couldn't take it. She fumbled through her bag for change, heading for the pay phone on the other side of the parking lot. Did not know whom she would call until she found herself dialing information for Michael Kelsey's number. Her change depleted, she used her parents' MCI card number to place the actual call. He answered on the second ring.

"You know," she said, and she thought her voice would break, "when I turned you down, the idea was that you would be so heart-broken, you'd send me flowers every day and camp on my doorstep until I agreed to a second date. I thought your generation was supposed to go in for women who play hard to get."

His laughter on the other end of the line cheered her, put some strength back into her legs. "Just like a twenty-year-old. Assuming my world would end because a moody girl decided she had something to prove. It's enviable the way the young exaggerate their own importance in the world. Once you're my age, you realize you aren't all that important."

"But I'm not your age," she said. "So I choose to believe that you've thought of me nonstop since we last met. And I'll have you know I'm twenty-two. And a half."

"Well, I wouldn't say nonstop," he began, "but I have thought of you. They weren't the kindest of thoughts, Kendra. Where are you? Why did you call?"

"I'm in the lot outside a gas station in Kenilworth," she said. "And I called because I have nowhere else to go."

"Give me the street," he said, and the lump in her throat rushed up to sting her nose. "I'll be right there."

She saw his black Porsche approaching from three blocks away. He drove too fast and swung into the gas station without getting into the turn lane. Kendra got in quietly, drenched with rain. She stared at his cell phone, discarded on the dashboard, to avoid looking at him.

"You smell of sex," he said, and handed her a sweater. It was burgundy wool, neatly folded. He had obviously brought it for her since, apart from it, there was no clutter in the car.

They drove to his apartment. Kendra sat on his couch while he made coffee. Decaffeinated. Kendra had never seen the point in drinking decaf, but she accepted it, and the warmth made her teeth stop chattering. They had spoken less than two sentences to each other since he'd picked her up. He looked as though he'd been planning to work at home that day: papers were piled in stacks all over the apartment, and he wore an old flannel shirt that might have belonged to his father. After she finished the coffee, he handed her a blanket.

"Why don't you go to sleep? I can go in to the office to work."

She stood and started peeling off her wet clothes to wrap herself in the blanket. Michael seemed oblivious to her as she undressed. He did not even comment on the fact that she didn't wear underwear; men *always* commented on that. Kendra brought her hand up to her rain-soaked hair—though she hadn't even washed her face since the previous morning, the likelihood of her being hideous enough that even her cunt was uninteresting was slim. Of course, he might still be angry about their botched date, though he wasn't acting mad.

"I'm sorry I made you come out in the rain on Christmas Eve to get me."

He didn't seem to hear. "So you just had a fight with your new boyfriend and ran to complain to your mother. Since she wasn't home, you called me to get back at him. Close?"

"No."

"In that case the argument must've been with Henry, and it's him you're getting back at. Mmm, he has been temperamental lately, but I never thought you took him that seriously."

Though his guess was still off, she heard the words as though they were truth, told herself it was what had happened.

It thrilled her, the way he poked fun of her father as though he were a harmless child. Pleased her so much that she stepped closer and leaned her head against his chest. His heart beat steady and strong. Reassuring. Almost instantly, he stepped away.

"Right now, you need to sleep." He took her by the shoulders. "You shouldn't think that because I don't have sex with you immediately, I've lost interest. There's plenty of time for that." He smiled, but it was not a flirtatious smile, rather a pensive one. "You're an expert in the choreography of pursuit, you ought to know these things. This dance has just begun."

She slept in his bed, which reminded her of a hotel room or the display bed in a shopping mall. Unused, as though no one had touched it in weeks. The sheets and duvet were completely unwrinkled, but did not smell or feel as if they'd been put on recently. She wondered if he was in the habit of sleeping elsewhere, and why he had offered to let her stay if he had another woman with whom he was practically living. She had only just started to calculate reasons and possibilities when darkness enveloped her and she dropped into a stiff, heavy sleep, as dreamless as any she had ever known. Still and urgent, and when she woke her head ached like she'd been pressing it into the pillows with the weight of bricks. Michael sat on the floor near the bed, though she didn't notice him until his newspaper crackled; she glimpsed the phrases *Wag the Dog* and *Operation Desert Fox*. The clock next to the bed indicated it was eight in the evening.

"It's late," she said. "When did you get in?"

"About an hour ago."

"Why didn't you wake me?"

"What for?"

"It's Christmas Eve." She struggled to sit, didn't make it. "Don't you have . . . plans?"

"None. My daughter is in Florida with her mother, visiting her grandparents." He turned the page of his paper again and fresh fear clogged her windpipe—he was a middle-aged man, an attorney, hard facts were his forte. Postponement of impeachment debates and votes, results of impeachment debates and votes, an end to the cease fire as Serbian forces killed more ethnic Albanians, bombing again in Iraq. Since she'd left home at eighteen, Kendra had owned no TV, did not read the paper—in what spare time? Here in the real world, it was all people talked about: Clinton's cigars and banal adolescent naughtiness; Milosevic, the new, inadequate Hitler; Sadaam with his disease warfare that hadn't caused or kept her father from getting AIDS. All men who wanted what men wanted: big fame and bigger dicks. She could not believe these dangers in newsprint were more real than the Dark Angel of *Serenade* (had Michael been playing Tchaikovsky too?), yet how, to a man like this, could she be seen as anything other than hopelessly sheltered, hopelessly behind, unable to ever catch up?

But when he spoke it was only: "Are you hungry?"

To this, her answer automatic, always, "Not really."

"You should have something." He got up and left the room. Kendra stared after him, waiting for her breath to calm, but the blackness came again before he could return.

*   *   *

May 1994

The next morning, her speed was missing. She ransacked her room, as if it were possible she'd have put it anywhere other than the usual place. As if it would be better that such a thing should be possible, anything, anything being preferable to this. The image of him next to her bed the previous night played before her the way she relived mistakes after every class — easy things — knees drifting apart during bourrées en pointe, *sloppy spotting in the whip-like* fouetté *turns she used to love. Ever since Otto she'd been so distracted. Kendra knew her speed was gone. She would have burst into tears, but was too afraid. What good were tears when every time you really needed them, you were too afraid? Downstairs, her mother was calling. The tone in her voice gave everything away. She shouted, "Kendra Ruth! Come down here now, I mean right now!" Kirby, in the hallway, scurried to her room to hide until school. She too was afraid, even though she was not being addressed as Kirby Ann. Kendra's father was silent, as all traitors are silent. Seven thirty — he may have even already been gone. Kendra breathed fast on her bed, willing flashbacks of the bag in his fingers. How had she not noticed? How had she just let him go like that? What had she thought he was doing there?*

She would be punished. What fate is fitting a high school girl who depends on pills to get her through hyper-competitive New Trier, ballet class, rehearsals, nights with Otto with her tights around her knees? Why hadn't her father waited until she was out to use the key? No, such camouflage would detract from any mission of treason. The moment of truth is when the betrayed looks into the informant's eyes, and knows everything has changed.

Kendra went down the stairs to face her mother. She would be punished, harshly. The battle had gone to her father. There was still the war, though; what is any family if not a war in progress? She could quit now, accept this loss as final, or simply accept the impossibility of clean triumph. Make her peace with a compromised win.

* * *

It was eleven thirty by the time she was dressed and ready to leave. He had been on the phone for some time while she slept, but whenever she tried to rouse herself enough to listen, she sank to sleep again before deciphering the first sentence. His voice, the whistle of a kettle, shuffling papers, the low tinkle of Chopin on his CD player: these were backdrops for her dreams. A perversion of Baryshnikov's poet pursuing his muse in the *pas de deux* of *Les Sylphides*. Gliding, twirling, maniacal in his triumph, full of vibrant, frightening splendor.

Michael Kelsey walked her to the elevator in bare feet. There had still been no physical contact to speak of between them. He pressed the down button and turned to look at her. Her head was not quite clear.

"It would be good to see you again," he said. "When you're feeling better."

Something in her body released.

"There's something you should know." His eyes stayed fixed on hers. "Your prima ballerina routine, your whims and moods turning on a dime, those things are all very charming. But I can be a very demanding lover, Kendra. Those games won't hold water with me."

Her voice, when it came, was distant. Funneled as if through the fun tunnel of a playground: churning, dizzy. "What does that mean?"

"Not what you're thinking. Let me specify up front— anyone you see or sleep with when you aren't with me is your business. I don't have a lot of time, and I rarely see the same woman more than once or twice a month." His words, the hallway with its fuzzy brown carpeting, everything, had taken on a surreal quality. She might well still be tripping. He hadn't answered her question, so she stayed quiet, waiting for him to go on.

71

"What I mean is that when you're with me, if you're with me, I require that you put all your trust in me. Trust I haven't done anything necessarily to earn. My sexual tastes may be different from other men you've known, and they aren't particularly negotiable. As far as it goes, whatever way it goes, it's all or nothing."

His words conjured ideas, kinky ones. Swinger's parties, leather outfits, bestiality. There was something in the way he looked at her, though, that made her understand these images had little to do with that of which he spoke.

"How do I judge if I can go along if I don't really know what you mean?"

"You don't need to know. You only need to be willing to try, every time on a day-to-day basis. I'll know if it isn't right. You could tell me of course, but you won't have to."

"Oh, *really*? Do you propose to read my mind?"

"No. Only to watch you. That's enough."

A heat rose up in her legs: arousal or fear? The first of many occasions to wonder, *Why am I here?* He smiled when she looked up. "Well," he said, "then you aren't going to say no. I'm glad. As you most likely know, I'd have been very disappointed."

"I haven't agreed to anything yet. You don't know what I'm going to say."

His eyes stayed on her, but he said nothing. The elevator came; they stepped in together. The cage smelled strongly of overripe oranges. She would remember that—citrus and sugar, an unsettling incongruence, with him, the scene. Michael leaned against the wall, his eyes turned away for the moment. She began to breathe again.

"You know," she said, "you make me very nervous."

"Really? You don't seem all that nervous."

"No? And what do I seem?"

"Intrigued mostly. A little pissed off."

A desire to undress him came over her, surprised her. She looked at him angrily as though he had somehow planted it in her head. Then laughed softly at herself.

"Yes, well maybe I am a little. Intrigued."

He took a step toward her, then another, until his body touched hers lightly. She lifted her face to him, and he put one hand firmly on her lower back, moving her closer.

"Good. We'll go reasonably slow. I'm not trying to scare you. Come here. Closer. Yes." He reached over to the buttons on the wall, pressed STOP. All motion ceased instantly. Kendra's heart began to pound in her chest. "Now that this is settled, we can get to know each other better."

Analysis

Yet, bizarrely, what offends this narrator is that the sexual relations did become reciprocal and engaged — that the hero aroused the heroine as much as she aroused him, that he touched and caressed and praised and eventually gave her pleasure, several pleasures. For as the hero becomes more sympathetic as a human being — less contemptuous, more remorseful about his own behavior, more generous in his sexuality — he also (according to the narrator) incriminates himself even deeper.

— Adam Gopnik
on "The [Starr] Report," in the *New Yorker*

Isabelle's Room

IN THE WINTER, THE scent of the shop was cold, but in the summer, the sweet-sour fragrance of mothballs and traces of old perfume rose up at the door to greet me. I remembered that smell and carried it always. Even now, when it was snowing outside, I experienced it wafting to my nostrils, the aromas of other lives released beneath the steam iron Mrs. Kelsey pressed down onto delicate, paper-thin fabrics not created for the sturdy, aerobicized bodies of today. Our muscles, our robust flesh would split right through the seams. The Victorian Era, the shop's specialty, bred bedridden women. Encouraged, even forced frailty. Isabelle's Room dealt in vintage acquired primarily through estate auctions—the clothes of the privileged dead. Dresses, robes, blouses made of materials costly in their day and costly to restore now. Mrs. Kelsey did the restorations. She was an artist: a transcender of time and manipulator of the body's disguises. It was a piracy of sorts; the pieces the shop acquired weren't, in a reverent world, meant to be worn. My dress was purportedly from Queen Victoria's court, though it had not belonged to anyone important. This mixture of history and anonymity appealed to me, grounded me, but still afforded the adventure of the unknown.

I walked into Isabelle's Room with the gastrointestinal sensation of being on a plane during turbulence. Though I had spent all the night before on the toilet, I was so empty now that I recognized the feeling of queasiness for what it was:

some long-pent, irrelevant love. My anus stung when I moved—rawness and angry bacteria. The sensation felt exposing. Behind the steam presser, Mrs. Kelsey's assistant was coated with a thin layer of moisture. About nineteen, the girl seemed a refugee from another time: so impossibly pale it was unimaginable she had seen sunlight since the inception of her work here. She wore her dark hair in a knot at the nape of her neck. The slightest hint of curl was visible around her temples, from constant exposure to steam. The girl's arms (I did not know her name; we had never spoken) were bare under a blood-colored velvet vest. I found her lovely. I harbored an irrational terror of her.

The girl did not acknowledge me until Mrs. Kelsey came into the room. Immediately I was struck by the comparative vibrancy of the older woman's skin, which seemed out of place beside the alabaster girl and yellowed fabrics, despite the shop being her own. Her child. Over a body I annoyingly found myself thinking of as "ripe" or "Amazonian" (this in an awed sense), Mrs. Kelsey wore a distinctly un-Victorian, fire-engine-red kimono dress that flamed only slightly brighter than her hair. Unfeasibly, the hem whispered against the floor when she walked; her legs were long. Towering over me by half a foot, with blatantly D-cup cleavage and full, apple-hips, the specter of her was even more impressive within the confined delicacy of the shop. Some women, even at forty, especially at forty, are just too beautiful. They can get away with anything, flaunt everything and survive. I recalled immediately Mrs. Kelsey's oft-proclaimed, irreverent fondness for rich foods and butter. So unlike my own, wanly beautiful mother, whose life seemed a denial of all things physical: food a bland necessity; fashion and scents more about keeping up appearances than pleasure. I considered Rachel. Mrs. Kelsey's charm would be difficult to emulate, yes, but easier than my mother's martyrdom to attain.

I had cancelled two dress fittings already, but had finally been persuaded by my mother that the wedding plans must move ahead. After all, how would my father feel if I deprived him of the opportunity to walk at least one daughter down the aisle? After all, despite doctors' talk about three-drug cocktails, none of us knew what would happen. The disease had already taken hold; his weight loss and lethargy had originally been attributed to depression, but it was now clear he had been ill for some time. He'd resisted beginning aggressive treatment for two months, stalling over telling my mother. Crucial events should be stalled no further.

I stood in the doorway while the assistant rose from the steam presser and headed in the back to get my dress. Mrs. Kelsey stared at me oddly. I wondered if she knew about my father. For as long as I could recall, she had been part of a loop that allowed her greater access to the lives of my parents than I was usually granted. But the look on Mrs. Kelsey's face was not discernibly one of sympathy. I shifted uncomfortably in my wool coat. Had the impulse to run and grab her by the knees and weep until she took me in her arms. Absurd. Yet she had a daughter who was only twelve, who must upon occasion cry in her mother's arms as twelve-year-old girls are wont to do. My thoughts ran something like: *Always I must expel something.* I stood, sweat swiveling down the sides of my body so that I dreaded taking my coat off, wondering if I could just defecate and cry and sweat myself away until I disappeared.

"Elise will work with you today, Kirby. I have a bit of a headache."

"Do you want an Advil?" It was a ridiculous thing to say, as silly almost as the impulse to be held. As if such a woman would not possess her own Advil. As if she—a Garbo or a Kelly—would ever take such a banal drug as Advil in the first place. No, she should be sipping some remedy made of poisons like absinthe. Smoking opium while reclining on a fainting couch, drinking Coca Cola concocted with cocaine. I looked at Elise with my irrational terror. The girl was tall too, almost as tall as Mrs. Kelsey, though she had flat breasts like Kendra's. Everything in the shop had always been either larger or smaller than I, rendering me the wrong dimensions altogether. Too ordinary to warrant history's having left its imprint on me.

I said (you know your patient, can't let anything lie), "So have you talked to my mother lately per chance?" When at Isabelle's Room, I said things like that, *per chance,* as though they were part of my ordinary speech.

Mrs. Kelsey's head snapped up; the movement, given the length of her swannish neck, seemed dramatic. The gesture reminded me of Kendra dancing, though with a tape measure, Kendra's neck was no longer than my own. "Yes, Kirby, I have. I . . ." Her head ducked again, and this did not remind me of my sister, and I felt strangely better. "I'm sorry about what your family is going through. I know you must—" The phone rang. She looked at it with naked gratitude. Elise (could it really be that I had never heard the girl's name until now? Or had I heard it every time I entered the shop, then forgotten upon departure due to its failure to suit the beautiful creature to whom it was assigned) moved toward the counter. Mrs. Kelsey stopped her. "I'll get it in the back. I'm expecting a call. Kirby, we'll talk later, all right?"

Her dismissal struck me as an act of calculated ruthlessness—a cruel extension of my parents' secrecy. Yet her strong back, hunched as if to hide, looked not ruthless but unspeakably fragile as she turned and fled toward the invisible phone that would save her from me.

I would chase her. I could chase her. Why, in a hundred years, would I ever chase her?

My heart pulsed like a boom box while Elise gathered fabric around my ribs tight, securing it with pins. She said, "You've lost weight. Dieting for the wedding?"

"The Irritable Bowel Diet." Oh, I should've said, *It's the My Father is Dying Diet*, which sounded tragic, not icky. I twitched. "Maybe I'll have to cancel the wedding if I melt away."

"That'd be pretty anticlimactic for us. Leigh's done more work than usual on your dress. It'll probably be the last wedding she ever does before she leaves for Colorado."

The 'ever' perplexed me; Mrs. Kelsey's mother and stepfather lived in Colorado and she visited often. But Elise's firm, working hands gave me goose bumps, soothed the blow of Mrs. Kelsey's dismissal. I spoke mainly to preoccupy her— to make her work last longer.

"Colorado?"

"She's spending August there," she dropped her voice, "but she might stay longer. She's thinking of relocating. Her parents retired there, I guess she wants to be close to them."

"Really?" An odd thing to want, surely. "Why?"

Elise shrugged, a pin between her teeth. She plucked it out: "Maybe she finally wants to get away from that ex-husband of hers. She's been avoiding his calls. I wish *he* were the one leaving."

I sucked in my stomach further. Felt less intimidated by this ethereal girl now that her tone revealed our common

gina frangello

admiration of Mrs. Kelsey. I leaned forward and confided, "I
don't want her to go either. I've always thought of her as a
second mother. I mean, we're not close anymore, but when I
was younger I worked here too, and before that I babysat her
children all the time, and she'd give me advice and tell me
stories about her life."

Elise eyed me suspiciously, hands halting. "Leigh only has
one daughter. Rachel."

Straightening to my full height on the platform before the
mirror, I felt almost majestic. A lump formed in my throat at
the thought of this exodus to the mountains, although many
years had passed since my one sweaty summer at the shop,
since my babysitting days. Ordinary disappointments, in the
wake of my father's announcement, had been cast in a gray,
heavy light. I smiled, an inappropriate gesture given what I
was about to say, but I could not help it.

"The other one died. She was only a baby. It was SIDS —
totally unexpected. That was six years ago. Her name was
Isabelle."

The world loves a dead child, isn't that true? The dead
child resides at the top of the tragedy pyramid, just above a
terminally ill lover and miles away from less poetic
catastrophes as physical handicaps, poverty, and rapes. The
failure of the Kelsey marriage was generally credited to stress
following the loss of their second child, a pinkish, colicky infant
who already showed signs of looking like her mother. Though
my parents maintained this was not exactly the catalyst — the
Kelseys had been unhappy prior to Isabelle's death — their
tragic cachet made them especially attractive to others
following their separation. Women and men alike strove to
rescue them from their real or imagined despair, reaffirming a
message particularly offensive to me in my shamed secrecy
over my father's illness: those of us with the bad taste to lead
lives of *inappropriate* tragedy are rarely the material of which
obsessions are made.

Despite her glowing skin and bursting-with-health body,
even I could see that Leigh Kelsey had the smell of melancholy
on her. But in truth, she'd given off that scent since long before
the death of Isabelle. It was one I knew well and had come to
associate with any radical displacement. But unlike my father,
whose displacement stemmed from the fact that he had grown

79

up neither urban, nor affluent, nor even Northern (and whose melancholy was thus spatial), Mrs. Kelsey's displacement was temporal. She seemed to be going through the motions of breathing, eating, seducing, long after the rest of her species had become extinct. My mother said this was why she had "such an unhealthy" preoccupation with ghosts as to deal in other people's clothes and to name her shop after a dead baby (to be fair, Isabelle was a family name—her mother's and great-grandmother's too). She felt more at home among them. Though this disconnection had but little to do with the death of her second child, that tragedy made it acceptable for others to take note of her strangeness, to discuss it among themselves. The Kelseys were *both* odd people. Their common reserved nature and (uncommon) beauty had rendered them an oft-envied couple prior to their separation. They were generally deemed a perfect match. Obviously, looks can be deceiving.

I called Kendra again that night. She'd moved out of Otto's place and into a studio on the Gold Coast that our father had somehow picked out or procured for her. The details were vague. I'd never been there. She rarely answered her phone, but I still tried to reach her at least once a day. The one time I'd had lunch with her since Christmas, her hair covered a strange, scratch-like burn on her left cheek, and she looked skinny in a jagged way I was certain even Balanchine himself would not have relished. She was teaching intermediate ballet at our old school, to girls at approximately the point of training I'd attained when I dropped out. Her other goals were diffuse: obtaining the jealously guarded advanced class, getting a gig at a "better" school in the city, studying "easy" modern dance so she could quit teaching altogether and get back on stage, and putting "something" together for a young choreographers contest sponsored by Hubbard Street Dance Company. Her hands holding her menu shook. She'd had a silver pill box full of Vicodin, obtained from Otto no doubt as she had consulted neither orthopedic surgeon nor physical therapist in months. She fingered one white pill for an unsettling period of time before finally swallowing it down with Pinot Grigio. Our lunches went untouched, and though I'd paid, I sent her home with the leftovers. What difference did that make when I would end up on the toilet, and she looked like she never planned to eat again?

Tonight Kendra answered the phone on the third ring. If ever she were going to answer, she did so after the third ring. She said, "I was just about to call you," before I could identify myself, and though I recognized the lie, I enjoyed her twin-e-pathy too much to say so.

I said, "I can't stand the way your apartment is decorated, so I called to offer my help."

She laughed appreciatively. "Okay. If we're going to play—what's wrong with it?"

I closed my eyes. Imagined a stuffy, pre-furnished, short-term-leased one bedroom meant for out-of-town businessmen who would order in pizza, then pick up hookers on North Avenue and screw them in rental cars in an alley. Each detail rained an assault on my sister's aesthetics, even if she were oblivious because all she was doing was smoking pot and popping narcotic painkillers and maybe snorting blow. "Well, first we've got the hotel-like, muted, mauve interior," I began. "Matching sofa and loveseat—coffee table from Ikea with a glass top. The carpet is Berber. Your comforter has orange in it—that's all I have to say."

"You have *no* idea how eerily close you are."

"Yeah, well why don't you invite me over sometime and let me enjoy the horror myself?"

"No." Voice flat in an instant. "You shouldn't be here."

I couldn't fathom any reason why my constitution was too delicate to withstand a mauve interior—or even an orange comforter—so I assumed she meant it would be best if we avoided each other altogether. This was exactly what I'd suspected. I chose words carefully: "K, I know you're upset and don't want to talk to anyone, and that's totally normal, but I still wish you'd let me in, because Aris doesn't understand the way you must, and I'm going out of my mind."

I didn't hear her breathe. I waited, but it was like she had fallen asleep.

Finally: "You're underestimating Aris. I don't understand any more than he does. A stranger on the street would be more help to you right now than I can be."

Though her obtuseness made my larynx twitchy with the desire to shout, I kept my tone gentle. "I doubt that. I'm already *in* therapy, remember, I get my fill of spilling my guts to a stranger. Sometimes I just need my sister. We don't have to talk about Dad all the time—I don't really want to either—it's

81

the other stuff I want to tell you." I waited for her to ask *like what*, but not very seriously. "Like how much I don't feel like having a wedding right now. Do you even know how lucky you are not to have to put on a dress and smile and accept vases and fondue sets and go on a honeymoon to Greece to see Aris's stupid family? My life is one gigantic farce."

"Let's go skiing," she said. "We haven't been up to the cabin this winter. We can bring Guitarist and Aris if you want, but I'd rather go alone. We can sit in the hot tub."

"You shouldn't ski with your back still in pain," I said maternally. As soon as I heard her sigh, I regretted it. "We could go hang out though," I amended. "We could sit around the fire."

"With or without Aris?"

"You and Aris should spend more time together. You're going to be related soon enough and stuck with each other for good, after—"

"You mean he wouldn't let you go away without him."

I glanced around the loft as though Aris, who wasn't even home yet, would overhear. "Hey, something weird happened today," I blurted, to derail any impending anti-Aris speech. "I went to Isabelle's Room to get fitted, and Mrs. Kelsey knows about Dad but acted really schitzy, like ran into the other room to talk on the phone and totally avoided me. People are cowards."

"The woman had an affair with him, Bee. Give her a break, she could have it too."

A chill tickled my neck as though my sister had carefully lifted my hair and exposed my nape to the wind. "How would you possibly know that? What, did Dad come up and say, *By the way, K, I slept with Leigh Kelsey?* You sound just like Mom. The woman was his friend."

"Oh, you're right. Just because he and Mom sleep in separate rooms, and she's not infected, doesn't mean he ever had affairs or anything. He got it at the dentist, I'm sure."

My breathing was irregular. I could feel it, burning through the bones across my chest, the valves of my heart. She exhaled, so hard I could almost smell the smoke from her cigarette, disrespectful in my nostrils. "Okay," I conceded, "I know Dad must've had at least one affair, or seen a . . . prostitute maybe. I'm not lost in some *Brady Bunch* mythology of our family. But that doesn't mean that he and Mrs. Kelsey ever—"

"Michael told me."

No noise came out.

"Michael Kelsey."

"Please, give me that much credit at least." I twirled the phone cord around my fingers, tight enough to turn them pink. "Do you think I don't know you well enough to realize you get everything you want sooner or later?"

"You knew?" My imagination, or did her tone beg for validation, for complicity, even forgiveness? "Bee, you already—"

"Yes, all right. I knew."

And I had. Knew then that I believed in destiny, that destiny was not and had never been my friend. Knew that they were lovers, had been lovers-in-waiting for some time, that my father had his lover too, that possibly she was ill, that the origin of the virus would never be found. That everyone had been fucking everyone except the people they were married to and me, but yet I'd smelled, sensed, suspected it all along. The body count was mounting. The visceral detachment of my not-at-risk flesh was unbearable. I would rather have thrown myself in on the pyre right then. Would rather have ended in ignorant blindness, like a turkey gawking up towards the sky in the rain—I would rather choke and drown.

Instead my sister giggled like the twelve-year-old she'd once been, like somebody whose father had never been unfaithful or ill, like a woman so wracked with infatuation the world could explode around her and she'd feel nothing but an illicit thrill. "He's nothing like I expected."

Within an hour, Aris would be home from work, and I would make dinner, and he and I would watch TV, and that night I would listen to him snore and feel his body radiate heat and I would be trapped but safe under the heavier bulk of his arm, there to shield me forever. Within weeks—if not days—this thing with Michael Kelsey, if it were even still going on now, would have burned out, and he'd be added to my sister's list, her most challenging conquest, but still a temporary salve to whatever invisible wound made her run year after year and man after man. Then it'd be the three of us again. I would no more go up to our parents' Wisconsin house alone with Kendra; that much I already knew. I could at least offer her this.

"I'm *glad* you finally nailed him," and the multi-faceted knot of grief in my stomach for our father and for the loss of my insular cocoon of twinship with my sister, made room, as always, for another lump of jealousy at another of her forays into waters I'd never dare chart. "With everything going on, you deserve a little bit of fun. I hope you stomp on his heart."

How to Survive the Plague

IN THE DICTIONARY that got me through Northwestern, I couldn't find jack under *Pneumocystis carinii pneumonia, histoplasmosis, coccidioidomycosis, miliary* or *extrapulmonary TB, Kaposi's sarcoma*, or *cryptosporidiosis*. So, Kendra having hung up so she could get ready for a date with Michael Kelsey (the pervert), I took to the Internet for clues to my father's future. Afraid to print information lest Aris discover the evidence (of what? I wasn't sure), I copied snippets into a notebook I'd once used in a History of Psychology seminar. Blurry-brained with images of my father's hands in Mrs. Kelsey's flaming hair, the dignified lines of his mouth flung grotesquely wide, tongue flapping at her crimson nipples, I made anagrams of disease names as mantras to settle myself. None convincingly formed "HIV will become a manageable disease."

In the notebook at my side I scribbled: *Protease inhibitors are the most powerful class of antiretroviral drugs and should be employed whenever aggressive treatment is indicated. New research indicates that protease inhibitors and non-nucleoside drugs, combined with older nucleoside drugs, may completely eliminate HIV from the blood.*

So my father would live to be ninety, though without much action—or maybe he could layer up on the Trojans this time. But wait a minute, not so fast, don't sign that check, there's—

Something you should know: *Ritonavir is the most difficult of these drugs to take and may trigger cross-resistance to Indinavir. Saquinavir has the least cross-resistance and should therefore be employed first. Should problems occur with Saquinavir, it may be changed to either Indinavir or Ritonavir.*

If at any time during our program, you are having trouble following, the making of flash cards is encouraged . . .

Oops, an update: *Saquinavir is now suspected of cross-resistance with Indinavir.* Your call is important to us, please stay on the line. *Cytomegalovirus (CMV) infection or viremia may also occur following initiation of Indinavir or Ritonavir plus nucleoside analogs. Mycobacterium avium complex (MAC) may strike shortly after beginning protease inhibitor therapy. MAC involves marked leukocytosis and lymphocytosis, focal lymphadentitis, and fevers up to 106 degrees.*

What this means:

Poor Daddy. Big funeral. Dead man.

Gee, Mom, only kidding:

Symptoms are usually reversible once the therapy is ceased.

I'd caught him once, I realized abruptly, in the dead of night, just getting home from her. Guilt was sticky on him like a film leaving trails where he walked. I'd stopped my raid of the refrigerator, stared in confusion. But he mistook me for Kendra. I wore her nightgown, a gray Calvin Klein sheath that reached my ankles. He didn't address me, didn't say her name, but I knew by the way he looked that he didn't realize I was me. Later I would tell myself I'd seen the anxious love in his eyes that he reserved for her. But when he spoke, he used offense as defense. Said, "I thought we discussed this. Did I make myself in some way unclear." It was nothing resembling a question.

I said, "Dad . . ."

Perhaps it took me too long to respond to his inquiry. I saw his fingers grip the kitchen table where my water glass rested, then, at the sound of *my* intonation, twitch jerkily away. Kendra was not in any kind of trouble I could remember. His words were nothing I understood.

I had just turned eighteen.

• *One to four percent of HIV patients experience deep, painful, destructive ulcers in their oropharynx and esophagus, leading to anorexia and extreme weight loss.*

• *Opportunistic infections may cause ocular damage and permanent blindness.*

- *Once CD4+ cell counts fall below 75 cells/mm³, morbidity from MAC often causes serious decline in quality of life, generalized wasting, fevers, and diarrhea.*
- *With CD4+ cell counts below 50 cells/mm³, CMV infections may occur. Commonly associated with retinitis, CMV may also involve the central nervous system, adrenal glands, liver, pancreas, and gastrointestinal track from the esophagus to the rectum.*
- *Adverse prognosis of hepatitis is associated with HIV disease.*

Postscript in the notebook: *Vaccinations for hepatitis appear to be effective for people with HIV.*

Postscript in the black of night: *Noncompliance will clearly jeopardize any treatment plan. Possible reasons for noncompliance include: side effects of drugs, difficulty of regimens, depression, and dementia.*

Oh Daddy, if you've been blue (and can't remember why) . . .

- *Four to seven percent of AIDS patients suffer from dementia. One-third of adults with AIDS eventually develop some neurocognitive deficit.*
- *The presence of AIDS-associated dementia has been associated with decreased survival.*
- *HIV has been associated with both mania and depression. This often begins more than one year prior to a clinical diagnosis of AIDS.*
- *Depression has been associated with decreased survival in HIV+ men. This could be due either to poor health habits or low compliance with treatment.*

Into the notebook: *Previous history of depression is believed to predict emergence of pre-AIDS depression.*

I said, "Dad . . ."

Without a word, his back retreated into the darkness of the hall. The way he hung his head in obvious shame made me sorry for him, rubbed against something like a scrape in my chest. I did not yet imagine his guilt as actual. I wanted to call after him, say I was sorry I wasn't Kendra, that if he liked, I could pretend and he could punish me for her elusive or imagined infraction. He had never hit me, not when we were children, not even when he was drinking. Perhaps I imagined the twitch in his fingers, the deliberate, difficult restraint with which he clutched the table. Perhaps that was not his intention at all.

How could any man have needed more than we offered? My mother and I who lived to please him, my sister whose rebellions were performances as sure as her dancing, staged for him, an audience of one. A triad of planets around his sun, we were not enough for him. Not enough.

Pros of Three-Drug Therapy	*Cons of Three-Drug Therapy*
It could save your life.	*You might actually live.*

SOMETHING BURROWING in my ear woke me. A moment of discombobulation, then a sharpening of focus: slick leather beneath my body, gone warm and sticky under patches of skin. And Aris. He tickled my stomach while the burrowing deepened, crooned, "You *luuuuv* it," in a voice halfway between a schoolyard bully's and that of an old woman pampering her kitten. I jolted up, pushed his hands from my stomach and ears, drew myself up tight to cover any vulnerable space. "Stop, you dork!" But I was laughing.

His finger extended again, seeking my ear canal. Aris's hands were huge—*man hands*, Kendra called them, after the *Seinfeld* episode where Jerry dates a gorgeous woman with hands so gargantuan he naturally has to dump her. I swatted him in terror, my own arms piddly and ineffectual. "Get your meat paws away from me!"

Aris mimicked my flailing arms. "Tyrannosaurus Bee," he pronounced, pinning me under one knee and again shoving a sausagey finger in my ear while I yelped. (Could he feel my ear wax? Didn't this gross him out?) "You *luuuuv* it," he said again; and though I yelled, "You're an oversized infant, get off, owww, you're hurting me, quit," and so on, he was right. I did.

He was making atonement. We'd had a hideous incident the night before, all hell breaking loose like nothing before in the years we'd been together. As was becoming my norm, I'd spent nearly six hours on the toilet that day; my Levsinex, since my father's announcement, had ceased working altogether. When I came out of the bathroom, I admitted, stammering, that I'd been fired from my latest temp job—an assignment with BBDO, a big ad agency downtown—due to inability to remain at my desk. I suggested in desperation that maybe I should try acupuncture or start going for colonics. Aris responded like a bull to red. He'd thrown things—even *The Virtue of Selfishness*—and went to the phone to call my mother and ask her to explain to me that there was nothing whatsoever wrong with me other than an inability to cope with stress. Finally, remembering that my mother was no longer at our disposal for such matters, given that her own husband was dying of an illness very much *not* induced by stress, he'd apologized and slammed the phone down before throwing it too. It smashed against a pseudo-wall, knocking our room divider clean over. I began to scream. Aris stared as though I were somebody he had the misfortune to be stuck in a broken elevator with, the hysterical girl who needs to be smacked silly in a disaster flick. He said evenly, "Kirby, I would never leave you with your father ill. I want you to know that. But we can't go through with the wedding with you in this condition. There's no way, just no way." He sank onto the bed, head in his hands. I was stunned to think that a moment prior I'd been afraid he might strike me. I *had* been afraid he might strike me, hadn't I? Why else would I have screamed? I couldn't be sure. I wanted to cry, but worried it would alarm him further. I said, "No, please. Oh God, no, please."

Now, after the strangely furtive and intense sex that follows anger, I lay atop his body, which stuck to the couch in the same sweaty places my own had an hour before, and told him with trepidation about Kendra's sleeping with Michael Kelsey. When he didn't seem nearly as aghast as I felt, I grew brave enough to divulge her revelation that our father had carried on an affair with Leigh Kelsey, just as our mother always suspected. "I thought she was paranoid," I said. "Mrs. Kelsey's so glamorous, I guess I knew my dad had kind of a crush on her, so I figured that was what my mother was reacting to. I mean, I didn't think Mrs. Kelsey would actually *have* him, even if he wanted to. I figured his feelings were moot."

"You always give women more credit than they deserve," Aris said. "Why do you think the Kelseys got divorced? You said he's always been a cheat. Why should she be so pure?"

I didn't know, only that I'd assumed she was. I sat up on Aris's legs—he felt solid as a boat—and reached to scoop my sweater from the floor.

"So okay, maybe both Mr. and Mrs. Kelsey were fooling around, and who knows, one of them contracts HIV. Then what, she gives it to my father? Is that what you think happened? Then what about Kendra? *She* could be at risk by sleeping with Michael Kelsey—is that why you think she's doing it? She's so upset that she's become self-destructive?"

Aris looked confused. "Well, actually, uh . . . it's really hard for a woman to give AIDS to a man. That hardly ever happens."

"So what are you saying?"

"I'm not saying *anything*. I don't think the Kelseys have anything to do with your dad's problem. I mean, I know your favorite thing to do is to analyze things to death so everything has some elaborate, complex cause and effect, but I think you're kidding yourself with that one."

Suddenly I couldn't stand to be naked anymore. I pulled Aris's sweater over my head instead, knowing it'd fall longer and cover me to mid-thigh. I stood over where he lay wrapped in his cocoon of certainty, so warm in what he thought that he didn't need clothes. And I knew.

"You think my father is gay. You've thought so since we found out—all this time."

Aris sighed laboriously. "I never said *gay*. I'm just saying, let's face it, lots of men have one or two experiences, especially when substances are involved to lower inhibitions and all that. I'm just saying it'd explain things a lot easier than your psychoanalytic self-destruction theories. Or a man getting AIDS from some affluent, Gold Coast, seamstress mom."

My skin felt bubbly and hot, self-conscious as if I were a child whose parents were poised to explain the birds and the bees in painstaking detail—with props. I'd have happily pried out an eye to escape this conversation. "Um, Mrs. Kelsey doesn't live on the Gold Coast," I deflected. "She lives in Old Town."

His brows pulled in as though I were speaking Hebrew.

"Look," I tried to make my tone impatient rather than nervous. "Don't you think being a cheater is bad enough? Is it really necessary that my father be a closeted homosexual too? I mean, last time I checked, it was politically incorrect to assume that only gays catch AIDS."

"He could have tried intravenous drugs," Aris consented. "Maybe sometime when he was trying to get off alcohol. There was that heroin revival in the early nineties, you know."

"My father is not a member of some Seattle grunge band!"

He rolled his eyes exaggeratedly. "Who's talking stereotypes now? I mean, like your sister never tried it? And she was a ballerina—they're supposed to be these ultra-feminine, pristine goddesses, right? But look at her. She doesn't even like men, and all she wants to do is get high. She gets those tendencies from somewhere—it sure isn't from you or your mom."

I was speechless. I'd heard my sister accused of being many harsh things—spoiled, bitchy, slutty, arrogant, heartless—but never had I imagined a day she'd be accused of not liking men. In an instant Aris had woven a bizarro-world, one in which the exact opposite of reality reigned. My father, rather than being a womanizing alcoholic, was a gay junkie. My sister, at whose feet every man we'd known since childhood fell—including my first boyfriend and our father's best friend—was a man-hating lesbian. And in this bizarro-world, as perverse as any in which Jerry, George, and Kramer spend afternoons at the library, Aris and I had become the perfect, healthy couple, somehow immune to the rampant dysfunction around us. His vision was oddly compelling. How easy things would be if life were as he saw it. I stared at Aris, reclining there, a man on his big leather sofa, his petite fiancée in distress and in need of answers, and for the first time in our relationship, I pitied him. He wanted to make the wheels of my mind stop spiraling. He was not trying to be cruel. He wanted to create for me a world in which things happened for reasons, in which people were good or bad, strong or weak. A world like *The Fountainhead*, in which men were men and women were women, and a man with AIDS or a woman with attitude three feet thick (that had not been cured by any number of aggressive male penises) could only mean one thing. And I, teary and sick last night, supine under him a half an hour prior, could only mean one thing too. But I knew (though perhaps I hadn't until that moment) that I was far from what he thought.

"It'd be perfect if Kendra secretly dug girls," I said, mild as a bunny. "It'd be ironic."

"I wouldn't be surprised if half of ballet dancers are lesbians," Aris happily agreed. "It's like being a priest—you're surrounded by your own gender. You're encouraged not to marry, to be married to ballet. Every once in a while, you can use a guy to deflect curiosity. Why do you think Kendra's pissed off about our engagement? She probably assumed you were like her too."

We sat in silence for a while. The room was dark. I thought about getting up to make a drink—a gin and tonic, maybe— but told myself I'd better not or Aris might accuse me of being a heroin addict too. I giggled a little, but when he didn't join in, I cut it out.

"I've been thinking," he said, his man-hand rubbing wide circles on my back, the wool of his sweater grinding into my skin in a way that was not unpleasant. "Maybe I should come to therapy with you sometime. Maybe . . . maybe my being there would help. Ever since you've been going, you've gotten worse instead of better. No offense, I mean, I know you were a psych major and you want to go to grad school and everything, but don't you think that this lady is just coddling you? You can't just go listen to somebody saying shit like, *It sounds to me like*, and, *What I'm hearing is*, and spill your guts and wind yourself up with these wild theories that keep you from seeing what's really going on. You can't spend your life hiding on the toilet to avoid the light of day. Maybe my going could . . . refocus things. Seeing you this way is killing me."

I felt a churning heat in my stomach. A distant awareness told me it should be anger, but I did not pull my body away from his rubbing. I imagined my ears were still full of his fingers and I was deaf. I envisioned myself relating to you what Aris thought therapy was like, and how you would laugh, and I let him rub my back and told myself this was a fair exchange.

"Maybe you could come sometime," I said, though I'd no intentions of bringing him to see you, ever. "I'll ask Dr. Friedland what she thinks."

"I only want to help," he told me. "I love you. Whatever makes you comfortable."

I said, "I love you too." We both believed me.

Fragment

If you can't be it, fuck it.

—Kathy Acker,
My Mother: Demonology

Michael Kelsey came by at nine and rang the buzzer but did not come up. Parking was difficult on the Gold Coast, and he rarely entered Kendra's apartment unless he was planning to spend the night. Spring underway, Kendra wore an ankle-length Betsey Johnson dress, which she'd purchased thrift for ten dollars. Black, splattered with red flowers, it had an empire waist so that she resembled a member of King Arthur's court, sneaking through the mist to meet her lover. Michael's Porsche decidedly spoiled the effect. It was like that between them: any illusions of romance splattered before they even got off the ground. It was the most comforting feeling she had ever known . . .

But wait. Three months had passed since the evening he pushed her face into the elevator carpet rough enough to leave burns on her cheek. Three months, and the world stage had shifted: Clinton had been acquitted of obstructing truth or abusing power or having an erection; instead NATO bombed Yugoslavia because Milosevic's erection was for blood, not young pussy, and had gotten out of hand. Now Kendra obstructed truth, and Michael had erections possibly induced by abusing power, and surely one did not just wake up in the middle of such things. You *do not become a charted country overnight.* No, no. *It happens slowly. In parts.* And so she remembered no specific beginning, only various curtains as they rose and fell. Only this.

At the restaurants he took her to, neither of them ate. They ordered things, but within the first several weeks of their involvement already they had wasted enough food between them to throw several large, catered affairs. Michael said she distracted him, that he ate more when she wasn't around, but she didn't quite believe him. She had the feeling he was always distracted. That she was merely the most deliberate of his distractions, designed to be so, meant to keep other, more disturbing ones at bay.

Though her mother and Kirby swore she was wasting away, Michael told her he preferred her body to those of more voluptuous women. Their first real night together (not the one in the elevator but later the same week), he'd pulled her arms away from her chest and stretched her out on his bedroom rug, studying her. "Perfect," he'd said. "Though I'm partial. I've always thought the exaggerated frailty of ballerinas made them the most exotic creatures on earth. Of course dancers are deceptively strong, stronger than most men. And with endurance that's astonishing." Then—an afterthought—"Large breasts and hips just make me think of mothers."

"Is that why your marriage failed?" she had asked. "Your wife became a mother?"

He shook his head. She wondered if he was thinking that in fact his marriage had fallen apart when his wife *ceased* to be a mother, at least to their second daughter. She realized she had likely asked the question to provoke his speaking about Isabelle's death and felt surprised since she had no desire for him to confide in her, to learn whether he were capable of grief. But he said only, "Well, maybe that was part of it. Some people just aren't meant to be married. My wife and I were both guilty on that count. It's harder that way—no one to blame."

"My parents blame you."

"My wife was everything I could ask for: beautiful, intelligent, creative. Mysterious even after years of marriage. And I was the one who had repeated affairs. So maybe Henry and Gail are right. To any extent that it counts."

The thought of his chronic infidelity turned her on more than worried her. No, turned her on *instead of* worrying her. Only with effort did she wait until after sex before asking, "So how many women are you sleeping with besides me?"

He was lying on his back on the rug; one outstretched finger traced her spine. "Why would you ask that? Do you really want to know?"

A shrug. "I was asking to be polite, I guess. You ask about my life."

"That's because you're young, and it's always interesting to see what will happen to young people. I'm older and I've already been happened to. Besides,"—and he took his hand away—"unless I ask, you never tell me anything."

"Why should I? You already know too much about me from my parents." But she scooted out of his reach, as if to indicate that the withdrawal of his fingers was by her own choice. "If you don't want to talk about your sex life, though, that's fine."

"No, as a matter of fact, I don't mind at all. Right now, there's only one other woman I see, with any regularity anyway.

She's a lawyer too. Mostly we go to each other's boring functions. Sometimes we fuck. Not very often."

"Why not?" She twisted around to see him. "Is she ugly?"

"No, Kendra." A smile, but paternal. "That isn't why."

She flopped onto her back too, stared at his white ceiling, his white walls. "Don't look at me like I'm unaware there are any other reasons not to screw. It's just that when the opportunity presents itself, those reasons never seem real. Only a lack of attraction can actually save you."

"Fair enough. And she's very attractive. But I'm not particularly attracted to her. Maybe that's what you're too young yet to get. More and more, they're not the same thing."

This time she didn't answer. He rolled onto his side, tracing circles around her breasts and moving up her neck to lightly touch her face. He moved in to kiss her. She stiffened.

"Don't do that. It bothers me."

"What does?"

"I don't like to have my face touched. Even kissing bothers me unless it's right on the mouth or a casual peck on the cheek. Having someone touch me up close like that, my face, it makes me feel like I can't breathe."

He withdrew his hand, lowered it back to her stomach, brushing her skin softly. She leaned her head against him, relieved now.

"I like this about you," she said. "You make me feel normal. No one has ever made me feel normal before. You don't care about things other guys find perplexing or scary. You just accept them."

"I don't know if you'll always consider that a virtue. My ex-wife called it indifference. Most women don't appreciate it after a while. The truth is, I like things that are odd but I don't want the burden of reasons. I'd rather imagine my own."

"Good," she said. "Because I don't want to tell you real ones."

"I don't think you really know the explanations yourself."

"You may be right. But if I did, I still wouldn't tell you."

"You're too impatient," he said. "Wait. We have time."

There was nothing but time. The schedule Kendra had kept since adolescence—daily class, rehearsals and outside coaching, sewing pointe shoes, not to mention constant appointments with physical therapists, masseuses, and acupuncturists—receded without a trace. All that remained in the wake of her dedication and discipline was a series of complicated grooming rituals, it now being Michael for whom her legs were always waxed, hair always styled. The purpose behind such sustained efforts seemed obtuse at times since Michael did not adhere to a classical aesthetic of Beauty, but preferred various states of broken-down decay. Still she knew instinctively: nothing can be desecrated that does not originate in a state of purity. Kendra could not offer innocence, neither in body nor mind, so she felt compelled to at least offer beauty, which, in sex as in ballet, is often mistaken for the same thing. Besides, every morning she needed restoration the same as if she had taken class, pilates, and rehearsed back to back. Even if she'd received a massage the day before (Michael made sporadic surprise appointments for her at Urban Oasis), she was worn down again. The accumulation of him mounted in her. Threatening. Until she would be that much easier to break.

There was nothing to be afraid of, though. The meticulousness of friends always surpasses that of strangers. A friend takes more care. More consideration. Would she want it any other way? There was nothing to be afraid of, no, nothing, she knew. Nothing to be.

Where are we then? Oh, yes, the second month.
Yes, two months. *Slowly. In parts.*

At the Dance Center, the world was different. There she had no Michael, no grown men at all. There she was enveloped in the constancy of *pliés, tendus, frappés, ronds de jambe en l'air, développés, grands battements*. There her mind slowed to adagio, balancing before the inevitable, heady allegro. Her girls were beginning pointe; a few she already allowed to keep their pointe shoes on for center work too. The gifted ones. The ones like herself, who would soon move to schools in the city, as she had, or boarding schools for baby ballerinas, as she did summers and would have year-round had it not been for Bee. Those students watched her with eyes attentive as any lover's, mirroring her with an earnestness that made some tender agitation rise up her throat in a rush and soften her voice like somebody in love. Those girls wore buns everywhere, carried Diet Coke or Evian, smoked covertly in gaggles after class. Never, ever ate. They worried her memory, made everything she had been and done at twelve seem as though it might have turned out any of a dozen ways—as though there'd been infinite possibilities to every choice irrevocable now. Their bones were lovely and light. Their elbows, larger than their upper arms and slanted out at unnatural angles like the broken wings of birds, filled her with a longing joy. They did not menstruate. They did not care about orgasms, or, yet, about men. In two years, three, they would be lost to her, gone from Kenilworth and from the insulated frenzy in which a young girl's body-limits can be stretched and defied all within the confines of dance, and that is enough. She nurtured their hope without trying: she had once been a student at the Center and gone on to dance for NYCB. She had lived their dream. She was perfect except that they would be *more* perfect and not allow any pain or herniation to stand between themselves and perfection—she was perfect except that her body had failed her so she must be weak. A teacher in Evanston, Illinois, was to be adulated but surpassed, she knew, even if in truth the chance that even one of them would make it as far as she had was almost nil, and she was nowhere now so what had it really been? Every mother tensely believed her child would be the one. Ballet mothers were the enemy, any teacher knew, except Kendra had not had one and so thought all that relentless expectation would have been nice. In the studio without grown men she was "Miss Kendra," an adult—and adults, in the eyes of the children who worship them, do not have dying fathers, do not grieve. The Dance Center was as it had always been, a haven of hope and nostalgia and glass-edged realism too, and in the moment the pianist began playing, girls lined up at the barre, she might have been one of them, except that when she was, she had never loved herself so hard. To adore when once she had been adored did not suit her. Ambivalently, she schemed every day to quit.

Nights with Michael Kelsey were equally ambiguous. There too exploded moments of unrestrained joy. Not from sex (though she came, too hard and too often, she did not imagine anyone could describe their sex as "joyful"), but in the hours that followed. Lying on his carpet wrapped in pieces of the clothing he shed when they made love, propped up on pillows from his bed, his duvet slung over them. Then a sense of accomplished purpose left her sore and warm. Like after performing a grueling but successful variation she had often been happy. Sometimes he rubbed her feet. Sometimes they didn't touch at all, but she didn't care, felt no real inclination to snuggle up to him like a puppy for whom affection must take the place of collaboration. Just like the supported *temps levés en arabesque* from *Giselle*, among the most difficult partnering required in any ballet, great physical and mental boundaries had to be overcome if sex were to become art. Looked at right, the choreography of her nights with Michael rendered everything reversible. Created new angles and facets, some sharp and cutting and taking all her breath away and hurting. Some illuminating vibrant colors in the dark.

Three months. There were things she knew about him now that meant she did not have to be afraid. Things he told her even though they sounded vulnerable and almost tragic, and she could not be trusted in such situations and he knew that too. Like how he had not wanted to end up at the firm, to end up like her father or who he was now at all. He'd studied the philosophy of law and wanted to be a professor like his father. But when he graduated, there weren't a lot of jobs for law professors, so he starved and lived off various girlfriends until something happened and he needed a change. The something had involved a woman and Kendra did not know her name but she knew the woman was dead. She could tell by the way Michael spoke about her or did not speak about her, it was the same thing. It was clear the woman died and that he blamed himself or wanted to. That was when he moved to Chicago, which was safer on all levels than New York where he'd gone to law school and starved while waiting to be a law professor — Chicago was safer and Kendra, if her parents did not live here, would know that too.

There were things she knew about him. That he'd dropped out of college during his second year just the way she had, only for his one year off he'd lived in a co-op and read philosophy in the dark. He read Hegel and Bataille. He read in the dark because the mood was better. His girlfriend at the time would nag him about how he was going to go blind, and he didn't want to turn on the light, but he believed her and had to dump her so she wouldn't be around to say I told you so. Now he didn't even wear glasses. He would have, though, had he kept the girlfriend around — Kendra said this and he agreed. He'd smoked a lot of pot then and wore his hair long, and she thought he was probably adorable but he said no, he was really skinny and never washed the hair so it hadn't looked that great or anything, it was just long. When she thought how Michael at twenty sounded not so different from Guitarist, and how maybe Guitarist could grow up to be Michael, she became inexplicably afraid. Not of Michael exactly, just the thought. Maybe of the acknowledgment of time, of such enormous change.

There were things she knew about him. There were things, but sometimes she was still afraid. Sometimes, in the moments while she sat waiting in her apartment for him to pick her up for dinner, she panicked and swallowed two Vicodin before he arrived—just in case—the way she'd once rubbed Benzodent on her toes before a performance. Or moments teaching class, when a demonstration pulled her body in some reminder, some arch, some bend, some strain that stretched her skin taut over a bruise. Seconds in which she thought she would not be able to do it again, whatever it was they were doing, whatever it was they were not really doing yet but were only preparing to do. If she were already hesitating, what would she do when she was really in it? The time was imminent. But she never picked up the phone and told him not to come, and when he rang her buzzer and she went down to him in her black dress with the red flowers and she saw his Porsche he was neither choreographer nor *danseur* but simply her father's old friend. A partner who offered no promise of anything tender that might confuse her, of anything except why she was here and what she was, and at that moment never fear but relief washed over her. Spring was underway by now. The man who had been her lover for three months leaned against the hood of his old car; he greeted her with neither flowers nor a kiss, but a smile. Always that. And there would be nothing turning in her stomach. She would feel a glowing, icy steel. It would be the most comforting moment she would ever know.

You do not wake up a charted country; it happens slowly. In parts.

They are her words, you realize. Not mine. They are all her stolen words after all.

Michael Kelsey was watching her. It was too easy with him just to drift off. Because he didn't mind, because he enjoyed it even, being able to call her back only when he so chose. He spoke her name (never an endearment, never anything but her name, and then only when they were not in a scene, during which times he called her nothing, addressed her as nothing, so she could not be sure whether she existed in the first place). Her head shot up—a jerk. She was on his bedroom floor alone, surrounded by containers of mostly untouched Chinese. Wearing his shirt and nothing else. She had spilled soy sauce on his rug; he had noticed, she was sure, though he neither acknowledged the spill nor glanced at the stain. At the doorway, he held a cup of tea, nothing for her. Didn't ask what she was thinking—no, never anything so general, with as much room for evasion—only said, "The last time I saw you before you left for Julliard, that boy you call Guitarist arrived unexpectedly and wept in your foyer. Afterward Henry and Gail were jumpy as cats, as though you might refuse to go away and leave him, and Kirby was so envious all she did was glare at you. All *you* did was flirt with me across the dinner table."

"Stop that," Kendra said, laughing. "You must have thought I was ridiculous."

"No, it was beguiling. Besides, you weren't as obvious as that, I'm mostly teasing. I had no idea whether you made any distinction between me and anyone else." He came to her, setting the tea on the night table. Took one of her feet in his lap. "I still don't."

"You mean that maybe I just flirted with everyone I met?" She settled into his fingers. "Mmm, maybe I did. Maybe I only remember you because you were always there."

"And now?"

"I really don't know." But she shut her eyes. Silence.

"Don't worry," he said. "I'm not asking for any declarations of loyalty or looking for you to tell me that you think of me when I'm not around."

"Of course not. You don't ask for things that you aren't about to give back."

"Yes I do. All the time. But there are too many other things I want to ask you for. Besides which, you know full well that I do think of you."

Eyes still shut: "Michael, I haven't the foggiest idea what you think about."

"I find it intoxicating when you lie to me like that."

"I'm not lying."

"You are. But it doesn't matter. It keeps me clear on what we're here for, on what you want from me." He let go of her foot, slid his hand higher along her leg. "And I'm well aware that none of it even remotely involves my touching your face, so you don't have to worry."

Her eyes snapped open fast. "You make me sound so calculated. Do you really believe my motives are so simple?"

"Sometimes I'd like to. Paradoxically, I also like that you want me to believe otherwise. It makes me think you won't tire of me that quickly."

"Is that what you guess will happen?" She heard benign curiosity in her voice—not the way she meant the words to come out. "That I'll tire of you and go on my way?"

"I would be deluding myself to think otherwise considering the difference in our ages. It's all right, though, it might be a good change. I find myself growing weary of women so easily that I bore myself with the predictability of it." He pulled her down to lie on him, their bones hitting together, muscle and sinew, nothing soft between them to lessen the sting of his words. Of his utter confidence that she would leave him and he would enjoy it. His arms wound around her back tightly, his breath hot in her ear. "None of this matters, though. Right now, I only want to make love to you. Now, I only want you to scream so loud my neighbors will call security. What would it take to make you do that? What will I have to do?"

Fair trade. A scream in exchange for information: about the affair between his ex-wife and our father. Its character, timing, duration. In exchange for silence in all areas she did not wish to discuss: the death of his infant daughter, the death too of his apparently adored mother when he was only seventeen, anything to do with his surviving daughter, age twelve. A scream in exchange for remaining a star, brief hours on his stage of cruelty, a scream a small price to pay for the satisfaction of—you will forgive my lack of imagination— such clean transference. But what did he derive? What on earth compelled the scream of a mere girl to be so valuable to him?

If I see her as that, a *mere girl*, it will exonerate me too. If the expectations upon us are low enough, we will be thought to have coped with our circumstances commendably. Everything is relative, you see.

She didn't mind his handcuffs as a rule. When he lifted her to the bed and snapped them cold around her wrists, securing her to the wrought-iron headboard, she didn't complain. Even when he opened the drawer of his night stand and removed the fat roll of silvery duct tape, spreading it evenly over her slightly parted ankles and the fitted bed sheet, several layers thick until she was completely immobilized, she didn't struggle. Why bother? She assumed (what else?) that he intended to screw her for a second time, as soon as his body was willing, and desired her bound to tease her better. When he turned out the lights, her eyes blinked in abrupt confusion. The outline of his body, picking up clothes off the floor. In the time it took to wrestle with whether to ask what he was doing or to play it cool, he exited the room. She demanded, "What the hell . . . ?" The front door breezed open, clicked shut; his key turned in the lock. Beside the bed, his clock read 11:16. No response.

Though her eyes quickly grew accustomed to the dark, night vision offered little except shadows of lights reflected on his wall from the outside. The sounds of cars decreased, Lake Shore Drive a ghost town past midnight on a weekday. Naked, cooled semen leaking from her body to dampen his sheets, shared sweat from their sex earlier dried to a prickly chill on her skin, Kendra shivered without a blanket. She kept herself from dwelling on the growing numbness in her arms by nursing images of fire, unforseen tragedy. It was not that she actually feared any such disaster as that she hated Michael Kelsey for not fearing it on her behalf. Imagine firefighters bursting into the room—she wouldn't be the first time they'd had such a show, she was sure. Conjured her body through their eyes, objectively. Devoid of past or personality, she might as well be any whore. Like the anonymity of fucking up when she'd been merely one among identical rows of corps dancers, the knowledge offered some comfort.

Where had he gone? For a cup of decaf at some all-night café? To another woman's house for a midnight fuck? Was he angry over something she'd done? Was this actual punishment, or only an extension of his original, stated desire to make her scream? An experiment: nothing personal. She should have cried out like he wanted while he pounded into her earlier, should never have held out in stubborn silence. Yet even here, bound to the bed, she might have wept, might have allowed him the satisfaction of re-entering the room to find her in hysterics, begging him to release her. She saw herself cowering in his arms and letting him kiss her tears away. Would he do so, or would he laugh? It didn't matter; her eyes stayed dry as bone.

At 2:11, his key turned in the lock smoothly, without any penitent nervous fumbling. He did not come check on her. Kendra didn't call out either, too furious and terrified by that point to even consider it. She heard him in the living room, turning the pages of his newspaper, occasionally getting up to go into the kitchen. Her stomach growled; her heart did flip-flops in her chest. She oscillated between anxiety that the tightness of the cuffs had cut off her blood flow (and these palpitations were the precursor of a heart attack), and *hope* that her circulation was so disturbed she would simply pass out, wake unrestrained elsewhere. Anywhere but here.

By the time she heard the whistle of the kettle, the clock next to his bed read 3:33. The sound went on for a long time, until she wondered whether he had left again, why he didn't go to turn it off. At last the screeching stopped, and he appeared in the doorway, switching on the light. She blinked (stupidly, stupidly), the brightness hurting her eyes and disorienting her. He was holding his small, glass teapot. Sat next to her on the bed, running a finger from where her hands lay limp against the headboard, then down to her stomach. Lower still.

"Are you tired?" he asked.

"Not really." Her voice did not break, did not even waver. The solidity of it shocked her more than anything thus far. "You've gotten me used to keeping odd hours."

He smiled almost warmly. "Be careful. Insomnia is addictive. Once you learn how much time is wasted in sleeping full nights, you never recover."

His absence of any apology or explanation soothed her. "Why don't you just use sleeping pills?"

"I don't take to medication. It makes me nervous."

He rested the teapot on her stomach. Scalding hot; she jerked away, causing some of the liquid inside to spill up through the spout onto her skin. She drew in breath fast. "Shit!"

He bent to lick the water off. "No. Don't move." He replaced the pot, higher, near her breast. Kept his fingers on the handle for balance but let the bottom make full contact with her skin. Her face contorted; she let out a noise a whimpering *Uhhmmmm* — but didn't dare thrash.

"Good. So tell me then. What do you and that Guitarist do in bed?"

The burning had spread instantly to her entire torso, causing her to sweat. She wanted to kick violently to throw off the fire, but her legs, long since without feeling, were still taped and immobile. The burning invaded her everywhere: under her arms, between her legs, pricking at her insides with hot needles. She was sure the skin of her chest must have singed completely. If he didn't lift the teapot soon, she would begin to shriek, go insane. Her mouth twisting—dignity melting into desperation—horrified her. It was a relief to speak and force her lips to move normally, just to make any kind of human sound.

"Why . . . do you . . . ask?"

He lifted the pot. She exhaled in jerks, too fast, like someone drowning. "No particular reason. I'm just curious."

The spikes of pain had gone prickly, lessened just enough. "We make up songs." She kept her teeth clenched. "But he always falls asleep before the end. Maybe I should try this."

Michael laughed. "What kinds of songs?"

"With *words*. Nothing you'd be interested in."

"What makes you think that?"

"Fine. Nothing I want to talk about then."

"All right. Now lie still." He tilted the pot so a small stream hit her thigh. Her body twitched: a sudden shock, sharper than the pot against her flesh but also more fleeting. Afterward a throbbing heat, simultaneously intense and numb. A red patch began to form.

"I think it sounds nice," he said. "Singing in bed. A bit quaint for my tastes, but nice." He smoothed her sweat-damp hair off her forehead. She wondered if he expected her to ask why he was doing this. "My ex-wife used to repair dresses in bed. It drove me crazy, like something my grandmother would have done, but now sometimes I miss it."

"It's ridiculous that you were ever married." Quick, before the next wave quelled her. "It amuses me."

Another splash of water hit, right on the breast. She thrashed again despite herself. "Yes, I know it does."

Tears welled in her eyes. She closed her lids tight against them, not long but long enough for him to notice. Still, they didn't fall. "How . . . how long are you going to do this?"

A small trickle fell on her stomach. "You can ask me to stop if you like."

"I can ask a lot of things. That doesn't mean you'll do them."
She sucked in her breath from another series of drops. Couldn't
speak. The tears leaked now. He waited for her silently. "And
if you would, I'd rather save requests for things that matter."

"I'm glad." He rested the pot on his knee, then removed it
quickly, putting it on the night table. "And intrigued. You'll
have to ask for something now. Anything."

Immediately: "When I'm here and awake, it's your job to
entertain me, not to read the paper a room away. If you won't
agree, I expect you to take me home permanently."

He nodded. "That was very rude of me." Ran a finger down
her arm. She didn't feel it. "I won't do it again, I promise." He
picked up the teapot and poured, more this time.

"Shit, ow, shit."

"You curse entirely too much for someone so articulate."

"Fuck you." A flurry of blinking and trying to breathe,
wondering how much longer she could hold out without
pissing on his bed. The thought of doing so almost made her
bust out laughing. He reached down for a corner of the duct
tape at her feet and pulled, one long rip that released one of
her legs, pulling off a tiny strip of skin. The tears fell faster,
though she made no noise. Blood ran down her ankle, not
much more than a nasty cut from shaving, not *significantly* more
painful than a bikini wax. Still the knowledge of it, her blood,
made her freeze.

"Open your legs."

Heartbeats overlapped, slammed into each other. The
noise filled her ears; she could distinguish nothing else. He sat
immobile, watching. She did it. He bent and licked her slowly,
the pot still dangling in his hand. She thought about wrapping
her leg around his neck and attempting to choke him. After a
moment, he straightened and moved the teapot between her
thighs, not quite touching. She could feel the heat radiating
from the glass and knew if he did not act soon, she would
begin to sob from fear. She locked her jaw again, but kept her
legs spread. He stared at her, eyes gray and achingly familiar.
She closed her eyes.

"Just do whatever you're going to. I don't care." Her lids
stayed shut, waiting for the fall, lips pressed together in
anticipation of the pain. After awhile, she felt him rise from
the bed. She opened her eyes a crack. He carried the teapot to
the other side of the room and left it near the door. When he
returned, he stretched out next to her.

"Your nerve will get you into trouble someday," he said. "But not with me. I find it far too appealing to do anything that would drastically deter it."

Relief flooded through her like water, like a climax she could not hold back. She tightened her stomach muscles, raw and weak, to restrain herself, prayed she would be let up soon, soon before she couldn't keep her bladder in check. His assumption that she would even consider getting into a similar situation with someone beside himself stunned her.

"You know," she said, "your hair is beginning to gray, after all. I thought it wasn't, but if I look closely, I can see it at your temples."

His eyes on her grew curious, intent. "You'll have to show me. In the morning."

"It is morning, Michael. It's been morning for hours."

"Yes, well when the sun is up then." And he lowered his face between her legs again, his fingers slowly tracing the shape of the burn on her thigh.

Where is the line? There is no line. If there ever was a line, it's long since been trashed. Let's thank Kinsey's methodology, let's have a toast to Henry Miller and Anaïs Nin fucking in their studios in Paris, let's thank *Naked Lunch* and the cult of the cock, Madonna and her carrots, and don't forget *Story of O*, oh even *Vogue* knows perversion chic is in, even *Vogue* knows kink's the way to sell, but don't forget your morals, doc, it's okay to come but something nasty's still supposed to happen to the big bad sadist in the end, he should lose an arm or get beat up by a fat girl or something and it takes a lot more than some duct tape and a pot of boiling water to shock a with-it individual these days, sure, don't worry, I know you must be a with-it individual, in fact you probably have your own handcuffs too, fur lined cause really it's the mind trip you're after, not the pain, you're not a freak, and you have special cleaning fluid for your multi-speed vibrator, and you don't own a dildo and strap-on, but you've had affairs with people who do, and your husband or your girlfriend or your brother or your son once went on a business trip or a college back-packing excursion or a suicide mission to Hamburg or Berlin or Amsterdam and brought you back a riding crop, and your friends have found it at parties when they were drunk and asked if you used it and you blushed and acted kind of coy so they all thought you did even though maybe you were embarrassed that in truth it's only there for show. I know I can't shock you. I know you saw *9½ Weeks* and you're a good liberated liberal and pornography is no stranger to you. And did you know that you can access kiddie porn on the internet — of course you did, you're computer literate after all, and you came across it one day when you were looking for some information on the Virgin Islands or cats or that disease you think you might have. It's under the heading KIDDIE — look it up if you don't believe me, and if you don't know it's there, your son and your daughter do. Look it up if you don't believe me, and if you don't know it's there, your father does. Look it up if you have the stomach, and if you can't stand to look at it, then you're in the minority, you're a freak, because we all love a good car crash, and you'd better catch an eyeful now cause it might be outlawed real soon. I can't shock you, don't think I'm trying. Maybe you get wet when you read a sex scene. Maybe I get wet when I write her sex scenes. Maybe I can smell you, your jaded hormones and slippery genitals, all the way from here. Maybe you will come thinking of my sister: you'll imagine her wearing my skin, forget I've referenced her longer hair, the anorexic sharpness of her bones, the defiant tilt of her chin. You'll forget that she has no tits to speak of. Maybe it's your own body you'll think of in his black and white checkered bathroom with piss as weak as water from so many cups of herbal tea running down your back, your face, your tongue. My sister knew how to have a good time. Don't worry about the ammonia that stings the welts on her ass, the cuts on her wrists. You're the doctor, this is your fantasy, the inconveniences of her body can't touch you. Everyone knows psychiatrists, like philosophers and the clergy, don't even *need* bodies in order to understand or condemn ours.

I am wasting my time. Don't you see: *I* need you in her body. Would I be able to take you there if it were my body that needed crawling into? Could I get you inside if *I* were *she*?

Sometimes I hear myself. Catch myself. Sometimes I hear that what I'm trying to tell you after all this time is nothing short of: It *should have been me.*

Analysis

Sex in America is S&M. One cannot
outmaneuver complicity.

—Kathy Acker,
Interview

Aris Shrugged

Oh Aris gettin' married, but he ain't a happy man.
Oh Aris gettin' married, but he ain't a happy man.
Got himself one sick lady, gots a problem with the
can.

(Lyrics by K-hole, music by Guitarist)

AS SPRING WORE on, the flirtation of summer—or its threat—charged ever closer. Two men occupied my thoughts. One was my father, who continued to show no response to the allegedly miracle-working drugs his doctors had touted, and whose health had given way from stagnation to rapid decline. Not, of course, that he was a compliant patient. We all understood that. In a socialized-medicine state, he probably would not even have been considered an appropriate candidate for such a high-maintenance plan. But in the United States at the turn of the century, money permitted a man the luxury of hope without others spitting in his face. My father's face was dry, but he was dying all the same.

My mother had announced that the only thing to do was to push up my wedding. Who knew what kind of condition my father would be in come October, and though I doubted ceremony ranked very high on his list of concerns anymore, my mother decided that if he could not walk me down the aisle, it would kill him then and there. July, everybody knew, was a fine time to have a wedding. It was, of course, an altogether better time if one had planned the event two years in advance, when churches, reception sites, and catering companies didn't laugh in one's face. Pushing the date up would mean losing a great deal of money, but then it no longer seemed feasible to have a large wedding anyway; the guest list was cut in half. My father would not be a sideshow, my mother told me, as though I had suggested it. He would not pay for everyone he knew on a first name basis to come and take a front row seat in watching him die.

I could not, I suppose you'll grant me, argue with that.

The other man on my mind was Michael Kelsey, who, in addition to sleeping with my sister on a disturbingly regular basis for nearly five months, had become the bane of my fiancé's existence as well. Since my father's indefinite leave-of-absence from the firm (cancer, everyone said), Michael Kelsey had volunteered to pick up the slack in supervising Aris's new-wing project. For all intents and purposes, this was a move the other partners probably interpreted as charitable. Nobody else wanted to be bothered. Had Mr. Kelsey not intervened, it was most likely Aris would simply have been dismissed, and someone from a high-powered architectural firm brought on. Instead, Aris now had Michael Kelsey standing in doorways staring at him, looking vaguely troubled as though, given his ignorance of architectural design, he could not be quite certain of the problem, but knew beyond a reasonable doubt that one would emerge in time. He made Aris explain the plans repeatedly, but each time seemed preoccupied and confused and said something cryptic like, "Didn't you say you were running over budget?" when Aris had never said any such thing (though it was true), then walked out before Aris could answer.

"That asshole is breaking my balls for the hell of it," Aris lamented every night. Michael Kelsey's name floated around my home, reverberated off the high ceilings of the loft. "He hates me because I'm marrying you. Kendra's probably told him you think he shouldn't be let near school yards, so he's taking it out on me. *I* don't care who he fucks. She probably went after him anyway. You're blind to your sister, but I know that type. If he weren't such an arrogant sonofabitch, I'd feel bad for him. He's the one who'll get burned."

"If you keep cutting on my sister, you can leave," I said, though I didn't contribute half of the rent and my name was not on the lease. It was the sort of thing some women can say, know we can say, no matter where we are. One small semblance of power.

Aris pressed his lips together and blew out hard. "He never even mentions Kendra—you should tell her that. I mean, your families are practically related, and I'm marrying her twin, right? It only seems civilized. Like, *Kendra and I were at a movie, Kendra said to me the other day* . . . I even tried once, though she won't believe it if you tell her. I said we should all go out for a drink sometime—I thought you'd like it if I could, you know, normalize everything and make it less scandalous—but he laughed in my face and then said in that blank Mr. Spock tone, 'What an astoundingly bad idea.' I didn't tell you 'cause I knew how pissed you'd be."

"I don't want to hear about that perv," I said. "I have to listen to it enough from Kendra and act all giggly and sisterly instead of puking—I'll bet he's been waiting ten years for there to be a crisis in our family so he could swoop in and take advantage of her. I'm sure he wants to seduce me too and only hates you because you're in the way. He probably has a ménage-a-twin fantasy and is afraid he'll need Viagra by the time you and I get our divorce in ten years."

Aris sank onto the enormous, black leather sofa. It was our only piece of furniture that could hold us both simultaneously, aside from the bed. I wasn't sitting. I was walking around fast, drinking white wine with ice cubes in it, which Aris hated and wouldn't let me do anywhere except our place when we were alone. The wine was going to my head because I'd expelled everything else that might absorb it. The scale that morning had read 111—nine pounds lower than I'd weighed in a decade. I would need to go to Isabelle's Room for another fitting.

He said, "Do you think we're going to get a divorce?"

"What?"

"That's what you said. Is that your vision of the future, us splitting up in ten years so you can screw around like your sister? What, are you only marrying me so you won't have to work and can live off my money? Because if that's what you've got planned, you can think again."

I burst out laughing. "What money? You have no money!"

"I make a hell of a lot more than you do temping once a week and wasting your degree."

113

"Yeah, Howard, you're a real maverick, I forgot. Don't worry. Michael Kelsey will be reabsorbed into the black hole of mediocrity, and you'll be left to reign supreme over the utopian land of the new wing."

A splash of liquid hit my foot. Panic rose: had the whole lower region of my body finally given out entirely, and I'd voided the way you do when you're about to die? But when I looked, my wine glass was upside down. Cold liquid seeped through my black ankle-socks. One ice cube lay, deformed from meltage, at my right big toe. I kicked it. Glanced back at Aris, who sat silently, shock marring his mouth like clumsily wielded red crayon. My skin crawled.

"You're right. You do need therapy. I guess I didn't want to believe it so I didn't see."

"Oh, I'm in a bad mood so now I'm mentally ill?"

"I can't say if you're mentally ill. But right now you're not anyone I want to know."

A foot between my ribs. Thud. Tears started pouring down my cheeks. I hated them; they weren't real.

"Yeah, well. Hey, I see your point."

"Look," he said. "You win. I'm leaving. I don't want to live in war."

"I thought that's what it's all about. Ayn Rand, Nietzsche. 'That which doesn't kill you makes you stronger' blah blah blah. I thought you wanted a noble enemy. Isn't that the idea?"

"No," he said. "The idea is to finally love somebody enough so that it's all right not to have to hold on to those ideas anymore."

I tottered a bit, stepped on the ice cube and slipped. My butt hit the floor. He didn't come to me. The sole of his left Doc Marten was torn. I was still there when he closed the door.

The phone is an umbilical cord tangled around the necks of mothers, daughters, sisters, strangling us close into a kiss. Since Kendra long ago tied a knot in her end of the cord, food flowed all the quicker between my mother and me. When I called my mother with a wet ass and told her Aris had, for the first time in our relationship, walked out on me, she said immediately, "He only left to cool down. I wouldn't worry, he dotes on you, anyone can see." This was our mother-daughter ritual—had been for my last three years of college, then for months when I'd first moved into the loft. My insecurities were legendary, repetitive, and usually inconsequential (which did little to quell them). My mother, ever patient, had her lines down pat.

"Something's wrong with me, Mom," I muttered. "I'm not afraid he's cheating on me or anything like that this time. It's me that's the problem. I can't seem to . . . be nice."

"Of course you can. Aris knows we're all a little on edge. But he's a good man, and I know you'd never be short-sighted enough to allow the stress of Daddy's illness to drive him away. It gives your father such peace, believing one of his daughters will be cared for."

"Maybe I don't want to be cared for." But tentatively. If that were true, wouldn't I be celebrating right now, changing the locks, hoping my fiancé would never return? I felt the opposite of celebration. I felt anxious and undeserving and generally ill.

"Darling," my mother said, "I'm going to be blunt with you, for your own good. Relationships are full of compromises and sacrifices you may not feel like you can make. But believe me, it's no improvement to be alone in a big world where nobody gives a damn about shy girls who try their best to be invisible. It's no fun explaining on first dates why you spend half your time in the ladies' room. Your father and I are burning through money fast—we can't even afford your therapy anymore. I'm your mother and I love you. Trust me."

"I can't believe what I'm hearing." Yet if I were stunned, it was her *honesty*, not the sentiment that floored me. "You don't think anyone else would want me. You're saying I'd better be glad I've found a body to cling to 'cause he's the best I can do."

"There's nothing wrong with Aris! He's a wonderful catch."

"But you think he's the best I can do."

"I'm thinking of your father," she demurred. "He's so looking forward to the wedding."

"Well, there's a good reason for me to spend the next fifty years with Aris—so Dad can have a nice afternoon!"

It was something Kendra would have said. My lips closed tight to keep further acid from leaking out. My teeth clacked, the chattering thing they used to do whenever Kendra smarted off to our father, whenever she said things that never quite evaporated but followed us around, tangled and stinking in our hair. "I'm sorry, Mom, I—" Yet if I thought anything, it was: *Dr. Friedland would tell me to trust and explore my feelings.*

115

In the gulf of silence, my shifted alliance leapt up like a blade, severing the wires between my mother and me. Across the distance separating Kenilworth from Bucktown, your presence blazed a blur of static through which words were funneled, garbled, misunderstood. All I could think was: *Next time.*

"You can be invisible in marriage too." I heard myself, blindly determined. "You made every sacrifice—left school when you got pregnant, worked to put Dad through law school—you were perfect. I never knew how you managed. But now, I guess I don't know *why* either."

She didn't speak. I'd shocked her, I knew. We did not say such things, acknowledge unfairness or regret, not she and I. That was my father's and Kendra's forte, reserved for the intensity of their anger, somehow beyond real life. I had no idea really whether my mother was in the least bit angry at the infidelity that must have led to my father's disease. I didn't know even whether she consciously acknowledged the connection, nor did I know how she lived, daily, crowded among so many grievances and fears. Not only rage at what had been brought into her home, but surely also fear of infection. Or maybe, by this point, imagining a life alone without him, she almost hoped for it in some covert corner of her heart? What were the chances: pregnant with twins after only a couple of indiscretions, no HIV after years of sex? Or was it true, what Kendra said, that he'd avoided her bed for ages—or that she had barred him from it?

I heard her blow her nose, imagined lipstick rubbing off with the frantic wipe of a Kleenex. Felt her fear—a cold, martyr's grip—that my father would catch her, that she would burden him, had usurped his ownership of grief. But when she spoke, her voice was bright. "Aris would never stay out all night. What's his favorite food, his favorite of your outfits? Of course he loves you, but men are funny. They always need a chance to salvage their pride."

"They'd better if they're the only ones entitled to any." It didn't come out a joke at all. A memory had popped up like a flash card in my head: the four of us in the old Volvo station wagon, driving up to Delavan the first year we'd owned the cabin. Kendra was saying, *When Mom walks into a place and the floorboards creak, she says, Now this is a home! But even if elephants were stomping on the floor, if Dad heard a creak, he'd say, Condemn this place! It's not new!* I sat holding the receiver, uncertain as to why I'd recalled such a meaningless incident—I'd never thought about that episode before. Was it real? But I remembered, also, laughter. My parents getting the joke. And our homes, all of them, from Cincinnati to Kenilworth to Delavan, adhered to my mother's tastes. Wood, wood, more wood; bathrooms and kitchens that needed work. I remembered my mother laughing, tinkly and confident and in conspiracy with her barely-teenage daughters. *Men make a lot of noise, but women always get our way.* Now, quietly, "Under the right circumstances, being invisible is not so bad."

"Mom," I said, "do you still love Dad? I mean, I know you love him, but do you—"

"I spoke with your sister yesterday, and she promised to come by this weekend. I had to call her three times—she didn't return any of my messages. I haven't mentioned the weekend to your poor father, he'd get his hopes up like he always does. Could you talk to her, Kirby? It means so much to him. Could you just do . . . *something*? Make sure she comes?"

"Yeah," I said, and I guessed her deflection was my answer; that whatever remained between my parents lay beyond my reach. Perhaps such insularity *was* love, or at least the thing that passed for love. Nothing more than a woman in her hundred-year-old house, flawlessly nice, yet irrevocably past the shared laughter of a family joke. I made my voice bright. "Gotta run, I have a negligee to pour myself into and a soufflé to pop in the oven. How's that sound?"

Chiding: "I hope you don't talk to Aris with that kind of sarcasm."

Ha ha. What do *you* think?

Floorboards in lofts creak. Not only did Aris and I have no real dividers to section off what we needed to think of as "rooms," and not only did the brick walls shed, ensuring that our floors (and socks) were always coated by a thin layer of rust-colored dust so we spent our lives sweeping, but we could never, ever make an inconspicuous move. Aris returned late. My mother was right; he would never have stayed out all night. For one thing, I had little idea where he would go. He had no family in Chicago, and no friendships where you call late and ask to crash on a couch. Always I had suspected that he'd been with other girls during our years together, but I had to admit that if this were true, they couldn't have been the sort of affairs that led to much. I was never in any doubt concerning his whereabouts. Even Kendra said I was being stupid, that men like Aris didn't like women well enough to keep a string of them around, that he was lucky he'd managed to bond with one and wouldn't want more. As I heard his feet—shoes removed so as not to wake me—wading through the dust and creaking against the tenuous floor that helped keep our world separate from those of our neighbors, I believed her and loved him with a fierceness more alarming than pleasant. I imagined myself bolting up and running across the loft into his arms. The image struck me as an excerpt from my sister's life, with one of those dramatic actor-dancer-musician boys with whom she was constantly breaking up and getting back together. My back stayed pressed flat against the mattress. Aris's body lowered onto the foot of the bed, and I lay too still, the kind of stillness that is only achievable through resistance. He sat, didn't move to take off a sock or unbuckle his belt. Didn't move.

"I didn't think you'd come back." But it was not remotely true, and I didn't know why I'd said it. It started everything off wrong. I sighed, and that was wrong too. My flesh sank against the mattress, deflating.

"Kirby. I've been doing a lot of thinking."

"Please." I sat, but his back was to me, and he couldn't see that I was naked, the way he always wanted me to sleep, the way I refused to remain for long after sex, claiming I got cold. "Aris, don't leave me."

His back sunk. "That's all anything is to you. Will I put up with things the way they are, or will I abandon you? What about *you*—the way you've become—how you talk to me?"

"I'll change. It's my father, you know that. It can't last forever. I'll get used to it, or . . . it will end some other way."

"I don't think it's your father, I think it's Kendra. Your father wouldn't incite this kind of behavior. This is petty and ridiculous, like girls in junior high. Kendra doesn't like me, she thinks you can do better, she wants to steal you back over to worship her, so you disdain me."

"I *love* you. You're the only man I've ever loved, the only man I've ever had anything with, been anything with. Look at me. Please."

He turned half around on the bed, but his lips, when he saw me, curled with what I feared was disgust. "This is it exactly. Look at you. Like you're going to take your clothes off and everything will be better. That's Kendra. That's everything I hate. That's not you."

"You hate my body? You hate making love to me?"

"No—*no*, but listen. If I were to succumb to you now, it wouldn't be making love. I'd be allowing you to manipulate me, and that wouldn't do either of us any good. I have to be strong for you instead. That's what you need."

"You're right." Something relaxed under my skin. "That *is* what I need. I'm lost."

He exhaled hard—I realized suddenly that he'd been holding his breath. "What do you think I'm here for?" Almost pleading. "I'd never let you fall. You have to give me a chance. I can take care of you through this crisis. Your parents know it—they don't have to worry about you because you have me, and it gives them peace of mind. Your sister is the only one who doesn't want things this way. She doesn't want to lose her hold on you."

"Aris, you're wrong about Kendra. She hardly calls me, she never comes over here. She doesn't care what I do. You have to forget about her."

"She doesn't do those things because *you* do. You chase her. That's what she likes."

"You make it sound like you think she's some evil machine out to destroy us."

He averted his eyes. Moved closer and inched the sheet down past my stomach so that my triangle of hair was exposed. He twined his fingers in it, stroked it. I kept my legs pressed together tight. Tried not to fidget.

"Your sister is a stranger to me. I don't dislike her personally, I just want what's mine."

"Am I yours?"

"Don't you want to be?"

"Does that mean you're mine too?"

His hand fell away. "What kind of question is that? A husband and wife belong to each other. They should connect on a deeper level than a shared bed and catered wedding and gifts. They should support each other and take care of each other. Everything I do is for you."

"What about for yourself?"

"I want to be the best I can be, sure. But it's for you."

"Why me?"

"Because I chose you."

"But why me?"

"Because I love you."

"But why me?"

He pulled the sheet back further. Pushed me back gently, prodded my legs apart with his knee. "Here, let me show you."

"No." I clung to him hard so he couldn't achieve the distance necessary to see me well. "Tell me. Why me?"

He kissed me, purposefully hard. "Because you saw it in me, Bee. You saw everything I wanted to be. You believed in my vision—I knew you'd support me even if others were against me. You didn't want me to follow my father. You wanted me to be me. At least you used to."

"No—" I pulled away, yanked the sheet back up with a snap. "I don't mean what I did for you. I mean what about *me*?"

His silence chilled me; in the dark he could have been any man at any point in time. He kissed my mouth again, but more tentatively. Took hold of my breast. My nipple stiffened, not with arousal but something else. "Bee, honey, what is this? What do you want me to say?"

He could see me now. Lowered me again, his hair against my chest, his mouth suckling, hands not searching but moving automatically to a practiced destination. I pulled back, tighter, tighter. But between his body and the bed, there was no place left to go.

Fragment

There is a charge
For the eyeing of my scars, there is a charge
For the hearing of my heart—
It really goes.

—Sylvia Plath,
"Lady Lazarus"

The Artful Dodger was a corner bar in a recently gentrified neighborhood where people not being kept in their fathers' love shacks lived. In an area of the city where Kendra, given her usual penchant for struggling-artist boys, would probably have chosen to live too, blending in among the vestiges of thrift-store clad, Wicker Park hipsters with a comfortable anonymity. During her brief hiatuses from NYCB, the Dodger had always been her Chicago bar. Guitarist lived only a few blocks away, in the attic of one of the sole unrenovated houses remaining, belonging to a Mexican family with four loud children and a very loud dog and many loud friends who hung out on the back porch wearing cowboy hats and drinking beer even in the winter. Kendra always suspected that Guitarist viewed living above such a rowdy family—like painting houses despite his college degree—as the pre-condition of calling himself a Marxist. Not that he said as much; part of his home-grown Marxism entailed that he was not supposed to notice when they played music at 2:00 AM or littered the yard with cans. Still, he acted subtly as though any compliment he paid them reflected more upon himself. Kendra, on the other hand, since leaving the Russian-tinted, Czar-inspired and communist-perpetuated world of ballet, felt like a veritable poster child for the moral perils of capitalism. Crap income, yet living on the Gold Coast courtesy of her father, dining out four nights a week courtesy of her lover. What would Guitarist make of joining the ranks of men who supported her? Once an artist, the most dedicated of workers, a symbol of all he admired, her current lifestyle seemed by comparison silly and gauche.

Kendra had not had a period in eight weeks. She had been vomiting up the vestiges of dry bagels (the entirety of her diet when not with Michael Kelsey) prior to becoming afraid to eat at all. No cash cushioned her checking account. Now how silly and gauche was that?

She went to the Dodger with every intention of borrowing money for an abortion. That is why she went: to ask. It is important to stipulate such things. To ask, and because she needed a drink. Because she needed *to* drink, to be around people who were drinking too, not Michael Kelsey who always had one glass of wine, or one scotch, and then watched with benign curiosity while she exceeded his intake five times over. Guitarist, at the bar as always, talking to the Southern bartender and two obvious regulars, could always be counted on to consume his share.

gina frangello

Guitarist rose when she entered. Embraced her in front of the jaded-looking bartender and two chain smoking fat chicks, all of whom stared not out of interest but because there was nothing else to look at, the bar being otherwise empty on a weeknight. He led her to a far corner and sat on the same side of a booth as she, holding her hand like somebody who had lost his best friend. It was not a romantic gesture. He had, in fact, lost his best friend. She looked at him for a long time, straight on, until he had to look away, which was easier than looking away herself would have been. He said, "K-hole. Long time no, you know. What's going on?"

Kendra appreciated the question. She wanted to talk. She wanted to talk the way they always had during the past eight years, though she was now irritatingly conscious of the fact that she'd known Michael Kelsey two years longer than that. She wanted to tell her best friend about what she'd been doing. About *whom* she'd been doing. Kendra had not spoken truly openly about her affair with anyone. Three long sips into a vodka martini, she found she could not stop.

She said: "I don't know how to explain exactly—Michael likes things his way. He's always very polite about it, of course, but there it is just the same."

She said: "Like the very first week we were fucking, I brought my own coffee to his apartment since no way could I face mornings without caffeine. But when he brewed a pot the next day, he still served decaf, and when I reminded him again, he said he'd run out of filters entirely. Ever since he's made only tea."

She said: "He has this fucked-up knee from a car crash when he was seventeen—I think it was maybe a quasi suicide attempt after his mother died—and sometimes his joints still swell up when he's playing racquetball and he gets desperate and sees his doctor. There's this entire stash of painkillers in the medicine cabinet, but he only takes a few and the rest sit there rotting because he doesn't like how they make him feel—control freak—so there are, like, three bottles of Vicodin in there, two are expired but I mean who gives a shit, I just keep putting them in my Advil bottle five at a time, I don't even think he's noticed yet."

She said: "When he does figure it out, I'll be subjected to some kind of arduous torture he'll pretend is punishment for my crime, but the truth is he'll totally get off on knowing I've been stealing from him like a common whore. I mean, I don't

123

mind or anything, I want the pills, I'm more than willing to oblige."

"Arduous torture," no joke, that is a direct quote. What was she thinking, you may wonder, divulging such details to an ex? Well, probably something like, *If I told Bee the whole story, that little goody-goody would run crying to Mom in two seconds flat.* Everyone needs somebody to confide in. On the other hand, what did her former paramour make of being the recipient of this little soliloquy? Probably something like this:

Guitarist sat beside the girl in the booth and thought he would like to slap her in the face. It was not the first time he had entertained such a thought where she was concerned, but the first time the thought made him miserable rather than aroused, because it suddenly struck him that if he had smacked her face every time he wanted to do so, she might be sitting in a bar somewhere talking to some other poor sucker about him instead of subjecting him to this bullshit about a fortysomething asshole who worked with her father and was probably bald and fat and wore Hawaiian shirts to kick back or some other terrible thing. (He had in fact met Michael Kelsey on two occasions, both of which times Michael was, coincidentally, wearing the same gray Armani suit, but he remembered nothing of it, having been only eighteen at the time and anyone past college being invisible to him.) He looked at Kendra and, although it was impossible that she weighed even one hundred pounds, although what little she had once had in the way of tits had diminished entirely so that there were merely two pubescent buds poking forth beneath her halter top, although her hair looked in need of a wash and was stuck like an enormous ball of yellow twine atop her head by a mangled-looking chopstick (how did it stay in there?), he found her the most lovely, horrible creature he had ever seen. His mind filled with images that frightened him: twisting one of her fragile stick arms behind her back until she wept open-mouthed while he fucked her; leaving bruises around those huge hollow eyes so that she looked a piece of damaged meat, not fit for consumption. Clearly it was her fault that he would think these things, sitting there admitting that her new sugar daddy liked to spank her with the soles of the shoes he wore to work, that he had left bite-marks down her back and then taken her out to dinner in a backless dress bought for the occasion. Did she think he, Guitarist, was inhuman? Didn't she think stories like that would make him sick, would make him want to do it too?

While Kendra rambled, four different people came to their table in the back to buy weed from Guitarist, who sometimes sold in early evenings when it was dark and quiet, but although he pocketed fifty dollars a shot, he found the presence of these barfly potheads a serious imposition. He found the fact that he, instead of being a successful attorney with a Lake Shore Drive apartment, was a barfly pothead, a serious imposition. Kendra had her hand on his knee. He was sure she hadn't noticed, so intent was she on analyzing this man, this friend of Mr. Braun's, with the sort of zeal she usually reserved for remaining enigmatic when one of her lovers was trying to analyze *her*. This turn-around was too much. Guitarist moved his leg away; her hand dropped to the vinyl booth with a weak smack. Then he pulled her by the hair and kissed her hard enough to smear her lipstick all over his mouth.

He said, "I want to fuck you. Now. However I want. You can't sit here and tell me this shit like I'm a eunuch. I was there first. Why should this guy get more of you than I ever got?"

Kendra looked more confused than contemplating going to bed with him could possibly merit. He yanked her hair again with an attempt at savagery, and hissed, "What? Are you in love with this prick?"

"Of course not." Then, with a bottomless weariness, "God, I hope not."

"So what difference does one more fuck make between friends?"

"None I can think of."

"Then let's go. You can tell me any stories you want once you're naked."

"Yeah, whatever. Just let me finish my martini first."

"I've got vodka at my apartment, baby."

She shrugged. "I can't taste any vermouth in here anyway. That's good enough for me."

*   *   *

March 1990

Rachel was wailing—a clear signal of Kendra's deficits. That was all it was, a child's crying: the sign of someone else's inability to love. From the master suite, though, the baby could scarcely be heard. Mrs. Kelsey must enjoy that, her room a sanitarium, a haven of peace. Kendra moved quickly, not trying to stop, unable to stop. Bureau, armoire, closet . . .

The drawer beside the bed, the top drawer beside the bed. Kendra stared: these weren't just naked girls lounging, not like the pictures in her father's magazines, pretty ladies with everything smooth and pink and open. Here women were stretched out raw and at unsettling angles, prodded with penises and things just meant to look like penises, invaded with the handles of coiled-up whips, spread eagle or asses in the air, asses in the air waiting for things she had not really known about. Not anticipated. In the drawer next to the bed. Kendra suspected that was where you kept things that were shared: not where a man hides his fantasies or secrets, but where a couple stores their ticket for transportation to someplace other than where they are, to someone other than who they have to be. Impossible, though, inconceivable that any woman wanted to see these things. How could anyone enjoy looking at the promise that her own body was meant first and foremost for pain? It might have made Kendra cry if she were a child anymore, if she remembered how. Instead, it made her not hear the door. In not hearing, all of her could go into seeing, as though if she looked hard enough at the page she could see through to where she would someday be, to what she was made for and how to escape it.

Mrs. Kelsey, a woman who knew things Kendra did not, who knew how not to be a woman so that she could get off on women's twisted bodies, stood watching Kendra search those bodies for the answers she needed and feared. She said, "I am standing in the doorway of my own bedroom. It is time for you to put that down."

Kendra did not put the magazine down. She held it to her chest: a last ditch hope. She meant to whisper, wanted to cry, "Why are all the women hurt? Why can't you see the men's faces?" Wanted to beg, "Tell me why this is sexy, I need to know why this is sexy." But in her silence Mrs. Kelsey approached her, mistaking her for a deer caught in headlights rather than a seeker on a quest. Removed the magazine from Kendra's hand with one definitive swish. Mr. Kelsey was in the nursery, the baby quiet; Kendra's face began to boil. Stripped now of her grail she felt merely caught red-handed, sweaty and young before an unfathomable beauty.

Mrs. Kelsey said, "Here. Take your money and wait in the living room until my husband is ready to drive you home."

It would not be the last time she accepted money for doing something wrong, but the first; Kendra felt a thrill. The corridor of the house was dark. She left the master bedroom, would ride back to

Kenilworth in a silence Mr. Kelsey would never think to break, being unaware that she loved him. But did she love him anymore, when he might be the face just beyond the camera's reach? Her wait was long, their voices muffled. Only rooms, only feet away, he knew what she had done. She found she was shaking. Were they calling her parents? But when he approached and she rose to meet him, Mr. Kelsey said only, "Are you ever going to tell me, on one of these boring drives, why you always look so sad?"

"No." Kendra stepped through the door he held open for her, into the humid air. They walked, in a silence she suddenly recognized as complicity, out to his car.

*   *   *

There is something disheartening in watching one's beloved make a fool of herself. It produces a hardening effect. One may react with hostility, with a desire to see the beloved object punished for having dared lose her dignity. A vicarious shame. Believe me, I know.

There is no doubt in my mind that Guitarist entered his attic apartment wanting to see Kendra Braun humbled. That he craved even to hear her cry—this being what she had coming, for behaving like such a ninny over some old man when he himself was in love with her and had been for so many years it was long since moot. Two hours later he fell into a deep, horrible sleep to escape her. If he never woke up again, that was okay with him.

Things had not gone as planned. In the picture in his mind, when he slapped Kendra for the first time, she would hold her hand hard to her face and whimper a little. Then he would push her down and tell her what he was going to do with her while she begged him not to. Then he would do it anyway and she would bawl—but since she was obviously into that sort of thing, something he berated himself for never having before ascertained, she would also come. Perhaps as part of the picture, she would even get tired of this aging man of hers and come to *him* for what she needed. Then his life would be a giant porno flick starring himself and his oldest friend. If in reality, Guitarist was not so naïve as to imagine things would turn out so perfectly, then at least he anticipated one hell of a night ahead.

The first time he slapped Kendra in the face, she just stared at him. Her look said, *Are you demented?* He slapped her again, across the same cheek. This time she flinched, and her hand did rise up, but she said, "What the hell are you doing? You know I don't like having my face touched, what's wrong with you?" He said, "Tough," in a voice too throaty and contrived to be his own, and threw her on the bed, which was actually a mattress on the floor. He pulled up her long skirt and began to spank her, glad that Kendra rarely wore underwear since he did not think he had the presence of mind to remove any had he found it there. She sighed, as if she had just discovered she was going to have to wait in a very long line to have her driver's license renewed. He smacked her ass again, and her body twitched, but she stayed silent. He said, "Jesus, baby, aren't you going to play along?" She said, "I don't have to, you're playing by yourself." He hit her once more and she said, irritably, "Oww," and pushed her face hard into the pillow, refusing to move. He was grateful for her stillness so he could reach for the condoms. She rolled onto her back expressionless as a fish. He slid on a rubber and said, "K, come *on*," and she said, "Are you over it now?" He said, "Why else would you tell me all that shit if it isn't what you want me to do?" She said, "Every time you watch a shoot-out in an action movie, do you go and gun ten people in the head? I thought you were my friend." This infuriated him, and he lunged at her, pushing her onto her stomach and fucking her as aggressively as he could, listening with relish to her occasional, unwilling grunts. Her pelvis arched away from him as if to escape—he dug his fingers around her hipbones as tight as he could. He felt glad. But then her body went slack and she wouldn't moan anymore or respond, and he said, "K, are you all right, I'm not really hurting you am I?" and she said nothing, just stared straight ahead at a picture of the two of them at prom in a frame on his wall with a bunch of other pictures, several of which she was in, and his dick went limp as lukewarm cheese. He pulled out, muttering, "Man. You are hard. Why do you have to be like this? Man."

Kendra lay on her side not responding. She lit one of his cigarettes. He said, "What's all this about?" She said, "I'm not your nine hundred number. Do you have any weed left?" He rolled her a joint and watched her, wrapped in the chilly satin of his vintage robe and staring at a *Simpsons* rerun on TV, the one where Homer keeps going back in time because of the toaster. Sometimes she laughed aloud, and once she said, "Hey,

Guitar, would you want to go back in time? I'd probably be burned as a witch. Remember my first opening night party when you tried to explain quantum physics to all us pirouette-headed dancers? Maybe parallel realities are real and we're still at that party right now. That'd be better, don't you think, than just this?"

Guitarist felt it entirely possible that he did not know where he was. His dick hurt. He crawled under the covers, leaving her awake, and fell asleep the minute his head hit the pillow.

It was one in the morning when Kendra got up, pulled her clothes over her tender body, her cunt raw from the fiasco several hours earlier, and removed the wallet from the pair of worn-thin, baggy trousers discarded at the foot of the bed. There would be, she knew from having watched sales earlier, at least two hundred dollars inside. She had no pockets, so she slipped it into her purse along with her stolen Vicodin. It was late to take the El, but she figured she could catch a cab on Ashland. She did not kiss the figure on the bed goodbye as she stood up and headed out, barefoot so as not to wake him with the click of her heels on the stairs.

A Saturday night, mid-June. The Saturday in question was the day before Kendra's twenty-third birthday. As far as she knew, it had never occurred to Michael that she might *have* a birth date. No difference: they always spent Saturday nights together, unless prior arrangements otherwise had been made. Tonight he would distract her, tomorrow Bee as always for their birthday ritual. Finally come Monday, she would have to call and schedule her abortion. No more special occasions until Kirby's July wedding—no more excuses to stall.

Saturdays were weighty because Kendra never saw Michael on Sundays, Mondays, or Tuesdays. He had Rachel on those nights, every week. Her mother had her from Wednesday to Saturday, one extra day, which amounted to many extra days over the course of any year, much less any life. Michael was not thrilled that they did not alternate, but he never made a fuss: he was lucky his ex-wife had agreed to joint custody without their having to go to court and drag each other through the mud, which, he told Kendra, would have been too easy, too humiliating for everyone. He was happy to have his three nights, though it bothered him that his ex-wife relinquished them so easily—as though maybe she didn't mind being alone for half the week, or being with whomever she was not alone with. This, he said, made him feel he should have made waves, because an extra night every other week would mean a lot to him. Kendra acted understanding when he said this, more understanding than she would act under any normal circumstances—than she would *be* during any normal conversation—hoping he'd get the point and steer the subject away from his daughter, which he did. In this respect too, he was not one to make waves.

At eight o'clock in the evening, the outside end of his usual window of arrival, Michael still hadn't shown. The apartment growing pinkish with sunset, Kendra poured a vodka tonic and sat on the couch drinking it, to wait. As she picked at a stray thread on a sofa cushion, it occurred to her that her father had doubtless screwed innumerable women on this very piece of furniture, and Michael had known about it all along. She hastily drained her drink in one sip, stood, and attempted a double pirouette to distract herself. Between the pregnancy and the liquor, her center was way off. Across the room, the red light of her answering machine stared back unblinkingly. Rachel, no doubt—Michael would drop her for Rachel on a dime. God forbid his precious daughter be lonely if her mother had a Saturday evening soirée and there was no junior high sleepover to attend. Michael would rush right over to rescue her, not even remembering the existence of his cell phone, not caring anything about Kendra and her petty birthday and inconvenient need to eat. The refrigerator was empty, so she made another drink and took it into the bedroom, away from her father's fuck couch. She'd bought her own mattress; that was one thing she'd made sure to do. Michael's daughter, right now, was probably sitting on the couch in his apartment, the couch whose arms he'd bent Kendra over so many times. Or bouncing on his bed inches from where Kendra's legs had been duct-taped, from where—no, what would she be doing on his bed? What the hell did Michael *do* with his daughter anyway, on a Saturday night no less? What the hell could a man like him and some barely-adolescent kid possibly share?

*   *   *

July 1990

Those pictures haunted her. You know they did. She moved her hands fast thinking of them, wondering how something that made her lungs breathe fire could make the heat between her legs burn so good. The aloof Mr. Kelsey metamorphosed into the camera-man, the dick, the whip all at once. His wife into a work of perfect, soiled art Kendra knew she'd never grow to be. Her own tits in her child's hands were pointy, her legs too short to carry off five-inch heels without looking like a baby whore. She wondered if she'd ever be a whore. In the crack that had flung open with those magazines, the fissure from which she could now view the world outside her family, all things had become possible. All things had become logical. What was going on, what she once thought would end her life, was merely part of the order of things. Something she was meant to enjoy. To consume. Revelations did not come cheap, Kendra knew. When you were granted one, its source inevitably became someone you were forever indebted to.

*   *   *

The sensation of being watched. Kendra bolted upright—the room stayed black. Late. She did not remember drifting off to sleep or how she'd come to be in bed, naked but for pink dance tights. Michael sat in the corner of the room under her floor lamp, flexible and soundless as a cat, reading one of her books, Gelsey Kirkland's first memoir. He wore a suit another woman had obviously purchased—it was not of his taste—but the tie was loosened and his jacket thrown carelessly beside him. A lock of usually neat hair hung in his eyes. He glanced up when she stirred, and he smiled a sweet smile as though he were happy to see her. She wondered if he had put her to bed, covered her with the duvet. Her esophagus began to palpitate.

"What time is it?"

No answer. A page turned. Despite his erotic appetite for the emaciated bodies of ballerinas, Kendra was certain her lover had, prior to their relationship, taken slim interest in the confessions of self-destructive dancers. She was not sure whether to feel flattered or invaded.

"How long have I been sleeping?"

Still he did not approach her. "Long enough for me to say happy birthday."

Kendra squinted at the bedside clock. 2:32. She was officially twenty-three. A relief; it might be calming to have the age difference between them finally one year less than twenty. Still, if she ever reached his age, he would already be . . . no, the idea of Michael in his sixties, seventies, unsettled her. Inspired a sudden impulse to jump up and throw her arms around him, but the memory of how she'd waited for him earlier, growing progressively more plowed and unsteady on her feet as she attempted to go through a barre, kept her still. The memory of—

She stood fast, pricks of light bursting before her eyes. "What are you doing here? You weren't here, you didn't show, you—how the hell did you get in my apartment?"

He laughed. "It took you awhile to put that together. Exactly how much did you smoke before you passed out? Those short-term memory lapses will get you every time, Kendra."

"I didn't smoke anything." A lie, and he could probably smell it. "Or maybe I did, maybe I drank two vodka tonics, took a Valium and smoked a joint. What did you do, pick my lock to save me from myself?"

"I have a key."

"No you fucking don't. I would never give you a key."

"Maybe not. But the woman who stayed here before you did."

A chill ran through her veins. She felt her legs buckle; her body forcibly moved back a step, farther from him. The smell of something else in the apartment: meat, as if he'd cooked. If only it weren't dark, if only she could see. It felt appropriate that she might start to cry, that if she were normal, she would start to cry. *Oh, God. Oh . . .*

"Why did you tell me that? Jesus, Michael. Give it to me."

He reached into his pocket and took out the key. Held it forward for her to take. She found that she could not approach him, sank back onto the bed. He put the key on the bookshelves. Came to her, sat down.

"It's not what you think. Though that, of course, would have been entirely possible too."

"If not your wife, then who?"

"Remarkably someone you don't know. A friend, that's all—we were *all* friends. When he ended things, she called me. I came to see her. She gave me the key. She'd forgotten to give it back to him and didn't want it—a symbolic gesture more than anything else. Henry had his own key, and he planned to give up the apartment. I never thought to actually return her copy."

"Did you fuck her too?"

"That night or ever?"

"Oh. Oh, I see."

"I can't see how that's relevant."

"Neither can I. So. What was her name?"

"Her name is Veronica."

"You've got to be kidding."

"Maybe I am."

"Why did he leave her? Did she get pregnant?"

"Most likely he left when he became ill. But I have no inside track on his motivation—Henry's become a missing person. He and Gail are holed up in Kenilworth in that house as though sickness is a mark of shame. It's archaic. It's the way my parents acted when they found out about my mother's tumor in, what, 1972 . . ."

"Don't talk about our parents, I don't want to talk about that."

"Fine with me."

"You had no right to come in here without my knowing. I could have had another man in here—you have no right to sit in the dark like that, watching me sleep. You know that."

"I know it, yes." A laugh. "But I brought you a birthday present, and when you didn't answer the door I figured you were out, so I used the key to surprise you."

"I don't want any present more than my privacy."

"So now that you *have* the key, why not come in the kitchen to see what I got you?"

She stood again. She didn't want to. Wanted him to leave, wanted to be alone here in this apartment her father and some woman called Veronica or not called Veronica had soiled. She thought of her feeling earlier, that Michael had been complicit in her father's infidelities, and knew she would vomit again. The waves were already rising. She needed more weed to push it down, but couldn't light up in front of Michael. Not now. Something had changed. *Boots propped up against the door.* She had not heard the key in her lock. He would be waiting to trap her. She could not think how. Her stomach hurt, her back hurt, her ass hurt. How?

The kitchen was full of groceries. Full of things she liked, as though her mother had done her shopping instead of just this man she fucked. Bagels and flavored cream cheeses and Cheerios and skim milk and hazelnut coffee and fat-free cookies and broccoli and bok choy and udon noodles and frozen yogurt. As far as she'd known, Michael had never bought food in his life (his apartment certainly never housed any); she was reminded again of his former role as a husband, that he was a father still, and, unlike she, knew about buying food products unavailable at Walgreen's. To think he'd summoned forth that old part of himself for her, that part he usually rejected—that his very affair with her symbolized a rejection of—seemed at once dangerously foolish and disarmingly touching. Abruptly she recalled Guitarist, a morning in New York at the apartment where maggots had taken over her kitchen. The first day of his stay, she'd awoken to find him standing on a chair, scraping larvae-like bodies off the ceiling with paper plates and stacking them neatly in the trash. So she wouldn't have to, so she could brew coffee, maybe even eat. That was it, the moment his declarations of devotion finally ceased to sound abstract and dramatized. She'd broken up with him before the end of his stay.

Now she faltered under the arch that separated her kitchen from the living room with the tentative alarm of a virgin crossing the threshold of the bridal suite. Better Michael had *brought* her maggots than to force her into the proximity of such overwhelming food!

He stood at the counter, as earnest as she had ever seen him, holding a bag from Taco Bell. "The regular food is for my peace of mind, so I'll know you aren't starving when I'm not around. This is your present, here—I got your favorite unhealthy take-out."

"I'm—" Absolutely nothing in her repertoire seemed right. "Not hungry right now."

"Of course," he said. "Of course you think you aren't going to eat either. But you are. I know you haven't had anything all day, I know you were waiting for me to take you to dinner. You aren't going to fight me, Kendra. The only thing you're opening your mouth for is to eat this disgusting burrito that I have no idea how you can like. Are we clear?"

Her feet unfroze—familiar ground. She snatched the bag from his hand. "You can't make me eat this! You're not my father, you're just a guy I screw."

He didn't move from the counter. "Whatever else I may be, I am a man who has never visited a Taco Bell until tonight." Firm, but with a gentle cajoling that scraped her ears. "And you are a woman who needs to put something in her stomach before she gets sick on vodka and pills. And if I have to tie you to a chair and feed this food to you bite by bite, I will."

Her gut, sour with booze, felt too empty to accommodate nourishment—but she wasn't empty, of course. She would be soon. The smell of Taco Bell made her stomach clutch in recoil; she hated herself for wanting to eat for him. Her parents had done this sort of thing when she was a pubescent ballerina, eager for self-starvation. They had never won, finally realizing that she would remain at the dining room table until she died if they didn't let her leave without touching their fatty pork chops or scalloped potatoes. The look in Michael's eyes, though, sparked a hunger that could trick her nausea, could break her. She laughed nervously. He did not crack a smile, did not look awkward or confused, just stood there, staring at her. She giggled harder. Sputtered, "I'm pregnant. I can't eat anything, I'll puke it up. I haven't had my period in nine weeks and all I do is vomit. Just give up, Michael. I'm sorry. Just go."

He said only, "Are you through?"

Apparently, she could not be. "Oh, yeah, that's right, you wouldn't believe me—you think I'm on the pill. Uh, sorry, that was a lie. Since you've broken into my apartment, you might as well look around. Go ahead, ransack the place, you won't find any birth control pills. I tried, but see they make me fat, and as you're so intent on pointing out, I've got some *issues* with my weight. But I really, really hate condoms, don't you? They make, what would you call it . . . intimacy . . . so difficult. One's got to live dangerously, isn't that what this is all about?"

It took only one sweep of his arm to grab her, push her into a kitchen chair. Her ass pounded against the seat hard, making her cry out sharply at the impact on her bruises. She tried to stand, but he kept one hand on her naked shoulder; she could not move. He dropped the Taco Bell bag in front of her on the table. Said, "I never claimed to doubt you. I also don't care if you spend the next four hours vomiting until you fill this kitchen. You are going to eat. I don't care if you're having triplets, understand. Open the bag and unwrap your dinner. Go on. Now."

Haltingly, she rolled a Burrito Supreme from its foil. He knew she did not eat meat. Tears welled up in her throat, pinched her nose. Her voice wavered: "Michael—," but he ripped the bag open to reveal the rest: cinnamon crispies, a carton of milk. He picked up the burrito and tore off a piece, held it to her mouth until she accepted. The tortilla was cold and soggy but wonderful, the beef tart and tangy as her memory of it, the pasty-cream of refried beans smooth in a way real Mexican restaurants never got quite right. She couldn't swallow, though, choked on the first bite. He sat beside her at the table, watching. A sob expanded in her throat, without any relief of tears. Choking, her tongue pushed at the mass, hand covering her mouth. When the spasm ran out, she felt dry and parched, but the bite, nearly liquid by then, went down. He held out another; her tongue tasted his fingers beneath the messy, falling-apart food: solid. When she finished the burrito, she accepted a few cinnamon crispies, placidly licking sugar from his fingers before turning her eyes away, silent. Michael must have been satisfied; he set down the bag.

"Let's try this again. Is the baby mine?"

She tried for a laugh. "Oh, who the hell knows? Could be—you've got frequency on your side. Maybe not, though. You're old, that sperm count's probably not what it used to be."

He didn't smile. Didn't flinch either. Put a hand over hers—she pulled hers back fast. Lowered her head onto the table, face down on arms. In a moment, she felt his lips there, soft. His breath on her hair, his hand enclosing her fisted one. This time she was too tired to resist. The lard from the beans felt heavy in her abdomen, like rocks she'd spend days trying to shit out, but she was always constipated—not like Kirby who couldn't stop going; it was a miracle Bee didn't waste away. But Kirby ate like a pig, stuffed herself docile. Michael's hand was warm, the temperature a body should be. Her own fingers had been cold to the point of numbness lately. She let her fingers twine through his for the heat, nothing else.

"I wouldn't like to see what any baby of ours would turn out like," she said into the table. "A mutant. Fucked up genes."

"Kendra. Look. If you're screwing men all over Chicago unprotected, I ought to know. It's got nothing to do with ownership. I use condoms when I'm with anyone else. We've known each other a long time, and that makes things seem . . . But hell. I've got a kid."

"Stop it," she said. "Don't talk about—"

"Why not? For the best fuck of my life I'm not supposed to *mind* playing roulette with real bullets? Well, I'm sorry. Those stakes are too random for—"

136

"I said stop!" She rose—unbearable to be here anymore, half-naked at the table, the cold of the metal legs brushing her calves. He did not let go of her hand. When she tried to jerk free, he pulled her instead to sit upon his knees, perched ridiculously like some oversized bird whose wings were damaged and could not fly away. With his free hand, he guided the carton of milk to her lips until she parted them. Her throat felt locked; wetness spilled a sticky path from her chin and soiled her tights. His fingers that had intertwined with hers moved to the white film dotting her chest, smeared the excess around her left nipple like finger paint. Once again he tilted the carton, this time guiding her head too, when to come up and swallow. More drops trickled, but some of what he tipped out made its way down her throat. When the last liquid was drained, she kept her mouth open, suddenly afraid for the game to end, for him to abandon her to whatever ugly thing would seep from her empty mouth next. But Michael reset the carton on the table.

"All right. Now your meal is finished. Now, if it's what you want, I'll leave."

From the insides of milk-soaked lips, impulses bubbled: *I'm not your daughter, I'm not your charity case, go ahead, get out.* From somewhere else, she heard herself speak.

"No. I'll be good, I swear. Please, Michael, don't go."

Analysis

Your body
Hurts me as the world hurts God.

—Sylvia Plath,
"Fever 103°"

Second Dream

I AM IN KENDRA'S body and I am in New York. A letter arrives from our mother reading: *Your father is dying. You abandoned us long ago, but now that it is almost over, you may come home—if you like?* Suddenly I am at the airport. Terrified to board the plane but I force myself, a symphony of my (sister's) muscles clenching during the ascent. Gravity clings to my stomach so I'm rising out of my body, trying to hold on to the seat, clinging to flesh, higher, higher . . . I don't remember landing. Outside O'Hare, a man meets me in a long black car—a limousine. Two naked women are visible through the lowered window. He says he has been hired to take me to my father. I don't trust him and say I prefer to walk, but he insists that on my own it will take another month to reach my destination. Inside the car, the man lets one woman suck him off while the other does her nails. None of them speak to me. At my parent's house, nobody is home. The man leaves for the cemetery, but I climb the stairs all the way to the attic room alone. There I start reading magazines while sprawled out on the bed. Like I have no place to be. I feel calm, almost sleepy. The magazines are piled high next to Kendra's bed—*my* bed, I remind myself. I don't count them, but it is clear there are thirteen.

The Joy of Symbiosis

THE EVE I TURNED twenty-three, I stayed up late. It was not a volitional act. Next to me, Aris radiated steamy heat like a furnace; every time I shifted in bed, damp warmth wafted from beneath the sheets to envelop my lungs. I couldn't breathe. Sometime after three, I found myself sprawled on the coolness of the leather sofa alone, Kendra's and my birthday book in my hands, flipping through the pages—twenty-two thus far—surveying our faces for changes, markers. Sticking, as always, on the day we turned fourteen.

The change was jarring. Over the first thirteen photos, Kendra and I had gradually evolved from indistinguishable babies whom even our parents could not tell apart without little name tags written meticulously by our mother on the inside-labels of all our clothes, to children with matching-but-different-colored outfits and identical haircuts, to pre-adolescents beginning to assert our individuality—Kendra's hair remained long while I'd hacked mine off (forcing our mother to rush me into a salon for an emergency clean-up). It was not that I alone chose to "separate"—our decisions were wholly democratic then. We'd flipped a coin, and I'd lost. In fact, Kendra was the one to pick up the scissors first and chop off my ponytail, so when we let the rubber band out, strands fell at psychedelic angles we thought looked "alternative" and befitting of the fashions that year, 1986. Still, even sheared we shared the same body, the same face, so that when we pulled our hair back to sleep, our parents confused us, lying together whispering at night in one bed.

The year we turned thirteen, we posed in front of our still-new home in Kenilworth, proud and lithe, hips jutting out like sassy Lolitas, legs wiry as the budding ballerinas we were. That year, we wore our hair in buns on purpose, so that we'd look *more* alike. We were in a new school, a new environment, and our twinship was novelty again—we had a whole new audience. We were back to tricks we'd given up in Cincinnati at age six.

At fourteen, Kendra looks almost the same, except her smile is gone and she is scowling at the camera. She was under threat of having to miss ballet class—the constant warning whenever she would not do what our parents wished—if she did not allow her picture to be taken. Her face is thinner, on the tenuous brink of becoming a woman's face, full of angles and shadows. Her eyes are directed, just slightly, towards me. But next to her, she could not have seen the mirror to which she was accustomed. In the photo, I have gained twenty pounds. My hair is limp and nearly plastered to my head in a way that, even at this distance now, calls to mind habits unhygienic. My face is blotchy with spots, Kendra a pale ghost next to my redness.

Alone on Aris's sofa, I scanned that face for the zillionth time, hoping for some connection. My fourteen-year-old eyes, however, averted from the camera and cameraman, our father, remained out of reach. The next several photos—fifteen through seventeen—showed more of the same: me, fat and startled, Kendra's increasingly striking cheekbones and haughty jaw line, marred by sarcasm. Then, for our eighteenth birthday, nothing. That year Kendra would not pose. She was headed for New York—they had nothing to bargain with anymore.

We resumed the tradition ourselves on our nineteenth birthday. The absent year must have marked some kind of transition, for on the edge of nineteen we were twin-like again, despite Kendra's professional dancer frame and my own, typical-college-freshman body. We both wore our hair long and straight, and though she was striking, the world by then her stage, in some ways I was the prettier, the more all-American of us. I was rounded in a nice way finally, a way that pleased men, that was more approachable than my sister's bony, graceful armor. Though guys still flocked to Kendra, at Northwestern I began for the first time to be noticed too, away from the comparative lens that had followed me all my life. Away from our parents. We took the photo on my first visit to New York so that we would never celebrate a birthday apart. Otto took it, actually, since he also could not bear to be away from Kendra on her birthday. But in the photo, I momentarily do not hate him. I am smiling again—we both are—free.

Kendra was the one who made copies of all the photos in our parents' twin-book, stuck them in our own album and entrusted them to me. Though she didn't know it, I always sent my mother copies of the pictures we took from age nineteen on, so she could continue their collection with or without my sister's blessing. By then, we knew Kendra could be bizarrely private and subject to inexplicable bursts of anger. We did our best, all of us, to placate her without completely surrendering our own treasured ground.

I jolted awake at 7:15 when Aris slammed the door to leave for work. I was still on the sofa, coverless and shivering from the air conditioning, head pounding with images from a dream about my father's death—a dream I was pretty sure I'd had several times before. I immediately grabbed the phone and called Kendra.

She sounded scary. Her voice was gravelly like she had laryngitis, but instead of slurring words with sleep, her speech came too fast the way it did when she was high. I hoped she had not yet been to bed, that she hadn't taken to doing whatever she was doing first thing upon rising. Manipulative with exhaustion, and stressed over the promise I'd made my mother that I would somehow get Kendra into their house, I said, "I think we should take our birthday photo with Dad this year. It may be the last birthday of ours he sees, and it'd mean a lot to him."

My sister, ever contrary, vetoed me quick. "I have no time for a big family production—it's summer recital rehearsals. Chaos. I'll be lucky to even squeeze in a quick breakfast with you. Over the next few weeks I might as well set up a bed at the Dance Center."

"Oh, I doubt Michael Kelsey would allow that. I'm sure *he* ranks high enough to fit in your busy schedule. He's probably buck naked next to you right now."

"He just left as a matter of fact. He picks Rachel up at nine and wanted some sleep."

"I thought you said he never sleeps."

"You must be the most literal person on earth. I meant he doesn't sleep much—if he never slept at all, wouldn't he be dead?"

"How should I know? When a forty-two-year-old man is able to keep up with a twenty-three-year-old woman, who can say what other superhuman feats he may be capable of?"

To my surprise, she did not respond with her usual annoying giggle whenever Michael Kelsey's alleged sexual prowess was broached, but rather said darkly, "Mmm. Who indeed."

"How's tomorrow?" I blurted, afraid she might reveal something I'd have to object to.

"I don't know," she hedged. "I need to crash. I can't when Michael's here, I might talk in my sleep . . . or whimper or something. You know I have nightmares around our birthday."

"You have nightmares all year round, Kendra. We both do."

"These are worse."

"Not worse than mine?"

"No." Resignation—almost defeat? "Nothing could be worse than yours."

"Hey," I said, "are you okay?"

"I just keep dreaming, like . . . everything there is to dream now."

"That Dad is dead," I finished.

"He was dead," she agreed. "And you all went to the funeral without me."

My heart flipped into my esophagus, beat there like a frog. "There was a man."

"The man was Michael."

"Uh-uh, in *my* dream, it was just a man. He took me to the house."

"Yeah, I know what he did."

I wanted to slam down the phone. "No. No you don't."

We were silent. Not digesting, not really. We were embarrassed. Our fears, our fantasies, our pains were not our own—there was something humiliating about that.

I said, "You'll come tomorrow, right? I'll pick you up. You have to, I won't see you today. I'll only see you tomorrow. I'll only take a picture at all if we can take it with Dad—"

"So do you ever watch Aris sleep?" she interrupted, urgent. "Do you ever just sit there and watch him sleep?"

"Huh? Sometimes. I mean, not really. I don't know. Why?"

"Because if you loved him like that, I needed to know. If you did, I'd be sorry I've been such a bitch to him. If you did, I'd be happy for you. But you don't."

"For God's sake!" I snapped. "Just because we had the same dream, don't act like you can read my mind. I shouldn't have to watch Aris sleep so you won't be mean to my fiancé. You should be nice as a matter of course, out of respect and love for me. I don't have to prove anything to you about my feelings—I'm marrying him, aren't I? Isn't that enough proof for—"

"You don't have to marry him just because he wants to, you know."

"I know that! Do you think I'm an idiot? Why are you preaching like this—like your sneaking around to screw Dad's best friend behind his back while he's sick is any better?"

"Guess what, Kirby. It's not a competition. No matter what a sham my love life may be, it won't make yours great. As long as you keep thinking my problems can cure yours, you'll still be trapped. I should know."

"I'm not—" I stopped, forced my voice lower, commanded my lungs to fill. "Trapped. I'm not. Really, K. I'm sorry—I know you don't like Aris, I know you want it to be . . . that this isn't what you hoped would happen. But I'm fine. Focus on yourself, how you can be there for Dad even though you feel guilty about what's going on with Michael, how you can stop your own choices from getting in the way of your own life. Honestly, don't worry about me."

"You'll be shitting today," she said. "You watch. I brought the taboos up—I said the things that are true and you can't face it. You don't know truth but your body does. You'll spend your own birthday on the toilet because you refuse to listen."

"You are not an oracle, get over yourself," I said solidly, as solid as she. The past weeks had been good ones bowel-wise, and I was invincible. "I'll see you tomorrow, okay? It'll be our first year posing with different hair colors. Dad in between."

"You're wasting your breath—you're wasting everything. Happy birthday, little sister. Guess it's still up to me."

White or Rye?

AT MY APPOINTMENT with you on Monday, my body obeyed her. The wires of my brain bent my will to her prediction: my bowels spasmed and churned, not on our birthday exactly, but the very next day, when it mattered more. Desperate in your waiting room, I grabbed the key to a restroom mercifully down the hall, grateful I would not have to expose even this to your scrutiny. Kendra had caused this, cursed me. I wept on your wood-lidded toilet, wondering how I always managed to *forget* the pain the moment it subsided. Did my tears wash away not only my dignity, but my memory, thereby enabling me to go on believing humans were more than animal and waste? I cried hard. Shoes appeared under the stall two down, pumps of expensive, probably-Italian leather, too grown-up still for me to identify with—I told myself it didn't matter what those feet, that brain, that woman thought of me, being only a pair of businesslike shoes. Only another body with the same capacity to be broken, only a woman, so who cared? But when the voice spoke, naturally it was you: "Are you all right? Do you need your medication?" I bawled, "No!" Amended, "Only could you please leave?" You did so, silent as good manners. The pain expanded, another body inside that would gladly split me in two, turn me inside out to escape the fermented smell of my inner skin. When it rode out of me in waves of agony and panting, it struck me at last: this perverted birth I gave daily had never been mine, but my sister's prophesy for me. Sick, weak, an embodiment of whatever idiotic "denial" she believed plagued me, I had *become* the pitiful simulacra of myself that existed in my sister's mind.

Minutes later you sat, notebook on lap, eyes on the clock. I had wasted half the hour, and we always ended five minutes early, but you did not reference this. You never attempted to render my defecating body common property. You respected my privacy in this small sense and behaved, despite our encounter in the bathroom, as though I were late for some other, unspecified reason. Perhaps I might have been stuck in traffic. I usually loved you for this, but today I needed you to understand that it was my sister's magic you'd been hired to tamper with, to disarm. That *she* was holding me back, had trapped me in this shit-and-tear-filled, cramped veal-box of a body with some twinly voodoo. Of course to articulate this would have seemed mad. For the past twenty-four hours, I'd planned to tell you of the unsettling dream-telepathy between myself and Kendra, but found now that I could not bring myself to even mention her name. I was afraid to voice her power. Instead, I offered you the dream I'd had just the night before my appointment—equally disquieting and even more bizarre.

"I've been having more nightmares. Sometimes my dreams are so perverse I think I must be seriously disturbed."

"Or maybe they only indicate that you're sad," you countered. "And imaginative."

"What if I really am crazy, though?" I asked. "And you're so busy not wanting me to feel bad about myself and playing cheerleader for me that you've forgotten to be a blank slate so I can find things out for myself—how screwed up I may be? What if feeling better about myself is that last thing I need and I end up in an institution because you're placating me?"

You looked at me with naked confusion. "What would give you an idea like that? You're a highly functional young woman—Irritable Bowel Syndrome has never led to anyone's institutionalization, I assure you. For what, the inability to sit at a desk for hours without going to the bathroom? I know your condition is scary, believe me, but neither it nor vivid dreams add up to the chemical imbalances that equal so-called 'insanity.'" You smiled gently. "And if I'm supposed to be a blank slate, I apologize, but I certainly don't feel like one. Especially not with your family. You pain me deeply, if you want to know the truth."

"I'm not sure I do."

"All right. That's fair."

"So in the dream, I'm being massacred." Abrupt, all business. "I've done something wrong—let's say stolen someone's property, or let's say I'm a witch. The whole town is meant to massacre me. They're chasing me. This is a medieval kind of scene, I should specify. I'm in a freaky empire-waisted dress with my breasts pumped out, I have on one of those pilgrim chick hats. I'm mixing my time periods, I know—my subconscious isn't very well versed in history. Anyway, they catch me. The town is walled, so there's no place I can go beyond a certain point. They back me up to the wall and somebody brings the stocks. Once I'm in them, bent over and stuck, they lift my dress, and I think they're going to flog me. I'm scared 'cause I'm really afraid of pain. But instead someone I can't see takes out a knife and starts to carve my butt, slice it like a piece of meat. I can't remember if it hurt. After, my mother is brought forward. She doesn't seem particularly upset. They give her a chair—it's all very civilized—and a glass of milk. They turn my stocks to face her so I can watch her eat my butt, sliced up into a ham sandwich."

"Wow."

My skin jumped. "Oh, great—you just said I wasn't nuts, but now my dream totally weirded you out. That's comforting."

But already you were dusting yourself off, charging again at some bull I couldn't see. Chuckling, "I'm sorry, Kirby—that response was directed at myself, not your dream. It suddenly hit me that we've spent so much time discussing your father and Aris that I've allowed your mother to be lost in the shuffle. Your dream just made me wonder what emotions you associate with your mother that might come to play in your subconscious. Say, guilt?"

I shrugged. "Why *guilt*? Doesn't it seem more like I must be really pissed off at my mother if I'm dreaming that she's punished by being forced to become a cannibal?"

"That's interesting. Can you tell me more about her being forced? Because the way you described it, it sounded almost as though she was the accusing party and was allowed to get revenge—"

"By consuming my flesh?" My teeth knocked together. "You mean the way the families of victims are permitted to witness executions." I shivered. Something was the matter with me.

147

"Well, I'm not saying that's what the dream is actually about . . ."

"No." I felt myself nodding. "Maybe you're right—maybe I should feel guilty where my mom is concerned. She has so much on her plate, but I'm always whining to her, being sick and insecure so she'll take care of me. I've never been able to let go—Kendra says that all the time."

"That's what your sister thinks of your relationship with your mother. Has your mother herself ever indicated that she finds you a burden?"

"Oh, she'd never say anything, she's too polite." I paused. "You know, I think being in here is good for me. Kendra can be kind of harsh, the way she puts things, but maybe she's just saying the same things you're trying to tell me, only I won't listen. I'm just—" my voice wavered and I hated the sound of it, let loose a bitter chuckle—"listen to me losing it, that's exactly what I do with my mom too. I'm so selfish it's sickening. My poor father is going to die, and my mother's going to be a widow, and do you know that when I go to their house, I'm always all nervous, like I'm going to touch the counter and contract AIDS or something. My family always thought of me as the weaker but nicer twin, but really, I'm not nice at all. My dad's secretly ashamed of me, and if my mother realized the truth, she would be too."

"Kirby." You leaned forward, hand grasping my wrist, fingers bonier than seemed appropriate. A lactating mother of wire mesh rather than one whose snuggly fabric I could cling to as I happily starved. "What brought this on? I promise, in no way was I implying that your mother wants to punish you in real life, or that you have any genuine cause to feel guilty. I don't believe those things, so giving you the impression that I do was the furthest from my intention."

I didn't answer. Didn't extract my wrist. Felt like a fool.

"Are you all right?"

"I just . . . I haven't felt very well today. I'd been better, I even thought . . . but now . . ."

Withdrawal. The air where your fingers had been was softer than your touch, but less vital. "I understand. Do you feel like you can go on, or would you like to switch gears?"

"I'd like to talk more about my mom if you think it's important. Really."

"Okay." You settled back. "Then why don't we step back and look at the feelings it brought up, my suggesting that you might feel guilty in your relationship with her? What happened between us just now—your sudden anger at yourself—feels important."

"I just got scared." But my mind was foggy now; I couldn't feel anything. "I mean, God, my poor mother! My father's cheated on her, and Kendra has no respect for her, but she has to deny any feelings of hurt or betrayal in order to hold our family together. I think about that a lot, and what you said made me feel like I'm just one of them, like I haven't been a good daughter to her—I've drawn lots with them instead. But I'd never do anything intentionally to hurt her. We're really close, even though sometimes she doesn't . . . I don't know . . . respect me."

"Do you respect her?"

"All I've ever tried to do is emulate her."

"Except when trying to emulate your twin, which meant the exact opposite behavior?"

"Maybe . . . I guess. My mother hides everything—if feelings leak out, they're passive-aggressive. Kendra's pure aggression, yeah. But she hides stuff too, her anger just deflects it."

Your feet on the floor rose to tiptoes, as though you wanted to pounce. "And at the center of all things hidden, there's Dad, right? If your mother has been a martyr to him, then your sister seems to be the one who rejects him *for* her, who's symbolically unfaithful through distance and her secret affair with his friend. Hmm. You mentioned thinking your dream indicated anger toward Mom. Do you ever resent her for lacking your sister's power?"

Your epiphany, though, had left me behind. "No. I don't hate my mother for not being narcissistic like Kendra—you asked if I respect her, and I do. I wish I could be *more* like her. I'd have fewer problems with Aris if I knew how to, I don't know, empty myself out for the sake of something larger, for a relationship to work." Your eyebrow rose. I crossed and uncrossed my legs. You watched like I was Sharon Stone in *Basic Instinct* and you were Otto—our one and only movie date. Frustrated, I stood, pretended to smooth my skirt. Flopped down again.

"Do you want to know the truth?" I sighed. "This feels like talking to Kendra right now. Like you're withholding information and then trying to lead me to it like a horse. Did it ever occur to you that the secrets you're keeping confidential for my father might cure me? Do you think it's healthy for me that you know more about my family than I do—how I should feel and what should drive me? Why can't you just tell me the truth?"

You nodded; instantly my heart bolted with the kind of fear I'd felt yesterday in the fleeting moment I'd believed Kendra might be about to reveal some hideous intimacy between herself and Mr. Kelsey. I should have known better. You said, "A few moments ago you indicated that I was telling you truths you didn't want to hear, just like your sister, and now you're saying I'm like her again, but this time for withholding truths and manipulating you with them. Yes, I've seen your father professionally, but it strikes me as extreme that you'd think this would provide me the information to 'cure' you, or that you'd believe I'm intentionally denying you this cure. Is that really something you'd like to say to Kendra?"

"Kendra is one gatekeeper, sure." The timer on your watch went off. "But that doesn't mean you're not hiding things too."

"If you had your way," you began, almost conspiratorily, "how much would you want me to tell you? What back-story do you need for the cure? How much information is healthy?"

I stood again to leave for real, motion obscuring my notion of danger. "Everything."

Summer of Wisteria

THE SHOP GIRL STOOD coated with a translucent layer of Aveda-scented sweat, watching Mrs. Kelsey pin me. Her eyes felt hot, as if she realized I had (several times) seen her around Bucktown, with her friends at cafes or strolling down Damen in her beautiful skin, and been too intimidated to say hello. It was not lost on me that I approached all relationships with women on a basis of intimidation and envy—and only constant exposure could lull me into relating *to* them at all. I was not sure on what basis I approached relationships with men. Aside from Aris and my father, I did not really have any. Hadn't since Otto, which hardly counted since our affair (if one could call it that) had consisted almost entirely of my watching his too-loud band slam around in a garage, then giving him clumsy, ineffectual head and being weirdly silent afterward. When I first told you about Otto, you said it was no wonder I had difficulty trusting men given that my first boyfriend dumped me to develop a seven-years-and-running obsession with my twin. But I, always the pathological liar, did not admit what a drag I'd acted like during the actual dating part, how I kept eating and eating until I'd gained fifteen pounds by the end of our third month together; no, nor my frequent tears and crazy, desperate letters to my paramour, obsessing that he'd find another girl, one who followed the band and possessed a tiny waist or bigger boobs, until finally he had to dump me because I was a psycho, I was *Fatal Attraction*, I was the kind of girl who might just up and off myself one day and no normal guy would want to be there when I did. I didn't tell that part. No, but by now I was afraid you knew me well enough to guess.

Mrs. Kelsey rarely exuded sweat. I'd noticed this a long time ago, while babysitting. She would go for a run and return a bit windblown but dry, firey wisps still crisp around a hairline of deep, hot auburn. Now, in the sweltering shop, she smelled of wisteria—not perfume but sachets, which she had been setting out in display drawers. Periodically she wiped her long-fingered hands on her ruby-red sheath dress, as if to eliminate moisture that did not exist.

Those long fingers were on me. Tucking, pulling, pinning. When she pricked me with a pin, I smiled. You know I did nothing, asked nothing. Her fingers were careful and careless at the same time. They adored my form under the dress because they adored the dress, her re-creation. I ached for her never to finish, and when she told me to get changed—we were finally done, I would be a perfect Victorian bride—I gulped in breath so deep I thought the pins would pop right down my back. But she left one hand on my waist where she had been holding me, kept it there longer than anyone could deem necessary, her touch soft with sadness and something I dared to think the residue of love. I blurted, "I need to—just five minutes . . ."

She said, "I have some coffee on in back. Come on."

It was not the season for hot coffee indoors. Not, certainly, in an overheated shop (which I was certain possessed air conditioning that this woman opted, for reasons of atmosphere, not to turn on). Yet I nodded. Followed the sound of her dress swishing around her legs, Elise's eyes trailing me, guarded but far from disinterested, as Mrs. Kelsey closed the door to the back room.

"I've wanted to speak with you too," she said not at all convincingly, with an awkward gesture for me to sit. That she could be shy of me was beyond my fantasies—but was this shyness or simple dread? "I think of you a lot. Of how you might be . . . coping with all this."

I surveyed the nervous aversion of her eyes, that fluttery swan-neck that seemed to arch and rise and sink to whatever position best approximated safety. All wrong for her words: she seemed less empathic than ashamed. The connection Kendra and Aris had been pushing clicked in against my will— she could have it too. I said, testing, "He's in bad shape. It's terrible to watch, especially now with the wedding and all. But that's nothing you have to worry about."

The hurt on her face was too instant to conceal. "I apologize. I didn't mean to intrude. I thought that was what you wanted to talk—my mother had cancer too, you know. She lost a breast. In fact, Rachel's paternal grandmother died of a brain tumor, oh, ages ago, Michael was younger than you. The disease is isolating, but other people do know how you feel."

I stared, unable to imagine in a million years what I was meant to say now. Though I had heard of this cancer fable from my mother, it had never occurred to me that I might be called upon to perpetuate the lie. My hands wrapped around the hot cup of coffee, china so delicate I feared the heat would crack it in two. I finally managed, "Isolating. Yes. Nobody is honest. We all pretend everything's fine one minute, then panic and push the wedding up two months the next, then make plans for remodeling the house next year. It's insane. It's . . . unbearable."

"Waiting is the hardest part," she offered, an expert. "I tend to think it'd be easier if we could just accept and let go. The living have such fear, the dying must find it offensive."

My brows crinkled in tight enough to hurt. Why she would say such a thing to me was clearly inconceivable from any angle. I stammered, "At least waiting offers hope."

Mrs. Kelsey smiled mildly. "I haven't been able to bring myself to go see him. Your mother and I met for lunch, and we've spoken on the phone. It's her I feel most badly for. This is just what men do, Kirby, it's cruel but true. They always manage to leave us taking care of them. I should thank God Michael left before it could happen to me again. I couldn't do it a second time. It reminds me too much of my own father. I wouldn't wish that on anyone."

Leigh Kelsey was the daughter of a Holocaust survivor. In light of this, her bizarre proclamations a moment prior suddenly carried weight and meaning. Her father, a Polish Jew, had seen his brother, her uncle, die right in front of him. Other members of the family perished too. When the camps were liberated, her father went placidly to live with cousins in Brooklyn. There he had three suicide attempts in ten years and was finally institutionalized for the better part of Mrs. Kelsey's youth. Her mother, a French Catholic (American born), never obtained a divorce, though she lived with a string of other men from the time her daughter was quite young. I remembered these stories. Mrs. Kelsey's voice had always been clear, words perfectly enunciated, as she told them. She had always smelled like rose water, in her fresh and lemony kitchen that never contained any food. Her active preschooler and milk-smelling infant seemed rosy and (foolishly, in retrospect) charmed. Now, surrounded by the clothes and smells of the dead, her history bore new credibility. I wondered whether she were right, if once my father died, my body would feel lighter. Whether then Kendra and I could stop insulting each other in hopes of deflecting our real pain. Whether then I could love Aris again, or think I did.

Mrs. Kelsey settled back in a white wicker chair. The sun through the window hit her like a spotlight, made me squint. "Yes," she said decisively, and I suspected her mind had turned to Isabelle, yet she focused on her father to evade that pain. "Faster is always preferable. Sudden, unexpected tragedy is impersonal, neither the dying nor the survivor is tested as much."

I said, "I'm in therapy. I don't know if my mother told you."

She laughed, so unexpected that I too tittered foolishly. "Did you think I was trying to play your therapist, or were you thinking I need a good shrink?"

"I . . . don't know. I've wanted to have this conversation, but now that it's happening I don't know why we're having it—I mean, why you would think it makes sense to have it. Why would my father's illness—or my emotional response to it—mean anything to you?"

She folded her arms across her chest, a warrior drawing a line. "Come on, Kirby. We're both adults. I don't make a practice of telling people things they already know."

My thoughts were balls of bile. In an instant, I hated her, sun goddess shooting off red flames from dress, lips, hair. Husband-stealing bitch. "Oh, so you're like my parents. You throw around clues, but as soon as a question arises, you pretend I'm the one playing games so you won't have to own up to anything. What a big joke."

"Yes," she agreed, standing to signal my time to leave. "But it's a joke to which I, in particular, am entitled, and may even call myself the punch line." A paradoxical smile. "All I really

154

wanted to say is that you've always meant something, been a friend . . . another daughter to me. Please remember that, after everything."

"After *what*?"

She swung back the door briskly; I saw Elise's eyes dart up, then down quickly, feigning ease. Remembered myself at fifteen, watching Mrs. Kelsey peel off her wet swimsuit after one of our beach days with Rachel. The knowledge that I shouldn't look had made it so her water-puckered nipples, the swell of the damp underside of her breasts brushing her ribcage, were momentarily all that existed in the world. Her curling hairs at the intersection of inner thigh and hipbone were shaved to a thin line so identically the shade of the luxurious mane on her head, I knew then the color was not natural. This effort fascinated me, made me marvel at the precision of sex, its rigor. My jealousy—of Mr. Kelsey?—surged hot as fever. The possibility that a lover would someday enact such rituals to ensure my desire made me feel faint.

"I'll see you at the wedding," Mrs. Kelsey said, moving to let me pass. "You're going to be a lovely bride, Kirby, more so than even I could have predicted. Your mother will be so proud."

Beneath my grannyish sundress and turquoise cotton underpants, my pubic hair lay untrimmed: pale, dishwater brown. And I knew as I exited the wisteria haven of the shop (though no doubt you will say I must have known all along) that my engagement to Aris was merely a compromise, the sort adults have to make, the sort one hopes will pay off in the end. For years, I'd blithely assumed I lacked the intensity for anything *more*. But once, long ago, I had dared hope. And I swear to you: in that moment, with a stabbing not unlike my usual sickness, something like hope began to roil anew.

Last Exit to Kenilworth

UNBELIEVABLY, KENDRA was already waiting outside when I pulled up in front of her sterile Gold Coast brownstone. Disheveled on a windy corner, in ultra-dark, pedal-pusher jeans with wide cuffs (we were both too small for anything to ever be the right length), she did not look at all the femme fatale Aris was continually painting her to be. A man's suit-shirt that must've belonged to Michael Kelsey (Otto surely didn't own one) was tied at her stomach revealing the tender knot of her belly button, pale for this time of year. Years as a dancer had taught Kendra to value the translucence of her skin; I had never known her to lie in the sun. As if to confirm this delicacy, she got into my car complaining of the cold. It couldn't have been less than seventy-five degrees. I was sweating, sun beating down on the windshield as I drove.

We were heading to our parents' house, remarkably only three days after our birthday, to have our photo taken with our father. Two snapshots, actually—Kendra insisted on one of us alone, for our collection, and our mother could keep the one with Dad in hers. Nonetheless, I was proud of having won, of having got her here. Watching out of the corner of my eye, I did not linger on my sister's bones. I pretended we were the *us* of a long time ago. NPR news spoke of other, greater problems, peacekeeping efforts in Kosovo; my life felt giddily small in comparison. Here we were, two girls cruising up Lake Shore Drive in up-to-the-moment capri pants, hair whipping in the wind, anonymous to history. I wondered if our imperviousness would wane when the creator of our history — our father — slipped away. My hand reached out to change the station, to find some retro hour and a song from our grade school days. In the picture in my mind, my sister and I were singing, voices hard and resolute against the wind.

Kendra's fingers, blue-tinged nails visible beneath the unbuttoned and too-long cuffs of the shirt, stopped my hand. "Keep it," she commanded, voice monotone. "I'm tired of music and all its lies. Nothing works out the way it does in ballet. Loss has no romance, death is permanent, and innocent people get stuck in the crossfire when villains get what they deserve."

I was unmoved by her crankiness at being dragged to Kenilworth. "So? That's the choreographers' and politicians' problem. You always said music was the only truth."

She snorted, but didn't stop looking out the window, clearly bored to death by her own melodramatic proclamations and completely unwilling to engage in debate over them. My vision of us, young and alive and carefree on the Drive, melted like a stupid puddle on the road.

"Do you ever think that maybe Dad got what he deserved?"

It was, if anything, a long overdue question, one I'd been anticipating. I had prepared my answer a hundred times.

"I think AIDS as a retribution for infidelity is illogical. I mean, the religious Right believes it's a punishment for homosexuality, and you're the first to disagree with that kind of holier-than-thou causality. Disease is random. Thousands of men cheat. Dad never abandoned us — look, you're involved with a man who cheated on his wife *and* dumped her. If this were justice, there'd be diseases for Milosevic and Pinochet, not straying, middle-aged men."

She listened, expression hidden behind leopard-print sunglasses. When I was finished she said mildly, "Does the fact that he's sick *erase* his destructive acts then? I mean, if illness isn't a punishment for his behavior, if that paradigm's faulty, then why is it an excuse?"

"I think you should leave excuses to Mom." But I was shaken; since when did my sister refer to 'faulty paradigms' and believe in retribution for extramarital sex? Though her rhetoric might have been the by-product of bedding a Marxist and an attorney, the vehemence of her anger at our father's infidelities was beyond my ken. "If Mom can get past it, we should too."

"Yeah, well, I'm not asking Mom. I'm asking you. Where you really stand." She turned off the radio, one quick flick of her bony wrist, and stared. Even in therapy, my opinion was not awaited with such fervor. Certainly this was a first in *real* life. I did not know what to do.

I parked outside our parents' house. The car was musty; I was having trouble breathing; I desperately needed a bathroom. Kendra did not seem inclined to budge. Her body had gone stiff as rigor mortis. We sat in a stagnant silence I interpreted as hostile, each refusing to give in first to the other's will: mine to flee her combative philosophizing, hers to expose my denial, or at least force my body to reveal its weakness and inferiority to hers. Then, a sudden full-bodied jerk, the gesture louder than any word so that I too jumped, cried out when her arm reached to clutch mine, as if even though sitting she feared she'd fall. "K? What is it?"

"I can't go in there." She was moving now, almost compulsively, squirming in the bucket seat. "No way. Why did you tell them we'd come?"

"Kendra, I had to." Slowly, to a child at the doctor's. "You haven't seen them in ages."

"But I can't. My heart is beating too fast. I think I need to eat something."

"Well that's a good reason to go inside. Mom's making us a belated-birthday lunch."

"Ha fucking ha," as though I intended wit. A finger to her pulse, lips moving in a silent count. "I don't feel right. I think I'm going to faint."

The image was absurd—Kendra swooning in my Toyota like a damsel in a corset. I had seen my sister dance her first solo at the Met on an ankle so swollen she'd had to borrow a bigger pointe shoe. Smiling all the way. My hand groped for her forehead to humor her. Clammy ice. Her pulse fluttered in her temples, manic beating of wings on a cage. I recoiled.

"Maybe you should go to a doctor."

"I don't think I can move. The car is spinning, I have to lie down."

My own heart jerked: start—stop. "Mom and I can take you to the emergency room."

"Don't leave!" She rolled her window down with great effort, leaned her head against the door, arms curling around her body fetus-like. "You take me. Just you."

"Kendra." Patiently, over her long, shuddery gulps. "What about seeing *Dad*?"

She grabbed my arm again: points of nails, balls of bone. Between clenched teeth: "I don't give a shit about Dad." Her rage was palpable; I could touch it, feel it under my skin, as out of control and speeding as her thudding heart. And for the first time I understood: this was not just an act to keep up her image as the imperious, prodigal daughter—*she means it, she is telling the truth.* I was afraid she would pass out then, that the energy of such hatred might be enough to destroy a body so slight. I gunned the motor, peeled out into the street. I didn't care about them either, their disappointment, waiting, or surprise. Didn't care about him, thinner and half-stoned on medication, wondering where we were. I would take her to the airport if she told me to, would take her to die alone in my arms on Mars.

Her breathing no more even once we'd left the block, her voice that of a child I recognized: "I'm pregnant." Then, my doubt a given, heartbreaking, "It's Michael's baby."

"Oh, God." Hand to hand across the gulf of bucket seats meant to maximize personal space. I clung too tight, her knuckles bore into mine so they grated like my engagement ring did sometimes, smashed into my flesh when Aris's meaty hand held mine, and I usually whined for him to stop. I knew I was hurting her too. But we both just held on, neither telling the other to let go.

To Bleed or Not to Bleed

Entering Evanston Hospital's emergency room, Kendra and I provoked stares. Even with my mutated dye job and her losing weight so fast no mere irritable bowel could make me catch up, we remained conspicuously identical. Just pretty enough so that when doubled, we could be mistaken for stunning. Yet it was also true that each flaw, benign on a single woman, could appear almost freakish by virtue of its adjacent replica: eyes too big, mouths too wide, cheeks and jawbones jutting—doubled, I often felt more alien than feminine, and it went without saying that Kendra, with all her efforts to live as far from my face as possible, agreed. Now, though, she leaned against my sturdier frame willingly; I felt guilty staggering a bit under her slight weight. We paused at an unoccupied desk. A mimesis of my body, she too squinted under the fluorescent lights and fumbled in an also-black clutch purse before simultaneously snapping her own sunglasses into a (less expensive than my) case. I imagined us in aerial view, a detached observation camera: who was supporting whom? We were both in trouble; that much the world could see. Everybody loves a beautiful woman in trouble. Everybody loves beautiful sisters sharing a secret. What bystander would guess that our secrets were mutually guarded from the other? The extent to which we were each other's trouble? Nurses and doctors blurred by in streaks of pale blue. But people were always willing to help us when we were together: to give directions, take extra time. If I were to leave, would her splendor fragment, devolving her into an ordinary woman alone? Or was she singularly responsible for our shared phenomenon—did it follow her when I was not around, so only I was rendered ordinary in her absence?

Behind a curtain sectioning off an examining cubicle, Kendra wrapped a hospital gown around twice like a sarong. She knelt Japanese-style on the examining table, complaining that her tailbone grated against the metal if she sat normally. I fingered the flimsy padding over the table, imagined her atop twenty mattresses, disturbed by the lump of a small vegetable.

She said randomly, "Ha ha. I'm like the Princess and the Pea. Funny, since my life is more like the Whore and the Big Ass Sharp Sword."

I wasn't entirely sure what she meant, but I knew when I got into my self-deprecating trips, I didn't always make sense. I usually thought Kendra immune to the kind of self-loathing that plagued me, but given her moment of telepathy, any likeness between us seemed feasible.

"I don't know if I can take this after all." She waved her skinny arm in my general direction, her braless nipple visible through the gigantic armhole of her gown. "You sitting there all faithfully with placid concern on your face. Bee's Beatitude." I saw her swallow hard.

"*You* made me come." But it pleased me slightly, that she saw me as invulnerable in contrast to herself, that this insecurity made her want to lash out. Or was she just trying to get rid of me so she could call someone else? "So, um, does Michael Kelsey know about this?"

"Why, were you hoping for a double wedding?" She giggled, drew her arms inside her sleeves, embracing her bare torso underneath the gown so that it resembled a straitjacket. "What a made-for-TV movie—you could go back to blond so we could change places and trick our husbands-to-be . . . well, as long as we didn't let the camera inside Michael's bedroom, 'cause you know, this kind of movie would never let a nice girl like you end up *there*. Who knows, maybe Dad would even be relieved there was finally a real man around to keep his rebel daughter in line. He'd walk between us down the aisle—we could hold him up if he felt weak. A real tear-jerker."

"You're being totally obnoxious," I said, "and I know it's just because you're scared."

"Whatever. Michael knows."

I waited, but she did not say more. It seemed evident that he'd doubt the baby was his—I wondered whether he had even offered her a dime. Did he have no fear of her going to our father? Did he have no shame? I imagined her telling him, all her little girl fantasies doing battle with her cynical side—perhaps the double wedding was a hope she'd secretly nurtured. What girl didn't dream, however covertly, of being a lovely bride, all her ugly history erased by ceremony? "It doesn't matter," I swore. "You don't need him—any of them. I'm here."

"I know." She tweaked the end of my hair. "Thank you, really." Then, instant wide-eyed alarm: "Wait. You don't think I'm going to *have*—look . . ." Her eyes locked on mine, mirror to mirror. "Listen closely, Kirby. Only three of us in this world could fully realize why I can't have this baby. Please, please don't fuck with me."

I felt my eyebrows scrunching up. "What? I'm not—"

"Bee. You do understand why—"

The nurse came through the door.

Negative.

"I cannot believe," I said once outside in the chilly shade of hospital buildings, "that you never bothered to take a home pregnancy test." My arm was clasped around her shoulders almost violently: love grating on bones. "What were you thinking?"

She squirmed but I would not let go. "I went nearly ten weeks without a period; it seemed the only probable cause—"

"Yeah, well, now we have another one, don't we?" *Anorexics don't menstruate,* the nurse had explained, looking at me and not my sister. And me nodding: a solemn mother at the parent-teacher conference of a problem child. But what the hell was I supposed to do next?

"We should go have a drink to celebrate," Kendra burst suddenly, jerking away from my embrace. "We never had one on our birthday—hey, do you have your camera?"

"Don't you think we should call Mom?" I had never wanted so badly to see my mother—to turn this over to her somehow.

"I told you." She crushed someone else's grayish cigarette butt with the platform toe of her sandal. "I'm not going there."

"That was when we thought you were pregnant with Dad's partner's love child," I countered. "Now that we know you're just too skinny, we *should* go let Mom feed you a meal."

"I said I am not being chauffeured back to Kenilworth to eat some contrite, well-behaved lunch in that mortuary! Mom probably made her nasty chicken salad with mucusy mayonnaise and crusty booger walnuts—we'd just have another debate about poultry, only you guys would all stare at me like if I won't eat meat now it's because I've got a *disease* . . . no way."

"Kendra—"

"You were being so nice. I knew it couldn't last."

"The fact that I love you enough to care makes me *un*-nice?"

"No. But the fact that your love can't be unconditional—that it's always worried and testing—means I can't trust you."

"K—" Shrill protestation. "Of course you can. I'm thrilled you're not pregnant—I'm not siding with Mom and Dad. Don't shut me out. I felt your heart racing, and if you aren't pregnant, you must be sick. Anorexia can make the heart act funny, I've read about it, everybody knows—you could die. Ammenorrhea is a sign for us to take this seriously."

"Look." Hands shaking out a pristine, white cigarette. "I didn't bug you when you didn't bleed, so why can't you extend the same courtesy to me?"

"When *I* didn't . . . ? What are you talking—?"

"Forget it." She turned her back, stalked a few feet away, but then abruptly spun on her heels. When she reached me again, her eyes had gone softer; she took my arm. "Come on, Bee. You know the only dancers . . . *any* athletes who get periods are on the pill. I thought since I'm not taking class, and I was normal for awhile . . . but now I'm not—big deal. My cycle just isn't regular yet. It hasn't given up ballet, even if the rest of me had no choice. Please."

"You can't con me. Look at you—you're emaciated! I know something is wrong. I love you—I'm not going to let you hurt yourself."

"Okay," she said agreeably. "So we'll have more lunch dates and you can watch me eat every bite on my plate. You can even order for me. But please, go to Mom and Dad's today and just let me go home. It's been a long, scary few weeks. I need time to myself right now."

We waited together until I boarded the flimsy metal elevator to be sucked up toward the parking lot. But once I was up on the level where my Tercel was parked, I rushed impulsively toward the south wall of the lot and stared down over the concrete barrier about as high as my breastbone, my eyes scanning until I found my sister: a lone figure on Central Avenue, headed for the El that would take her back to the city. She stopped abruptly, facing north, unaware that I was watching her, to finally light her cigarette with difficulty, wind continually extinguishing her matches. She resembled nothing like the dazzling figure I'd watched so many nights, defying gravity under bright lights on a stage. Soon I would be with our parents, explaining, forever explaining, though already I knew I would not tell them the truth but some safety lie to protect her—and them. I stood, wind whipping my face, planning my story. Kendra disappeared, en route to her train. I wondered where it would have to be going to carry my lost sister home.

Fragment

Guilt always hurries towards its complement,
punishment: only there does its satisfaction
lie.

—Lawrence Durrell,
Justine

Every time her phone rang, Kendra was alarmed and repulsed by how much she let herself believe it would be him. Instead, Kirby again; Guitarist with another *mea culpa* for his lame-ass rapist trip; her mother with more martyr bullshit. Never before had she waited longer than the three days Michael spent with his daughter before hearing from him again. Now, five days and counting . . .

She could not feign shock. Those groceries in her kitchen had nothing to do with eroticism, nothing to do with sex. Though she and Michael had never discussed any rules governing their arrangement, had nothing resembling even the loosest of contracts, clearly their last evening together had been indisputably out of bounds. He'd crossed a line when she wasn't looking, had come to believe he was entitled to rights over her body more precious than anything she'd allowed him to take with his duct tape or his dick. His transgression violated her as surely as dancers felt violated when a choreographer assumed proprietary rights over their bodies not just in the studio but also in bed. The key, the watching her sleep, the force-feeding (or that he'd manipulated her so completely force was unnecessary) was unforgivable. Part of no deal.

That was not all. Michael had not signed on for a weak little girl to rescue—Kendra was supposed to be tough, impermeable to his penchants, resilient in her cocky youth. He wanted illicit, not a basket case he'd have to spoon-feed like a sick animal—like his dead baby. Not some waif naïve enough to get knocked up and coming undone without a riding crop in sight. But then neither had she sought a nurturer who cared if she ate, if she hurt, if she begged, *Don't go*, or added, *Please.* She knew he knew: she had fucked up too.

She hadn't set foot in her stocked kitchen since he'd left on her birthday morning. Now, five days later, her throat still ached like sandpaper from how far down she'd shoved her toothbrush the moment he closed the door. In the clarity of a five-day fast, she'd come to understand what her father had liked about the apartment he'd rented for a woman called Veronica who might or might not be dying. All the rooms had locks. She'd noticed during the night, her first without Michael, and even though it was customary to spend three nights apart, his absence felt like a gaping wound she alone was responsible for cleaning up and bandaging. She'd realized in the night, silence an invitation to memory. She had pushed through darkness, its weight tangibly heavy, to awaken, fog lifted, standing in the middle of the kitchen with legs apart and braced for a storm. Too much: the solitude, the hunger. Scraping at her organs until the red of her could leak right out onto the floor in lieu of her missing period, her missing baby—a testimony of what it was to be empty. She longed to cry, but tears required liquid, nourishment and salt. Numbness rode through her limbs in familiar waves; she held fast to the counter, whispered aloud, "It's okay it's all right I'm okay." Then simply, "Don't just don't." All the doors had locks. An apartment built for life in a world that could not be trusted, for people who knew they could not be trusted. She found the keys all in one drawer labeled with tape—another woman's writing. Her body worked fast, slammed the kitchen door hard enough for something in this city to break. Locked it, slid the key back under as if to reach a prisoner inside. Relief flooded her veins like a shot of tequila (she realized she'd stupidly forgotten to take the booze out of the pantry before locking herself out of the kitchen). She didn't puke that morning despite her frantic movements. No puking since Michael left—she'd told herself at first that the baby just wanted to be rid of him; then that it was not a baby, merely a dilemma. No, she had the money, so not even that. Never mind now: a bad joke.

Five days without the distraction of mealtimes and no sustenance beyond self-analysis (plus a sporadic nonfat latte) can change one's perspective. Walking out of the studio after her three thirty intermediate class, Kendra's step felt light. Relief throbbed in her chest in the urgent fashion of someone who has narrowly escaped being run over by a bus: hip grazed, sore and stunned, but determined to alter her course. Even the lack of a period seemed fortuitous now that no pregnancy was involved. Blood was dangerous. Besides, since Michael, she hadn't had a hell of a lot to spare. The condition of her bodily fluids was bound to improve further as soon as she gave Michael back his Jeep, which she'd been using for almost a month for her commute to and from the Dance Center. It'd been parked outside her apartment when they parted, and in order to get it back, he'd have to call—unlikely since female neediness was more inconvenient than owning only one car. No matter; she would drive the Jeep back to his apartment, let the doorman call him down to retrieve it. He knew her well enough to guess that if she'd rather take the El all the way to fucking Evanston, she wanted out too. The plan relaxed her, though the projection of never being touched by him again rendered her blood heavy like it wasn't flowing right through her arms. Her empty womb was a sign: Michael was still healthy, she could feel it. Whereas her own nausea, vomiting, lack of a monthly cycle despite nearly a year without dancing ... her body was breaking down, showing early symptoms of infection, a defective immune system. If they parted quickly, he'd have no idea how close she'd come to killing him.

Eyes burning from brightness before she even hit the Dance Center's door, Kendra rummaged for her shades without luck. Outside in the expanse of white sun in the parking lot, impeccable in a white summer suit, Kendra's mother stood, not leaning against her car. The Saab was parked right next to Michael's Jeep. The absurdity of such timing was overwhelming. Sunglasses shielded any expression in her mother's eyes. According to Bee, their mother did not sleep anymore; her hair was falling out in clumps despite B-12 shots. Kendra saw only that ten years of previously indiscernible age had settled onto her face these past six months like the aftershock of an earthquake, and though her mother, who'd been a pale and lovely child-bride, was the same age as these ballet moms flooding the parking lot in their Keds and SUVs, she looked like a haggard vision from their own painful futures come to warn them. Kendra stopped moving forward. Her mother too stayed motionless; a surplus of feet sprang up between them. Around their separate bodies, frenzy continued until vehicles pulled away and the parking lot was empty, left to them as if for a showdown in a ghost town.

"I knew something was the matter with you. I knew you had turned your back on your father for some reason I couldn't conceive. But I never in my wildest dreams suspected this."

The grief in her mother's tone made Kendra's heart thud against the cage of her chest. Too fast, thump thump, gratitude and hope. Maybe Kirby *had* said something. No, asinine—what would she have—oh God, could her mother have *guessed*? Thump.

At Kendra's silence, her mother gestured to the Jeep. "Do not play dumb with me, young lady. Your sunglasses are on the dashboard. Your father and I paid for those glasses, as we've apparently paid for everything in your life."

The tone was not sadness after all, but fury. Too late, Kendra's racing heart left no energy for fear. She held out hope: "Yeah, but you couldn't have known about Michael 'til you got here, right? So? Why did you come to find me?"

"Why!" Throwing hands into the air as if to say to an invisible audience, *Where shall I begin?* "You have some nerve. Not to show up to see your father for the first time in two months, then to leave me to handle his weeping. Does that please you, to know you made your father cry? Oh, and it wasn't the first time. But the buck stops here, miss. I've taken over the finances—your poor father's too sick and depressed to cover up your deceptions anymore. I know where you are, I know what he's done, and I want you out of that apartment today, now!"

Kendra blinked, her confusion surprisingly real. "Wait a minute. How does Dad's fuck apartment translate as *my* deception?"

A hand nearly as pale as her mother's suit, a hooded albino cobra, rose and struck her across the face. Kendra reeled—there was not much weight to keep her rooted—and stumbled into the Jeep. The slap did not hurt nearly so much that she was not moved by the irony of Michael's stupid car breaking her fall. She started to laugh. "That wasn't very Christian of you, Mom. I bet it felt good, though. I bet you liked it. I bet your fingers are itching to do it again."

But her mother was already choking up, the purity of her rage a moment before distilled. "What did I do wrong that you would be so hateful? How could you turn out like this, so vicious, when your sister is such a kind girl, would do anything for her family?"

"I don't know," Kendra admitted. "I must have taken after Dad."

"That's a lie! Your father has never been a cruel person! Whatever he's done, you can't believe he ever wanted to harm anyone, least of all you. Maybe you had a right to your anger once, I'll give you that—no man should raise a hand to his children, no matter what the Bible says *or* if he's drunk. But some tragedies supercede old grievances—no man is perfect either. For years you've been playing the victim, but your true colors show now."

Kendra's bag lay on the ground. She felt her cheek throbbing to a swell, the pain trying—failing—to register amid her incredulity. "You're talking about that night. You think that's why I'm so—here I've been telling myself that you, I don't know . . . *blocked it out*, while you've been using that night to explain everything you don't like about me for over five years, but never cared enough about me to breathe a damn—"

"I will not rehash this with you. I will not stand here and play a game of vilifying your father when it's taken every ounce of my strength just to hold my marriage together. Do you think I have the time to pity you because your father took a belt to you once in your entire youth? For God's sake, my husband has AIDS, you selfish brat!" Her mother's face shone red with strain and sun, clashed with her white suit. "You will be out of that apartment immediately," she proclaimed, a fierce angel doling out justice. "I am calling the landlord to give notice that I'm breaking lease. I'll be handling all family finances, and aside from the firm's health insurance, which you have until the end of the year, you are one hundred percent cut off. I'm on my way to the accountant's—understand me, there will be no allowance, no rent. If you aren't ashamed of exploiting a dying man whose presence clearly repulses you, then there's nothing anyone can do for you. And as for this . . ."—she gestured at the Jeep again, a hysterical sweep—"everybody knows *this* is merely what that man does. He is far worse than anything you think of your father, because your father would never have abandoned his family. Men like that have only one use for a woman your age. He thinks it's titillating, taking a sick friend's daughter to bed. But if you think he'll take care of you once your father's gone, you deserve what you'll get."

The keys to the Jeep were still in Kendra's hand. She had, she noticed, been clutching them so hard they'd dug into her palm, not hard enough to draw blood but enough to leave a jagged, pink-purple imprint. "That's all I want, Mom. What I . . . deserve."

Her mother climbed into the Saab with the cumbersome limbs of a woman twice her age. Between them, the open window framed her face—the same face Bee would see in the mirror someday: so righteous, so afraid. Desperate to flee, her mother turned the ignition.

"You've gone to the right source then," she said.

The house smelled of sick. Heavy, rotting like a nursing home: the smell of a body only on loan. Kendra's mother had been incorrect—it had actually been closer to three months since she last saw her father. He'd seemed okay then. A little thinner, sure, kind of tired from his meds, moderately depressed, but then his ill moods were nothing new. He certainly hadn't struck her as a man on the verge of death. But this smell. She approached the stairs slowly, having let herself in. Imagined (though she knew otherwise from Kirby) that he was cloistered in an upstairs room like Joan Crawford in *Whatever Happened to Baby Jane*, at the mercy of her mother who would bring him Bibles for breakfast and invite the minister to burn incense over his prostrate body. The thought gave her a sharp pain in her chest. She began to ascend the stairs.

"K. Well. What a surprise."

The man behind her was standing. He wore a white rugby (did her parents coordinate their wardrobes?) and a pair of too-large Bermuda shorts knotted tight with a worn, tan belt. Emerged from the kitchen carrying a can of something called Advera that looked like a Slim Fast, though Kendra immediately guessed its purpose was exactly the opposite. He noticed her staring at the can and held it up slightly, like he intended to propose a toast. "It tastes like shit," he said, as though responding to a question. "I have to doctor the hell out of it just to get it down. But today I'm too tired. That's the thing, they want you to eat a lot, but most of the time I'm too tired or too damned nauseous to do it. Nothing tastes right. Your mother marinates my meat in soy sauce like a geisha. Otherwise it's too bitter, and I'm supposed to load up on protein. Today I'm lucky. My throat is sore, so I'll get liquids mostly."

She said, smiling, "I don't think geishas' talents lie in the kitchen. Those are wives."

"That's your mother all right—a wife." A laugh. Then, "What happened to your face?"

"I don't know how much stock I'd put in those shakes." She descended the final few stairs. "You've lost a lot of weight."

"Just trying to keep up with my daughters. The family that wastes away together . . ."

Fast: "Kirby's not wasting away. She looks great."

He narrowed his eyes. "She looks like you used to before all this . . . this whatever it is you're doing now. She looks like

171

you in New York, and you looked sick even then. Now . . . well, I suppose since you don't care to visit me, you're just staying connected in another way."

Her nose smarted. Stung so she had to wrinkle it, pinch it to keep her eyes from watering. "Dad, look. I know Mom's at the accountant's . . . disowning me, as it were. I came because I knew you'd be alone, because we need to—I mean, if there's anything I should know, more about how . . . timing . . . you owe me that at least. Here's your chance."

He searched her face, his eyes a study in perplexity. "You sound awfully cryptic, sweetheart. There's no big secret—I'm not trying to keep anyone in the dark, I proved too temperamental. I'll be dead before the New Year most likely. Is that good news or bad?"

Kendra's throat constricted. She looked sideways for fear of seeing him anymore. "Are you just willing that to be true? Why isn't that three-drug therapy working for you? Why isn't *anything* working? Is it just that you don't want to be here to see the fallout?"

Henry leaned against a wall. Above his head hung a plate bearing one of Kirby's childhood drawings. They'd had plates made out of pictures both girls drew—Kendra's was in the kitchen. Kirby's drawing contained a larger-than-life puppy next to an extremely small, blond girl. A sun with a smiley face beat down on them. The miniscule girl held a leash restraining the giant dog. This warped, child's vision of the world seemed ominous now. Henry staggered to the sofa, sank down. Pills on the table. Kendra scanned the room: pill bottles on nearly every flat surface spare the floor. Chills inched down her back. She felt conscious of her body's lack of substance as she moved into the living room to sit across from her father. She stared down at her legs, fierce panic rising in her. Her thighs did not used to be this small.

"I need you to listen to me," her father said. "Please, K, princess, just listen. Please."

"I'm here, aren't I?"

His head was in his hands. He would not raise his eyes. "I want there to be some magic thing I can say to you. I've spent my life trying to find some woman to love me enough to make my own skin bearable, but all along that was you, and I blew it with my stupid searching—I betrayed my family. When you were a girl, you loved me like that."

"Children can't make much of a difference to anyone." Her voice was not unkind.

"No," he insisted, "They should be able to. You should have been able to. It should have been enough. The drinking, the screwing around—I deserve everything you think of me now."

She said, "Wait. What exactly are we talking about here?"

"I need you to forgive me. Your mother . . . she's waited twenty years for the chance to take care of me, for me to rely on her for everything—this is the best thing that ever happened to our relationship. It may sound strange, but I'm glad to be able to give her this. But you—"

"What about Kirby?"

He swallowed a pill. "What about her?"

"Dad." Her voice broke. "What about Kirby?"

"I don't know where you're going with this." But his warning tone revealed otherwise. Then, nearly a whisper: "Now is no time to rehash—insanity. So help me, I thought better of you. And much as I love you, I won't stand for—"

"Bravo." Applauding, she stood so fast her hipbones popped. "Do you think if you convince *me*, God will let it slip by too? What if this is your last chance to get it off your soul?"

He chuckled thinly. "Why, I didn't know you believed in souls or God. How completely unexpected. Your mother will be so pleased."

"How dare you make fun of me!"

"I'm not." He began to cry. Suddenly, without any buildup, the sobs claimed him, wracking his bony back. "I'm envious. There's hope for you. So envious. You'll never know."

She was crying too. Yes, she had to be crying, but when she reached a hand up to her eyes, they were dry. A compulsion to sever something: her hair, his neck, dry and taut as a twig upon his shoulders. Her voice was quiet now. Steady. "Dad. Five years ago—"

"I should never have broken into your room, I know that. But I was terrified for you. You were so . . . I knew drugs had to be involved. I should never have spanked a girl your age, I shouldn't have punished you that way, shouldn't have gotten your mother involved. Please, princess. You're scaring me with this kind of talk again. Please."

"This is useless. This is—" She moved to leave.

"I'm falling apart!" He screamed it to her back, her receding form. "It's all come on me at once—I wasn't meant to be saved from this thing. I've got MAC, I've got wasting syndrome, I've got every damned side effect they can think up. I'll be dead before you know it, I'll be gone. I'm your father. I love you more than I've ever loved anything. You've got something special, I've always seen it, everyone does, it's more than ballet, you could have been anything, any kind of star. You still can be."

"Don't," she whispered. "Don't."

"If you leave here now, like this, you will kill me."

She spun on her heels to face him. How quickly he'd become a broken skeleton, flesh plotting ways to part with bone. If she stayed, it would touch her—his air, his smell. No, too late, it already had. Her fingers twined in her hair, gripping, pain grounding her just enough to prevent her screaming, from howling and being unable to stop. "What do you want from me?"

"Not forgiveness then," he sobbed. "Just closure."

"Then tell me one thing. Does Leigh Kelsey have HIV?"

"Overruled." He shook his head hard. "I'm allowed some remaining dignity, my life is still my own. You are my child, I'm not yours. I don't owe these pieces of my privacy to you."

"Your conscience is clear, huh?"

"You are my conscience, not Leigh. You're what wakes me up at—"

"What about Kirby!" Screaming—a banshee. "What about my sister you sonofabitch, what about your other daughter, what about her what about her what about Bee!"

"What do you want?" But his weeping only made her want to bring one of the dining room chairs crashing upon his head, to beat him with the severed wooden leg, to bring rising welts to his pale flesh and crack his brittle bones. "I don't know, I don't know what to give you. Kirby is fine. She—she never mattered to me!"

The oak door was too heavy to slam—swished slow, stuck halfway as always. Nothing but the silence of suburbia on a summer weekday. Her eyes could not stop blinking back invisible tears that did not even try to fall. Down the stairs, over the curved walkway to the Jeep. She drove. Another man's car, another man's apartment, another man's money to save her. And if he turned her away? *Stop*—paranoia talking, he'd be incapable of so gauche an act. *Just drive.* Another man's vision, another man's cock, another man's cruelty to save her. Clouds. Clouds rolled in. The storm would not be far.

In the lobby of his building, Kendra's hands shook so much that her chunky, silver bracelet banging into her watch jangled like a wind chime. She clasped her fingers around each opposite wrist and locked her hands behind her back to stop the noise. The doorman didn't seem to be listening. Didn't even really look at her while he made the call. Probably he was annoyed—he knew her, had been prepared to just send her up, but she'd refused, insisted he call first. He must have figured she wanted some big announcement, thought she was that kind. Finally he raised his eyes and said, "Yeah, he's in, go on up." She managed a slight nod and headed for the elevator. He'd already told her Michael was there, that he'd come home an hour ago. She imagined what he must think: how Mr. Kelsey's young plaything seemed nervous tonight. Off. Visualized herself with her hands around her wrists like a prisoner—rightfully so, given what she was about to—*No.* Tight, knuckles white, she walked, afraid to let go.

In the hall outside his apartment, she negotiated what to do with her arms. Heart pulsing quick at the back of her throat, she practiced making her breath come even the way she'd done in the wings before every performance. Poised to knock, Michael's door flung back before her knuckles could initiate contact. A girl stood before her like a hostess, one in hockey gear, a dark ponytail halfway down her back. The girl stared for a moment before smiling. But Kendra did not quite register. Familiar, implacable as a ghost.

"Kendra. Come in." Michael stood in the background; he held an object in his hands; he was trying to repair something. "You remember my daughter." Then, "Here, sweetie, try this."

A rollerblade. Kendra stood in the foyer next to an empty, lopsided coat rack. Rachel had one shoe off and was jamming her foot into the blade. Both she and Michael seemed pleased with whatever magic he'd achieved. He said, "Don't scoot around the rug on that thing, take it off," but she didn't listen, half glided, half hobbled back to Kendra, parting the fibers of the rug behind her like a sea. At twelve, his daughter was more attractive than any child could safely be. Rachel said, "Are you the twin who was my summer girl, or the other one?"

Finally something comforting, some anonymity. "The other one."

"Oh." Interest gone. "Dad, we have to go."

Michael turned his eyes to Kendra. "Maybe you should call Chloe and let her mother pick you up. I didn't realize I was having company."

Rachel frowned, "I think you'd better drive me. Chloe's Mom's always late."

"Don't be ridiculous, she's only a block away. I'll call, you can wait for her downstairs."

"No way, I'll be, like, fifty by the time she gets here. I'll grow dust."

"Collect," Michael said. "You'll collect dust."

"I'll *grow* hair down to my ankles," Rachel said, and laughed.

He picked up the phone. Kendra wasn't listening, couldn't hear anything through the ringing in her head. Rachel made a lopsided figure eight in the rug. Said to Kendra, "What are you doing here?" Then, without waiting for an answer, "You could come too."

"Come where?"

"To my practice—outside cause it's hot, see?" She held up her spare rollerblade, then shrugged, looked annoyed. "It's no big deal anyway. My dad always comes to real games."

Michael: "They'll be here in less than five minutes."

The girl bent to pull off her blade, jumped around on one foot looking for her shoe. Her movements were hard, jerky, like Kendra's students'. Exhausting to watch. Kendra slid around her, her own feet light as a cat's. Rachel intercepted her path.

"Are you dating my dad?"

Good God! "Tell me who you're dating and I'll tell you who I'm dating."

Rachel snorted. "Nobody dates at my age."

"Yeah, I know. You guys just make out behind the gym or something."

Rachel's eyes shot towards Michael in horror, whether because she'd been busted or because she found the prospect of making out repulsive, Kendra couldn't tell. The girl, though, had tits. The same size as Kendra's—she was only a couple of inches shorter too, maybe five one. They could exchange bras, clothes . . .

Michael half-smiled at his kid. "Don't look at me like that, I was twelve once too. But if I catch you with any boys behind any Latin School structures, you're dead. Now go."

Rachel tossed her head—her ponytail cracked like a whip. "She's way too young for you, Dad." Kendra's stomach flipped. But in the next breath, "Say hi to Kirby, okay? She used to take me for ice cream every time she came to my house. I was really little, but I remember."

A catch in the throat. "Yeah. She remembers too."

Unfair, the way something Kendra had never wanted to see could leave a hole when it disappeared. The way a child left a hole, the way a woman filled in gaps until nothing of the child was left. The silence following Rachel's departure swelled like an injury between them. Kendra felt herself backing up, away from the grown man with whom she'd been left alone.

His hands were on her. She hadn't seen him coming, had not seen anything but Rachel's absence. Michael backed her against the door and kissed her with a force that strained her neck. She jerked away. He took hold of the back of her head and turned her face toward his. When he moved his mouth slowly over hers again, she did not resist. The trembling under her skin was humiliating; Kendra wrapped her arms around his neck vise-like, pressed against him in the hope that contact would ease her shaking. He pulled her to the floor with him, mouths hard and hungry, but as soon as she wrapped one leg around his waist, he pulled away. Stood.

"Would you like some tea?" he offered. "I don't have anything to eat."

She got up and sat on the couch, a safe distance from him. "What's the matter with you? Why did you let me up here, why do you think I called first? Why didn't you send me away?"

He ignored her. "I have chamomile. You could stand something to calm you down."

The possibility that she could put anything into her stomach without barfing all over his rug was negligible. "Yeah, as a matter of fact, I could. Got any Valium?" He stared at her. "Didn't think so. Oh well then, guess I'm fucked." She sat on her hands. Wanted a Vicodin, but they were all the way across the room where she'd discarded her dance bag at the door. Plus she couldn't just go get them out and take one—not in front of him, not unless she wanted . . .

Michael said, "I'd offer you a painkiller, I hear they're popular for sedating effects. Of course, in your condition . . . though I suppose that's already moot."

"It is."

"No matter. It seems, in either case, that I've somehow run out."

She got up, crossed the room. Pulled a silver pillbox from her tote bag and shook out two white pills. "On second thought, I'll have that tea. These work faster if you wash them down."

"I'm afraid I can't have you taking those tonight. You can keep them, after all I wasn't using them. But put them back in your bag for now."

She closed her fist over the pills, tight. "Look, did you hear what I said? My mother already came to see me today at work. She was standing there next to your Jeep like she'd just glimpsed the anti-Christ. Maybe we should just start placing bets on who'll get to my father first, his wife, or yours once she hears about tonight. What do you think, where are the odds?"

"There are no odds," he said. "Nobody will tell Henry anything. He's ill, remember? If I'm reading you right, probably a lot sicker than I realize. Nobody wants to upset the dying." His eyes stayed on her, unblinking. "He is dying, isn't he?" And when she would not respond, "So tell me. Would anyone—yourself excluded, of course—tell a dying man that his daughter and his partner are fucking on his impending grave? You might as well keep your worries in perspective, Kendra. It's your father who's in danger—your little secret is safe."

"My secret." She popped the pills dry. "That's funny."

"I'm glad you're amused. But speaking of perspective, tell me. Neither of us is married. You may be young, but you're well above the age of consent. If my knowing your parents precludes ever revealing our relationship to anyone on the planet, I'd like one good reason why."

"*Relationship*?" She snorted. "No, actually, you're so right. I shouldn't be upset that Rachel knows. Maybe she and I can even be friends. We'll go on picnics and to the zoo and do girly things together like shopping—I can take her to Taboo Tabou and get her advice on which dog collar you might dig. What was I thinking, making a fuss?"

"Because there are certain things she obviously cannot be privy to does not mean you have to be total strangers. It's not as if we never do anything ordinary—"

"We go to dinner. That is all we do besides fuck. We eat, and not very much. That's it."

"That doesn't have to be it."

"It does, and you know it."

He surveyed her there, crouched on the floor. "All I know for sure is that you're too damned afraid to even consider the possibility that I might be human, not just some robotic asshole playing a role to make you come."

The whistle of the kettle screamed. Michael went to pour two cups; she followed him into the kitchen, blood hot in her temples, unable to stop. His composure, the slowness of his motions agitated her so that he seemed alien, nothing she had ever known. That he would imply a future together after the weakness she'd shown on her birthday eve made her fear he might be mocking her even now. He turned and handed her a turquoise-colored cup, steaming over. She snatched it, slammed it on the counter. The pressure behind her eyes pushed harder against her sockets like hot bubbles trying to explode. If only they would, then the pain might stop.

"I came to return the little bourgeoisie-mobile. Now I'll go." Her body didn't move.

He leaned up against the refrigerator. "This game is tiresome. If all you're after tonight is for me to fuck you and give you some release you can't seem to get any other way, I'll be glad to accommodate. But next time, call from your apartment first. Don't show up in my lobby and then act as though my sending you away was actually an option. Don't expect the privilege of interrupting my life whenever you choose if you have no desire to be part of it."

No. All wrong. A roaring in her ears.

Kendra picked up her teacup and whipped it at him, hit him square on the right shoulder so hard he reeled sideways into the counter. Yelled, "Shit!" boiling water assaulting his bare feet, splattering in an arc along the black and white tile floor in all the space between them. His jaw clenched tight, to keep from crying out again or from cursing her, she wasn't sure. She backed under the archway joining the kitchen and living room. Didn't move. Wanted to whimper, *I'm sorry*, the asymmetry of the water stain on his gray T-shirt terrifying, provoking an image of the burn beneath. Reckless, too reckless, not the way he was with her, not the way this was supposed to be. His foot, bare, burned red already. She covered her face,

179

heard him struggle with his breath: furious, uneven, then steady. Deep. She peeked above her fingers, then lowered her hands fast altogether, repelled to find herself in such a recoiling pose. His shirt was off, wadded on the counter. The burn on his right shoulder shone wide, splotchy as a Rorschach inkblot. Rash-like splatters littered his chest. He had to be in a great deal of pain, but his eyes, when she dared glance, were calm. His voice almost pleasant.

"I should really put some ice on this. But first, will you do something for me?"

He would tell her to get out, immediately, before the explosion behind her eyes could occur. Without him the bubbles of pain would keep expanding but never burst into the relief of tears, though she might knock her head into walls, might rake serrated knives along the tender undersides of her forearms, anything, anything just to feel. *He* could force a release. Though he hadn't pushed her to breaking yet, it was only because he was waiting, savoring; he hadn't really tried — that much she understood. If he chose, he could reign her collapse into the confines of an erotic dance, draw perimeters around her choreographed *mort* as sure as a ballerina rises from a death scene once the music stops. Without him, tears would be elusive or unstoppable. If she did not cry immediately she would die. If she cried without him to tell her when to start and when to stop, she would die. Pressure mounted, numb gray agony. *Please, Michael, please . . .*

"Go pick out a belt you like and bring it here."

A flash of hope. Then, despite her desire, fear. She chewed on her lip. "I . . . can't."

"If you'd rather I do it, that's fine. I'd like to give you a choice, but if you prefer to leave it to me, we can do it that way too."

Now she held his gaze. "Are you burned or are you deaf?" Hands no longer trembling, there in solid fists. "I told you, I am not in the mood."

"That's fairly apparent." He actually smiled. "And ideal. After all, common sense would indicate that if you're only disciplined when you think it sounds like a rip-roaring good time, that discipline might . . . how shall I phrase this . . . lose its meaning."

"I wasn't aware we were on a quest for meaning."

"No." He took a step toward her. "Nor was I."

Her body backed away again, automatic flight. "Or discipline for that matter."

"Well luckily for you, I'm flexible."

Mornings of him, naked and dripping water from the shower on his rug; he selected suits and ties and belts with an ease that thrilled her. Even when she was too tired to join him in the shower, she always cracked an eye to watch his daily routine. He'd noticed, understood that she feigned sleep and never called her on it. Did he guess already which belt she would choose? Cherry brown, gold-buckled, picked up in Italy when he'd gone with his wife and her parents a decade ago. Thicker than the slim ones he wore with suits, heavy yet still supple. In a moment she would ask where he kept his belts as though she'd never paid attention, and he would instruct her, politely, as though he had no idea of her lie. Her transparency was unbearable. Still, when she finally relented she would sigh: the generous mistress indulging her lover's sexual demons. Would dare hope he'd never realize how much she needed what he was about to do.

"You won't own me because of this, you know. It's nothing. All you are is an interesting lay. You amuse me, that's it."

"You don't mean that. Well, yes, you probably do right now, but I'll try not to take it personally. Except the part about being a good lay and amusing you. I certainly try my best."

"Oh, I know you do."

"You're wrong about trying to own you, though. I just find you fascinating to watch."

Behind her eyes, pent-up dams yearned to spill. Anticipation gripped her, terrified and mad. Of redemption, of bliss.

"Liar," she promised. "You wish that was all."

So. Telephone wire, tangled, drawn from a drawer. Wrists in front of, not behind her body—that way she couldn't panic when things got bad and try to cover her ass. Stomach down, bent over the dining room table backside facing the door—if his daughter were to rush back, having forgotten a lucky rabbit's foot, this'd be the view. Heat in her stomach: an ulcer, a tumor, a forest fire out of control. Question: What to *say* while her lover carelessly fingered an Italian belt, doubled it over preparing to beat her ass? Answer: "Not yet. Talk to me a minute first."

181

But he: "You won't be talking long. And I can do two things at once, you know."

So. Sharp against ass and thighs, weight on hipbones grinding under impact. Teasing snaps, searching, then same spot—bruised like fruit. Again. Shards of glass piercing skin. Repeat: fire, red, an inability to distinguish the exact location of each blow. A mercy. Faster—like nothing else now. Counting strokes to keep focused, dividing numbers, half for each breath: in, out. How long? Burning coursing from epidermis to deepest organs, colors exploding on impact, screams flowing: no rhythm, no order, no language. How easy. The world. Gone.

Only: *Please, don't make me, don't let me, please Michael, no—*

Sobs crushing at the back of her throat, collapsing muscle and bone. What he'd wanted all along, so clear, the only thing she knew, the clarity blinding. What they had both been waiting for, her pure line, her empty stage, this inevitability that before he was through she would become whatever he meant to make her. Everything rode her like a wave until it burst out, shaking her body, wracking her against his tight restraints. Too hard, not a dam but volcano. Weeping bubbled from her mouth: molten lava, full of phlegm and sweat.

I'm sorry I'm sorry I'm—

Then nothing. One raw nothing.

Home.

Sunlight.

Head on his lap, still on the living room floor. He held the *Chicago Reader's* "News of the Weird" in one hand, played with her hair carelessly with the other. A moment to register the reason for pain on the backside of her body. She closed her eyes again—inconceivable to look at him now. Recalled blood slashed on the carpet alongside his daughter's soiled figure eight. On his Michigan sweatshirt too, streaks she saw behind her eyelids. Souvenirs of the night before. Michael, slowly unwrapping telephone wire from her wrists and ankles as he'd waited for her to stop hyperventilating. His command once her breath returned, "Turn onto your back," and her own raspy pleading, "You do . . . can't move, oh . . . hurts." She'd curled into a ball by the time he'd finished whipping her, but he turned her over matter-of-factly as if she'd asked him to unzip her dress. Rug fibers invading broken skin. Whimpering as his hand parted her knees, as his rough entry jerked her against the carpet, leaving lethal tracks. She hadn't tried to say no. Of course he was going to fuck her, what else would be the point for him? Oh God. Her plan had been simple: return his Jeep, exchange no bodily fluids—what kind of person was she? Weak; too weak to get tested, to confront her father beyond veiled pleas, to consciously acknowledge risk at all before thinking a baby involved. Far worse than weak. She opened her eyes.

Michael must have sensed the change in her body; the tensing, abrupt adaptation to a pain unnoticed during sleep. He looked down at her. Did not smile, but held her gaze. His fingers still intertwined in her hair: a light massage against her sore scalp—she shivered. The gesture, strange and out of place amid bloodstains, made an impulse to sob rise up again.

"If I ask you a question, will you answer it?"

"You can ask me anything."

She turned her face into his stomach. "Have you taken it this far before? Last night. Is this just something you do with your lovers? Did you with your wife?"

He moved to run a hand along her cheek, stopped himself before contact was made. Hovered just a centimeter above the bruise her mother had left behind, the bruise he'd not yet asked about. She felt the heat of his body, radiating. Wanted to tell him it was okay, he could touch her face, he could ask, but she didn't—it wasn't, and she couldn't allow him.

"You underestimate yourself with those questions, or pretend to. As though you're a passive receptacle for my urges, as though you don't have everything to do with the outcome yourself." The muscles of his thighs shifted. "The answer is yes, a long time ago. And the answer is no, only with one other woman before you. She was older, with a husband who never looked at her, never touched her. I suppose she wanted to feel more alive or to get back at him, I never asked. For me, it was a matter of having found a willing partner in a game I'd always wanted to try—I didn't feel anything for her except a benign sort of pity that by the time I left started to feel too much like disgust. It was nothing like this. Nothing like us."

"What does that mean?"

"You know what it means."

Her stomach growled. "What about your wife then? With Henry? What did they do?"

Michael withdrew his legs, but carefully. "Always back to that. Look, I'm sorry to disappoint, but there's nothing much to tell. Leigh's imagination tends toward self-invention, not sex. When I first met her in New York, she was a not-very-successful model going by the name Lisa Stone. She had a Brooklyn accent and an amphetamine habit—we slept together twice and called it a day. When I saw her again, six years had passed. We'd both fled the East Coast for Chicago as a result of separate but equally idiotic tragedies, both of our own design. She'd married and divorced and was calling herself Leigh Anderson. There'd been speech classes and time spent at Gold Coast teas, but she fucked exactly the same. Now Leigh Kelsey lives in the Victorian Era and yearns after a dead child neither of us wanted—" He looked at her then, a look she had never seen. One that said, not without fear, *I cannot believe the things I say.*

She answered, "Don't. It's okay."

"When you marry someone like that, Kendra, sex *is* a fantasy. It just wasn't mine."

"Maybe she needs her fantasies to escape her father." She did not know why she said it, did not care about Leigh Kelsey, about anything he had discarded, much less some other woman. "A concentration camp survivor and all that. So much ugliness. It's a lot to live down."

Michael laughed. "Yes, sometimes she tells that story. And I hate to be the asshole who would spoil such poetry, but Leigh's father was born in New York. He was a diamond dealer who got sent to jail when she was a kid. He was out within a year, but she never saw him again."

"Jesus." Inexplicable, inexpressible sadness. She knew he too must have once been saddened by this, but his sorrow had long passed. "Wow. And I thought I was fucked up."

"No. You . . ." His voice came low, thick with something. He drew her onto his lap again, lifting under her arms until she lay against his chest. Spoke into her hair, "I can't change what's happening in your head right now. I'm not planning to try. But as long as you want to, or need to, you can leave your body to me. Where the two meet, well, we'll just have to see."

She sat fully. The effort was considerable, but looking at him was fine, easy now, though she didn't want it to be. "I know. You don't have to pet me anymore. I'm not upset with you."

"What is that supposed to mean?"

"You know what it means."

He withdrew his hands. "I think it means you don't want me to touch you. But rather than admit it, you're trying to make me believe I'm only doing it to placate you, figuring if I'm not exactly convinced, I'll at least be too embarrassed to admit my real reasons. But it's all right. I can certainly see your point. And I won't touch you if you don't want me to."

A visceral desire to kiss him overwhelmed her. To make love on the dried, red patches on the rug. Too late to stop derailment anyway—she smiled despite herself. "I don't mind if you touch me. But I'd rather you find something more interesting to do than play with my hair."

His eyes on her grew curious. He stood, helped her to her feet. She grit her teeth, knew her legs wouldn't work right, not today, not for days to come. She would hobble, need to drink, to down Vicodin to be comfortable enough to sleep. Would teach her students by dictation. Still, she could not take her gaze off him. He had seen everything. Something toxic and swollen in her core was gone. The belt a deliverance, grace and bodily fluids. She savored her pain sweet in her mouth, a morsel of knowledge. Nothing mattered now. He would go with her, he would *willingly* go with her: she believed this. She was not alone.

He said, "Kendra. How do you feel?"

The admission was simple. "Better."

Analysis

Does not everything depend on our interpretation of the silence around us?

—Lawrence Durrell,
Justine

Pandora's Schachtel

MUCH TO OUR MOTHER'S surprise, Kendra attended my shower.
Twenty or so women, mostly my mother's friends, gathered
at Mrs. Kelsey's Old Town house. They bore pastel-wrapped
presents and spoke not a word of disease. My sister's slip dress
accentuated her dancerly thinness, but the loose hair flowing
halfway down her back gave her a wild look markedly
divergent from her ballerina-bun days. She'd also finally
commemorated the end of her career with the tattoo she'd
always wanted—ballerinas couldn't mar their bodies—and
when she (inadvertently?) flung her mane aside laughing, the
fresh, blue-black Miro on her right shoulder blade lay encircled
by an equally fresh human bite mark: a sign, I now realize, to
the initiated. As if on cue, Mrs. Kelsey sought her out, and
though they seemed only to be making small talk about the
shop and the Dance Center and whether either was dating
anybody ("Commitment is bad for my complexion," Kendra
said, oh and how they both laughed), I sat on, tongue-tied,
helpless to extricate myself from conversation with boring firm-
wives, Presbytery ladies, and great aunts from Ohio. My ears
didn't function. I failed to hear what was spoken to me,
straining instead to catch the light banter of which I so wished
to be a part, yearning to wear my sister's sophistication like a
cloak so Mrs. Kelsey would see that whatever interest she had
in Kendra was reflective only of more profound affection for
me. My mother came to sit beside me. I imagined she'd
detected my wandering eye just as she detected my father's

years ago, and had come to play watchdog. Though her own gaze moved over Mrs. Kelsey with something akin to reverence, I felt nothing kindred but rather an alarming spark of resentment. I imagined your voice: *She's lost so much, do you really expect her to let you go too?*

Kendra was the hit of the party. She drank too much punch (and ate nothing at all), then unwrapped my presents and handed them to me with the flair of a *Nutcracker* veteran so the guests spoke as much of her grace as of anything I received. During the hour I spent ill in that rose-fragrant powder room, she entertained all with her woeful tale of imminent eviction and asked blatantly whether anyone was looking for a tenant. When I emerged dehydrated and sullen, our mother stood on looking equally green-yet-pale. A master of escape, Kendra kissed my cheeks and departed with the other guests, leaving my mother and me alone with our hostess.

Straightening up, Mrs. Kelsey arranged things just so. Though a service would take care of the cleaning later, the reorganization of the house was hers. I saw her go to the refrigerator and take out three apples (she must have put them in there to clear room for the buffet), and set them carelessly into an old, earthenware bowl, then place them in the center of the table. The effect was close to magic—as magical as Mrs. Kelsey herself, with her impossibly red tresses and flamenco-styled dress to match. That dress hugged everything, permitted no rough corners, no bumps in the road. I watched her, watched my mother watching her. How could Mr. Kelsey prefer my sister, an emaciated, breastless version of *me*, to this Spanish courtesan? Once I'd acclimated to the truth, I found it hard to begrudge even my father his indiscretion at Mrs. Kelsey's hands. Yet perhaps anything could grow old if familiar enough, and Michael and Leigh Kelsey had shared too much breath in the night, seen each other on the toilet once too often, for such gestures as the arrangement of fruit to bear meaning. I feared: nothing beautiful lasts.

My mother had been on her best behavior all day, formal. Hard to believe that there had been a time, four years during my adolescence, when she and Mrs. Kelsey had been the closest of friends, our home full of complicit laughter over the phone. The two couples had even gone to Europe together for a month when Kendra and I were in eighth grade. I'd heard about the trip not from my mother, secretive as always, but from Mrs.

Kelsey, who'd loved to tell me things my mother would not. From her I learned that they had languished at a spa in Baden-Baden naked on a coed night, anomalies all of them among the fat, sagging German couples and malnourished, hairy and smelly backpacker-youths. In Spain too they'd gone nude on a beach; Mrs. Kelsey had those photos pressed into a decorative book, separate from the other pictures, but she'd shown me. "It's valuable for you to understand that your parents are young, good-looking people with their own lives and sexualities," she'd instructed. "Some kids forget."

Of course I saw my mother naked all the time, but looking at my father and Mr. Kelsey unnerved me until I let my eyes drift and discovered that seeing Mrs. Kelsey made me feel special and good. I was fourteen; if she'd been sleeping with my father already, I'd never have guessed. From where I stood, she only had eyes for her husband. They were less tentative than my parents—their (clothed) photos showed them kissing, and when I babysat, Mrs. Kelsey's vases were overflowing with flowers Mr. Kelsey picked for her in other people's gardens "like a schoolboy," early mornings when he never slept but went out walking. They were both so pretty I took for granted that they were supposed to be more romantic than normal people.

Two years later, once Mr. Kelsey started cheating, Mrs. Kelsey stopped confiding in me and turned to my mother alone. I spied on them, drinking gin and tonics in our yard the spring they first began talking about not being so dependent on their husbands and opening a vintage clothing store together in the city. I'd leave my bedroom window open to catch the drifting voices. In that fashion, I'd first heard of Michael Kelsey's "unusual tastes." I wasn't shocked; this was after Kendra had told me about those magazines.

"So here we are in front of a line full of strangers, and his carry-on sets off the metal-detector, and when it's searched, oops, out comes a pair of handcuffs that are obviously not for me or they'd be in the *checked* luggage we're sharing. I don't get off on them but I thought he'd at least try to use them on the trip to cover his tracks—he didn't even bother."

I'd known little of sex toys, but I wasn't stupid. Imagining made me burn with a sharp, itchy embarrassment, got me touching myself the way Kendra did when she heard our parents making love—an ordeal which had always made *me* curl into a ball and hide in sleep's dark denial. The frenzy of orgasm provided less relief than the death of sleep, though, so I stopped.

Now, Mrs. Kelsey once again starring in the fantasies that played behind my eyes at night whenever Aris touched me in the dark, I gathered presents into Pottery Barn and Marshall Field's bags knowing when next I saw her, I'd be married. My anxiety confused me—as though it made any difference. Wanting badly to leave, I heard my mother's voice the next room over, low and intimate, formality gone. "Men are weak, so I knew it was up to me to tell you. I don't know how long ago you last—if *you* should be—Michael, too. I don't want this on my head."

Tiny hairs popped up on my arms; I braced my feet. Didn't breathe.

And Mrs. Kelsey: "You're worrying yourself sick for nothing, Gail. Henry told me he has AIDS right after the New Year. I never disclosed it to Michael because it wasn't necessary. There's nothing to be afraid of there; he's not infected either, he's been tested a dozen times. I should know—I insisted. Your daughter's safe." After everything, she commanded: "Trust me."

The Maidservant's Warning

"KIRBY," YOU SAID, two weeks and a day before my wedding was scheduled to take place, "how did you feel when Aris said he might not be able to marry if you didn't bring him here?"

By now, eight months into treatment, I had learned to take your questions seriously. To hang on the implicit interest. *How did I feel?* Well, panicked for starters. My wedding had been staged like a grand finale to my father's life; his heart must've swelled with gratitude each time he saw my shrinking form on their doorstep, eager to go over some final touch with my mother. His sallow bride of a daughter: dutiful, careful to hide my fear of their toilets, their kitchen knives—anything to which his fluids or blood might have somehow been exposed. I never allowed fear to stop me, though I spent my nights countering terror by scribbling concrete medical facts off the Internet. When asleep, I dreamed of myself robed in white and holding him close during his final hours. Making him understand that I had never been merely an understudy but the one who'd seen him through. How did I feel? Well, Aris was here, was he not? Across from you, straight-spined, ready to save me from the lethally estrogen-charged combination of you and myself. I felt. If Aris did not agree to marry me in two weeks' time and give my family this last ounce of hope, I felt in serious danger of killing him.

Pros of Couple's Therapy	*Cons of Couple's Therapy*
It could save your relationship.	*Your relationship might actually live.*

"I um, understand his point of view," I began. "I've been very . . . rude to him lately."

You: "Can you look at Aris? Can you tell him that?"

I looked. It might very well have been the most unforgivable thing anyone had ever asked me to do. "Aris, I know you need to see if I trust you enough to share this part of my—"

"I thought she'd be relieved," Aris said. "I'm shocked to be here—I thought she'd see my giving her an ultimatum as an easy out and use it as an excuse. It's seemed so clear lately that she's not excited about the wedding—or me—even though I haven't changed at all. I mean, why would she have made this kind of commitment to begin with if she didn't mean it? Believe me, she didn't hesitate either. She grabbed that diamond and stuck it right on her finger and ran off to call her mom before I could blink. But then she started having diarrhea and crying every time I open my mouth—I told myself it was stress—her dad—but it started before then."

My mouth must've been hanging open. You were nodding at him sympathetically. I sighed as hard as I could; you moved your eyes to me inquiringly.

"He cut me off! You asked me to tell him how I felt and he put his feelings in my mouth, and now you're nodding and not even telling him he can't do that. I took counseling—I know interrupting isn't allowed. Men always interrupt women, it's statistically proven—"

"That's Kendra talking," Aris interrupted. "Ever since Kirby's sister came home, all I hear is how I'm a Neanderthal dragging my woman by her hair off to my cave. She can't accept that Kendra's planting these hostile ideas in her head because she's jealous and probably gay."

"Oh, now who's the broken record? My sister is not a lesbian."

"Both of you, let's back up. Kendra's sexuality is not the issue here."

Aris and I silenced meekly. Good Northwestern grads, we revered authority—we made me sick. I kicked the leg of my chair. Once. Twice. You darted your eyes to me. I stopped.

"You're wrong," Aris said finally, and I admired his balls, momentarily wanted to blurt, *Honey, let's leave, I can make this work, I can.* "Kendra *is* the issue. Her dad too—it's this Braun thing, like you have to screw up your life and be miserable and bitter in order to fit in. It's not the AIDS or the stress of illness in particular. It's the whole way that family lives."

"Do you see the way he talks about my family?" I spun in my chair, made a huge point of eye contact with Aris. "Honestly, why do you stick around if we're all so pathetic? Do you even love me anymore, or do you just want to prove you can save me from them? Because lately I feel like I'm just one of your projects, some way to prove yourself as the Superman or Hero or whatever—like since things aren't going well at work maybe you feel emasculated, so—"

"Do not bring my work into this."

I blinked rapidly. "Why *not*? You blackmailed me into bringing you to therapy but now you don't want my therapist to know that Mr. Kelsey fired you because it's embarrassing?"

Silence. My eyes fixed on the wall, afraid to look at you, to see shock in your eyes at how I was acting. Afraid you were no longer my ally. Why in my desperation had I ever allowed this man to violate my one sanctuary? My eyes grazed your bookshelf: *The Fountainhead.* Had it always been there? Or had you bought it in anticipation of his visit? To enlist his aid in curing me? Silence, silence. My flesh crawled.

"Aris," you began, "do you think the fact that you've recently lost your contract with the law firm is influencing your attitude toward Kirby and her family?"

"Absolutely not." Aris ran his hands through his hair; it fell back into its exact same shape. "Though I'm beginning to wonder if she's glad I lost my job, the job that was paying our rent. She's sure happy to rub my face in it. That project was everything to me, my chance to prove myself, to make a name outside my father's and do something right. But she doesn't care. That's love for you, Doctor. Someone around to laugh the loudest when you fall on your ass."

"You know that's not true!" I spun back to you. "His Howard Roarkean masterpiece was a damned fire hazard. We're broke, can't pay for our honeymoon. Real funny, ha ha."

"Losing a job is traumatic, Kirby." Your suit skirt, an *Ally McBeal*-ish mini, rode up as you crossed your legs. Had my father entertained sexual fantasies featuring those legs? He dug redheads after all. Had he ever imagined you while making love to my mother? "I know you don't want Aris to believe that you enjoy his pain. Could you tell him otherwise, now?"

I stared. *Not on your life.* But Aris, strangely, saved me.

"The ironic thing is, Kirby moans about how I insult her family without even realizing I'm envious of how easy she has it with her dad. When a poor man makes money, he wants to spoil his kids rotten to prove he can. My father didn't have to prove anything—everyone kisses his ass, so he expected me to be the same. Go into his business, think like him, talk like him, but I just couldn't. I acted like I had some other plan when in reality there was nothing. I figured out that if you're arrogant, if you convince people you've got a vision nobody else can see, no one can hurt you. Then I met Kirby, and for the first time I let myself believe I could let my guard down, live another way. Have that sweetness, a normal family, somebody who'd always support me. But ever since Kendra came back, I see where I stand on the food chain."

You were rapt. "You've come to doubt whether Kirby loves you as much—or as unconditionally—as you need to be loved, is that what I hear you saying?"

Aris bobbed his head like a puppy. Not even a snicker at the *I hear you saying* part. He gazed at you, a gutted fish on a line.

"Oh great," I said. "You've turned my psychiatrist against me, are you happy now?"

"That isn't what's happening, Kirby," you said. "You know I care about you and that in trying to get at how Aris experiences your relationship, my goal is to help you. But if Aris is going to start coming here, it will be a goal of our therapy to help him too. That's only fair."

"Oh, sure, everybody has to help Aris," I agreed. "You know, those ex-poor-kids like to spoil their daughters, so they buy their fiancés fancy jobs that talent alone wouldn't merit."

"Kirby!" You took my arm; I yanked it back. "This sarcasm is counterproductive. Why are you so threatened by my concern for Aris? What's the source of this pain? Is it that Kendra usurped everything you ever—"

"Stop blaming her! Everybody stop blaming her!" I covered my ears.

Aris was on his feet now; he pulled me by the shoulders into a tight embrace. "Hey. Kirb, stop freaking out. Look, I'm sorry, I won't come back, okay? Calm down."

"No!" I bucked away, threw his arms off. "You know what, Aris, you said you wanted to help my therapy, and surprise—

you have. You've helped me see it's all a big fat joke! I'm still shitting constantly, I still feel sick. I bought into *this* just like I bought your illusions of grandeur, always hoping someone else can save me. Hey, a breakthrough! I'm out of here."

"I understand your frustration," you began cautiously. "Truly I do—there hasn't been the symptom reduction either of us hoped for by this point. But please, don't make any decisions at least until after the wedding. You should allow us those two weeks—for closure if nothing else."

"I don't have to give you notice. My father pays *you*—I can leave anytime I want."

"Honey." Aris held out a large hand, capable of choking me, of smashing in my face. "You're hysterical. You're being extremely rude. You don't know what you're saying."

"Try this on for size," I said, backing toward the door. "You are nothing but an ordinary man with no special talents. See— I'm cured! Now that we've cleared that up, do not ever, ever patronize me again. Is that clear, *honey*?"

You both stared. You may have stared. I did not see you. The stairs, no time for the elevator. Fifteen floors. If necessary, I would pound on the door at the bottom until security heard and let me out of the stairwell. Or I could stay inside forever, no matter. July rain. A late July wedding. I was free, *free*. Spirals of identical steps, all leading to no place I had ever been. Through the walls, I heard the echo of thunder. Somewhere outside, rain came pouring down.

Looking for Madonna

RAINDROP-SLICKED fingers made the tablets sticky; I had to shake my fingers against the open window to get the pills to drop. Driving sixty down Lake Shore Drive, tossing Levsinex one by one, everything was clear. Yeah, Aris and my father had it all mapped out. Though they agreed on little else, all along they had agreed on the subject of me. Agreed the Subject was an Object. Agreed the object was an item over which to barter: my father would give Aris a job that could make his career, and Aris in turn would put me through grad school someday when I'd pulled myself together enough to be a psychologist rather than a client. In the event of that day never arriving, Aris would knock me up and buy me a large house on the North Shore close to my mother (unlikely he could afford it since he'd gotten himself canned, but hey). Aris and my father nodded in unison when discussing my Irritable Bowel Syndrome, their common enemy. "Kirby," my father assured Aris, "has always been high strung." Aris drove to Walgreens to pick up my prescription for Levsinex; my father had called you personally to ensure my getting an appointment even though, the world being what it was, appointments were in high demand. They were a tag-team, I their mission. They both loved me, but it was clear I was without a productive direction. Not everyone could have a productive direction, so it was important that everyone have a father or husband with one. My father was more aware than anyone of the importance of male guidance. Aris, as he had just testified, deeply missed this element in his own life, though his father's success constantly stalked him, albeit from afar.

Caution: fathers in mirror may be closer than they appear.

I stood in the rain. The hero of a feel-good movie, the man who'd come to his senses and was about to win back the girl. Or *Stella Dallas*, staring into my daughter's happy, untouchable window. I was nothing I could explain. Despite rain, the world remained inconveniently bright. July—it would be light until eight or nine, was now only 7:06. Aris was probably driving home alone in his daddy's old Beemer, cursing my family. Right now, though I had no way of knowing, Kendra was at the Artful Dodger letting the Southern bartender pelt her with martinis, hoping Guitarist would come in so she could explain her unforgivable theft of his wallet, which she knew from his many wailing messages that he assumed had been ripped off at the bar by a stranger and not taken from his apartment by his oldest friend. Only years later would I correlate our motions: as I stood in the rain staring at the window of Isabelle's Room, my sister was staring at a head of Elvis suspended above the bar along with a bunch of cheap voodoo beads. Elsewhere in the city, Michael Kelsey may have been coming home from work surprised not to find Kendra home awaiting his call, but then he might not have called and if he did perhaps he didn't give a shit where she was—who knows, we're not in his head. I stood in the rain. My hair plastered to my skull: a sorry excuse for a seductress. I did not know how to be a seductress. On the south side of Armitage, surveying Isabelle's Room, I waited for the woman I loved to emerge so I could do what they did in movies—stare or start to cry and wait for everything to be all right. I would say, *I missed you*, except there was nothing in my life I'd ever had enough of to miss except Kendra, and that ache dulled long ago. I would say, *Tell me the secret of how to be a woman, I'm lost.* I would say, *Be my mother, I need a new one.* I would say, *Your thighs, your hair, you are trying to kill me.* I would say, *Oh.*

Leigh Kelsey did not emerge. I waited across the street in the rain, but she was not inside the shop. Elise exited alone. Seven o'clock closing during the week, tonight she ran late. She wore a dress of thin cotton, 1940s style. Barely beige, it reminded me of the dress Kendra had worn her first night in Aris's loft last November, only Elise's veins glowed right through her pale chest where the dress dipped low, so the effect Kendra created with a splattering of blue flowers—that of being able to look right through flesh—was real. The girl carried bags in her arms, clothing to be carted home and repaired. She turned the key behind her, rain pounding her sheer dress until skin and fabric merged into one. In a moment, she'd be gone.

I was standing next to her when she turned around. She jumped, charmingly. "I came to find you," I lied, like a man. "I wanted to see you. Will you come with me."

Not a question, but she treated it as one. "What do you mean? Where?"

"I think you're beautiful. You're her lover, aren't you?" My head was spinning: nerves, dehydration. Possibly she would smack me, would spit on my shoes, would start to laugh.

Instead: "Why should I tell you?" Then, a smile, a smile, "I *wish*."

"You are."

"Why do you keep saying that? Are you?"

I kissed the girl. Kissed her the way I had never kissed anyone, the way I used to breathe after coming up from diving into cold, deep blue. Panting, but no noise, no air. Against the slippery glass of the door, against the sprawling name of a dead child, bags crackling behind her thighs, her one hand still clutching them. She pulled back despite nowhere to go: me or impenetrable glass.

Her lips moved: "How did you know, did Leigh tell you about me, why would she talk to you about me? You're getting married, why are you here?" Her mouth the broken, tart skin of a plum—I bit to find sweetness within. Arms hard against her, around her, my hands scraped the wall.

"What's it gonna be, Elise, you've got the key right there in your hand, are you gonna poke my eyes out with it or are you gonna let me in?" Fierce as the big bang, life rushing everywhere. I murmured, "I've watched you, I know you, nobody had to tell me anything."

And she: "You're crazy—I can't."

I: "You *are* her lover, tonight you are her lover."

She: "Come on then."

Soft as unexpected rain, mouths opened, necks strained: You are Leigh, tonight you are Leigh/You don't know me, Kirby /I know you, I know you, you are me.

Here. Darkness, a sudden eclipse. Yes, yes, hurry. A hard and beautiful night.

Case Study

... who knows why a man, though suffering,
clings above all other well members, to the
arm or leg which he knows must come off?

—William Faulkner,
Absalom, Absalom!

The patient recounts being under enormous stress in the forty—eight hours leading up to The Incident, particularly regarding where she would live once the end of the month arrived . . .

On the other end of the line, Michael's daughter said, "Why did you answer the phone?"

"What are you talking about?" Three in the afternoon and she was in Michael's bed, the apartment quiet, sun beating in like artificial light, irrelevant with the air conditioning. She was not quite awake. "Like I'm going to just let it ring?"

"That's what I do. There's an answering machine."

"So you want me listening to your personal messages?"

The daughter seemed to think. "I wouldn't leave anything personal," she decided. "Anybody might be there."

Kendra's head felt heavy. The room smelled too fresh. It was possible the cleaning woman had come, dusted right around and over her. She thought she remembered the vacuum, lulling her deeper into sleep.

She said, "Your mother must date too, right? Why are you weirding out about me?"

"You're too young for my dad."

"Yeah, you already said that."

"Well it's true, okay, so why don't you stop seeing him?"

No cigarettes, there were no cigarettes on the night table. Michael must have taken them; he did that sometimes, hoping she'd be too lazy or broke to buy more. She gulped cold mint tea from a dirty cup, heart racing, was it the coke or this conversation, *little bitch,* exhaled hard.

"Look, you've got it all backward, Rachel. You should be glad your father's running around with somebody half his age—this way chances are he'll never remarry and you'll never end up with a wicked stepmother. Count your blessings."

"My dad doesn't believe in marriage."

"So what are you afraid of then? What, you want me to be old so you can be the only young girl in his life?"

Silence. Then, "You say freaky stuff. You're supposed to be nice to me."

"Don't take it personally. I'm not nice to anyone."

"You're nice to my dad." But if Kendra burst out laughing, if she choked, it went unnoticed. "Everybody is. Even Chloe flirts with him, it's totally gross and stupid, like—"

Anything to stop her: "Chloe of the mother who's always late. Mmm, maybe it's Mom he's after. Maybe nobody's safe and you'll have to be paranoid about every woman you know."

But the girl seemed to prefer this prospect. "Chloe's mother is pretty. My dad's had tons of girlfriends her age."

A quick yank and the bungy slid out of her hair; she ran her fingers through the strands, some falling out and sticking to her fingers. "You're a real charmer, Rachel, I could talk to you all day. But I was asleep, so why don't I tell Michael you called and you can hang up now."

"No." Kendra felt her skin twitch—fear that the girl would refuse to let her go, that she would have to slam the phone down in order to escape. But Rachel said only, "Don't tell him I called. He might be mad that you answered his phone. Just forget it."

Dial tone. She was left to the heavy aroma of pine cleaner, to warm and cool spots on the bed sheets, a tactile glory against her bare legs. The phone was beeping, reprimanding. Kendra hung up too hard, had to replace the receiver. What the fuck was Michael thinking? How had the loose plan in her mind escalated to this point: that she had become the first woman besides his wife to own a key to anyplace that was his since he moved to Chicago fourteen years ago? How had he imagined she was up to the task? Since the night after he'd used his belt on her, she had come and gone at will, had barely seen her father's former apartment with its ghosts and its stale food still locked in the kitchen. But Michael's space was even less her own, and sharing it was not unlike being in a hotel, with delivery instead of room service. Nothing spare twenty different varieties of herbal teas sat in the cupboard. He owned a television, but she had never seen it turned on, just as she had never seen him asleep in his bed instead of on the floor. Kendra relocated to the bed after he went to work, and sometimes his sheets were new. Other times, they were marked by his daughter, who used three pillows and pulled her socks off at night so they ended up tangled in the duvet. Whose bungies slipped out of her straight, dark hair while she slept. The girl had no scent yet; her possessions were the only proof of her existence. Did she require no nutrients to sustain her, desire no Diet Pepsi nor spend her summer vacation watching *General Hospital* on the always-cool TV whose remote had been in exactly the same place since March? Did she never use the room, the *bed* that was down the hall and struck Kendra as not even a hotel room but a ghost town? Kendra pretended the socks and bungies were simply her own—used them, sometimes took them out of the apartment and left them at the Dance Center for her students—but Michael never mentioned it, as though Rachel had an endless supply of such expendable items. As though her father's bed were necessarily a black hole.

There were things she knew about him now. He spent the middle of some nights working underneath old cars, had two besides the Porsche and the Jeep. Though she'd never seen him do this, some mornings when she joined him in the shower she found him covered in grease, his body, lean and slick from water floating off oil, indistinguishable from any mechanic's.

She'd long known his favorite composers to be Chopin and Mahler, but recently had learned that he had a brother, one year younger: a music professor in Oregon whom Michael hadn't seen in eight years.

There were things she knew.

He had never been penetrated, either by flesh or artificial means.

Those bungies and socks disappeared at Kendra's hand, but no one, no one said a word.

There were things she did not want to know.

No matter how often she saw Michael change his clothes after work, the shock of who he was never fully wore off—of how vaguely alarming it seemed that she should be privy to his nudity. He turned to catch her staring. He wore one of his few pairs of boxers and an unbuttoned steel blue shirt, long-sleeved but linen. One foot slid into a soft-looking, gray and blue sock. "Are you hungry?" he said.

"I can't go out. I've been here so long I've run out of clothes—I haven't showered."

"Whatever you want."

The other sock was on now. He went into the bathroom. She heard him urinating into the toilet, not bothering to close the door. The desire to watch overcame her; she went in after him and perched on the sink.

"Your daughter called," she said after the toilet had been flushed.

"What did she say?"

"That I'm too young for you, that you have a string of girlfriends, and that her little friend Chloe thinks you're the bee's knees."

"Oh, is that all?"

"Actually, no. That I shouldn't answer your phone."

She waited, hoping he'd say, *That's ridiculous*, or even concur, *She's right, you shouldn't*. Then defiance would be in order, and she could tell herself she'd picked up the phone to bug him, not because she thought she had any claim. He said only, "Children are liabilities in relationships. Women try to ingratiate themselves to Rachel, promise to take her places so later I'll have to call them when she asks about the dunes, the stables, the circus. A child is a trap."

"Yeah, well I probably chewed your leg off for you then."

He looked at her curiously, but did not ask what she meant.

"Michael." Not bravery that surged through her, but the fear of running out of time. She'd heard animals could smell a storm in the air. Patients in hospital beds knew when the time had come to die. Kendra watched him, his legs roughly the same length and width now as when hers were shorter, smaller, without any womanly shape. He was putting on his pants.

"You shouldn't let her sleep in your bed."

He did not ask what brought this up. Did not ask how she knew where Rachel slept at all. Did not so much as glance her way or blink. "Why not?"

"What a stupid question."

His laugh floated, airy. "How uncharacteristically traditional, Kendra. I'm charmed."

"You never even turn the lights out. How can she sleep?"

"You're right, Leigh complains I send her back tired. But children of divorce don't need rest so much as proximity. It reassures her, her crazy dad sitting on the floor working, reading, watching over her. And I'm selfish. I'll be sorry when she doesn't need me anymore, when I become a nuisance instead of a comfort. They grow up fast. Look at you. God, look at me."

No answer then to this, his sudden nostalgia for his boyhood, a longing perhaps for the protection of his own mother, for reconciliation with his father, also dead. She felt vaguely guilty, vaguely duped. Inexpressibly weary, despite all her sleep.

"You look sufficiently beautiful to be seen in public," Michael said flatly, eyes moving over her. "But if you prefer, I'll bring something back for you. What do you have a taste for?"

"Nothing," Kendra said. "But never mind. I'm coming."

*　　*　　*

May 1994

"You are to come straight home," her mother said. "Straight home and to your room until your father gets back. I don't even want to look at you, do you understand." They would talk about "it" later. Later, when Bee was at swimming. Later, when her father was home.

Numb and dazed, Kendra drifted through her day. Minutes crawled to hours: school halls vibrated with voices and the slamming of lockers; her tailbone grating against desk chairs for meaningless fifty-minute intervals. How easily she had been tricked. She didn't know what her father was up to, but it was clear all would be revealed soon. Whatever this was, this set-up: a chess game of blame and accusation, of defense/offense. Whatever she had coming. His plan.

*　　*　　*

The patient writes that, some fifty-two hours before The Incident, her lover leaned only slightly across a table they had waited an hour and a half for and said, "I'd like to see another man fuck you. I'd prefer a stranger, but if you feel markedly more inclined toward someone you know, I'm willing to let you make the arrangements."

They were having dinner at Meritage in Bucktown. Blond wood, cool metals, rare tuna, good wines, long waits. Like everywhere they went, it was all the same.

The fantasy of Michael watching her, naked and writhing under another man, had come to her often in the seconds that preceded orgasm. Usually this consisted precisely of him instructing a third party to do to her the things he did, to hurt her and then make her come, while he sat back and observed, getting off. To hear it from his lips, though—to have the fantasy dragged into the realm of the real—stung worse than a slap. Yes, his preference of a stranger was sound logic: a stranger's alliance would be solely to himself, not to either of them. Nothing could be staged. Any aggression or arousal exhibited would be genuine. Still, Kendra found unknown men frightening and distasteful, and knew Michael was even less fond of strangers than she, so that she would be asked to fuck one could be construed as nothing but an insult.

Options played in her head: Rising to leave, *You despicable misogynist.* Or, half-smiling, *Have you been getting into my coke, Michael?* Finally, holding back tears, *Would you really want that, really like to see another man humiliating me, putting his dick where yours has gone, will go*—how stupid could she be after everything? "So. Why this sudden urge to share?"

She caught his smile at the mere thought. "I tried to think like you," he teased. "I figured that when I'm touching—partnering—you myself, so close, my powers of observation are compromised at best. All art forms require occasional distance—a director to witness the actors, a ballet master to assess the dancers' weaknesses, right? So shouldn't I be able to experience you as outside of myself to learn you better too? Why wouldn't I desire that?"

"And me? What do you think I should feel about fucking a random Joe and getting myself beaten up a little in the process, all for the sake of furthering your creative expression?"

"Should? I thought you *would* find the prospect intriguing. Theatrical and transgressive at once, which, I think it's fair to say, is quite your taste." He shrugged. "If you find my proposal too scary, that's your call, of course."

She exhaled a stream of smoke, not bothering to face away. "I hate to disappoint you, but you're way too civilized to be scary. I mean, sure you'd probably fire me for good if I ever refused to star in one of your little productions, but big deal. You'd never screw or hit me against my will—you'd consider it tasteless. I'm perfectly safe."

Grinning broadly, "I thought we'd already established that I'm not about to dump you."

"Yes, well that's easy to establish since I'm not about to say no, isn't it?"

Sudden stillness. The retraction of his crooked grin. At that moment, the patient recalls stabbing out her cigarette and striding to the ladies' room, conscious of his eyes on her back. Her mood was suddenly elevated. She clarifies that, in those final days, nothing pleased her more than her lover's hard-to-elicit, nervous silence.

* * *

May 1994

Mostly, her parents talked in front of her. Kendra sat in her father's study like a Brady child, a retro gag out of some parody movie. Hands folded, a study in how to look contrite when your father has stolen into your bedroom like a thief in the night and confiscated your speed. They decided her fate in businesslike tones. Grounding for two months, the purpose of which was to pull her from daily ballet class. Clearly it was this obsession with dance that had her turning to speed to keep thin, keep her flying through the air with ease. Dance was the enemy; they would reclaim their child. Only occasionally did her father remember to turn her way and address her as "you." As in: "You'd better tell us immediately if your sister is involved in this little drug ring too." But no, her mother shook her head, "Kirby would never do something like this, I know her. If she knows what Kendra's been up to it's probably breaking her heart."

There were moments in which to be silent. Moments in which to sit on hands, to bite tongues hard enough to bleed. Kendra sat on her hands. She bit her tongue; her mouth was dry; she felt no pain, drew no blood. Across the desert of her mouth, words blew out.

"You don't know your own daughters' asses from holes in the ground—especially Kirby! If she were on speed, maybe she wouldn't be fat and silent because of you and him!*"*

She shot to her feet, but her mother pushed her back down, a hand sharp on her shoulder. "Oh, no, we're not finished with you, Kendra Ruth, not before you—"

A growl rose from Kendra's belly: a fury's prayer. She flew at her mother, claws out, teeth bared. Her mother backed into a corner, screaming. Hair coming loose, fistfuls . . .

At the intercession of one heavy hand, both women ceased their frenzy. Kendra's lipstick smeared like a wound in her father's palm, left her mouth streaked with red. Her mother's back shook with sobs, turned against her unrepentant daughter. Kendra's father did not reek of booze. Four years of sobriety must have granted him time to peruse the Souse's Sourcebook *for tricks like straight vodka, peppermint Life Savers. Tricks like righteous indignation. Kendra's mother, hands covering her face in a posture of defense, tried for a gasp but couldn't muster one. No use pretending Kendra hadn't deserved so harsh a slap, and more.*

No use pretending she did not deserve whatever was coming. And more.

*   *   *

The truth of morning defies metaphors. Kendra wore Michael's robe, read a *New Yorker* distractedly, his glass table-top allowing the glare of black and white checks on the floor into her peripheral vision. By the light of day, she could not shake his Third Party Proposal from her mind. The night she'd just spent seemed a sordid hoax. She was ashamed now to have allowed Michael to kiss her mouth, to stay inside after he'd come, collapsed but propping himself up on his elbows to talk, breath and hope in her face. "We should go on vacation," he'd proclaimed, spontaneous as a child. "Camping out West. No drugs, no cigarettes. You don't need them, I promise to keep you entertained." She'd countered, "I don't think I should be alone in a woods with you. There's no telling what you might do." But laughed a consenting laugh, couldn't keep her smile from spilling everywhere so she had to turn her face away in a flimsy attempt to hide.

He stood at the kitchen door. Naked, wet from the shower—how had she not heard it running? He stared at her, his eyes moving down her body to her feet, bare and braced on the checkered floor—a queen or a pawn? He moved his eyes along the floor to the space in front of where he stood, indicating for her to come over to him. She started to obey, then stopped short.

"I had a terrible nightmare about you," he said, not approaching her.

"How quaint. I didn't know you dreamed."

Without touching, he moved past her, sat on one of the stools at the counter. His dick was at half-mast, its noncommittal state irritating: either way he couldn't be accused of anything. He took a sip from her cup next to the teapot. Flipped the *New Yorker* to the page after where she'd stopped reading and looked down at the print intently as though trying to make sense of it.

"What's with you? Was I so horrible in the dream you're not speaking to me?"

He closed the *New Yorker*. Lowered his head in his hands so that he was still staring down. "I can't do this right now." But she could not be sure it was her he was addressing instead of himself. "I can't do this with you. I don't want to be this, this *way* we are. I dreamt I was drinking with Henry, quaint though you may find that, and I was trying to justify to him why I didn't call you after you told me you were pregnant, why I didn't go with you to get the abortion and take you to a decent doctor instead of whatever half-assed clinic you most likely chose. I didn't have any explanation as to why I could've been such a shit. Then I woke up and remembered—you wouldn't have me anyway. You didn't want my concern or even my money. I was shut out, just like after Isabelle died. I was irrelevant, *I* hadn't wanted a baby, I didn't count." He raised his eyes. "And I realized, I don't care what roles we play in bed, kink doesn't justify this disdain for each other's feelings. Jesus. It's only sex."

She did not know what to say. (Give me a break, would *you* know what to say?) It was the most she had ever heard him utter in one mouthful, electrifying and terrifying and too much to swallow. His dick was soft now, and that scared her more, that there was no turn-on in what he'd said, that it had nothing to do with sex. She wanted him to be lying. Wanted this to be an attempt to break down the last frontier of kink: tenderness. When no perversion lay unturned, what could be more perverse than honesty, than intimacy? But there were *plenty* of perversions left unturned—just last night he'd mentioned one of them—and this was not about sex, it was about death, and no matter how she tried, they would never be the same thing. This was about a man twice her age who'd been introduced to death young, younger even than she would be introduced to it, who had already accumulated three female bodies at his feet—mother, lover, child—and perhaps, perhaps, could not stand the knowledge of one more. But who'd ever said their baby would have been a girl? Of course, there was no *their* baby, never had been, so perhaps the only girl was her; perhaps she was the body he was trying to dodge. Perhaps she was the second chance he'd been waiting for.

She said: "You are not going to like this."

She said: "There was no abortion; it was a false alarm."

She said: "Once I found out, I was so pissed you hadn't called that I just didn't tell you."

So this was what shock looked like on him. Him, this man she'd known since girlhood, whose pornography had once schooled her to understand the implications of her darkest, most secret fear. This man who had made her cry and come within moments of each other, who'd sat calmly on the edge of the tub while she vomited ammonia into his toilet. This man whose expensive dinners had been the only thing standing between her and self-starvation, whose voice in the dark promised to be a stand-in for death so that she wouldn't have to die.

He moved into the other room to put on his clothes. She heard the familiar sounds: the hum of his zipper, the buckling of his belt. He re-entered the kitchen where she stood exactly as he'd left her, her feet in fifth position, pulled in tight. She longed to curl up on the floor, close within herself, but was wary of even that much movement. Michael's face was harrowed. Hurt. Tired. Old.

Shout, hit me, anything but this silence . . .

He, of necessity, spoke first:

"The smartest thing we could do at this point is back off. We've already done more damage than I'd let myself believe. If we keep on this way, it's inevitable that we'll hurt each other more—and worse. I'm telling you because I don't trust myself. You're young, you deserve more than this. Walk away intact while you still can."

But: since childhood, the patient had been contrary. But: things never seem as destructive when we're in the middle of them. So: instead she did what she had never done. Ran to him, threw her arms around him, buried her face in his neck and pushed his hands inside the gaping robe. "Stop," she begged, the desperation in her voice greater than any he had ever beaten out of her. "I'm not young, I've never been young, you know that, you know me. *I* trust you, I've always trusted you. I don't care about the future. I don't have any regrets."

And then his hands were on her breasts. You know they were. Cupping her ass, fast as snakes circling the narrow breadth of her body. Between mouthfuls of her skin, he murmured something like, "You haven't been intact for years, have you?" And she groaned, shuddered, "Not since you've known me—I'm used to it." Skin to skin, mouth to mouth, bone to bone: nothing left to do but surrender. Hard, as fast as they could. Nothing left to do but laugh.

Later she went to confession at the Rainbo Club in Wicker Park. Her soul was on the line in more ways than one, and this was the most manageable of them, the most concise avenue for gaining some small ounce of her integrity back. She sat on the floor because the Rainbo was crowded on Saturday night. Hot, smoky, thick with skinny bodies like her own: with unwashed hair and re-worn clothes. It unnerved her, how all signs of physical and mental deterioration that might, in a different decade, have served as some kind of warning sign, were instead, on the brink of the millennium, merely the ultimate indicators of hip. The bodies around her, maybe they were hurting too. Or perhaps they were only truly cool. She could not tell, was not sure she was interested. They were noisy, they smoked so much that even she could not breathe (it was better here, so near the floor). She waited for Guitarist to arrive: scrawny, scruffy, smelly from the mothballs his clothes had sat in before being carted to whatever thrift store he'd bought them at, from hand-rolled cigarettes. Stupid German. She waited near the floor, not smoking because she couldn't stand to here, not when a cigarette was a membership card, a badge of the bad-girl persona she'd never striven for when she was young and dying to be a ballerina (though all dancers smoked too). The culture of youth and her role in it had never borne any meaning, and this too seemed unsettling—that she could blend in while feeling so removed.

What she had come to do was jump to her feet at the sign of her confessor. Her fingers chiseled their way through the crowd until she stood before him, blurting a story about how she'd been supposed to meet someone here but the girl hadn't shown. He did not question her. Nobody cares about the activities of women among themselves, about their meetings and small disappointments. He did not say, *Hey, I'm glad you're making some new friends.* Hugged (but did not kiss) her tentatively with, "I thought you hated my ass, baby."

She lit a cigarette after all, tossed her hair over her shoulder. "Come on. No big deal."

"What then, we just talk every few months these days?"

Acrid smoke swirled in her head; she wished she'd sprung for a drink. Laughed throatily, just the way he loved and hated. Demurred, "I'm busy. You know."

She was wearing leather pants. Guitarist commented immediately, touched them, hand running down the slope of her hip; she could barely feel it beneath the thick casing. The pants were a present, the latest thing in Chicago (though already old hat in New York). Still, not only for hookers and perverts anymore. She wore them with a tube top, under which she wore no bra. She wore them with platform sandals, inside which her toenails were painted the color of blood in a vial, blood without undue contact with oxygen. Her lips were the same color as her toes, though this could not have been clear to Guitarist, who was not currently viewing these body parts in close proximity (likely he entertained hope, for the first time in two months, of doing so soon). She came to him in the skin of a fantasy, of a lover. Touched his arm with deliberation; did not mention her old-fart fuckfriend. She said, "I missed you." She said, "I hate this bar, let's leave, I want to talk to you." She said, unbelievably, "Please."

Kendra was shocked to find that he had moved. All the way to Andersonville, north of Foster. Only by strange coincidence had she caught him at the Rainbo; he'd been in Wicker Park that evening jamming with his new band. He said the word *jamming*, and Kendra could not help but think how her current lover would never use language like that. Guitarist had gone by his old haunt hoping to run into friends he hadn't seen since moving. Andersonville had its own bars too. Some of them were cool. "I'm getting too old for the Wicker hipster scene," he said. Everyone in the Wicker scene said that from the time they were twenty, Kendra had noticed, though many of the men were in their thirties and apparently still too turned on by the smell of a girl dusted with pool chalk, H, and smoke to really leave. Andersonville was quiet; they would be able to hear Patricia Barber without blaring the CD player, they would fall asleep to Kurt Elling the way they used to in the place he lived before he lived in the apartment with the loud Mexican neighbors he could not complain about without jeopardizing his politics. Kendra imagined kissing him in the cab they'd hail on Division Street—there were many cabs on Division Street to meet the demands of condo dwellers horrified to use their cars for loss of increasingly precious parking. But no, Guitarist had a car now too, parked somehow right outside. It was so much his that he kissed her against the passenger door, until she finally wound her arms around his neck and felt her sin disintegrating. Felt her burden just melting away.

*   *   *

May 1994
   Perhaps, only once, her mother said, "Henry, no."

A good old-fashioned whipping. That was what he called it; Kendra had to laugh. "Too easy on you for too long." And who could argue? Kendra wished for a cigarette, would have lit up there in the house, let his crazy smoke detectors deafen them all. Her mother stood by trembling, his command of "Gail, stay out of this" further eliciting Kendra's disgust—and the memory that she could have opted for this privilege of neutrality as well. They would have to move quickly. Get it over with, whatever he was going to do, fast before Kirby returned.

"If you make me stay home from ballet, I'll run away. You think I'm an embarrassment now, wait until I have to sell my body on the street for money. Or maybe it won't come to that. I'm sure some of your partners would like a piece of me. Maybe they can set me up."

Kendra's mother sobbed. Her father's voice was gentle. "Gail. Honey. Leave the room." Not a command now but permission. The possibility had never before occurred to Kendra: that there would be no witness, that what she'd known could happen would no longer be abstract, but the knowledge would still remain hers alone.

"A good old-fashioned whipping, that's what you need to teach you some respect."

The sudden realization that she did not understand pain, that she feared it. "Mom—" But her mother's feet ascended the stairs, a punitive goddess whose back turned after judgment. No, a wild thumping in her chest, her throat, her ears, Stay. The will to fight surged through her body; his hands on the belt around his waist, sure and slow. "Mom!"

The house screamed silent, an answer to her own duplicity. Thrashing limbs, wild movement, the final verdict on who ruled whom. "Mom, come back, I'm sorry, please!"

"It's too late for that. Don't make it any worse for yourself—be quiet, please." The incongruence of his pleaded warning. "You left me no choice. Don't make me come to you."

* * *

The car stopped in the middle of the street. Kendra said, "Drive, somebody will hit your new car, drive." Guitarist, though, was busy, saying things to show he still had a heart. Things that meant it could be broken like, "You wouldn't do that to me, you know I'm in debt, you know I need every cent I make, you wouldn't fuck me that way, I know you." But in a voice that was loud, that was frightened, that indicated he was sure he did not know her at all.

She said, "You do know me, that's why I didn't spend it, that's why I'm giving it back."

He did not seem to hear. Drove fifty miles per hour on Ashland, swerving around double parked cars, old Nine Inch Nails screaming on Q101. "Head like a hole," they screamed, "Black as your soul," they screamed, "I'd rather die than give you control." Kendra thought, with a detachment that worried her, *He should control himself better, that's his problem, no control.* She thought, *I could never trust myself to him.*

The car screeched to a halt. Her body jerked against the shoulder belt. Guitarist shifted into park and grabbed her purse—a Kenneth Cole bag with a broken zipper and two lipsticks and cigarettes and a joint and the piddly amount of Vicodin she had left in her silver pillbox and the wallet that belonged to him and the one that belonged to her that had less money in it by far. They were near Roscoe, just past the recently closed Blind Faith Café where Michael had sometimes taken her when he wasn't in the mood for dressing up and martinis and waiting in line. Michael liked the smoothies there, he liked the macrobiotic plate; she was not sure what she had ever ordered. If only she could be there now.

Guitarist screamed, "Why the fuck did you steal my money? You owe me at least that much of an explanation! I thought it got ripped off at the Dodger, I've been ragging on the bartenders freaking out thinking maybe it fell out of my pocket, you know nobody was in there that night, nobody could have fucking taken it, but no, I would never have thought it was you!"

"I thought I was pregnant and needed an abortion but I was wrong." Then, hoping to distract him, "They said I just don't get my period because I'm anorexic."

But he was not distracted. He was not interested in anorexia, especially since he was never planning to see it naked again. "We used condoms, I always use protection, it would have been his, wouldn't it, you were stealing my money to cover aborting that rich old fucker's kid!"

Kendra whispered, "No, no, there was no kid but it could have been yours, don't you remember that night in Kirby's loft when we couldn't find any—"

"That was eight months ago!"

Silence. That was before she'd ever slept with Michael. Impossible that anything at all happened that long ago. She sat, stunned.

There'd been a time. Their bodies tangled beneath the ratty afghan his grandmother had made. They'd giggled. Dropped acid and stared at the fractals on his computer. Watched *Seinfeld* and ate ice cream off each other's stomachs and talked about what they'd name their kids. She called him, *my boyfriend*. They exchanged earrings and said *I love you* every time they said goodbye. It was what people did. It was normal. It had never scared her.

"Get out of the car."

Who was he, this *man* with a car and an apartment up north and this venom on his face? He still held her bag in his grasp. She reached for it, and he said, "No way, fuck that, you see what it feels like, go call your fucking daddy-substitute collect and tell him to pick your ass up."

"He isn't at home. He had to go to a party."

A sneer. "Oh yeah? Why didn't you go? Is he ashamed of you?"

Her voice cracked. "My mother is supposed to be there."

Too late. No compassion to soften his mouth, not even interest in her scandal. He put her purse behind his back. She was this close to crying. All of a sudden, she was always this close to crying. She did not think he had ever seen her shed a tear. If she were to start, would he notice it as anything unusual? Would he change his mind?

He said, "Stop sitting there. I told you, get out."

"I need my purse. I'm not leaving until you give it to me."

He leaned across her and opened her door with a pull and a push. She lunged past his body to grab the handle of her bag, but he pushed her back, knocked it out of her reach. Her tits flattened against his palms; he held her at arms length, pushing her to the door. Now, now the tears were coming, though no sound accompanied them. She tried to swing to hit him but his arms were longer, she was too far away. She shouted, "Fucker! Stop it!" The blubbering had begun, she couldn't stand it, almost got out of the car to keep him from seeing, but she couldn't, couldn't leave without redemption, couldn't leave without one friend in this world besides the man who'd *started* all these repulsive tears. Couldn't leave without somebody to fuck her in front of Michael so it wouldn't have to be a stranger.

"Guitar, how can you do this? It's *me*. Let's just go home. Yours or mine, I don't care. Anything you want, let me make it up to you."

215

Finally there was a trace of sympathy on his face. "How could you offer yourself to me? Don't you know you make me sick? What kind of shameless slut have you become?"

A tremor ran down her back. The pity on his face was worse, far worse than the hatred. She had imagined him pushing her out onto the curb so she'd land ass-down in the gutter. But no, she got out on her own legs. He reached into her purse and threw her wallet into the back seat, almost reluctantly now. Then handed over the rest of the bag.

"You know," he told her through the open window, "this is much worse than our breakup. This is the saddest thing that has ever happened to me."

She watched him disappear, purse handle slippery in her grasp. "You're lucky," she said.

No cash. No credit. Kendra could not call a taxi and pay once she got home—she had no money aside from what was in her wallet, and any cash Michael had would be on him. She could walk. Down Ashland to Chicago, that would be safe, but once on Chicago she'd have to pass Cabrini Green. Two hours until she'd get back to Michael's apartment building on Lake Shore Drive. She was decked out in black leather pants, a tube top, and platform heels. Outside the realm of Wicker Park, she looked like a prostitute. Already, it was almost midnight. Kendra went into a corner bar on Ashland and Roscoe, populated with Lakeview frat types, and headed for the pay phone in back. Her parents' calling card number was the same—she was somewhat surprised her mother hadn't changed it lest their devil-daughter employ *their* thirty-five cents to keep herself from being raped on a midnight stroll. She was aware that she had some nerve feeling indignant about anything. On her way from the phone, a guy in a baseball cap caught her around the waist and moaned, "You're not leaving are you, you just got here." Kendra thought seriously about asking him to buy her a drink. But something about his fingers disgusted her. Something about the mere idea of fingers disgusted her. She said, "Sorry, you can't afford me," but couldn't go through with it without laughing so he'd know it was a joke. He called after her, "Oh, oh, you've broken my heart," and she wondered if he might be harmless after all and if he had a car, but by then her ride was coming so she went outside to wait.

Aris took thirty-five minutes to arrive. The loft was approximately ten minutes away. Though he had answered the phone, it had never occurred to Kendra that he would arrive without her sister in tow. When she got in, he grumbled that Kirby hadn't even heard the phone ring and that he didn't see the point in both of them missing a decent night's sleep over Kendra's ridiculous absent-mindedness. She had, of course, told him that she'd been at this bar on purpose, that her friends had taken the first cab to go north and she was to take the next, but after they'd gone, she realized she'd spent all her money on drinks. Aris thought her stupid enough that he'd feel no need to question this. She imagined what he thought of her in her leather pants and bicentennial-styled tube top: like some bimbo starlet auditioning for a part in *Boogie Nights*. Except she'd never be hired with her tits—he'd struck it lucky on that end of the twin-deal. Of course, he had problems with Bee's tits too, not aesthetically but relationally. Probably he thought those problems were Kendra's fault. Probably he was at least a little right.

Kendra said, "Well, you're out now. Do you want to go have a drink?"

He said, "Don't you have anyplace to *be*?"

"Like where? Michael's at a party. My mother is there. His ex-wife is there. Everyone is there but me."

"Well, that's understandable," Aris said, not unkindly. "He couldn't invite you and antagonize them."

"Oh, he invited me. I just wouldn't go."

Aris snorted. "That guy is such an asshole. No offense, but man." He looked around as if he might be thinking about where they could go. His voice dropped a bit—perhaps inspired by her confiding in him about Michael's party. "I've been meaning to ask you something anyway," he admitted. "Yeah, sure, let's go someplace, I could use a drink or two. None of your freaky bars, though, I didn't bring my polyester bellbottoms."

"And I didn't bring my Gap khakis, so unless you want people to think you hired an escort . . ."

He kind of laughed. "Maybe this town isn't big enough for both of us."

She shrugged. Cracked the window to light a cigarette, but he stopped her. She glanced at him sideways. He was unshaven, a little dirty looking. He looked better that way. Kirby probably didn't agree. His hair stood up at odd angles.

After-sex hair? No wonder Bee was sleeping so soundly. Kendra had never seen Aris's hair rumpled before.

"We could go back to Michael's."

"Won't he be home soon? He'd think that was kind of weird, wouldn't he, me drinking in his house in the middle of the night? He fired me, you know. He thinks I'm a raving idiot."

"Yeah, well, you think he's an immoral asshole, right? So do you want to or not?"

"What about your place?"

"I don't really go there anymore."

Aris looked at her strangely. "You two are living together? Does Kirby know?"

"It's not living. I'm just staying there. For now."

Even at nearly 1:00 AM, the car was hot. Kendra rolled the window down farther. Aris sighed like a word. "Okay, okay, you can have *one* cigarette," he consented. "So, where does this Lothario live?"

There would be exchanges. Over Glenfiddich and ice that came right from the ice maker, an intimacy between them due to the illusion of impending family. The family they loved to hate. They had both been playing that game since childhood— it would be if they were to *like* one another that they would worry. Antipathy was comfortable. Over scotch and watery ice cubes, they discussed how her lover had fired him and ruined his career. How she had no career anymore either and therefore felt little pity. How being married was expensive and thus required a career, and how she couldn't relate to that either. An hour passed. They had made small talk long enough to become drunk. To turn the conversation to her sister, his soon-to-be wife.

"She didn't come home," he said. "After she ran out of the session, I went home to wait for her. I called you—I didn't know then that you don't live or stay or whatever at your own apartment anymore. I called your mother. I called that black lady Deborah from the temp agency, the one she has lunch with sometimes. Kirby doesn't have a lot of friends—I couldn't imagine where she'd gone. Then I did imagine. I couldn't, but I did. In the morning, she was home. I'd fallen asleep around five, and she wasn't there. Then she was in bed next to me. She said she'd driven around all night. I know she wouldn't do that—she doesn't like to drive; she always makes me drive even if we're in her car, even to your parents' house. She said she'd driven around all night. We're getting married a week from today—less than that, it's Sunday already. We're getting married in six days and that's all she could give me."

Kendra fetched him some tissue. She knew where everything was. She knew where cups were to make chamomile tea to calm him down. She knew where another bottle was to calm him even more. She'd invited him to sit like the furniture belonged to her. Her bare feet on the rug moved with authority. She thought, *If you bleed on something enough, it feels like yours. If you bleed on someone enough, it's the other way around.*

Aris was crying. All around her, men cried. Her father cried, her sister's fiancé who was nothing and everything like her father cried, her best friend said she was the saddest thing that had ever happened to him and cried all the way back to his Andersonville haven, she knew as sure as if she'd seen it herself. Aris wept angrily, swiping his eyes with frustration. He said, "I've never loved anyone besides Bee. It was going to be so perfect. We were going to be like nobody is anymore. We were going to be married to our first love. You're probably laughing at me, but I don't care. I just want you to tell me the truth, if you know where she was, if she's seeing someone else. Something's changed. I want the truth. You wouldn't understand that kind of faith in another person. But it was everything to me."

Kendra's lover never cried. Michael had told her: the last time was the night his mother died. Then it dried up in him; he couldn't do it anymore. Not at her wake, not when he wrapped his car around the tree and got to be unconscious instead. Not even later when his baby died, and that was when his ex-wife figured out he was a monster and kicked him out of her house, except he was planning to leave anyway, which just proved what a monster he was. Kendra's lover did not cry but wanted to see her fuck one of these other crying men. Wanted to see them make her cry, to let them feel strong for a moment in her weakness, to pretend he did not know she could eat them alive. Or maybe he was pretending to think she *could*. She was not sure what she was capable of anymore. Her would-be brother-in-law spilled tears over Kirby; Kendra never thought anybody would weep over Kirby—it always seemed the other way around. She had no idea where Bee had been, but was positive no infidelity was involved, and Aris was humiliating himself for nothing. "Bee doesn't have it in her," she assured Aris, "I got all those genes."

"But you share the same genes," he choked, so she poured him more scotch and more for herself too, because she had long since stopped knowing how to answer that.

No, Michael would not see them at first. The door opened into a hall, which led to the living room and the entrance to the kitchen. The dining room table was the only thing visible from the foyer. The bedrooms were down the hall—two, one always unused. His bed was queen size and had stories to tell that Kendra did not want to know. She was part of the story, only part of his story; he was out tonight with her mother and his ex and they were perhaps talking about her father, or maybe her mother was throwing a drink in his face and calling him Satan, or maybe he'd run into his lawyer friend who was attractive but to whom he was not particularly attracted and was fucking her anyway. After his outburst earlier, it did not take much to deduce the score. He wanted out, but due to his stupid guilt (prompted—*please God no*—by loyalty to her father?) he hoped to provoke Kendra into ending it first. As if that were possible anymore.

Aris had ceased crying. He was no good at it. He was merely drunk. And embarrassed. He'd said he wasn't, but she knew better. He drank more, as if in hopes that it would pass.

Kendra said, "Fortysomething-year-olds don't stay at parties until 2:30 AM, do they? We aren't even living together and he isn't coming home at night. Infidelity is cheap. Go home. Kirby's in your bed now, isn't she? That alone is almost more than anybody has."

"She holds me in disdain." Flatly. "You know that damn well. Don't treat me like a naïve kid you have to pat on the head and send back to Disneyland."

"All right then," she countered. "Don't go. You want to get back at her for some imagined crime? Stay here with me. Is that what you want me to say? Because I'll say it. Be careful what you wish for. You want to get back at her in the worst way you can imagine. Fine. I know she doesn't love you—I'd consider it an act of mercy. Michael's gone. Maybe I want to get back at him too. Maybe I want to pretend he'd care. Maybe he would. Here I am."

He approached her. Pulled the tube top down with one yank so it floated around her belly like a deflated inner tube. Her tits stared back at him, pubescent and invisibly soiled with other men's teeth and tongues. What he could not have anticipated, she knew, was their resemblance to Kirby's. No, nor that same stretch of bones across her chest, the same concavity of collar bones, the identical down of fine blond hair in the hollow of her stomach. She watched his want become urgent, fueled by likeness, by the perversion of likeness. Become need.

"Don't pretend it's all about getting even," he ordered. "Don't deny you've flirted with me from day one. You've always been jealous of Kirby's life. Admit it."

What did Michael look like running, escaping into the flesh of some faceless woman? Eliciting another's moans, decoding another body? Kendra wanted to be there in the shadows. Would have traded any hope of his fidelity just to be there now instead of here. She turned her back on Aris. Permitted herself the gesture of covering her breasts.

"Never mind. I've had enough of grabbing and pulling. If I want that, I don't need to commit high treason to get it. If that's all you've got to offer, leave."

But immediately he moved behind her to put his arms around her. Strong arms, bulkier than Michael's despite his lesser age, more fatherly in the stereotypical sort of way. Arms not without their merit. She felt, strangely in his embrace, as though she understood her sister better than she had in a decade. As if this were just the bridge she and Kirby needed. She knew she was deluded. She was nowhere close to right or true. There was nothing here she even desired, nothing except this illusion that had little to do with sex. Except the turn-around of Michael's surprise. Except doing the worst thing she could possibly think of doing so that finally, finally, *finally* there would be nowhere else to go.

"You want nice?" Kissing her neck soft as a tickle. "I can do nice. It's my specialty."

"That's funny," she said. "Kirby doesn't think you're nice at all. She thinks you're aggressive and pushy and frightening."

"Do I scare you?" Maybe he too was tired of being perceived that way, maybe he had a right *not* to be perceived that way. And though she of all women could not possibly perceive him in any way that would offer salvation, maybe he too had the right to want to be saved.

"Nobody scares me," she promised, guiding his thick, warm hands to the breasts he'd already studied so well. "I'm way too busy scaring myself."

So maybe it went like this:

Kirby had apparently told him about the no-underwear thing—on several occasions he'd even teased her about it—but now his hand shot down the back of her pants before lowering them, as though he could not wait to see for himself. Visually reminiscent of bear paws, those hands were remarkably adroit—practiced on Bee's modestly pantied bottom—and tight leather waistbands did not trouble him despite his bulk. Lights on, always on—in Michael's apartment it seemed an unwritten rule. It had never occurred to her, even in his absence, to violate this. Aris flipped her over. Because Kirby wouldn't, or because he couldn't bear to see his fiancée's face staring back at him? Stomach to the bed, pants stiff and squeaky. Crackling down.

"What the hell?"

She had, if you choose to believe her, forgotten the marks were there.

Aris backed away, her pants still around her legs, constraining her movement. When he'd first given her these pants, Michael had zipped and buttoned them up mid-thigh to bind her, folded the waist under to fill out any pocket of air that would allow movement; immovable leather against the furious pressure of thighs trying to break free. For a moment now she believed that if she whirled around it would be the same—a game she could read on her lover's face—but instead when she turned her legs tangled and, drunk, she fell to her knees off the bed.

Something like: "I know we aren't the best of friends but I want to help, I swear I do. Has he threatened you? Did he do this when you tried to leave?" Extending a paw to help her rise, not even the hint of a smirk on his charitable face. "Come on, get dressed. I won't look."

She swatted at him, pushed herself to standing, pubic hair jutting above the wide black V across her thighs. "You have *got* to be kidding."

"Now I see why you wanted to get back at him. Look, he's a maniac, he's not worth it. Come home with me. We won't tell Kirby anything about any of . . . us. It wasn't your fault, it was mine. I was drunk, and I didn't . . . know."

"For God's sake, Aris." Nothing recognizable in him. Without arrogance, smugness, *I told Bee you were a slut*, he seemed a stranger—a victim. She tried, "It's not what you think."

"Have you confided in your mother?"

"If you say anything to my family, I will kill you!" *No*, exhaling between her teeth, *too desperate, too in-denial*. She tried again, "Look, I want it." Yet though true (wasn't it true?), the words bore a hollow ring. "I like it," she explained, copping a smile. "Don't you ever want to?" And shit, not what she'd needed: a brutal hand yanking back her hair to expose her contorted face, or the force with which this body could slam her belly-down, *You like it rough, you'll get it rough, baby*. Her teeth chattered a little knowing how close to broken down she was already and what damage this body could inflict. Still, anything, anything was better than his—*Aris's*—pity. She encircled his thick thumb with her chilled fingers. "Nobody has to know."

"Don't talk like—I'd never want to hurt you—it has to be those painkillers, whatever you're on, this isn't what you really mean." He backed toward the door. Qualified, "If you ever want to talk, but not here, not now. Put your clothes on, Kendra, please."

"Fuck that," she snapped, "I don't have to cover myself so you won't be uncomfortable. You're the one who's deluded— if you don't want to screw, God knows I can't imagine any other use for you—slink back home to Kirby you pitiful coward, she hates you anyway, she'll leave you, it's only a matter of time, she just has to get her courage up—" She kept on shouting, though the volume of her voice made her feel insane, long after Aris had run for his life.

Then, only four Vicodin left. Alone in his room, Kendra counted; no chance this would be sufficient to grant her not waking until after Kirby's wedding. She swallowed them anyway, hard and dry, too weary to rise for water. Heart throbbing in protest—what if all the scotch *did* render the pills a lethal retribution?—she prayed, paradoxically, that her heart could hold out.

Time must have passed because it always does. A body in the room. Next to the bed, the blurred sound of clothing being shed. Darkness, perhaps due to shutting her eyes. The sudden cold of a duvet swept back, his weight on the mattress. She wanted to see him. Could not.

"I notice you've been entertaining."

Her eyes opened forcibly, there, yes; Michael was holding the empty bottle of Glenfiddich, had seen the glasses, two, only one with her dark lipstick. Her head hummed. In the bathroom would be other signs: his condoms broken into, a trail of inside-out clothes revealing stages of undress. She wanted to tell him. He was not holding the bottle or speaking anymore—had stilled. Poked her in the arm, "Hey, are you okay? What did you take? Can you hear me?" She could; somehow let him know she could, that it was fine, that it would pass. He sat on the edge of the bed, his thigh solid against her side. He was saying something like, "Just sleep it off, Kendra." Smoothed back her hair—horribly wrong—not what she expected or deserved at all. He was promising something like, "It is going to be all right."

*　　*　　*

May 1994

Too warm in the room. Too warm for spring in Chicago, a heat wave, a wave of heat inside her stomach that wouldn't be pushed down. Wouldn't go away. Kendra kept the comforter pulled up to her chin. Words did not sound right in her mind: comforter. Comfort her. The need for comfort was an embarrassing one, one to which only those persons who did not seek out trouble were entitled. But she was a warrior, a guarder of secrets, a substitute scapegoat. An avenger. She did not desire *comfort—she who would un-sire, she who was of the sire—she had made a vow to desire nothing except a turn of events. Events had turned. Her stomach had turned. Her skin had turned inside out, was raw and swollen against the flannel sheets of her bed. Not a warrior's bed. Under the blankets, her skinny legs itched and throbbed. It had been easy to get sent home from school—her fever was raging, her face ugly and pale. She was seventeen—no need to call her parents. "Go home," they'd told her. "Take care of yourself." Eighteen next month. Eighteen and a woman. Comforter: the word tangled in her mind, returned hollow and senseless. Surely a letter must be off. Her ass burned too badly for comfort. Too badly to rely on. Too badly to be a plan of attack. If only she could go back and change her strategy. She had misunderstood. Had thought she could feel pain not in her own body, the pain of another who was not really an other. She had been wrong. So wrong.*

It hurt. It was not supposed to be hurting, she was not supposed to be shaking, was not supposed to be pressing her arms so tight, wrapping her arms so tight around herself afraid she would fall in

224

somewhere, be swallowed up into this hot, sweaty comforted room where she was less safe than anywhere else but still she had told her teachers she was ill so they would send her home from school. It hurt, but not so much that she would die, and so there was still some hope of reversal. Still some shot of repair.

Footsteps on the stairs.

She lay still. No, she had already been still. Feigned dead. But this was what she had come home for—this was what she wanted. His feet heavy with conscience: what was he doing? Why was he here? The door to her room opening, and this time there was no protection, no boots by the door, no booby trap to trick him. This was what she wanted: her body bruised from his beating, prostrate on her stomach beneath the pink and white comforter, her comforter coming home to say he was sorry, to tell her he'd been wrong. But no, not after what she'd threatened, not after what she knew. His guilt would tip the scales in her favor. Her body still beneath the covers; his weight on the edge of the bed. She'd meant to be a messiah, to take burden from the poor and heap it upon her own shoulders. Her shoulders screamed with weight and tension. Body on the bed, warrior slain with an arrow. Kendra began to cry.

"Shh, princess," he soothed. "It's going to be all right. I was wrong last night, too harsh, you made me crazy, I couldn't think. I had to use the key, K, sweetheart, you understand that, don't you? I had to find out what you were on. Daddy will fix it. I know you're confused, those pills have confused you, but we're going to get you some help."

Finally, Kendra remembered how to laugh. The memory clutched her so hard she bolted up in bed, screamed through the laughter, "You're not taking me anywhere! You'll have to kill me first! I know what you are—I'll never leave Kirby to you! I've made my offer—that's all you're getting. I'll tell everything, everything, do you hear me? Don't you dare think you win!"

And then only this: one swift movement of his hand. The room was not cold, but suddenly felt so. Then only this: a girl warrior and a man who'd been broken, who had nothing left to lose. Then only this. One swift sweeping aside of the covers, letting in the air.

*   *   *

"Rough night?" Michael was next to her in the bed, leaning back against the headboard, one bare foot tucked under her body—for warmth? Sweet almond aroma from his tea made her stomach growl. Her throat was dry, her head pounding.

"I'm out of Vicodin." It came out a croak. "Will you get more?"

"No." He didn't look her way. His eyes seemed fixed, absently, on the top of the bureau. "Though I'm pretty sure that, for better or for worse, if you'd just see an orthopedic surgeon you could probably walk out with a few prescriptions of your own."

Kendra turned her head with effort to stare directly at his profile. No contact was made. He kept tapping a pen against a *New York Times* crossword. Quick staccatos, so unlike his usual measured nonchalance that panic rose in her throat.

"Nice disclaimer. I'm impressed. Did my mother coach you?"

"Gail didn't show." He extracted his foot. Stood. He had been to the East Bank Club, was wearing gray running shorts and an old Greenpeace T-shirt. His skin would be salty. "Listen, do you want to see *Rent* tonight? I got tickets for Rachel and Chloe for Rachel's birthday, but this morning . . . Rachel isn't feeling up to par, so Leigh's keeping her in. But you and I could go. I thought you might enjoy the dancing."

"I would."

"Good." His back was turned. "It's the least I can do to repay your consideration in not leaving another man's semen in my bed."

"That wasn't my choice."

"Then for having a taste for men who possess better manners than yourself."

Her body sprang to sitting. "You arrogant fuck. How dare you call yourself mannered? What are you even *talking* about? Are you honestly as much of a sociopath as you want me to believe?" Then: "My God. My God, what did I do? Aris."

He turned around. (He had, she noticed, been folding her crumpled clothes. No reason, no precedent for him to be doing this.) "What?"

Flatly: "I invited him here. I got him drunk. I knew I was going to. It was no accident."

A flicker of amusement crossed his lips. Disappeared. "What the hell possessed you?"

"What do you think possessed me?"

The smile came on full force now—smugness, she figured, at being invited into the game of deciphering her. He sat down on the floor as if to think better; she had to prop herself up on her elbow to see him. He was playing with the button of her leather pants now. Twirling it—the action made her nervous, but she did not ask him to stop.

"It's my fault," he concluded. "I annoyed you by not coming home."

She tried for a laugh. No. A sigh instead. "Oh, Michael. Everything is so urbane with you. You annoyed me, so I brought Aris to your bed. Well, that makes perfect sense because I was annoyed. Your not coming home all night after telling me earlier how we should back off annoyed me. That is how I felt, annoyed. Now it's all clear."

"How *did* you feel?"

"None of your damned business."

"All right then. We'll go with annoyed."

Her heartbeat thumped too slowly. Arms hung heavy and sluggish; she couldn't get in a full breath. The pills, she knew. "Just tell me one thing. Why did you have to be so fucking predictable? I thought this mixed message shit was for boys my age, for people still pretending they aren't capable of cruelty. You can't shock me. If you're getting edgy, if you want to walk, don't play games. Don't sleep elsewhere and then invite me to a musical. Just do it."

The metal button of her pants revolved, a tiny top between his fingers—spin, spin. "My evening was not predictable. I wish you were correct, I can't tell you how much I do. Your fantasies are invariably more palatable than reality."

"Are they? Well, I'm glad somebody sees it that way."

He was at the bed again, sitting there on the edge. How many of the pivotal moments of her life had taken place just this way: her body coiled beneath the covers in some state of illness or fear, a man there on the end of the bed, his weight causing disequilibrium to her insulated cocoon? She imagined the strength it would take to pull her feet up and, with an enormous force of energy and will, kick him right onto the floor. She imagined him lying there, startled. What would he do? But no, the scene would still play out the same. He would laugh, or he would stand up and smack her face until she cowered, or he would reprimand her for her childish behavior and shake his head in paternal disgust. Either way his dick would end up inside her; either way she would *want* it there inside her. The outcome was fixed.

She said, "How can even you look at me now? I threw myself at my twin's almost-husband. It doesn't get much worse—I'm the black swan, I'm the one the audience boos."

"Don't do that to yourself. It's pointless. It's beneath you."

"I've done a lot of things you say are beneath me. Many of them with—and to—you."

"I know that. I know it. But if you want me to help you demonize yourself, to say yes you're evil, you're a worthless slut for fucking a man your sister can't stand anyway, bad, bad girl, I'm not playing. What makes you think Kirby's a saint? How do you know what damage she might inflict if she faced life's shit alone the way you do everyday?"

He had done it at last. She could not speak. Stared at him, the gulf of confusion in her chest forming a protective moat around her sluggish heart. She did not say, *So I'm alone then?* She did not say, *Is that what I'm doing, making my sister face life?* She did not say, *Am I facing anything, here hiding under my bruises and my pills, with you telling me I am alone when I'm not, when your voice is as much my rock as Aris's engagement ring is Kirby's?* She did not say, *How, after everything, can you sit here and flatly refuse to see anything but strength in me?*

"Why don't we take a shower?" Almost gently. A hand on her hand. "It's getting late."

"I don't want you to fuck me." All she could manage. Nothing else. She stared at him, his changing eyes, the thinness of his face, the irreverence of the smile he was not showing, that waited for her maybe, not now but sometime in the future.

"Okay," he said.

Rory Kennedy's wedding was off. That was what happened when tragedy struck: weddings were cancelled. The bodies hadn't been found, but if a Kennedy was involved, everyone knew there wouldn't be survivors. Like a biblical parable, that family—a pox on their house. Carolyn Bessette-Kennedy and her sister Lauren were stuck in the crossfire; Lauren left an identical twin behind. That was the one Kendra felt sorry for, though she didn't know her name. Kennedys meant nothing to Kendra. JFK had been assassinated thirteen years before the bicentennial year of her birth, but Michael said he remembered. His family was Irish Catholic Bostonian; his mother had mourned fiercely, had come down with one of her migraines and been unable to cook or even touch the piano. Kendra couldn't relate—she'd been a dancer, not an American; she was a twin, those genes her country of two. How could she be expected to grieve this, these history-making strangers whose tragedies bore no tint of shame and warranted the mourning of a nation? She wondered instead if the bride were secretly glad, not for the deaths but for this sudden salvation. Did Rory love her would-be husband? Or, like Kirby, had she gotten her feet stuck in wet cement and couldn't unstick them without making a mess?

Kendra said, "How can my sister marry? She doesn't even like men."

"That doesn't seem to stop many women," Michael said.

They faced the screen again. Dangerous, this visual and auditory letting in of the world after so many months without TV. She regretted making him forego newspapers in her presence; print was a safer way to learn about death. Images of hugging mourners played. Of John John saluting his dead father, and Kendra imagined Michael, only three years older, frightened in a dark, silent, migraine-proofed house, with no idea he too would not grow up to be a hero. A little boy watching another boy on TV, a boy not really called John John saluting, locking in his fate. Michael had been lucky not to have to salute, to have a father who'd live so Michael could hate him, to grow into a man not a hero. Now the other boy was dead and here was Michael but who could say for how long? Who could predict how far the Braun pox would reach?

"What am I going to do?"

"Since you mentioned it," as if her question were logistical, "move in with me, I believe."

Oh, yes, there were things she knew about him. Basic facts. If she declined cohabitation, he would go on as though he had not offered it, no ultimatums; if she accepted, then found a better alternative, he would act as nauseatingly civilized as she always accused him of being and pretend to be happy for her. And if she merely could not stomach playing stepmom to Rachel, he would not object to her sleeping elsewhere on nights his daughter came, would not trouble himself over whose body she lay under then. Would never offer monogamy, would not consider her giving it as any gift of significant value. There were things she knew, no need to ask.

"Rachel doesn't want you with me. Your ex-wife could use an . . . arrangement . . . like that against you."

"Not a factor." He rolled onto his side to face her. "As it turns out, Leigh will be moving to Colorado permanently within the year. Even Rachel didn't know until . . . of course I insisted on telling her the truth immediately, once I learned. That's why she's too upset to celebrate."

Did Kendra's heart soar, or just lurch? "You're giving Leigh sole custody? Out of state?"

"Actually . . ." slowly, "Rachel will remain behind. She'll stay here for some long stretches while Leigh gets settled, then after she graduates she'll spend the summer with her mother. For ninth grade, she'll begin boarding school at Lake Forest Academy. I'll be able to drive up to see her anytime I like, and she'll still be here weekends. But summers she'll be out West, and during the work week, you and I would be alone."

Her throat closed on questions like a vise. The cleanliness of this plan felt wrong; Michael had never mentioned boarding school for Rachel, nor did Leigh Kelsey seem the sort of woman to abandon her precious daughter for cowboys and ski studs. There were things she did not know—that she had misjudged, that no one was telling her. And things she still knew, that no disappearing ex-wife or boarded-up daughter could change.

That erotic obsession was built on mystery. That she and Michael might not weather proximity. That he could end up being the one who wanted out.

He watched closely. "I only want to do this if you feel able to handle the risks involved."

Deadpan: "This isn't *Story of O*. Remember, in ballet nobody dies once the audience has gone home. I'm classically trained, so please, don't develop a Sir Stephen complex on me."

He burst out laughing. "Kendra, you never fail to astound me."

CNN droned on, relentless in pursuit of bodies not found—what would it take to be a body not found? Somewhere, another twin grieved.

"Ask me again the night of Kirby's wedding," she said. "I'll give you my answer then."

So maybe it went like this:
Exhausted from their afternoon without sex, they finally simply did cocaine.

"I'm not sure about this," Michael said. His hesitance thrilled her. "I don't do drugs well. They make me reckless and stupid."

"As opposed to methodical and manipulative like the rest of the time?"

"Exactly," he concurred.

"Where's your sense of nostalgia?" A giggly, schoolyard pusher. "Come on, Mister I-bought-a-Porsche-in-the-eighties. Tell me the truth, Michael, were you a Reagan Democrat? Or did a hard-on for Ferarro save your soul?"

He crossed his heart: "Geraldine all the way." Sincere as a Boy Scout. He'd never been a Boy Scout. Had played kickball in alleys, paid neighborhood girls to pull down their pants. Hadn't learned to swim until he was twenty. He'd never gone to camp. Now he wanted to take her camping. To bury her cigarettes in a hole and watch her go crazy from withdrawal. She wanted to let him. Better he should enter her world first, though, so someday, once they were living together, if he told her not to get high anymore he would have done it with her and it would not be like her father telling her, so she wouldn't have to say no. She was not sure he would ever ask her not to get high anymore. She could not imagine him saying it. She did not want him to require it of her, but at the same time she did.

"Just say yes. It's the last of what I've got. I hadn't done any in half a year, not since New York. This was a gift from a friend of Guitarist's who wanted to take me to bed. If you do it with me, I'll tell you if I went and if I liked it. I want to see you high. I want you to get reckless and stupid and make me promises you don't really mean. I'd like to believe you."

"Sorry," he said. "Even flying I'd know better than to tell you anything but the truth. You'd laugh in my face if I did."

"Maybe. Maybe I'd enjoy it just the same. I'm willing to bet you're an excellent liar."

He did not resist her. Probably he never meant to resist her. It was not the first time he'd done coke, she knew. He'd had a life without her, a past without her that was longer than the length of time she'd been alive. There had been nights with his ex-wife, nights with her father, nights with the lovers he'd accumulated while his ex-wife was sleeping with her father. There had been, yes, but maybe they were safer nights with safer people, people who hadn't seemed safe at the time but did now that he knew her. Maybe there'd been less at stake, less need to hang on to control. Yet he would not resist. She had given him things that transcended reason or simple submission. It was not gratitude; he was not grateful. But her recklessness precluded resistance. This was nothing. This was a matter of an increase in heart rate, a matter of heightened arousal, of a stimulated nervous system. He was a man whose livelihood depended on recognition of a fair exchange. He offered this paltry one without battle. Submitted.

"We'll do the rest later," she instructed him. "I want it totally gone by tomorrow."

Stoically, he gave himself over to her wish.

Though she'd seen *Rent* before, somehow she'd forgotten—or never noticed the first time around—how this insipid musical, based on an insipid opera, portrayed AIDS as nothing but a political stamp of approval, a PC calling card for the artsy and cool. Kendra was grateful for intermission, still unused to sitting in the audience rather than being onstage or watching performances from the wings. A boulder had lodged in her larynx, eyes burning too; she felt shamefully conspicuous among the anonymous crowd. Why, why had she come?

"I'm having a hard time standing still," Michael confessed during intermission. But when she slowed her own panther-in-a-cage pacing, he seemed to blend into the pillar he was leaned against, motionless as a statue, so she didn't know whether to believe him. A synthetic xylophone alerted them to return to their seats. Obediently, audience members filed past. Fear clogged her throat.

"We could cut out," she suggested.

"Why?"

A trick question. Mimi wasn't dead yet—how could they leave? Except unlike *La Bohème*, in *Rent* she didn't die, came back to life right there on a table. That was nearly possible now, here on the brink of the millennium. One could almost die and never get there. One could go on living for years. There was the assumption that this was progress. Kendra's father was a heretic. He was a dinosaur; he insisted on going the traditional way. He would neither grant his survivors hope nor prolong their agony. But Mimi was young and gorgeous. Everybody loved a young, gorgeous woman on the brink of death. Tickets sold at $67.50 a pop.

"Rachel and Chloe would have fallen in love with Mimi," Kendra said. "They would have wanted to *be* her." She pressed her hands to her sides to stop their shaking.

"Let's go." Michael abandoned his wine without having taken more than two sips. Set it down slow—it was all she could do not to race ahead of him out into the gray street. He seemed not to be allowing himself much movement, as though he feared that if he gave in to motion, he would not be able to stop. She did not want it within his control. He wasn't responding enough, was not the way she'd imagined him: manic, wild, without logic or boundaries. She wasn't sure drugs could do that, only that she needed it from him. Needed to see.

Rain drenched them before they reached his car. Hard, pounding, so that once inside they could sit there right in the open and measure the white powder out just so for their next lines. She let him do it—her hands were shaky from the show. Let him snort first too: tip his head back hard, swallow deep. The action was greedy and graceless; there was no way he could lend it dignity. But the rush was in him this time, she could see it. "Oh."

"Are you there now?"

Her body was in his arms with a swoop, close and wet. A kiss that tasted of New York, of dance class and youth, of black, black night. Something like, "Anyplace you want me to be."

"Good. Good."

"Where are we going, Kendra?" He had never before asked, not even for her approval of his own suggestions. Her heart raced though she had not yet done her next lines.

"To your office. Do you have the key?"

"Of course. There's a security guard, but we can sign you in under any name you like."

"Maybe I'll use my sister's."

"I don't think so. After last night, I'd prefer another theme."

Wheels spun to motion on wet pavement with a jerk. No matter, the street was nearly empty. She could barely see in front of her through the window. Lightning exposed the sky; thunder and the incessant drumbeat of jagged drops screamed warnings. Inside the Porsche, the air was thick with humidity, heavy with her perfume. The veins in Michael's gear-shifting hand bulged with blood coursing too fast, just right. Kendra leaned her head back at last, throat runny and sore and bitter, in anticipation of the ride.

Hysteria

I now believe that you and I are, strangely
enough, included among those who are
doomed to live.

—William Faulkner,
Absalom, Absalom!

Altar or Bust

THESE WERE THE words we lived with: perforation, stomach acids, sepsis. They could not define the body that lay behind the door we could not enter. These were the excuses we heard for three days: she's an adult, her choice, nothing we can do. My mother sat in a mauve chair the exact color I'd always imagined graced the walls of Kendra's apartment. How was it possible that I had never been to my sister's apartment? My mother shook, her body trembled in my grasp. She said things over and over and over: my fault, it is my fault, she always hated me. My mother spoke in the words of a mourner, the only words that made sense. She could not separate the living from the dead. I pulled my arms from around her shoulders to order, *Stop, stop, this is not about you*. But no words came, only my arms sliding back to my sides, empty. No sound.

Before dawn on a Monday morning, cocaine coursing in her system, my twin sister had somehow broken down the locked door to her unfeasibly well-stocked kitchen and systematically eaten until her stomach ruptured and she was rendered unconscious. That was all we knew.

Otto sat across from us in respectful distance. Three days, he'd been here. We waited, all but my father who couldn't come to the hospital for fear of germs. We waited like statues. At the Presbytery, the secretary, an old woman who sent my mother home with a fruitcake every Christmas, spoke into a telephone to postpone my wedding. *The maid of honor is sick.* The honorable maid would have died. Would have except Otto had shown up at her door to return her wallet—"She'd, uh, left it in my car." Her door had been open. My sister, everyone knew, had long held little faith in locked doors. He'd walked right in, headed for the bedroom. She was not in bed. The kitchen door was off its hinges. Suddenly, the unlocked door grew ominous. Otto had wished for a gun. He did not know how to use one, but thought, *If I nailed a rapist, maybe she'd forgive me.* He'd been standing there, half in terror, half in Jackie Chan bravado, when he noticed her bare feet splayed out across the floor.

These were the words we heard: surgery, fever, intravenous antibiotics. Conscious, unconscious, sleeping, awake. *Your daughter, your sister, your first love doesn't want to see you.* Go home, we'll call if there's any change.

At the Presbytery, the secretary said, *The wedding will be rescheduled. Probably early autumn. There's been a serious accident. Very serious, but we do hope everything will be okay.*

This was what we did: drank coffee, read magazines, watched my mother whisper, palm cupped over her cell phone, to update my father. Aris came between job interviews, loomed like a giant in the undersized chairs. His feet tapped; the leather of his soles pounded out a beat fast as my heart. At night, he sat outside the bathroom, offered to refill the pills I'd arrogantly tossed out my car window, and when I sobbed so hard I couldn't breathe, his arms around me were the only thing to keep me human, my wailing like an empty well, so hollow, so dry, but I couldn't stop. I shat and wept and fell asleep with exhaustion in his arms to wake up and go back to the hospital. I dared eat nothing for fear I'd shit there too. My skirts hung loose around the waist. I could not look at food without thinking of what she did, but in the evening my hunger caught up with me; I grew mad with it. Every night I broke my vigil with pizza, McDonald's, KFC. I was too weary to prepare meals, and Aris would hold me but he would not (could not) cook.

In the mornings, my mother's clothes were different as she cornered Dr. Rosenthal again demanding to be let into Kendra's room. In the mornings, Otto wore the same second-hand bowling shirt, hair pulled back in the same matting ponytail as he slouched outside the entrance for a cigarette break. He was the one who grabbed my wrist fast to keep me from sliding away, finally muttered, "Um, has anybody called, uh, Michael—he was the last to see her." But when I asked how he knew, he just wiped his nose on his shirt. Challenged, "She *looked* liked she'd been with him." And when I asked what that meant, he stared at me like I was playing some phony ingenue role. I conceded only, "They've called everyone invited. He's on the list."

In a safe church office, an old, fruitcake-giving woman in a floral printed dress recited, *I'm calling to let you know the wedding had to be postponed. It's a family emergency, a member of the immediate family is sick. Please, just hold on to any gift you may have bought.*

Across Chicago and the North Shore suburbs, would-be guests thought: *Poor Henry. Cancer, you know. Couldn't hold off 'til the wedding. That poor man is finally going to die.*

If she developed sepsis, her own IV could kill her. If her stomach acids had eaten away at her stomach and other organs, if her fever didn't go down, if her organs began to fail. Even if she lived, there could be neurological damage. Even if she lived and sustained no neurological damage, she might be declared a danger to herself and get transferred to the psychiatric ward. Even if she ever made it out of a locked ward where they followed her into the bathroom to keep her safe from herself, she would have a scar for the rest of her life where they'd cut through her stomach muscles. She could not eat or piss or sit by herself in the ICU. Could speak when she was awake, but they would not tell us what she said. If she said anything other than that she would not see us. My mother sent a cleaning service to the apartment Kendra had planned to move out of after my wedding. People whose name I would never know disposed of all evidence. Afterward, I would wish I'd gone to clean things up myself. I would wish I'd seen with my own eyes. That week, though, it did not occur to me. Otto tried to fill me in, tried to purge himself too by describing the scene. "It was unbelievable," he said. "You would not have believed so much food could fit inside such a tiny body." My mother answered for me, though. "It *couldn't*," she clarified, voice ice and poise and an intolerable level of grief. "My baby. My baby, oh God," and rocked away from me so I slithered from her grieving body toward more coffee and a shared cigarette outside with Otto. He cried into the unmoved and unmoving brick, admitted, "We had a terrible fight. I threw her out of my car, called her a whore and pushed her and tried to steal her purse." He qualified, "I wasn't thinking, she made me so crazy; she was crying and I was proud I'd finally made her cry." I stared at him. How many times would I have liked to throw my sister out of my car and make her weep if I could? I could not indict him. Couldn't console him either. I left him there against the building with the guilt he needed in order to believe he mattered in all this. I knew he did not matter. I knew that something mattered and that it was not any action of his. I could not place what the thing that mattered was.

Day four. Two days prior to what would have been my wedding. In lieu of vows of sanctity and forever, I had doctors in anonymous hallways, complicit elevator conferences far from the earshot of others. Dr. Rosenthal, blue-eyed and blue-robed, pulled me aside: "I've been wanting to speak to you alone. I don't want to worry your mother." All-business: "We couldn't help but notice marks on the backs of her thighs . . . and buttocks. Skin is broken and scabbed."

I looked away, muttered, "Oh, sure, Kendra's always injuring herself, she teaches ballet, she's reckless with her body, she roller-blades and rides her bike without a helmet—"

"Miss Braun, I'm no psychiatrist. But the motive of making some boyfriend sorry might go a long way toward explaining why she did this."

I shook my head. "No, Kendra doesn't even have a boyfriend, so that's not possible."

"Okay . . . or sometimes, women become very distraught following a sexual assault."

Very distraught. Oh yes, my sister must have been very distraught. I looked at him, this man of gray hair and blue coat and eyes cloaked behind glasses and invulnerability to bruises and lacerations and perforations and rape. I did not know how to make his language work for me. I wanted to cry, to embarrass him with a woman's tears, to fall safely behind what had always protected me in a way nothing like his blue coat and gray hair protected him but was the only protection I'd ever known. I wanted to cry but couldn't. I thought of her; her coldness gripped my throat. I thought of her and of how much I wanted to fall to the ground and weep at the feet of this man who had named something I was too petrified to name. Her possession of my body began with a bubble in my throat. Rising. A giggle.

"Kirby, maybe you had better go home."

The elevator door opened.

And you, of course, can testify: doctors always know best.

His number was listed, of course. He was a middle-aged man, one who made hundreds of thousands of dollars a year and lived in a high-rise with security and thick, almost soundproof walls. He had nothing to fear. I stood at a pay phone on Damen, because Aris had refused to give me his cell phone in case he got a call back for a second interview. I'd had to drive almost all the way home from Northwestern University Hospital, where my sister would or would not die, before I'd worked up the nerve to make this call. I stood at the pay phone across from Wicker Park, where the homeless men and yuppies with their Labradors were out in full force, it being summer and the night being hot. I had a sense of déjà vu, though I'd never used this phone nor called this man. The line rang four times before his machine picked up—I had expected voicemail. His voice confirmed the number I'd reached, did not speak his own name, did not say, *You've reached Michael Kelsey*, much less, *Hi, this is Mike.* But after he had given the number, a girl's voice—Rachel's, of course—chimed in, "We can't come to the phone, but you can leave us a message." Oh God, criminal, my intentions! I imagined her, though it had been years since I'd seen her, a dark-haired child, darker than either of her parents, eyes a brown that was almost black. But beautiful like them. Stunning, in the way her mother was blatantly gorgeous, not in the quiet fashion of her father, whose beauty was not so recognizable until he moved or spoke. I'd held her in my arms, I'd changed her diapers, and so instead of what I'd planned I could only choke, "Mr. Kel-this is Kirby. I need . . . would like to talk to—"

The machine dismissed me with a shrill beep—I'd waited too long. I hung up. Even though I was blocks from the loft and it was after dark and one of the men across the street called out, "Hey Red, hey pretty Red," I left my car where it was and walked the rest of the way home.

Fear of Snakes

ARIS, NATURALLY, WAS home. He was not, at least anymore, the type of man to stay out late, to get drunk, to stink my bed up with liquory sweat and mutter the names of other women in his sleep. He was waiting for me. Though he'd not actually ordered the pizza, the Leona's menu was on the counter; he'd merely waited to hear whether my stomach held up well enough today to handle dairy or whether I wanted pasta instead. His shirt was off—the loft was hot—and the bulk of his body alarmed me. At his sides, the mass of him grew soft, slid into a proverbial spare tire. Love handles. I imagined myself under Aris, grasping the fat on his sides and using it like a steering wheel to guide him into my body. In reality, it was an unwritten law that I should never touch the deposits of lethargy and age that marred his once-perfect football-captain's physique. Now, though, I wished my sister's body were so padded, so shielded. I conjured Aris on an operating table, sliced open, fat peeled back to get at muscle that needed to be cut, his spurting stomach in the stitching hands of a surgeon. Perhaps they'd toss Aris's fat into a bucket on the floor full of dirty surgical instruments: liposuction for free. Perhaps his heartier body could withstand such acts against nature. I stared at the Leona's menu. So much to choose from on a pizza alone: pesto, alfredo or traditional tomato sauce, stuffed crust or thin. So much in this world that one could eat.

Nonplused, Aris stared blankly at the TV, another retrospective of JFK Jr.'s brief, hot, tragic life. The whole thing enraged me in a cloudy, childish way—the assumption of mourning for a famous stranger. If Kendra had remained a ballerina, become a principal dancer, maybe there would have been some small sidebar of news about her as well, nearly lost among the Kennedy shuffle. As it was, she didn't merit even that.

I told Aris, in hushed tones, about the bruises. I added things Dr. Rosenthal had not said. "There's no way this could have been caused by any accident, everything is too localized. Somebody has to have beaten her. That's why she did this to herself. To make him sorry." I did not know why I felt such keen need to tie cords together, to make a perfect fit of motive and execution—as though Kendra had premeditated the results of her actions to the T. As though she would even have known such a thing could happen. Then, because Aris was a man, because he had worked with men, because he had seen the man who did this in that mysterious context of men-only and might therefore be privy to secrets beyond me, I begged, "Would he do that? Michael Kelsey? Is he a violent person? Or do you think it was somebody else—a stranger she picked up? Dr. Rosenthal thinks maybe she was raped and just didn't tell any—"

"Michael did it." Quietly. He pressed the mute button, but even without sound, any American could follow the program. We were all in this together, like it or not. My jaw shook.

"How do you know? Did he tell you?" Then, disbelief fading, it all seemed plausible—crystallized. Michael Kelsey bragging at work, how she got out of line and he taught her a lesson. The other men, laughing atop my father's impending grave. And Aris, Aris who wanted to fit in, who wanted to succeed, who hated Kendra anyway, blamed her for everything wrong between us . . . "What, you didn't think it was *important* enough to bother mentioning to me?"

"Stop it!" He rose from the couch, finger pointed at me. "I'm trying to tell you now—do you hear how crazy you sound, the kinds of spiteful conclusions you jump to about the man you're supposed to marry? What's wrong with you?"

Trembling, even my voice vibrated: "Don't . . . you . . . point. You're not my father."

"Damned right," he muttered. "I don't screw around, I don't get diseases, I don't hang out with men who beat up girls half their age to get off. But God forbid you even appreciate—"

241

"What I'd appreciate is your getting off your high horse and telling me the truth!"

"Bull. You don't want the truth, you want me to be the bad guy. Well I'm sorry, but the truth is that I know about Kendra's disgusting scabby ass because *she* told me about it and how she likes it and wants Michael Kelsey to do it to her. She wanted me to do it too!"

"Liar! You haven't even seen Kendra in months!"

"I saw her Saturday night, the night before Otto found her." His voice was calm, rational, suddenly sure in where it planned to go. "She lured me to Michael's apartment in the middle of the night and pelted me with scotch and stripped and waved her bruised-up body in front of me and said you didn't love me and wouldn't give a crap if I slept with her. That's your poor, victimized sister for you, Kirby. I begged her to leave Michael and she laughed in my face."

But being a twin had long ago destroyed all vestiges of compassion, perspective, and decency in me. I could manage only: "You saw my sister *naked*?"

He snorted. "It was no glimpse of paradise, believe me."

"You slept with her!"

Somehow he was in the kitchen, had moved his conspicuous frame from the leather sofa to my stool at the counter. "You actually think I'd want someone like that, under those circumstances? You think—what?—I picked up the nearest weapon and knocked her emaciated body around until . . . Okay then, that's what happened. I screwed her 'til her nose bled. Those bruises the doctor saw, I made them. Would that finally satisfy you?"

His sarcasm could not untangle their bodies writhing together in my mind's eye. "Hey, don't sweat it, you deserve a good lay, God knows we haven't had one in years. I can't be jealous after all—I did it too."

"Did what? You did what too?"

Sneering, I felt it on my face, in the curl of my nose: "Got me a girl, of course." But when he didn't react—I *needed* him to react—I couldn't stop there. "I mean, did you honestly think you could turn me against my twin with your stupid dick? How pathetic, to believe that thing between your legs makes the world go 'round, when all the time I—"

"Shut up!" The crash of kitchen stool into wall, wooden legs splintered, shattered; sweeping clean the counter, toaster clanking to the floor. Adrenalin tinny in my mouth; the singular effort of not cowering arms-over-head. I noticed I was still sitting erect, staring at him. Heard myself, "Yeah, *that'll* get me hot—big strong man. In fact, whenever I'm in bed with a new woman, I always ask her, *Hey, honey, could you, like, smash a chair—*"

I didn't feel the impact to the left side of my face until I was on the floor. My fallen stool pinned my legs; I was too surprised to push it off. Nobody besides Kendra had ever hit me. The side of my face swelled already; blood pulsed there, rushed to the site of the wound.

"Kirby, oh my God, I didn't mean—"

But I could still speak. "Do you feel like Howard Roark conquering Dominique, you boring sonofabitch—"

"Don't talk like *her*!" He lurched again, but I screeched, scooted backward and recoiled fetal-like, clinging to the leg of the one stool still standing, kicking him off. He fought me for the stool, yanked it upwards with powerful hands until I realized if I did not let go he would raise me right to my feet where he would have clear aim. When I surrendered, Aris veered a little; the stool shot above his head. He loomed so high above me I could barely distinguish his features through my one unswollen eye, stool poised to strike . . .

Instinct kicked in. Crouched low, face shielded, whimpering—I saw nothing else. The stool descended; chaos— I waited for impact. Following the crash, Aris's low, guttural growls, breath heavy, the animal *Arrgggrh's* of his frustration. Sounds of him pacing the kitchen. Slowly I opened my eyes, understood that he'd smashed the last stool onto the counter; its remains lay fragmented around me. I pushed myself up from the wood-splattered floor to see the great body of my fiancé leaning against the counter, his shoulders convulsing with sobs.

"Your family turned me into someone I don't recognize." Incredulous, a whisper. Tears dripped from his chin. "All this time, you were the problem, not her. *You* were the lesbian."

His name was on the lease. But in the world we lived in, under the laws we knew, I was not the sort of woman who would ever have to evacuate her home. So he packed his gym-bag with clean underwear, a toothbrush, shaving gear. And became part of the periphery.

When in doubt, drink. I started at eleven; by eleven thirty I was numb. Aris and I were not big partiers. We had no hard liquor in the house, so I contented myself with downing an entire bottle of red wine within forty minutes. My face didn't hurt anymore, though my head was starting to. The limitations of alcohol were disheartening; I found it hard to understand why my father had so believed it could save him. Finally, tingly and somewhat calmer, but nowhere near blissful oblivion, I staggered to the shower. Unlike wine, water could at least purify me of the rank stench of fear heavy on my body. I let it pour, dazed by the sight of Aris's shampoo, confused by his robe hanging on the door. My achy bowels were mercifully empty; I had not eaten in twenty-four hours. The loft was humid, the water hot, and eventually I grew dizzy, heart racing, so I had to leave the baptismal bath to collapse naked on the (my) tainted bed.

When the buzzer rang, my first fear was that it had to be Aris, regretting his pangs of conscience and coming to finish me off. Naturally, though, Aris had a key. More likely it was Otto, drunk from the Rainbo and wanting to crash on my couch instead of facing the trek back to Andersonville alone and depressed. I buzzed him in, wrapping a towel around myself clumsily and weaving to the door, which I flung open at the same instant a knock began.

The hall was dark. Michael Kelsey stood with less than a foot of space between us, staring at me. I immediately grabbed for my towel, tightening it around my breasts. Backed a step away, but he failed to avert his eyes in any show of even mock-politeness. Sweat beaded on my skin afresh. He had not crossed the threshold into the loft, and I contemplated slamming the door on him before I realized it was not my body he was gawking at but my face. He said, not tentatively, "So you finally ended that engagement of yours once and for all."

I touched my left temple, the swelling tender under my fingers. "You missed your calling, obviously. You should have been a detective."

"A black eye is a small price to pay to be rid of Aris, I'm sure." He stepped inside so I could (reluctantly) close the door behind him. Gestured to my towel, which I no longer clutched but which had mercifully not dropped to the ground in my drunken stupor. "Why don't you put something on that requires less vigilance on both our parts, Kirby?" A wry, crooked grin, one I too had known since childhood. "I promise not to steal anything while you're gone."

When I returned, robed in drawstring Gap workout pants and a white T-shirt (with bra), he was seated on the sofa. The TV was still on mute, and though he wasn't looking at it, I hastily shut it off. Once I stood in front of him, I lost all sense of what to do with my arms.

He instructed me. "Sit down."

Aris and I had never bought much furniture, but our sofa was enormous, easily accommodated four people across. Michael Kelsey sat compactly at one end, directly facing my decimated kitchen. I placed myself on the loft's one chair, almost twenty feet away from him.

"I don't want to intrude any more than necessary," he said when I failed to indicate why I'd called to mutter gibberish into his machine. "I didn't find out until a few hours ago. I'd assumed your postponed wedding was due to a worsening in Henry's condition, and that Kendra was dealing with the . . . baggage . . . associated with his dying of AIDS. I wasn't surprised not to have heard from her. Once I got your call, I realized I'd misread the situation."

"How did you find out then? From your ex-wife?"

"Gail. But only because I phoned her and threatened to go see Henry otherwise."

He confused me. "Why would my mother view your seeing my father as a threat?"

His eyebrows pulled in with curiosity. "Kirby, she knows about Kendra's involvement with me. She's known for weeks."

The butterflies in my stomach picked up speed. Empty or not, I had the feeling my body was not going to hold out much longer without a detour to the toilet. Despite my obsession earlier that evening with the discovery of truth, now I wanted only for him to leave.

"Kendra could get sepsis!" I hoped, I think, to frighten him, to guilt him into flight. "Or organ failure—she could die there and it would be your fault. You're sick! My poor mother, how dare you call her and flaunt your attempted murder of her child in her face?"

A long inhale. I watched the movement of breath in his stomach and thought of my sister, whose inhalations filled her chest instead, the way ballerinas are taught. Diaphragmatic breathing might make their stomachs swell unflatteringly onstage. Or perhaps there was another reason, one more to do with endurance than aesthetics. Michael Kelsey's breath was slow and even. With his slimness and grace and calm solemnity, wearing a cream-colored, collarless shirt with loose khaki shorts, he struck me as a monk in meditation. The fallacy disgusted me.

He began, "As an aspiring psychologist and her twin, you should know more than anyone that I'm not the totem father here. I pushed Kendra over the edge, okay, I accept that, so perhaps I should bear all blame courteously. But it's hard enough to face that, to the woman I love, I've been a mere repetition compulsion of Henry. No. I am far too angry to accept more."

"What a cop out! How dare you imply that my father is the cause of Kendra's binge? Our father worships Kendra, he can't help being sick! What gives you the right to waltz in here flinging psychoanalytic jargon around as some trick to make him share your guilt?"

"I find it hard to believe you're as naïve as you're pretending. But if you are, if you really don't know what I'm talking about, then I had better leave, because there is nothing I will say to improve your already troubled world."

Chill, chill, the tremors began again. Here was the last moment in which I could have jumped up and shown him the door. Here was the last moment in which I could have wrapped my ignorance around me tight as skin. My bones shook, the kind of shaking that made what I'd experienced with Aris a few hours before seem a flutter. This trembling originated so deep it was not visible on my skin. I looked into his eyes, gray and deceptively clear, this snake charmer who'd used his melodies to make my family secrets come slithering out from under a dark, wet stone. This boatman who had transported my sister to the shores of death and left me to foot the bill. I had never hated any person so completely. Yet if he had put his arms around me, my shaking would have stilled. The power he wielded was venom, the power of knowledge.

"Tell me. Tell me *everything*."

But after the farthest moment-long journey I had ever traveled, he offered only, "What Kendra does with her past does not belong to me."

"As though you don't know full well it's too late for discretion!"

Michael Kelsey stood to leave. "And you know full well that I have not been discreet."

I rose fast to block him. "You said you love her! If you do, you'll help me help her. Love doesn't mean saying what she'd want you to even if it kills her."

His smile was grim. "Yes, I always forget that to young girls, love is a Band-Aid that can repair even the ugliest of situations, casting them in a romantic light. The idea of my so much as touching Kendra makes you sick—you can't even bring yourself to call me by my first name—yet you hope to soothe your pain with the sentimental notion that my love, as per your definition of course, can somehow save her now. Here is the truth, Kirby. A twenty-three-year-old woman almost died. I had a hand in it." He glanced at the door, buried his hands in deep pockets. "And this conversation is a joke—I never said *love*, not in seven months. But then, Kendra's wise enough to get that love can't save us from anything. Henry loves her, look what that's done."

The bottle of wine on the coffee table was suddenly in my hand. I hurled it, still drunk and half stumbling; it missed his head but knocked him on the shoulder so he reeled back and wound up on the couch again, his other hand moving to check the assaulted arm. He made no noise of pain or surprise, gave no reprimand for my outburst, merely sat there as though he'd never risen at all. "I could kill you!" I screamed. "You think you can just say 'oh yes, I pushed her over the edge' and never think of it again. How can you even stand yourself?" Crying, despite my efforts not to, phlegm and strain. He watched me cry. Seemed unconscious of the fact that he was watching until I shouted, "Stop *looking* at me stop it stop it what the hell is the matter with you are you insane!" Then he lowered his eyes, still holding his battered arm. Remained seated as though knocked of all intentions to depart, eyes averted while I wept.

"Excuse my inappropriate curiosity," he said once I'd calmed. "It's just that you're more uncannily like her than either of you seem inclined to believe."

"Go to the damn hospital if you want to stare at my sister so badly! Just think, then you could torment our mother some more! Oh, but you wouldn't want to face what you've done to Kendra in person. She wouldn't look so sexy in a hospital bed, I'm sure."

"*Are* you sure?" Laughter, a short, scathing burst. "Then maybe you don't understand nearly so much about all this as you think you do." The fear on my face must have been visible, because he added, voice gentler, "Any man ridiculous enough to think he could save Kendra from herself would be wasting his time. That was never my place—she made her own choices. I would not patronize her by believing my feelings of guilt mean I had more power than I did."

"I want you the hell out of my house."

"A smart idea." Once more he got to his feet. Looked, I was grateful to note, significantly less collected than upon arrival, his movements less fluid now that his shoulder was hurting, that his mind was cluttered, perhaps, with my grief and blame. When he reached the door, he turned to face me again, but his gaze was no longer hard and deciphering. Instead he looked baffled, as though he had found himself on quicksand, ground sinking fast, and was out of time. He reached to block my slamming the door in his face, but his grasp felt random; he knocked the door chaotically, almost blind. *He is not even seeing me now.*

"Kendra will let you in soon." More than a promise— almost a plea. "If there's one crime solely on my head in all this, it's that I lost the nerve to name her demon, precisely when she most needed it named. Please, Kirby. Don't make the same mistake."

And my sister's lover left much as my own lover had earlier: amidst my silence and my rage, closing the door carefully behind him.

I STOOD AT THE NURSES' station of Kendra's new, non-IC ward and shouted my sister's name. Stood wailing like a town crier until the nurses came in droves. Stood as tears streamed from the puffed-up, purple meat that was my left eye. A monster in a loose lavender sundress, screaming, "I love you, I need to see you, please please please let me in!" Nurses' arms swooped around me; they smelled of antiseptic and powder and sour women's sweat. Of motherhood and hairspray and new chalky lipstick. Their arms were black and white and brown and fat and thin; I collapsed into them murmuring her name. It was early morning, pre-visiting hours. I had told myself, sleepless, that I could sneak through the halls unnoticed — an invisible twin — but no, sore and haunted, I was visible still. The nurses led me to the lounge, handed me coffee, swore to me that Kendra was getting stronger, that was why she left the ICU, there would be no sepsis, the danger had passed. "We'll get Dr. Rosenthal, he'll want to tell you himself. She could be home in less than a week, even if she's acting funny now she'll see you then, she's just ashamed, they get that way, the ones who hurt themselves, they don't want to hear I told you so." I wanted my mother. I never wanted to see my mother again. I wept, but although it worried the nurses in their aromatic and sparkly uniforms, it seemed a normative state to me. They soothed me. "She's very strong considering. It couldn't have been a suicide attempt, just an accident. She didn't mean to die. The ones who don't want to die sometimes end up just fine."

Dr. Rosenthal arrived. Emerged from around a corner, from another world of patients and family and frantic desperation, his blue coat and blue eyes and blue blood intact. I hated him. In that moment, as much as I hated Michael Kelsey with his quiet dignity and confidently mellow voice completely incompatible with the image of a madman viciously beating my sister's bare skinny prostrate ass until it was covered with bruises and crusty scabs. I hated this doctor for his indifference, for our anonymity to him, for his (correct) belief that our pain was no worse than any other pain he saw during any other day. I could no longer feel the arm of the nurse around me, a plump and pretty African-American girl a bit older than I, whose nametag read SHADISHA. I wanted her to hate Dr. Rosenthal too. I longed to bury my face between her breasts, to eat her skin and forget that everything I'd ever learned in Race and Gender seminars would indicate that she probably had a rougher life than I and should not by any law of reason be comforting me. Withdrawing her embrace, she said firmly, "I know you're hurting, but remember, Kendra's been through hell, and if you love her you'll be strong." Then abandoned me so Dr. Rosenthal could sit next to my shirking, black-eyed self, and he, the man who had birthed harmful knowledge and bottomless helplessness into my world smiled at me and said, "Good news. Your sister will see you now."

Entering Kendra's room, more than a twinge of fear. She was, I realized for the first time in twenty-three years, absolutely and irredeemably beyond me. I did not know the name of her battle; I did not know its terms. From the doorway, she looked asleep, propped up with pillows, her feet making small lumps under the blanket nowhere near the foot of the bed. Her face, devoid of her usual black cherry lipstick, was almost colorless, hair limp, neither styled nor in her ballerina's bun. A small bandage covered her (bluish) lower lip awkwardly, no place to really affix. I imagined her biting through her own flesh during her binge, blood mixing with the—but I did not *know* what she'd eaten. The scar from where they'd cut through her muscles to stitch her stomach lay buried under blanket and hospital gown. I was overcome by a macabre desire to see it. Could hardly contain myself from asking as I sat, tentative so as not to hurt her, at the edge of the bed. Her eyes remained closed, even as I felt her body register mine. Up close, her skin smelled wrong, not the Ananya perfume oil we used, nor our Aveda conditioner, nor her favorite Nag Champra incense (which I'd detected once even inside a borrowed pair of her shoes), but rather disinfectant. The alcohol stench of cotton swabs sterilizing skin.

"Well it looks as if I've finally gone mad," she said slowly, and smiled.

A catch in my throat like I might cry.

Eyes still shut: "Please don't. Promise, or I'll have to make you leave."

"I won't," I said. And two tears slid down my cheeks. She held her hand blindly out to me, and I grasped it—so frail it felt, and hot. How had I ever allowed things to go this far? Remembering a decade of family jokes ("Let's go out for Ethiopian, maybe Kendra will finally finish her food") and my envy of her litheness fueled my self-loathing. Knowing that this frail-limbed, hollow-eyed creature had been having sex with men at all was beyond frightening, but to know that she had been abused, regularly beaten by a lover she'd trusted since our girlhood, was unthinkable. It was almost upon me to decide that Aris had made it all up to torture me, that her injuries were not Michael Kelsey's fault. But though he'd made no specific reference to hitting her, violence had lain implicit in every sentence he'd uttered, an underlying given he couldn't even muster up the shame to hide. I clutched her hand tighter. She flinched.

"I'm afraid they'll put me in some psychiatric ward. Mom couldn't do that, could she? I'm over twenty-one, she can't just commit me, can she?"

"No," though in truth I had no idea, "of course not. Kendra, what's the matter with your eyes? Do they hurt? Why won't you look at me?"

The same wan smile flickered. "You're all beaten up. Dr. Rosenthal was afraid it would upset me. He wanted me to be prepared. But I don't want to see."

The nurses I'd so loved a moment before became traitors now, scurrying to tell Dr. Rosenthal not only of my emotions, but of my physically grotesque state—warning perhaps even that it might not be good for the patient to see me. Kendra's eyelids snapped back quick, without hesitation. "I'm being ironic, I think. Oh. You do look like shit. Couldn't you have dumped him before I had that hideous . . . dress . . . altered?" Her breathing heaved, far away and strained, robbing her language of whatever essence of *her* it contained. In a rush of panic, I inched my fingers to her wrist, groping for her pulse.

"It just comes on me. You don't think I'll die, do you? My heart feels so weird. Sometimes so fast, and now I can barely sense it. Can *you* feel it? Bee—"

"It's all right."

"That hurts." I let go of her wrist. "Everywhere." A pause, a storing of energy. "So did Aris finally get sick of us? Or did it work, did you make him leave?"

Did *what* work? But all I could manage: "Why does everybody immediately assume Aris did this?" Voice rising inappropriately: "I could've fallen in the shower after drowning my sorrows that you almost died. I could've been in a car accident while freaking out over what Michael Kelsey did to *you*. Aris is not violent—he never even punched the wall like some men do! He would have taken care of me. I just didn't love him back. It was all me."

(Cowed?) she lapsed into silence. My heart felt like somebody's fist was squeezing it tight then letting go, no steady rhythm by which to breathe. I waited for her challenge, *But he did do it, didn't he?* When her voice came, a trickle of water over gravel, she had lost interest in Aris already. "You don't get to talk about Michael."

"Talk about him? I talked *to* him! He came to the loft pontificating on how he doesn't feel the least bit guilty about beating you up and making you go insane and how dwelling on it would be a total waste of his precious time. That's his brilliant commentary on your being holed up in here—and he has the nerve to call that being in love!"

She sighed in agitation. "He didn't say any of that."

"He said exactly that."

"No. He didn't. You just weren't listening."

"He said exactly that before I threw a bottle of wine at him and I'm sorry I didn't hit him in the head and kill him."

Delighted: "You threw a bottle of . . . really? You didn't just want . . . you *did* it?"

An irrational surge of pride. "It only hit him on the side, his arm, but hard. I was drunk, bad aim. I don't care how sick you are, that man is a psychopath, he talks in riddles—no matter how he feels about you it can't excuse what he's done."

"I didn't know we were looking for excuses. But if we were, yeah, whatever . . . accidental attachment Michael may have developed for me would be beside the point."

She enraged me. Another conspiracy, just like the one she'd been in for a decade with our father. An unspoken, secret language passed between them, even in the absence of contact, the primary purpose of which seemed to be to exclude *me*. I did not believe her indifference any more than I believed Michael Kelsey's cryptic assertions of his "attachment." Yet they had developed some code that was operating on its own now, a belief system in which he loved her (and therefore had the right to be brutal), and she was immune to his love (and therefore could not be hurt by his brutality). No, worse. A belief system in which what they shared transcended love and made the basic tenets of decency, tenderness, and kindness seem insipid and banal. She could not be destroyed by his brutality because violence was *not* brutal, because what was savage was a purer form of love beyond . . . what? . . . bourgeois conditioning? I thought I would barf. I said flatly, "He thinks Dad is to blame for what's wrong with you. He thinks Dad is some sort of monster, like he raped you or something and that's why you're messed up now."

Her eyes darted nervously toward the door. "What the hell are you talking about?"

"He said it," I insisted. "He thinks he's got it all figured out. He thought I already knew, didn't think he was giving anything away because he figured, hey, one big happy incestuous family—I was probably getting it from Dad too!"

She pinched my arm to silence me. "Shit—what's the matter with you?" She tried to sit but winced, slunk back down. "I don't know what got into Michael, but you're scaring me."

"You have to talk to me, you have to tell me!" I was bawling now, though I'd promised, and she glared at me in a way that made me think clearly, *All hatred stems from fear.* "Kendra, did you give him that idea about Dad? Oh God, oh God. Is it true?"

She wrapped her arms around her torso, shivering in the thin hospital gown. The little remaining color in her face drained. "What are you doing?" she whispered, voice so low, so small she could have been a corridor away. "Our father is nearly dead, and you've picked now to lose touch with reality? Or are you hoping for me to give you permission to hate Dad so you don't have to be responsible—so you can stay sweet little Bee, only protecting your sister?"

"My . . . ? No." Rocking away from her, tears on my face growing cold. "I'm sorry, I don't know what I'm saying. Maybe I misread Michael. Maybe he didn't intend it that way."

"You mean," between clenched teeth, "that he didn't even say those things?"

"He implied it," I maintained. Then, "Or at least I thought he did."

"You mean," she said, "you're conning me? When all I ever wanted was to help you?"

"Of course not! I wouldn't—it's just you're always excluding me! I've always felt there was something I didn't know about between—"

"Leave. Right now, I mean it, I really will go mad if you say one thing more."

Desperately, I tried to touch her cheek, to pull myself in to embrace her, but she jerked back, hands springing up to cover her face: "Don't make me call the nurse."

I ran out of her room.

Leigh Kelsey came to the door in a man's midnight blue, vintage robe. Because of her height, the garment hung well, though the sleeves were long. Her legs, exposed below the knee, were bare, her feet clad in sweat-socks that clashed markedly with the robe. This irreverent touch lent her unfeasible grace a human, unintentional air that enraptured me all the more. Behind me, Old Town streets were packed with bodies sipping cappuccino at sidewalk cafes, strolling, shopping, begging for money outside Walgreen's. I stood on her stoop, a stupid, purple-eyed beggar squinting in the sun. She was not without mercy. She said, "Come in."

It was no coincidence that I had gone to her home rather than her work this spectacular summer morning. I knew her routine well—at least within the confines of when I might casually drop by the shop to catch her. I fidgeted in her foyer, overwhelmed by so much vintage wood.

"Michael and I were just discussing you," she said, and must have detected horror on my face because she quickly amended, "on the phone." I followed her into the living room, my Spartan, sterile loft suddenly cozy compared to her Victorian antiques. The first floor was awash in wine and jewel green velvets, meant to disarm. Did she keep private rooms upstairs for her own comfort? But no, she reclined easily upon the settee, at home. I muttered, "Why?"

Amiably: "He was just informing me that you think he's the anti-Christ. He, on the other hand, was surprised by your charm. I've been telling him for years how adorable you are, but he was never inclined to believe me." She smirked. "The eye probably helped."

"That's disgusting. Why would the two of you even—like I'm a shared trinket for amusement? This isn't *Dangerous Liaisons!*"

"Oh, Kirby, relax. Nobody is plotting the seduction of the virgin. And from my understanding, you'd hardly fit the bill."

Elise. My face burned. Hotter still at the thought that blushing was probably part of what she regarded as "adorable." She looked around the room like she might be hoping for somebody to miraculously bring us coffee. Rachel? But we seemed alone.

"I'm so sorry about Kendra. I didn't realize it was possible to split one's stomach . . . poor girl. She'll survive, though, despite my ex's record. This one's tough. She'll outlive him."

She spoke like we were in on a conspiracy. I wanted to understand, to feel the heady rush of a secret shared, but her words floated on my surface like oil on water, not penetrating.

When I failed to speak, she glanced down suddenly and tightened her robe. "Everything I've said so far has upset you," she murmured. "Let's start over. What did you come to talk about?"

"Not *him.* I don't care about him. I want to know about my father." In the morning sun, airborne particles of dust floated through my field of vision, though the wood surfaces of the room looked spotless. "He's too sick to help me," I blurted on. "It's worse with Kendra in the hospital. I was always afraid to ask him, and now I've waited too long."

"Ask your sister then. Michael's told her everything."

"Kendra doesn't trust me. She thinks I'll crumble. She hides hard things from me."

"You already know, of course. If you didn't you wouldn't be here."

"Yes, but how long?" Easy, the admission fell too easy. "How long did your affair last?"

She still looked away. Hair spilled over her profile, a startling highlight against the burgundy settee. Only the haughty French slope of her nose remained visible. She held her silence, leaving me to my sweaty angst, before abruptly rising to pour us each a glass of something (scotch?) from a decanter. She handed a glass to me, but I was not fond of neat, straight alcohol and merely stared at it. Hers disappeared in a swallow.

"The last time was after you'd gone to college—you'd only recently left. We'd carried it on several years but were sporadic by then. Michael and I were separated, filing for divorce."

"Is that why he left you? Because of my father?"

"I thought you didn't care to hear about Michael. Or is it that you want me to say yes, I chose your father over him? Well, I can say that if you like, but it isn't true. I never loved Henry that way. He was a good friend, and he loved *me*— your father has a talent for loving too much. After a marriage with Michael, I needed that."

"Did my father give you HIV?" A pause, one in which she may have guessed what was coming next. "Or did you give it to him? You told my mother that Michael isn't infected, but what if he is, what if he gave it to my sister? That could be why she did what she did."

Her voice stayed reasonable, friendly. "Henry has had as many lovers as any man of his kind. He's affluent with reasonable looks and charm. He doesn't need to hire women, but possibly he has anyway. I don't mean to be cruel. But the last time I slept with Henry was five years ago. He could have been anywhere since then."

I realized I had downed my scotch. "You aren't sick?"

"Of course not." One graceful whisk of her long legs and she was upright, patting the space next to her for me to come closer. "I'm fine. You don't need to worry about me."

My movements toward her were tentative, nothing like the fantasies in which I ran to be enveloped by the arms of a lover. Instead I perched hesitantly on the edge of a fainting couch beyond my ken, let her draw me in slowly, the flowing sleeves of her robe like a mother bird's wings. The robe's flap fell open to her pale thigh; sun beamed hot in the un-airconditioned house. There was nothing sexual in the moment. She held me with a nonchalant maternal camaraderie. She had never loved my father; she was healthy, and so removed from my family's body-count war. She pitied us, felt some vague responsibility to be more kind to me than was her nature. That was all.

I wanted to see my sister. The knowledge that, although Michael Kelsey had abused her, he had not condemned her to death, made me giddy and light enough to jump up into amateurish pirouettes, knocking over antiques. Sleepless, I was drunk from one scotch. When I moved to go, she stood with me, linked her arm through mine as we traversed the short distance to the door. Instantly, the frenzy I'd failed to experience earlier bit at me, crawled up through my legs and scorched my skin. The thought of her letting me go, releasing me into the breeze outside, left me thick with longing. I sidled up closer, leaned into her as much as I dared. The wind filtered through the open door, sifted between our bodies. It was then that I noticed the trunks at the top of the staircase: three, like prop luggage in a Merchant and Ivory film, waiting for some strong lad to appear and hoist them down. I murmured, "You're going away soon?"

"Mmm, yes, looking for a house and space for the new shop." She withdrew. "But please, do stress to Kendra that she can trust me to—I agree it's best Rachel know nothing of the binge. In case she ends up living with them after I settle, while she finishes eighth grade."

Lamely: "I wasn't aware my sister was planning to live there with or without Rachel."

"In all fairness, I understand her acquiescence was expected at your wedding."

"Maybe her binge was an alternate response."

"Maybe." A tinkle of laughter. "Fitting, if so, that when my ex-husband finally falls, it'd be for a self-destructive child more dangerous and unapologetically lawless than himself." A darkness crossed her eyes. "I saw Michael at a party the night before Kendra's hospitalization. He looked as haunted and desperate as I must have looked to your father, trying to crawl inside another body to escape the brutality of love. I told myself that by sleeping with him, I'd be passing on the generosity Henry showed me—I'd forgotten how impotent such gestures are to save anyone from the wreckage they seek. That's how foolish love is, Kirby. Avoid it."

She frightened me. I let the sun on her porch hit my skin. Down the street, Elise was approaching, a garment bag slung over her arm. For one sick moment, I believed Leigh had timed it just this way, until I recalled that I had come by unexpectedly, that I had been the one to stand to leave. Elise's eyes widened when she saw me, mere inches away from Leigh Kelsey's white skin. I backed onto the steps she was fast approaching. Leigh watched us, bemused, as I scurried down the stairs and onto the street at the same time Elise's foot hit the first step. The memory of the high arch of her feet, of the sensitivity of her toes under my teeth jolted me, made my underpants immediately wet, the pit of my stomach hum with some achy throb. "Hi," she murmured, and I responded quickly, "How are you?" But she never answered, already having reached the darkened doorway to kiss Leigh Kelsey swiftly on the cheek and disappear inside.

When I returned to the hospital, I received a message that my mother wanted me to call her at home. I was overjoyed to learn I would not be running into her in the halls. Already I'd concocted a story to explain my bruises—a fender-bender caused by worry over Kendra—but several toilet runs had resulted from subsequent fears that my mother might want to see my car, or worse yet demand that I sue the other driver. Soon I would have to confess to my wedding being off for good. I anticipated horror, accompanied by her telling me I was making the biggest mistake of my life and inferring nobody else would ever love me, quiet and invisible as I was. Then there'd be the inevitable efforts to persuade me that I was not in my right mind and therefore not capable—in such a stressful time—of making decisions about the rest of my life (and how I should thus defer to her judgment). Admitting that Aris had struck me, though it would silence her, was not an option. My parents thought me pathetic enough, and if I no longer entertained any belief that I'd ever loved Aris, I was still ashamed. His love too must've been flimsy if he could turn on me so completely during so dark an hour.

"Darling, thank God it's you," my mother breathed into the phone. "I need a friendly voice. Have you been to see Kendra this afternoon?" When I said I was about to go, she gave a long sigh. "Don't expect the best. She threw me out right in front of a nurse and Otto. He was on the bed with her, the two of them were playing dress-up like toddlers—he was polishing her nails! I'd brought flowers but she ordered me to leave, told the nurse to have me escorted out by force if I wouldn't. I haven't had the heart to tell your poor father—it was obscene."

"It's my fault," I muttered. "I upset her this morning."

"Oh, darling, don't try to pile this on your shoulders, I know whose fault it is all right. I could wring your father's neck! All the years he spoiled that girl, handing her money so she could drop out of school and play the star. He destroyed her. She's so disgustingly selfish she hasn't even given two seconds of thought to who's footing this hospital bill!"

Nervously I glanced down the hallway. Shadisha was laughing with another nurse; I turned away as though they'd glean my mother's tirade all the way from Kenilworth. My body as flat against the wall as I could press it, phone cradled between body and wall, I whispered, "Um, don't you think rupturing your stomach is a little severe a response to being spoiled?"

"If Kendra had to clean up her own mistakes, she wouldn't be so quick to land herself in the hospital racking up surgery bills God knows we can't afford. We've got enough to worry about keeping your father covered under the firm without Kendra exploiting her coverage too. After the way she's disowned us, we could have easily gotten tired of committing insurance fraud on her behalf, telling Blue Cross Blue Shield she's an employee at the firm—what then?"

"Mom! If that's the sort of pep talk you were planning, no wonder she won't see you!"

"No wonder all right," my mother said bitterly, "God forbid I do anything but shut my mouth and smile. That's my job, isn't it, that's what you all think? Even you."

Something in me bubbled and stirred—toil, trouble. "Well to tell the truth, Mom, if you wanted to tell someone off, I think you'd have been better off going to Michael Kelsey and telling him to stop fucking your daughter thank you very much instead of whining to me. From where I'm standing, it looks like *he's* the one responsible for breaking Dad's heart."

Silence across the telephone wires. My own words had knocked me quiet too. I imagined my mother, nestled on the North Shore in a house no wolf could blow down, safe from the chaos of the lake, the urban sprawl in which her daughters—and her husband's lovers?—dwelled. I conjured tree-lined Woodstock Avenue, picturesque haven of homes with wrap-around porches, one of which shielded her inside. Yes, there she was, hair snaking out of her chignon like a suburban Medusa—was my father nearby? Was that why she didn't speak, to protect him still? But no, from the depths of my mother's belly, a voice, low and broken, rose.

"Those doctors go on about anorexia and bulimia, personality disorders and such. But Kendra isn't mentally ill. She's an emotional terrorist. Her body is the weapon she's using to destroy this family. She is my child, I know her on a level you never will. Michael Kelsey is no match for her—no man is. She has the singular purpose of a fanatic, nothing will stand in the way of her vengeance. You've chosen the wrong side, Kirby. She hates you too."

I slammed down the phone. Automatic, as if my battered face, my lack of sleep, the scotch scorching my belly, had left me incapable of second thoughts. Yet for the first time in the decade since I'd left ballet, my solid center of gravity, there in my unruptured stomach, felt sure. I focused on the throbbing of my eye: a wound Kendra in her hospital bed did not possess. I could not feel her pain. Because I was not my sister, neither could I know if my mother spoke the truth about her essence. The totality of this disconnection floored me. My body tingled, alive. For the first time, I knew I would become another woman entirely. Only *I*, not *we*.

To my surprise, Kendra did not refuse me. Otto, as my mother reported, had gained admittance earlier, but he'd left hours ago for a painting job. A lady psychiatrist, Shadisha informed me, had also been by—a shrink from Northwestern's psychiatric ward, specializing in eating disorders. She had not stayed long.

This time, Kendra looked more like herself. When he'd learned she was out of ICU, Otto had once again stepped in as the good sister I'd failed to be—he had brought lipstick, her favorite brush, butterfly barrettes to make Marcia Brady hair. He'd brought a pair of legwarmers and his favorite cardigan with the sleeve for her IV arm cut right off. He'd brought wooly socks she'd given him once for Christmas—socks she'd bought for our father but then there'd been a fight because Kendra had been invited to join the Company and could not come home, so Otto flew alone to spend Christmas with her in New York. Now, she looked like a poster girl for a vintage clothing store for the disabled. He had brought cigarettes, though she couldn't smoke in her room and was too weak to push her IV around the lounge, so the Camel Lights sat like a prop, adding to the illusion that "hospital patient" was merely a role Kendra momentarily consented to play. The irreverence of her blood-lips and retro hair and newly polished nails (which he'd painted for her) made me pause in the doorway, hesitant to enter.

"These nurses are unbelievably camp," said my unbelievably camp sister when she noticed me. "Guitar has a theory that nurses are usually dominatrixes by night, but mine are so dowdy they must blow whatever empirical evidence he's compiled out of the water. They don't even understand the comic elements of Jell-O. They bring it in all jiggly and green and ridiculous on that plastic tray with a little carton of milk and buttered bread like in grade school, and I'm all, 'Jell-O is akin to Spam—like would you ever really *eat* spam?' But they just stare at me. I'm the bulimic girl. There's no humor in it. It's insurmountably fucking tragic."

I did not know what to say. Jell-O did not, at this moment, strike me as worthy of humor. Her lipsticked, wooled-up, bony body struck me as insurmountably fucking tragic. To hide my own dowdiness, I lay next to her. She took up so little of the bed it was almost like lying alone. I wrapped my arms around her as tightly as I could without hurting her, without her pulling away. She relaxed into my skin; I received this like a gift. Pressed my face into her hair.

"You never loved him, right?" she whispered. "Aren't you glad it's over? That's one good thing that came of my throwing my body in front of the moving train of your wedding."

I said, "You're worse off than I believed if you did this on any level to save me."

"I've never done anything to save anyone."

"I wish I could entirely believe that." I kept my head hard against hers, our hair meshing—why had I ever dyed mine to separate myself from her? It was all I could do not to take the scissors Otto had used to mangle the cardigan and hack off my offending red locks right there. Instead I surrendered to the smell of Ananya (Otto, for everything, was a saint), savored the womb-like interplay of our bodies, heightened by fear that she would soon pull away, make me leave. "It hurts so much," I murmured like a sweet nothing in her ear. "I would have grasped at anything to give your actions some reason. You have to understand that."

"I do." But I felt her body tense. "I understand that you don't believe Dad would really harm us. I know it was only because Michael . . . he had no right to pull that on you."

Schizophrenically, I heard myself protest, "Maybe he's hurting so much he couldn't bear what you did without assigning a reason."

"He can bear it," she said.

In the late afternoon sun, our shadow flickered and faded against the wall: a two-headed beast. She held on to my waist and begged, "Don't go. I feel so alone."

"I'm not going anyplace." Then, bursting, "*Why*, K? I mean, Dad is sick, it's awful, it's a nightmare. But you've lived virtually without him and Mom for years. Is it Michael Kelsey? Or leaving ballet? Why would you do this to yourself now?"

A nurse, not Shadisha, stood at the door excusing herself awkwardly, clearly spooked by our identical eyes staring at her. She carried a single rose and a card and handed them to Kendra, who made no move to open the card. The nurse nodded at me sympathetically before leaving.

"Aren't you going to look at the note?"

"I don't need to." She moved to give it to me. "Throw it out. No, wait," and snatched it, a violent movement, from my shaky fingers.

The card was nothing but a small square of white paper in a plain envelope. I was huddled so close to her body I could read it as clearly as she. *Definitely more compelling timing than* Story of O, *but I have never seen a woman go so far to make her point.* No signature, though I too knew who had sent it. My sister started to laugh. She gasped in pain, held her stitches, dropped the card onto the sheet. Tears ran down her face; she moaned, "Oh, shit, owww, it *hurts*," but giggled still, clutching my arm as if to channel her pain into my unamused form. The rose lay strewn across our laps; thorns pricked my legs. I shrank away. Kendra's wracked body had gone unreceptive to my pain, to my love. The moment we'd shared unraveled before my eyes, mocked somehow by Michael Kelsey, his bond with her an invisible wall.

"If you were as impervious as you're pretending, you wouldn't be here." But the point seemed obvious; I felt petty throwing it in her face. I extracted myself from the bed, shamed.

The rose tumbled to the floor with my sudden movement. My sister did not even glance at it. Instead her fingers groped, swift, revealing, to the sheet where she swept the card up between newly manicured fingers. The gesture told everything, more than I wanted to know, but even once she held the card in her hand, she gripped it so tight the paper buckled in her grasp: a talisman. I backed toward the door. I had stumbled upon something not meant for my eyes.

Their language did not translate.

May 1994

Otto had asked my sister to his prom after dumping me when Kendra and I were juniors, but the next year he refused to attend ours. By then he proclaimed prom "fascist," and Kendra and I "slaves" to our "New Trier conditioning." Kendra promptly broke up with him. Rumors ran high until a jock, too cute and popular to have to waste his time with an aloof ballerina with one foot in New York, asked her — it wasn't fair. My own date brought a cell phone on which he kept getting calls from an ex-girlfriend. Still, I was happy to see Otto ditched the way he'd jilted me — even if it confirmed that Kendra had all the power in the world and I had none.

Later, he came for her. At a post-prom party in a suite at the Marriott O'Hare, after Kendra had passed out with her black dress gathered tight around her hips and her thumb curled into her mouth, he arrived. I was playing Quarters at the plywood hotel table, laughing hard with three other girls — girls Kendra and I had known since grade school. My mouth was full of Doritos. When he banged on the door, I raced to keep him out. The suite was chaos: people piled on two beds and crowded in the bathroom, cable blaring, stereo on. Otto's Amnesty International T-shirt was torn near the neck. He pushed me aside like a cop, stood over Kendra, the curve of her ass a dangerous contrast to the thumb between her lips. Burgundy lipstick smudged on her knuckles. Otto stared down for a long moment, transfixed by this banal moment, this wasted high school girl. Then he hoisted her into his arms — somebody yelled to her date, "Hey, your damsel's being kidnapped, asshole," but he was praying to the toilet. I threw my body in Otto's path. I wore red. My hips did not block the doorway, so I stretched out my arms. Said, "You can't have her. It's our prom. Ours." Kendra's left glove slipped down her arm, hung at her air-thin wrist. She threw her head back at a horrifying angle, murmured, "It's okay, he'll take me to the picnic tomorrow, won't you, baby?" but Otto said, "Over my dead body." Then kissed her throat, arched like a dead sunflower stalk, and said, "Hey, Kirby, she's leaving soon anyway right? New York, it's bigger than the both of us and all that shit." My sister giggled as he carried her out, the spoils of war: light, decadent and heartless as a diamond or gold-sculpted trophy. My ears pounded, her swift betrayal nothing like a war.

Those revelers not expected home for curfew were passed out by the time the phone rang. The bedside clock read 4:43. Somebody answered. Somebody sober enough to remember my name and family relations. People kicked me. "Bee, lush, rise and shine, it's K." I went, "Unng." I had to pee. Hands pulled me to my feet. My dress had slipped around my waist like an inner tube so my bustier showed; the cups sewn in my gown flopped aimlessly. I staggered to the phone.

"Bee. Bee. I'm so glad you came."

"What do you want?" I said.

"I have to talk to you." Her voice was urgent, raw. "It's important, I shouldn't have waited 'til now to tell you. Shh, Guitar's asleep."

"Who cares? You're unbelievable, leaving me on our prom night for that Mr. Working Class Hero—like he doesn't live in the basement of his parents' big house and drive a car his Daddy bought. Tell him to give his car to the poor, why don't you? Then you guys can go write your manifestos on the evils of prom and live in the woods and own one damned spoon."

"I love you," she said. "Shh, shhh. Don't be mad."

"You're trashed."

"No!" (If Otto had been sleeping, he wasn't now.) I could feel her clutching the phone. I could feel . . ."Come to New York with me. You can't stay here alone. Promise. Please."

"Now I've lost my space on the bed because of you. I'll have to sleep on the floor—"

"We can get an apartment. You can get a job until you can apply to schools too. It'd work, it'd be easy. Just don't stay home."

"Why wouldn't I stay?" My voice loud now too. "Maybe I'll finally get some attention around here. Why should I follow you and play shadow all my life? Do you think I'm stupid?"

But she was crying. Years since I'd heard my sister cry. Usually she mocked me for it—no, that wasn't right, she never said anything. Just stared at me with a kind of mute disgust, and I understood that fear, the fear that she was looking into a mirror and my weakness might rub off. Now she choked, a fish tossed onto land. "Kirby." Struggling for poisonous air. "Listen to me carefully. You have to get out of here. Away from him. Please."

People were staring. I lowered my voice. "Away from—what are you talking about? Did you drop acid? You sound like you're trip—"

"Dad . . ."

But suddenly Otto was there, his voice in the background, "K, baby, what's going on, you don't really want to go back do you, I'll take you to your little picnic tomorrow, come to bed."

"Please," she sobbed at me. "He's drinking again, and you'll be alone, I'll be gone—"

Otto's voice cut in. "Who is this? Kirby?" So easy. Easy to
scream, Give me back my sister, *to beg,* Tell me, Kendra, tell me
what you're afraid of for me, tell me what you mean. *A*
Novocain injection in my jaw—I couldn't talk. Coward. I backed
away from the nightstand, uncoordinated; I knocked into the wall.
The phone hung askew; I heard her, "Kirby? Bee!"

"She's flying," *I said to somebody, a girl who was headed for*
Northwestern too. "Do my sister a favor and keep her from
embarrassing herself any further. Hang up the phone."

For years I'd relived that phone call, rare proof that Kendra
needed me too, was afraid to be without me. So scared she'd
blown our father's drinking all out of proportion: a threat
instead of a sad burden. My inebriated panic response seemed
irrelevant; I remembered only: *she loves me; she cried.* I'd
treasured her vulnerability—a talisman to warm me. Suddenly,
it scorched.

How to Burn a Witch

SHE HAD INSTRUCTED me to wait; she wasn't sure what time they'd release her. Probably they'd send that shrink around again for some last-ditch chance at probing the admittedly dark realms of her brain. Come January, Kendra's health insurance under the firm would expire; my mother had no intention of begging the senior partners for renewal. The consequent necessity (perceived by me) of my sister seeking therapy before the first of the year had been the catalyst of several fights between us—I hoped against hope that the hospital psychiatrist could persuade her. I waited by the phone. By the time I called to see what was holding up her release, it was dinner time on the hospital clock. I was told she'd left three hours prior.

According to Shadisha, to whom I demanded to speak, Kendra's last night at the hospital had been spent in inconsolable weeping. "The night staff didn't know what to do. Until then, she'd never even talked to them, she was unresponsive—which means calm." They'd given her a sedative, but Kendra was a regular user and failed to fall into the expected stupor. Threatened with an injection and being kept for psychiatric observation if she did not calm down, my sister meekly asked to make a call. "Afterward, she was okay. When I heard about it, I figured she'd called you—or that ponytail guy. You're the only visitors she's ever accepted."

Furious, I dialed Otto's number and found him not at home. I sulked around the loft assuming he must've picked

Kendra up and they were off at some bar getting knock down drunk, possibly with the intentions of ending the evening with an overdue (albeit sedate) lay. Not caring whether he had caller ID, I dialed his number every fifteen minutes stalker-fashion, livid as a jealous wife; I even debated going over to his apartment in case they were getting high with the ringer off. Here is denial, Doctor, in all its glory. Yet when Otto finally picked up after ten (unable to get a word in edgewise for a full minute as I unleashed my fury), his answer, "I haven't heard from her—she told me she was moving in with you," hardly came as a shock.

Michael Kelsey's 312-number was already committed to memory, so often over the past week and a half had I almost phoned him—to threaten his life, to commiserate, who knew? I couldn't go through with it that night either. I ached to call my mother, to surrender, *You're right—she's chosen him, she's left us,* but dreaded the possibility of hearing my father's voice; I was sick with guilt at being unable to dismiss Michael Kelsey's inferences. Two in the morning, three, five. I rocked myself on the couch, moaning as the cramps came on, finally screaming in rage (how had I been stupid enough to believe this disease would depart with the tossing of my Levsinex, the tossing of Aris?) as I surrendered to the toilet all the poison inside.

I was tired, so tired of this body. I was tired, so tired of this war.

Eight thirty when his car pulled up in front of my building. I was sitting in the window by then—had been for hours—waiting. High up as I was, I heard his door slam. In an instant of panic I ducked, irrationally frightened that he might see me. Only after a lapse during which she had not rung my buzzer did I peek above the windowsill again.

Michael Kelsey sat on the hood of his black Porsche, which was double-parked on the opposite side of the street. He wore a suit, which made the image incongruous, like a photograph in some urban exposition. Kendra was still inside the car, pale and barely visible between the sun's glare and the rolled-up window. After a moment, she stepped out and leaned against the door. He didn't move to help her, didn't look at her, just sat there on the hood, staring straight ahead. She remained still for a long time. Then went around to the front of the car, her movements deliberate but not obviously painful, and stood before him, just out of reach.

He got to his feet. They stood facing one another, neither of them moving. I was at too great a distance to know whether they spoke. Finally, he took a step toward her, then another. His body mere inches away from hers, he stopped. She made no effort to bridge the negligible gap between them, but her face tilted up. Slowly, he brought one hand up and touched her, brushing his fingers against her cheek. When she made no response, he cupped her face with his hands, lowering his head against her forehead and leaning into her, hard enough that she swayed a little, then steadied, face no longer visible between his hands, hair spilling over his fingers. The tenderness of their stance startled me, made the skin on my face burn. I wanted her to extract herself, but they leaned into one another for so long—a Gothic arch with only the smallest of spaces between their bodies—that it was I who turned away.

I didn't look back outside until ten minutes later when I heard the car pull away. The sun had retreated behind a mass of clouds; Damen Avenue was washed in gray. Kendra sat on the curb, a cigarette perched between her fingertips, people milling past and around her as she stared off at some invisible point that may have been the sky. He was gone.

By the time she reached the third floor loft, Kendra had lit another cigarette. It dangled from her fingertips, the nails of which were bitten down so Otto's week-plus-old manicure was obsolete. The sleeves of her crocheted sweater flopped over her hands so close to the slender white stick I feared she would go up in flames. She, a dancer since age seven, was winded from the stairs. Her cheeks stood out red from strain—Dr. Rosenthal maintained it would be weeks before her stitched-up stomach muscles healed enough for her to move without considerable pain. I let her in, my face no doubt the same mix of red and white as hers, my rage and confusion smoldering under some noxious notion that I should be solicitous of her lest she fly off the deep end again. But she was my twin: forced kindness was not part of our repertoire. Up close, mascara smeared black under her eyes; sex sweat rose strong from her skin; her hair matted wildly; her unlipsticked mouth pulsed raw-red and swollen. I itched to slap her until her stupid stomach muscles collapsed and she fell right down at my feet. She stared back, clear-eyed and unashamed as a witch. I said, "You look like crap."

"Gee, thanks." Glibly. "So did you hear Rory Kennedy's tying the knot today after all? Must've been meant to be, true love, huh, all's right with the world."

"Guess dying's no way to stop a wedding," I said. "Guess you have to try and seduce the groom and when that doesn't work split your stomach in two."

She smirked like we'd shared a joke. I wanted to be twelve years old. Oh, to be twelve and grabbing Kendra's hair, rolling on the floor with her in furious, nail-extended, hair-pulling, arm-biting frenzy. She had always clobbered me, but now, worn-down and skinny as a junkie, sleepless and scarred, I could finally take her. I wanted to be twelve and in our new attic bed, in our new house in Kenilworth, whispering after lights out. Our parents said we used to talk to one another in sleep, nonsense only, meaningless exchanges: *Did you see the hill?* and *But I wanted strawberry ice cream.* My sister had binged on ice cream, had tried to tear herself from my body and my world, found me so unbearable that even now when she had failed, she preferred the bed of a sadist to mine. I didn't expect she'd stay with me longer than a night or two before moving in with Michael Kelsey after all. No doubt she was here only to claim her possessions: four Hefty bags of clothes and books packed by neither my mother (who wouldn't set foot in the apartment our father had kept), nor myself (who couldn't face it), but by some anonymous service, perhaps the same that had cleaned up evidence of her binge. We could not handle her, my parents and I—we never had been able to. I had failed. Exhausted, I sank onto the monster couch that Aris kept postponing coming to retrieve. Kendra flopped next to me, refusing to acknowledge my anger. I said, "Tell me one thing. That's all I'll ask. Did he hit you last night? Did you get right out of the hospital and run to him so he could hurt you some more?"

She tilted her chin, that same defiant pose she'd used on our father. "All right. Yes."

I'd thought I expected as much, but after the scene on the street my conviction had lessened. I dared hope she was lying. I countered, "I can't believe you, you enjoy tormenting me," but she flipped back her sleeves and extended wrists red-rimmed and welted from bucking against too-tight restraints, blotches of purple where blood vessels lay too close to epidermis.

269

"You can check out the rest," she offered lazily. "I have to change anyway, you're welcome to watch."

"You need help." My voice ached to scream. "Something is hideously wrong with you."

"Yeah," she agreed with theatrically false epiphany, "that's exactly what I need! I need some incense-burning surrogate mom to tell me what a good person I am and how I should do visualizations of safe spaces or sleep with a doll when I get anxious. Maybe I should have done some pretty meditations on flower fields the night I binged—maybe then I wouldn't have ended up in the hospital. Or maybe I should have just gone the fuck home with Michael instead of to my apartment alone. Maybe *then* you wouldn't be treating me like an imbecilic four-year-old you have to take care of, like you aren't so busy on the toilet and getting beat up by the pussy loser you almost married that you can't even take care of yourself."

I would not let her goad me. "You're only hostile because you're scared to death."

"How interesting," she drawled. "What am I afraid of?"

"You're out of control," I explained steadily. "Not just about Dad's illness, but everything—food, sex. You spent years in a profession where everyone has a borderline eating disorder, but now you can't dance and you don't have the Company to help regulate your weight, so your lifelong denial of food has gotten out of hand. Everything's out of hand. You always liked bad boys. But Michael Kelsey isn't a boy, he's a man. At first it was a turn-on, he was kinky, you liked that—I'm not so staid or innocent as you think. But it's gone too far. Leaving you with marks that freak out doctors, needing to hurt you when you're so weak you can barely walk. You think you love him, but it's just an addiction, it's like the food. He's *sick*."

"Astounding," she said. "You're one hundred percent correct. Why didn't I think of it?"

"I can't possibly imagine."

She stood. "Look, I'm going to sleep. You can sit here and play Freud. Knock yourself out. You're boring me."

She was almost to the bedroom, almost to the bed I'd shared with Aris. Thinking of her sprawled in it—how had I ever managed to convince myself that Aris had been lying? Whatever else he was guilty of, I knew the truth: she had tried to seduce my fiancé. I didn't love him, but he was *mine*, and she had meant to make a shared joke of me, an irrelevance of me, as she had done with Otto, as she had somehow done with our father. I jumped to my feet heading after her, grabbed her arm and twisted her around so she faced me. She lost her balance and bumped my hips, but I withdrew; she had to reach to steady herself against the wall.

"You can't stay, Kendra. Mom is right about you. I've been blind. I've had enough."

A momentary crumbling of her mouth, the corners of her eyes. Then gone. "Fine."

I was not finished. Of course, I could not have been finished. "You've done everything you can to destroy our family. Dad will die miserable because you can't find one small space of compassion in your heart—you'd rather multiply his suffering by a thousand than deal with your own guilt and grief. You're perverse. You trust a man who makes a fetish of your pain before trusting anyone in our family, even me. You've turned Mom into a bitter martyr and ruined her for me too. I asked you point blank before if Dad ever . . . if he abused you in any way to make you like this, and you denied it. If that's true, you have no excuse. If it's not, tell me now."

My sister held tight to the wall. Though her eyes glassed over—with tears or the mere effort of standing—her mouth set a straight line, lips pressed so they all but disappeared. She looked ugly with her ratty hair and semeny smell and raccoon eyes. Like something to be cast on the pyre, or at least into the hall. Her voice rose, quavering but resolute, flawlessly cold.

"I have no will to mourn Dad. But I am not some product of his sins. My demons, whatever they are, are my own."

"You can stay with Otto until you're on your feet." I was not crying; I would no longer give her that. "He offered last night when I called looking for you. If you want another option besides Michael Kelsey, Otto's there. But we all know where you'll choose to go."

Hand gradually inching from the wall. "I'll send Guitar over for my things."

When she reached the door, though, my stomach rushed. I blurted, "This *is* for the best, Kendra. If we're ever going to come back together, we need distance . . . time apart to think."

She looked at me with pity so deep my knees buckled. I sank right to the ground.

"Have a backbone for once in your life," she said. "Don't forgive me."

I sat on the floor outside the door of my bedroom until long after the sun went down.

The Spectacle of the Other

THE PATHETIC ARE never more so than on Sundays.

On Sunday morning, six days after Kendra left the loft, Aris finally arrived with a borrowed truck and a former frat brother I recalled vaguely from freshman year parties, to haul away the couch I so despised. In his slouchy white shirt and faded denims, he looked handsome and harmless. By the way his friend smiled at me, I knew that I too appeared unchanged on the outside, could still pass for the sweet girl-next-door with whom Aris fell in love. Yet between Aris and me, the air was charged with electric secrets, ugly truths revealed, lovers' intimacies that now felt shameful. We made strained chit-chat about his new apartment, about the fact that I planned to look for a cheaper place, about the various drawbacks of loft living— "Remember how we used to vacuum three times a day to get rid of all the brick dust until we finally gave up!" he cried with excessive jocularity, and I laughed too loud. His friend guzzled my Evian straight from the bottle, and they had a slight trip-up on the stairs, but soon the couch was gone, Aris along with it. I imagined running into him in a few years, in a crowded restaurant, being introduced to his pretty, demure wife. Or perhaps in Lincoln Park, strolling with their newborn son. He would be working for some architectural firm, happy enough to be a grunt, part of a large company. They would take Caribbean cruises, pose for Christmas portraits, have plastic playground equipment in their green suburban yard. Already, as though the conclusion of his life was foretold, I felt a paradoxical mix of nostalgia and *Thank God that isn't me.* I could imagine explaining these feelings to no one but Kendra. After holding out for nearly a week, it took only moments following Aris's departure for me to at last phone Otto looking for her—then for neither of us to be at all surprised that she was not where she'd told the other she would be. An argument immediately ensued over which of us would call Michael Kelsey's and ask to speak to her. In the end, my sister's long-time lover agreed to call the man she'd chosen over him. He had little choice given my insurmountable horror of hearing Michael Kelsey pick up the phone and say hello.

"Tell her I don't care who she's sleeping with or whether she sees our parents," I begged, hating the desperation in my voice, hating chasing her so shamelessly. "Tell her I need her."

My phone rang an hour later. When I picked it up, it was only Otto again. "Well, I talked to him," he said. "For about twenty minutes." But when I went, "Eeww," he countered, "He was actually pretty friendly, like we knew each other already. He doesn't sound very old."

"What about my *sister*?"

"He hasn't seen her since the morning he dropped her off at your place."

"Bull! She's probably cuffed to his bed and he couldn't be bothered to get the key."

Otto inhaled—on a joint by the way he spoke holding his breath. "Baby, I doubt it."

"Do not call me that. A few crappy lays at sixteen doesn't give you the right-do you even care about Kendra, or now that you and Michael Kelsey male-bonded you're content to leave her to his capable, *friendly* hands?"

"You are so sanctimonious. All you'd do if you found her would be unload more fascist psycho-babble on her about how she's mentally ill!"

We fell into a humiliated silence. I was about to hang up when he mumbled, "I proposed. In the hospital, then again the day you guys fought and she came to crash with me. I said 'Let's stop this shit and get real jobs and some kids and maybe it'll straighten us out.' I offered myself up, and she left while I slept, without even a note. Do you want me to let her kick me 'til I die?"

Lamely: "I didn't know that."

274

"Yeah? Well *he* did. He knew all the fuck about it—the first proposal at least. He said it was nice of me and that it meant a lot to her. I should kill him, talking to me like that, like it was all so rational and laissez-faire and I'm not still dying inside that she said no. But I was fucking grateful too because he told me it meant something to her—*he* said it did, but *she* never let me know. She just said something like, 'Oh you know we can't do that,' and asked me to polish her toenails." He sniffed back tears, and I was glad that at least he'd held out; that unlike me he hadn't given Michael Kelsey the satisfaction of blubbering for show. "I love her so much it's an addiction. But I can't be a junkie all my life. I've finally had enough."

"This is no time to denounce your vices! Kendra's broke and suicidal, she could be—"

"She's probably just mooching off old ballet friends in New York 'til her stomach muscles recover from surgery and she can snag a job." He sighed, or maybe only exhaled. "She'll call in a few weeks."

"Or the morgue will call us!" Then, knowing I'd scared him, "Look, you're right, I'll try some people from NYCB, somebody has to know if she's in town. I have to do something—I'm not going to act fascist, I'm just worried sick. I swear to God, Otto. I swear to Marx."

"You don't believe in either," he said flatly. "You don't believe in anything. I'll make the calls myself. I don't trust you."

My father, after coming so near death that my mother and I dared, as people do, wish he would mercifully die and get it over with, began that autumn to improve. After a bout of pneumonia that nearly killed him in the weeks following Kendra's disappearance, it became clear that he would never adhere to the rigorous regimen that had only barely prolonged his life during the past year—his depression was too great. Instead of giving up on him, as would have been the case with a poorer man, with a few hasty interviews he was added to a new study on a treatment that required only two pills a day. By Christmas he was strong enough to begin work again, part-time at the firm. Nobody trusted him to bear the lion's share of a case; his health was shaky and might fail mid-trial. But the senior partners were charitable—they'd always enjoyed my father's residual Southern charm. *Remission*, the wives whispered among themselves at the office Christmas party.

275

Lung, I heard — or was it colon? Recidivism rates are brutal, you know.

My mother and I breathed an unspoken sigh of relief that Michael Kelsey had left the firm in September, thus they would no longer be working together, providing constant opportunity for Michael to divulge his treacherous affair. When I asked my father why Michael had gone, my mother became antsy and chimed up, "That man's always been eccentric, darling. He's probably run off to Santa Fe to paint wolves for all we know," but my father said quietly, with authority, "He had a more lucrative offer, that's all." We did not speak his name again.

We filled the void of Kendra in convoluted ways. At first, following Otto's inability to track her down in New York, there were tearful phone calls between my mother and me in secret. My father was still deathly ill. We dared not push his depression over the edge by admitting what had transpired, so we created a fantasy in which Kendra had indeed gone back to Manhattan, was waitressing and living with yet another long-haired, instrument-playing man, studying modern dance as she'd planned. In this scenario, Kendra was in contact with Otto, and occasionally me, but continued her irrational refusal to speak to our parents, so wouldn't provide me with an address lest I pass it on to them. Though my mother developed a peptic ulcer, and I spent much of the fall crying myself to sleep under the sedation of red wine, my father's depression, so unshakable over the past year despite his Paxil, began to lift. Kendra's rejection, perhaps, felt more abstract now that she was thousands of miles away instead of in an apartment forty minutes from his home (for which he paid!). He did not seem particularly hurt that she refused contact with him or my mother. He seemed — a fact that filled me with hatred — relieved.

It was easy, you see, so easy to deceive him. My mother and I were angels of mercy, handing the invalid whose love we craved pretty fictions wrapped in red ribbons: his prodigal daughter's bohemian life. We spoon-fed these tales into his eager mouth, watching him grow more vital by the day until his spirits were so lifted by his apparent recovery that he no longer required psychiatric meds. Until my mother's spirits were so lifted by the apparent recovery of the man she'd dismissed as dead that she did not call me crying to obsess about Kendra anymore. Instead she began to utter phrases like, "She's a grown woman; she made her bed; if anything terrible had happened we'd have been notified." Until she began to say when I called in tears and mad grief, "You have to move on, darling. You can't let Kendra's acting out ruin your life."

Leigh Kelsey died alone on a mountain road, driving back to her parents' ranch from a millennium party at a country club. According to friends in Colorado, she had not had much to drink. The roads were only mildly icy. Later my mother heard that Leigh's system had been full of muscle relaxants given for a ski injury, which may have exacerbated the effects of her few glasses of bubbly. Everyone thanked God Rachel was with her father at the time of the accident.

For a few days, my parents were wild with some sort of transferred grief. I knew they had both loved her, but the fits of sobbing, the inability to eat, the unwashed hair and musty smell of the house surpassed all reasonable proportions. I, on the other hand, went numb. Her death seemed random—not even tragic, since tragedy requires meaning, or at least a certain poetry to derive its power. She was a beautiful woman of vibrant health, making a fresh start out West with a just-opened shop and a new home undergoing renovations. She had a daughter and an assembly of adoring would-be suitors of both genders. The madness of her meeting such an end surpassed even the madness of my sister's actions: running to escape the death of a father who did not die, from a sister who worshipped her, from two men—albeit neither princes—vying for her love. I could call neither Leigh Kelsey's poor drug-mixing judgment nor my sister's rage-turned-inward *tragic*. But both losses tugged at me with the weight of the most crucial of subtractions, until I did not think myself fit for additions anymore. My parents' loud, audacious grief offended me, made me glad I could not summon their intensity, glad I was not quite entitled. What had this enigmatic woman been to me anyway?

I did not go to the wake. My fear was too great. But before the funeral, trepidation shape-shifted into heroic fantasies about finally facing Michael Kelsey again. All along I'd held fast to the belief that he knew more about Kendra's disappearance than he'd admitted to Otto, and though I hated him, this hope kept me going during long nights when I feared with trembling helplessness that my sister was dead. I imagined how at the funeral, he would see me looking so like Kendra that he would not be able to keep from approaching me, and I would confront him and force him to reveal what he knew or risk exposure to everyone for what he was.

On the day of the funeral, though, I saw him for only a minute and at a distance. Shortly before my arrival, Rachel— gaunt, but as lovely as her mother must have been at that age— flew into a clawing grief and began sobbing and shouting *Mommy* and could not stop. I came just in time to see Michael Kelsey carry her out to his car. She fought him like a crazed animal being caged—claws extended and whipping at his face. I watched him move purposefully with her body tight in his arms, his dark suit cutting sharp lines against the background snow, eyes on her transfixed face. Most likely he did not even know I was there. They drove away not in the limousine meant for the family, but in his tiny Porsche, Rachel cowed and slumped where Kendra had sat that last day. I rushed for the ladies' room immediately, not to cry but to vomit.

It was not the sort of moment in which one expects transformation. No, not even in the instant I saw Elise, crouched in a stall and sobbing with a raw abandon I envied as I had envied everything between them. I abruptly recalled the protrusion of her knees and elbows when we fell together to the floor of Isabelle's Room, our jumble of angular limbs betraying cluelessness, and how she'd tremored in fear then not unlike now. Though I did not approach her, she sensed me, and her tears took on the self-conscious quality of a private act usurped to the public realm. I felt, despite my numb sickness, that I'd been paid an enormous compliment. As though I had caught a queen in the act of shitting, her regality all the more precious for the secret contortions of her inescapably human face. My ache turned to barely containable, exquisitely contradictory joy. The prospect of comforting her seemed more romantic than any I had ever known. But not yet. I stood watching her, tingling as she tried in vain to compose herself, savoring the moment.

When my father grew well enough to figure out what treacherous protectors my mother and I were, he hired a private investigator to track Kendra down in New York. Naturally, the P.I. turned up zilch. After combing Chicago too, his expanded search revealed record of her on an Air France flight to Paris from O'Hare the previous August, the very day after Guitarist and I had last seen her. The EEC being as it was, further efforts to locate her proved futile—she could have gone anywhere without so much as showing a passport. She'd been gone almost a year.

Once again there were tearful phone calls between my mother and me, rationalizations to cover our shame. Why hadn't we considered an investigator earlier, when there was still a chance of tracking Kendra down? The short-term happiness that had conspicuously (if inappropriately) covered my parents since my father's improvement gave way to silence and resentment and separate bedrooms on opposite ends of the hall. In short, things were restored to their previous state— as they'd been before my father's diagnosis with AIDS. My mother bore his latest punitive silence with humble, accepting grace. As though she'd known all along that, if he hung on long enough, she would ultimately be uncovered as the one in the wrong.

I was leading a triple-life by then: temping by day, taking summer-session graduate psych classes at Northwestern at night, and cruising girl bars on the weekends. I was too busy and too glad of Kendra's relocation to Europe to give my parents' marital discord much thought. By now, Elise and I had parted company. Once, spanking her playfully, I'd suddenly pinned her down and hit hard, trying to make her cry. She'd accused me of "buying into the straight world's dominance-submission misogyny," and, though she was twenty, proclaimed me a "baby dyke" who did not know what I wanted. My heart did not break to lose her, a substitute for the woman neither of us could see again. But I wondered: are we all doomed to become what we most despise? How inextricably bound to the nucleus of desire is the molecule of our worst fear? Did I emulate Michael Kelsey—seek to become him—to turn an incomprehensible demon into that most familiar: myself? And Kendra? Was it my psyche she grappled with there, bleeding on his pitiless beige carpet? Was I that entity so horrific I could only be fetishized? Was I her darkest desire, that my tears might be hers? Am I *her*, is he *me*, am I— are *we*—our deepest fear?

I was exhausted. There were still sporadic calls during which Otto and I speculated as to how Kendra had obtained money for a plane ticket (in high season!), aware that the only people she knew with access to such funds were my father and Michael Kelsey. Clearly neither of *them* would have handed her the money to leave them. "Maybe she fucked someone for it," Otto suggested, but I pointed out that a girl who weighs ninety-two pounds soaking wet and has stitches, bruises, and can barely walk does not score twelve hundred bucks a roll. We couldn't fathom how she'd even managed a suitcase, though it appeared she'd taken nothing but the bag she'd brought from the hospital. The rest of her things remained hidden like a murder weapon in the trunk of my Tercel, in the same Hefty bags that'd been cleared from our father's city apartment. I was afraid to touch them, as though to do so would be to acknowledge her for dead. At least Kendra had forged a plan, however absurd. At least her death was not *guaranteed*.

A year is a long time to mourn. My term at Northwestern ended; I'd be starting graduate school full-time in the fall. I celebrated by calling you. I had decided (maturely, I thought) that as a future shrink I needed to make peace with my own quitting behavior as a client. I'd long since recognized my fury over your concern for Aris as thinly disguised shame that you were able to show him more kindness than I, the woman who supposedly loved him. I had been a fraud; now I was myself. I'd stride into your office with my long blond hair, my chic, un-matronly clothes, my red lipstick, and you would see how far I'd come. I might subtly allude to your not having realized I preferred women, and leave you with the knowledge that it was this, not Aris, that had been the failure of our work. Our meeting would be my final catharsis.

The night before my appointment, my stomach acted up as it still did from time to time. I tossed and turned on my new, cream-colored couch, fitful and too restless for sleep, music, or TV, awaiting the worst waves of the pain. When I found myself in the hall heading down the stairs to my car, I could not have said with certainty what I intended. Only once I opened the trunk rather than the driver's side door did I know why I'd gone out. From the dark, confined space, the smell of my sister rose to greet me. Her perfume oil and incense must've spilled, permeated the fibers of her clothes. I squatted and yanked the Hefty bags onto my lap with jerks, emptying the contents onto the ground. At the bottom of the third bag, I found them—her journals—though I'd not known they were there. Among dancer's autobiographies and biographies, Agrippina Vaganova's *Basic Principles of Classical Ballet* and a dozen books evaluating the Vaganova method; among books by and about Balanchine, about the history of ballet, the stories of great ballets, and the founding, workout methods, and anniversary years of every ballet company I'd ever heard of, they tumbled into my hands. Three spiral notebooks, every inch of paper covered with her writing: small, manic, changeable. Exactly like mine.

I sank onto the pebbles and broken glass and decomposing trash of the curb. That Kendra had documented herself this way seemed surreal. The cerebral was *my* forte. She was the physical twin: reckless, careless, the antithesis of my introspection. Never mind that she'd maintained nearly straight As at one of the most competitive high schools in the country while also dancing semi-professionally. Never mind that we shared the same genes. I opened a notebook at random, scanned: *You do not wake up a charted country; it happens slowly. In parts.* The tone rang familiar as my own train of thought—like nothing I ascribed to my sister. Did I misremember her? Had I ever known her at all? I sat shameful, lap strewn with her clothes: inconceivably tiny, overwhelmingly black. Then I picked up the journals and went home, leaving my sister's life hanging like the intestines of a gutted animal from my car.

Totem for Girls

WHEN I WALKED into your office on legs that could barely hold my weight, you immediately took my arm and led me to sit. My red-rimmed eyes were swollen like a boxer's, my hair knotted from a night of running my fingers through it anxiously as I read and wept, my clothes sweat-stained, unchanged from the night before. I smelled. You sat across from me with a quiet, maternal patience I had never recognized; I had the sensation in that moment that I—always—broke your heart. Perhaps this was self-aggrandizement, a narcissistic view of my own tragedy quotient. You offered Kleenex and reached out to touch my nasty hair. I pulled back, shocked and incapable as ever of tenderness. You retreated back to your own chair.

I could talk. Yes, I could always talk, couldn't I? I summarized Kendra's story for you, needing you to understand that it had become my own. It was a Gothic tale. One of a girl on the brink of womanhood, whose father had used a stolen key to enter her room while she slept. Like a thief in the night, he'd uncovered a bag of the speed that kept her energized for ballet and school now that she had a boyfriend and stayed out late, partying and engaging in constant adolescent sex. Her parents confronted her; she flew into a rage and attacked her mother, after which her father beat her harshly with his belt. The next day, penitent, he'd left work early and come home to see her, nursing her wounds in bed. He found her anything but cowed—instead she threatened vengeance, swore to destroy him. He'd thrown back the duvet under which she lay to strike her again. Instead. It was the month before our eighteenth birthday; she stipulates that she did not resist him. I asked meekly, "I don't know . . . does that qualify as consent?"

My tears had dried on my face like a mask I could peel off, a mask of what I'd once been. "According to her journals, he had sex with her five years before she disappeared. He might have already been infected. She was obsessed with that, wrote constantly about being scared to get tested—she could have AIDS. Maybe that's why she left, but I don't understand . . . how could she sleep with Michael Kelsey then, someone she worshipped since we were kids? Their affair was a bodily fluid fest—if she's infected, the chance he escaped seems pretty damn slim."

You remained silent, nodding. My sense of foreboding mounted; I knew with instant gleaming certainty that you had heard this story before. You began, "Maybe she thought engaging in a bodily fluid fest with him, as you've described it, would magically save her because he was all-powerful and therefore invulnerable. Perhaps only later, once familiarity led her to realize he had no special immunity, did she fear she'd condemned her lover to death."

My heart seemed to thud to a stop. "Are you saying she *was* infected then? Is that what you mean? Did my father tell you—did he confess?" But I choked, could not suck in air.

You leaned forward, murmured, "Take a deep breath, Kirby, close your eyes. Okay, breathe in. There, yes, out. Inhale, yes. Exhale. Good. In. Out. Open your eyes."

I didn't. Didn't want to see.

"My sister is dead, isn't she?" I whispered. "You've known and didn't tell me. All this time, you knew she was as good as dead."

My hand in yours. Dangerous, I knew from my own classes, dangerous to touch one's clients. Who knew what demons lurked, how they would react? But you knew me. For months I sat in this chair, babbling about Aris, my petty jealousies of my glamorous twin, my martyr mother whose ideals I could never reach. Oh, the time I'd wasted. Here I sat again, unprepared.

"I'm going to tell you something," you said. "I should not be doing this. I'm violating confidentiality and that's something I swore never to do. But we all make choices in life about what we can live with. And I'm going to tell you. Do you understand?"

Eyes open a crack, I nodded.

So you did. You told me a story I already knew. The one I'd relayed a moment before, about an amphetamine-dependent baby ballerina whose distraught father decided to snoop through her room for the drugs he suspected were the cause of recent strange behavior. Why he had snooped while she slept remained a mystery, but yes, you knew the story well. Then suddenly your version veered — ended not with a father's taboo consummation but with a daughter's fantasy. "He told me the whole thing, Kirby. I saw him several times a week when he got out of rehab. He admitted to his relapse of alcoholism during your senior year of high school, and also to striking Kendra in her room the afternoon after he'd spanked her. But once he'd slapped her, he ran out — sober, he had no stomach for violence. He was an addict who feared his daughter was an addict and hated in her what he hated in himself. But Kendra was operating under . . . delusions. She believed things had occurred, made accusations he didn't understand. I'm not sure she could separate fact from fiction at that point, or if and when she became able to do so later, but once he got out of rehab, the incident seemed to have blown over. Kendra left for Julliard. In all their subsequent fights, she never mentioned it again, but he and I discussed it many times. He was terrified for her but too intimidated to force her into therapy for fear of what she'd say about him. This was the early nineties, abuse accusations were rampant, everyone believed without question — and she was eighteen anyway, beyond his control. But that day haunted him. I believe he'll carry his guilt over beating her to his grave."

"What are you saying? That my sister is insane?" Yet my heartbeat slowed to a rhythm that made sense. *This* could be why she had allowed Michael Kelsey to whip her too, the beating always leading to consummation of a twisted sexual trauma she'd never realized with our father. Reenactment of a repressed desire, her urge uncontrollable, probably not even conscious.

"Among other things, I'm saying that if Kendra were actually HIV-positive, she'd have had a low T-cell count, and rupturing her stomach, being in a septic situation, would have plummeted her further. Doctors would have noticed. To survive an ordeal like hers, she must have been very healthy indeed. Despite all her efforts to the contrary."

My relief was fleeting. I wanted to hug you for asserting that my father was not a monster, but new images popped into my head—prostitution, violent one-night stands, even suicide—like psychic visions of the equally scary scenario you posed. If Kendra were so mentally ill, so sexually out of control, how could she survive out in the world, broke, alone?

You offered kindly, "Your father loves you. If he seemed to pander to your sister more, it was because he was worried about her. The trusted child is often the one ignored."

"How can you be sure he wasn't lying?"

"I can't. But usually the guilty don't volunteer clues against themselves. I never met Kendra, I never heard her side of the story. He told me freely, himself. He trusted me, and I returned that trust—I'm comfortable with my decision. Your father told me his daughter tried to force herself on him and it scared the hell out of him, and that was what got him sober."

"But what kind of person would—what daughter would try to seduce her father? *Why?*"

Your last opportunity for total honesty, before we parted forever. You arrived at only this: "Jealousy is the most destructive force on earth. Some daughters will do anything to gain an absent father's attention—or steal it from a rival love object, even if that object is imagined."

Leigh Kelsey. Oh, how *not* imagined her beauty had been, how threatening she must have seemed to Kendra, overhearing our mother's constant, fearful allegations of an affair; watching our father, depressive and guilty, surrender again to drink. But what would I know of it when I'd been too in love with Leigh myself to notice anything but the same splendor my father saw? My last remaining strength sifted right into the floor. I nodded. Of course, I understood.

We said goodbye. You told me to call if I needed to. I promised I would, knowing I never in my life wanted to see you again, not with all you knew. As I turned to leave, you added, "Kirby, I suspect you've always been attracted to the man who was your sister's lover. I often felt you were comparing Aris to him and judging your own relationship to be staid by comparison. Please don't allow Kendra's journals to prompt you into backsliding into that kind of thinking, much less into initiating contact with him. I know you may be tempted, I know you want to uncover the truth, but he sounds like a dangerous man."

Only then did I realize I had failed to tell you anything—not that I had gone back to school, not that my stomach had improved, not that from the first time I'd tasted a clitoris silky as a baby's toe under my tongue I'd never looked back. Not that I would have considered giving my life if Michael Kelsey could be dead. The profound gulf of misunderstanding between us seemed at last complete. I was too spent to make my case at this late stage. What was the point after everything, after nothing, now?

I nodded briefly and left.

The Boatman

THE TRAFFIC LIGHT shone red on Michigan Avenue, but when he saw me, all thought must have been suspended. My blond hair was past shoulder length. In the titillating almost-summer breeze, I wore a red halter and slim black pants with slit pockets across each hipbone. At one hundred and eight, I was still ten pounds heavier than the high end of Kendra's weight during their affair, but in the instant in which he should have hit the brakes, I knew he mistook me. Rachel was beside him — Leigh Kelsey had been dead nearly a year and a half, their daughter now solely his. I reeled back; a teenage boy grabbed my arm and yanked me out of the way. In a sudden snapping back to reason, Michael Kelsey's arm flew out in front of his daughter's body like a shield. My eyes, for a split second, focused on that arm, on Rachel's collision into it. I felt my throat closing, could think only some nonsense like, *If Kendra had seen this, she might have been able to stay.* The thought made no sense. A screech of tires, the crunch of metal. His Porsche collided directly into the passenger door of an eastbound car. I stood in a mass of onlookers. I felt like a voyeur. People milled around the cars involved; Michael Kelsey had not yet emerged from his, though I heard Rachel screaming. I could not tell whether the passenger side of the car he'd hit was empty, only that it was dented so the Porsche fit inside like a piece of a puzzle. Somebody was using a cell phone to call an ambulance. I dropped my bag containing a tube of Lancôme lipstick and some spray-on self-tanning cream. I ran.

I knew Michael Kelsey would call. I had long since moved out of Aris's loft in favor of a cheaper place and was not listed. But I knew that my sister's former lover would somehow access my number and call within a day of almost running over me with his car.

Understand: he realized who I was. *She* would have stood right in the middle of Michigan Avenue and let his car hit her. I remained the coward among us. She would never have run.

He called at eleven that night. I had still not figured out whether I planned to answer the phone and sat staring at it before grabbing the receiver frantically on the third ring.

"You know," he said, "ghosts are a road hazard and should be more considerate than to leave the house. Would it be trite of me to say I like what you've done to your hair?"

I said, "I thought maybe you were dead."

"No such luck. Though I have twelve stitches on my forehead you might find satisfying. Rachel had a fine time holding my hand and saying comforting things. It's good for her to witness the fact that sometimes people emerge still standing. Thanks."

"My pleasure. Now we have nothing more to say to one another." But I did not hang up. He didn't speak, as though waiting to hear the impertinent dial tone. Finally I blurted, "Have you heard from her, for God's sake? You haven't, have you? Otherwise you wouldn't have looked at me like I was the walking dead."

"You're correct. But then I wouldn't have taken Kendra's desire to leave seriously if I'd anticipated postcards or drunken phone calls at 4:00 AM from Riviera bars. If I'd received any, I would have told her to stop behaving like a fool and come home." The slim sound of his breath, a sigh both satisfied and resigned. "She is not a fool. I don't expect to hear from her again."

"You mean you *knew*? But you wanted to live with her. Even if you changed your mind, how could you let her go, not even tell her family? You may as well have killed her yourself!"

Nothing. In the lapse, I knew he was debating whether to reveal himself to a confidante as unworthy as I. His decision surprised me. "She planned to ask Henry for a loan. She'd have received one, of course, with conditions. He'd have insisted at bare minimum on knowing where she went, keeping her tied

288

via financial strings. I couldn't stand to have him buy his conscience that way, so I sold mine instead. Cheaply, as I'm sure you'd find appropriate."

"*You* gave her the money?"

"She was going to ask your father for two thousand. I persuaded her to take five."

"Oh God." My esophagus palpitated with an arrhythmic joy. Had he been there, I might have thrown myself into his arms. "She had reserves then. She could sleep in a bed. She could eat." That he didn't respond or in any way seize upon my momentary gratitude was somehow an insult. I stammered, "What happened between her and our father. You knew something. How?"

"It wasn't hard to figure out. I avoided it as long as I could out of loyalty to . . . or identification with Henry. But her aversion to my daughter, her questions about Rachel's sleeping arrangements, things she said when she was . . . not in control—" He caught himself. "You were playing dumb. That night while she was in the hospital. You pretended not to know what I was talking about. I should have realized slow on the uptake is not part of your genes."

"She left journals behind, I know *everything*. You're the one who doesn't have the story straight. She wasn't raped. She tried to force herself on him—seduce him—and maybe failed."

He started to laugh. The kind of laughter this close to a slap, mocking. "Only an arrogant kid who has never been a parent could possibly say anything so unfathomably idiotic."

"Oh, and you feel fit to judge what people are capable of, do you? You took a girl half your age who'd almost died and spent a night injuring her more and sending her back to me with welts all over her wrists and God knows where else!"

An abrupt thud of silence. I began to sweat.

"Kendra spent her last night at the hospital in an emotional meltdown," he said. "They had to restrain her—she kept trying to leave. It wasn't a psychiatric ward, it was the night staff of a regular unit. I guess they tied her wrists to the bed with some sort of flat, waxy string. If she hadn't fought them, it wouldn't have cut her. But of course she did."

"Liar!" But my stomach rose up with recollections of my conversation with Shadisha the day of Kendra's release. Oh God, I had assumed the worst about the welts, had come out swinging the moment she walked into my apartment. Had my suspicious interrogation been the final straw that broke her away from us forever? "No. No."

"Don't worry, Kirby." His voice was almost gentle. "She was probably just too exhausted to bother undressing to show you the marks that were mine."

I started to cry. Wait, can I scratch that part? Can I say it never happened, that I faced him down with stony pride, with assurance in my righteousness? He said crisply, "I wish you wouldn't do that," but I couldn't stop. So instead he began to talk, methodical, telling me he had gone to see my father days after Leigh's death. He'd announced he'd been sleeping with Kendra and laid out what he "knew." I listened, mesmerized and horrified. Could this be what had clued my father in to my mother's and my deceit, what tipped him off that Kendra had not been in New York all along? My brain rattled like a cage shaken roughly. "He did not," Michael finished, "seem very surprised about our affair."

"But he told you what really happened then," I managed. "He was your best friend for ten years, why can't you just believe him? Our father would never have hurt her—if he had, then she could be sick too! If he did, then she ran away alone to die!"

Separated by miles and wires, I could not hear his breath. I suspected I'd frightened him, but instead of feeling victorious, my world grew scarier still. When finally he spoke, though, his voice was not tentative as I'd expected but authoritative, as though I'd presented a momentary glitch. "Whatever her intent when she left, I believe the outcome was more along the lines of finding a reasonably interesting man to marry and procure European citizenship." Suddenly I *felt* his smile. "Kendra has an uncanny ability to extract proposals from men."

I caught my spontaneous grin too, my craving to believe. Desperately, of course, but this optimistic vision came too late to supercede the dark one he'd first sparked two years prior at Aris's loft, the one that led to quite a different outcome: my sister emaciated and near death, too ashamed of her infection by our father to show her face at home. This earlier truth was not one you recognized; not one, it seemed, that Michael Kelsey wanted to touch either. It was not the truth I prayed for, of her attempted seduction and delusion. Yet it was the truth of my bones.

Wearily: "I don't want to talk anymore. Why couldn't you have just been predictable and tried to fuck me instead of so much talking? All this time, missing her, didn't you ever think of coming to me? Then however you wrecked her, at least I'd finally understand what she felt."

"You do," he said. "*That.* Your need to crawl inside her. That's what she felt about you. It's why she threw herself in the line of fire—at Henry. And it's what tore you apart instead."

But what did he mean, laying Kendra's craziness at my feet? You'd explained to my satisfaction that our father's affair with Leigh was what drove Kendra to attempted seduction, actualized or not. Still, I didn't protest; I was too aware of my hostile proposition hanging in the air, insignificant as the dim threat of rain at the beach—nothing he needed to consider. Humiliation complete, I started to hang up when he said, "You look—sound—so almost exactly like her. How could I not want to touch you? Even your anger is poignant to me. But it'd be like jerking off on a picture of a girl I had a crush on in junior high. It would be grotesque."

Never in my life had someone said anything as unequivocally horrible to me. I was stunned. He dared qualify, "I'd like us to be friendly. But you despise me, and we have nothing in common aside from a familiar ache we don't choose to medicate in the same way. But I do regret the impossibility. I do."

"I think it's fair to say that you and I will always regret one another, Michael."

It was the first time I'd addressed him by name—the intimacy made me cringe. But he, nonplused, said, "Always is a long time to keep a vigil. Don't make me your cross, Kirby. It's misguided. Kendra did not sacrifice herself to me—that pain was not about us. We were lovers. We were *friends.* I don't have to explain myself to you, but I have never in my life wanted so badly for anyone to understand anything. I see I've failed. I just wish you could put it to rest."

"I know," I whispered. "I can't."

"In that case," he said, "I'm afraid I have made a terrible mistake. In that case, I have something you need to see."

Case Study

It is only towards the end of the treatment that we have before us an intelligible, consistent, and unbroken case history. Whereas the practical aim of the treatment is to remove all possible symptoms and to replace them by conscious thoughts, we may regard it as a secondary and theoretical aim to repair all damages to the patient's memory. These two aims are coincident. When one is reached, so is the other; and the same path leads to them both.

—Sigmund Freud,
Fragment of an Analysis of a Case of hysteria

The offices were quiet, dark, without a trace of movement. Kendra's hair had retained a shocking volume of rain; it spilled from the ends of her long strands, making the carpet beneath her feet squishy. Michael gathered her hair in his hands and shook out the tail he'd fashioned with two swift flicks. Drops splattered, and they laughed, complicit and furtive as thieves, leaning against the doorway in the blackness. His voice, shattering silence, spoiled the effect. He didn't whisper like a criminal, but spoke full volume like a king in a palace he owned.

"Do you want to see where Aris was planning to kill us all?"

Kendra giggled again. She couldn't stop. Though coke rarely made her so giddy, tonight she felt like a teenager high for the first time. Through the windows across the office, lights from downtown Chicago simulated the after-effects of thousands of flashbulbs. She glanced around half-expecting a hidden camera, but Michael had already scooped her up off her feet and was heading down the hall with her, the wetness of her hair forming rivulets that dripped from the point of his elbow. Her eyes quickly grew accustomed to the dark. The hall leading to Aris's fire-hazard wing seemed endless, longer than the aisle of First Presbyterian Church where Kirby was set to walk in less than a week. Kendra's period would be gone by then. It had come unexpectedly (who expected it any more?) in the car on their way here. No stores open this late on a Sunday downtown, she'd stuffed two Kleenex between her vaginal lips to catch the blood.

Thunder clapped in the sky, so loud she felt the boom in her chest. "I haven't been here, she said, "in a very, very long time."

"You've never been *here*. This is uncharted territory."

The would-be new wing was huge. Nothing but halted construction now: boards lying on a sawdusty ground, the smell of dust sharp in the air. Nothing that looked solid enough to even lean against, much less lie on. She stood where he'd put her down, unsure what to do amid so much open space, a man's failed venture. "I'm healthy again." A random comment; Michael's eyebrows raised in confusion. "My period," she said, suddenly serious. "It was gone for months and now it's back, so I must not be sick after all. It must have just been a fluke."

Michael had picked up a flashlight among the workmen's rubble and shone it on her. "Bleeding this one month doesn't mean you aren't far too underweight to menstruate regularly."

She rose a hand to cover her eyes. "You said I'm not too thin."

"I said that months ago. You are. Now you are."

"Turn that damned thing off."

He didn't, but set the flashlight down so the focus was off her face. Came to where she stood, sliding the zipper of her dress down and lowering the soaked material off her shoulders to her waist. She was conscious of the padding of his hands against her shoulder blades, the sharpness of her ribs. "Don't shrink any more," he said. "You'll make me afraid to touch you."

"Ha. You don't seem to think much about how small I am once you have a hard on."

The pressure of his hands against her bones grew greater. "You're wrong. How fragile your body looks, how easy it is to hold you in place, to hurt you, is a turn on within limits. But there's a difference between simulating nihilism and actually courting it."

A spurt of laughter. "'Women should at least know the difference between love and death,' huh? Adrienne Rich wrote that. I doubt you and she would agree on much else."

"If you move in with me, you're going to gain some weight," he continued, not smiling. "Nothing drastic—you know my taste. But I insist on a few pounds."

"Do you?" The tingling under her skin, cocaine and wet chill, grew hot. "So . . . if I fatten up, if I conduct myself properly in front of your daughter, if I can act like a normal person and pass all your tests, tell me, what do I win?"

Now the smile, now. "Is that what I'm doing? Testing you?"

"Mmm, let's see. What sounds like more fun to you: cozy dinners for three and tame, quiet sex that won't wake your kid up in the middle of the night, or helping me pay for my own apartment where nobody could hear me scream? It's not rocket science. You must think you have something to gain, playing it this way. Giving me no choice but right into the line of fire."

He kept his hands firm, his gaze, but tension gathered under his skin—unwillingness, she knew, to yield once again his need to know that their games were a *choice*; his embarrassment at trying to save her from himself, the hypocrisy. Maybe, also, a reluctance to admit that if she failed, could not stop playing the petulant child long enough to be an adult for Rachel, he would cut her loose, clean: his easy out. Whereas if she succeeded, mastered this role as she had

gina frangello

every other, there might *be* no clear end point, no falling curtain. Then, real risk would begin.

He kissed her. She let her arms wrap all the way around him instead of maintaining a vigilance to clutch his shirt, pull his hair, scratch his back, grab for his dick—any rough movement that could not be mistaken for affection. His body was less fluid from the coke, choppier, but she didn't mind. It would be fair to say the urgency implicit in his jerkiness touched her. It would be fair to say she was thinking something like, *Maybe we can transcend what we've been, maybe it really could be something more.* Perhaps she thought, in that moment, about saying yes right into his mouth, into his breath so there could be no telling which of them had spoken and which breathed the other in. But she had, you will recall, snorted two fewer lines than he, and her presence of mind, while shaky, was not completely gone. She knew he wanted to wait for Saturday. Until the wedding reception when they could meet secretly in a corridor, when she could whisper her covert acceptance in passing. When they could spend a clandestine evening in public before spending the night in his apartment that would soon be theirs, in the confused and reckless excitement that would surely follow her yes. She stayed silent. But the intimacy of holding him this way, of his allowing her to hold him this way, threatened to obliterate her will. She pulled away. Got down on her knees, where it was safe.

He was not even a little bit hard.

Kendra jerked as though she'd seen a ghost. It was entirely possible that she gasped. Not at all appropriately embarrassed, Michael moved away from where she rested in front of him, ready to suck him back to some safer realm. He said flatly, "I can't. I am . . . distracted."

A light of recognition switched on; she felt her shoulders relax. "Oh, what," she teased, reaching for his fly, "you're getting me back now because I didn't want to fuck this afternoon?"

"Kendra." He pushed her hand away—*he pushed her hand away.* "I have something to tell you. Get up."

She could not get up. Could not meet his eyes. She knew, of course, what he was going to say. Somewhere between her mention of his daughter and the moment she got to her knees, he had realized he was a fool. Somewhere during the seconds of hope she'd permitted herself, reality had hit him, and he had seen their shaky plans for what they were—absurd. *You*

295

cannot live with me, he would tell her. *I can't do that to Rachel, expose her to what we are.* Or more simply, *I'll tire of you if you're available constantly. I am tiring already.* Desecration should not coexist with the ordinary—she knew this. Had always known this would happen: a few months (seven was more than she'd expected) of intensity and transgression and heart-pounding need. Then the day when her bruises ceased to be sexy, when her welts became inconveniences that oozed on the furniture, when orchestrating such rigorous passion cut into his already scarce free time and left him with a cramp in the arm that bugged the next day at the gym. When the epiphany dawned that he could not respect a woman he had tortured until she howled like a beast, when he could not respect himself for having debased this woman into a creature so unworthy of respect. When she had nothing left to conquer anymore. Oh God. She could not rise from her knees; he had to help her. His face was dirtied with some transparent pain. She backed away. Heard herself, horribly, "Michael. Don't say it."

"I know that Henry has AIDS."

"Oh." An anticlimactic response to what had been her worst, unutterable fear. She wondered if she were in shock. "Um . . ." Did not know what to add. "When did you find out?"

"Last night. Leigh told me. After we'd fucked, which is beside the point except that it might be what inspired her to tell a secret she's been keeping for months—some memory of old intimacy. Now that I know, it's hard to believe I never guessed. It seems . . . so clear."

"You . . ." Her voice quivered like nothing her father's disease had achieved. "Made love with your ex-wife?"

He blinked. "I didn't want to come home to you. She was there, that's all. She was there looking her usual gorgeous, self-invented, fabulously shallow self, so I thought maybe she could fuck some sense into me." He half-laughed, short and angry. "Obviously, that didn't work any better than it ever had."

"Obviously."

He reached to touch her; she retracted her body just the requisite inch so his hand dropped unfulfilled. "Why didn't you tell me, Kendra? You knew I wouldn't go to Henry."

"So what?" Eyes flashing, she moved closer again, daring him to touch. "*You* know I don't like to talk about him. Do you think I care what he's dying of—that he's dying at all?"

"No." But he took hold of her arms, one in each hand, as though to prevent her from disappearing. "No, I don't imagine you would."

She stood impassive, felt no clarity of emotion. "Then why even bring it up—especially tonight? To rub my face in it? What the hell does it have to do with me?"

He shook his head, foggy from the drugs or her irrationality. "I'm telling you, Kendra, for any number of reasons, all of which you know full well." But when she rolled her eyes, he pulled her tighter, more of a shake—"Hey. What sort of logical system are you operating under right now? I'm telling you I *know* what you've been going through since he got sick. Don't you think I see how all this reflects on your state of mind, how it reflects on me and what I've done to—" His voice cracked: thick, choked, impossible. He dropped her arms fast, turned away.

"Coward." No trace of irony in her tone. "How dare you not want me to see you cry."

Though he faced her immediately, eyes in fact doing nothing resembling weeping, it was some time before he was composed to speak. "I can't give you something I can't give myself."

The fog had lifted. She felt rage. Grasped it, swallowed it whole. "Bullshit! That's exactly what this is about—what *everything* you've extracted from me amounts to. Deny that, and you dismiss everything between us."

"This shouldn't even be about us. I'm not your father. He's the one dying, and you—"

"God, *whatever*, Michael." She yanked herself away. "Look, this is nothing new to me—I've known for months, so excuse me if I don't want to trip out about it for the zillionth time just because you brought it up. You just found out that your best friend's a dead man, and fine, you're freaked and grieving and way too high—well, big deal. That's my starting point every time I come to you. For once you're not in control—you're smack in my element."

"You're wrong." Quietly. "I don't care about Henry."

"Great," she gave a quick clap, "then we're on the same page! New topic, please." She picked up the flashlight, shone it in his face; he squinted, hand rising instinctively. "Like that you fucked the femme fatale adulteress who bore your child, maybe? Just to be clear, now tell me if I'm getting this—I'm

297

not supposed to *care*, right? But—I hate to be a downer—what if I do? Should I dump you? Or . . ." a stage smile, "should I just give you a little test of my own?"

With sudden great fatigue: "And what is that supposed to mean?"

Her question. They had come full circle. She sensed her body straightening, so light she could float away. The words slipped out easily. She had known they were coming all along.

"When you play your games with me, you tell yourself you're offering catharsis. That's not just rationalization, it's true. But that's not why I want to do it to you."

Outside, the city shook under violent thunder. In an empty, calm, sawdust-smelling fire wing, Kendra Braun could think only, *He isn't fixating on my father now, his death and disease.* Her lover's attention had focused back onto her like a laser that bore right through flesh and bones. A surge of victory pounded in her ears; his response no longer mattered. The moment was already won.

But after a long pause: "I've always figured you would want to turn the tables someday, if only once. This is not the sort of circumstance, not the sort of night I had in mind."

And she: "Go on, Michael. Tell me with a straight face that you are not in the mood."

"I'm not going to say that. You can do anything you want to me. You know that."

"Actually I didn't. Until now."

He sighed. "Why lie? Why, when I finally get what this is about? You want to do to me what you never could to him—fine, I won't back out if you need that. But at least be real."

"You think I want to hurt my father for being sick? Why would I bother—?"

"I *know*, Kendra. I have known. There are no mysteries any—"

"Shut up!" Hand flying, fingers extended, colliding with the side of his face. "Don't say anything else! I stop talking when you tell me to. You do the same or this ends right here."

And he? He had always been the more literal of the two. It made him, she suddenly realized with nothing short of terror, far better at following orders. She would have snapped *Fine*, or more likely *Fuck you*, before grudgingly sulking into obedient silence. But he responded not at all. Adhered already to his end of the bargain.

She yanked the belt hard from around his waist and wound it round his wrists like a snake to begin.

*   *   *

July 1989

The noise her sister was making was like what Kendra imagined an animal would sound like in a trap. Hollow, so deep it made her marrow vibrate. She had to go to the noise. Maybe an hour before, she'd heard footsteps on the attic stairs leading to Bee's room. Feet too heavy to be her sister's: going up, coming down. Then, following the descent of heavier feet, the scuttle of her sister's stockinged ones, scurrying to the belly of the house. Bee had slammed the door to the first-floor bathroom as though it were not the middle of the night, as though she might not wake up everybody with such racket. As though, Kendra thought, she wanted to be heard.

Kendra rose from bed. The animal-sound in the bathroom felt like a magnet, pulling her so hard to the site she stumbled. How was it their parents did not hear? Clearly they could not be sleeping, they'd just been in the attic — but no, that was only one of them, one set of footsteps on the stairs. Inside the bathroom Kirby had grown quiet. Kendra's hand on the door gripped wet; she had not noticed she was sweating. Door flung back, she stood blinking in the dark to see. Flipped the light on fast, whispered for some reason, "Bee, it's me, don't scream."

Between the toilet and the tub, Kirby was working. Fast, jerky, rubbing the bar of soap against what looked to be her bed sheet. Kendra strode in and yanked the soap from her hands — Bee gave a small sharp cry that failed to rouse any movement upstairs. Maybe their father had passed out already, their mother's head also heavy against her pillow with the Valium she'd needed ever since they'd come to Kenilworth from Cincinnati. Kendra was not supposed to know, but she wasn't stupid. She'd even stolen one once and split it with her new best friend before school let out, but they kept getting in trouble all the rest of the day, couldn't pay attention, floaty and tired, incapable of algebra. A weekend thing Kendra decided, but had never managed to swipe another — her mother kept them locked away.

"What are you doing?" Soft, cajoling, the way you'd speak to a cat in a tree. Kendra had never heard her own voice come out like this.

"I got my period." Her sister was whimpering. "I didn't want anybody to know."

A demented thing to say. Kendra stared down at the blotchy circle of soap and blood that soiled the sheet. How long had stupid Bee been crying? The feet on the stairs had woken Kendra up—had her sister's wailing prompted her father or mother to go up there to calm her down? They'd given up on her no doubt; Bee was always bawling over something, ever since the move, ever since their father's drinking. Kendra pulled the sheet from her sister's hand. "Just go to sleep, leave it for Mom in the morning. She'll be happy. I'll get mine now too."

Kirby jumped to her feet, a startled deer lunging. "Leave me alone. You can't have yours too, it's only going to happen to me!"

"That's what you think, stupid. Everything that happens to you happens to me."

Kirby had the sheet now. Ran with it trailing behind her, scampered out of sight up the stairs. Kendra sank onto the toilet. She didn't have to pee, but wiped herself just the same. No blood. Not yet. Let Kirby keep her secret. Then when Kendra got hers in a few days or a month, she could say it'd happened to her first, and if Bee wanted to deny it, she'd have to admit her earlier lie. Kendra giggled. Then everybody would know her sister had gone insane.

*   *   *

What she had with her: one belt around his wrists. Another (from an extra suit hanging in his office—where they were now and where he told her she would find it) wrapped just above his knees and buckled tight. A sock (his) shoved over his hands and under the belt so he couldn't undo his bonds if she pissed him off, which she hoped she was going to do. A pack of cigarettes, nine left, and his silver lighter. A thin, broken-but-still-somewhat-too-long wooden board. His shirt, the body of which she'd threaded between his wrists, then spread him stomach-down over his desk and stretched his arms tight to tie the sleeves to a wooden leg in front, holding him in place. "Superfluous," he'd pronounced this last restraint, and it did look uncomfortable, likely caused every movement to pull at his shoulders making him feel his arms would snap. Legs bound, he could not very well have run away to begin with. He'd only have fallen thrashing on the ground, and he wouldn't have done that and she knew it and he knew she knew it. Now he could not thrash even if he wanted to. Probably he could still propel himself over the desk using his legs. But the effort would be a directionless one, spawned by

300

the kind of hysterical fear of which she thought him incapable. He kept his legs still.

Things worked against her. Though she was not very big, a lack of strength wasn't one of them. An ex-dancer, she was still muscled over protruding bones, and high besides. By now she'd also learned ways to wound that did not require much strength. It was not that he did not take her seriously either— she'd worried about that at first, feared one of them would just bust out laughing. But she was too mean for that and he knew it. What she lacked in experience she made up for with nerve. She'd started with a cigarette, paced and deliberate 'til there were small blots of blood all over his back—connect the dots—before moving onto the board.

No, she was not, that she could see, doing anything *wrong*. But Michael had been on the other end of this deal too often, with her and before her. It was like trying to analyze a patient who was himself a psychiatrist. The process held no mystery for him. He knew it for what it was, was too easy with it, quiet and calm when he could be but knowing exactly where everything would lead, how little his own will had to do with the inevitability of control giving out. He didn't struggle against it the way she did, but accepted her torture of him like a surgeon accepting gas before going under the knife—with an almost good-natured curiosity. She wanted to kill him. Knew too that in her position, this was a dangerous desire.

She talked to him in between her tasks. This was what he always did with her, and she realized now that he did it because silence was too hard, too awkward and too humiliating for both parties. She wanted to humiliate him that much, but the quiet was too much for her too. She mocked him if he made a noise, mocked him if he didn't. But even the mocking was better than nothing, than not acknowledging they were people who could talk to one another.

Occasionally, she asked his advice. "Backs are off limits, right? It's dangerous, or is that only the lower back?" When he snapped, finally alarmed, "For Chrissake don't give me a spinal injury with that plank you're wielding," she said, "Too bad, I'd like to hit you where I've burned you," and lit another cigarette to touch to his already-welted ass. That achieved a sharp noise, a frantic pulling in of breath that whistled like a hiss. His stoicism was crumbling, but slowly, more slowly than she could comprehend—she was much smaller than he, malnourished and with a bad back and a system usually saturated with depressants. She was pretty sure that already what she had done to him would have been enough to render her unconscious.

Sharp board smacking his ass again, she *felt* his body twitch, the throaty vibrations of his low moan. Sing-song: "Are you going to lose it for me soon, Michael? Or could I murder you without your figuring out how to make anything other than these mildly discontented sounds?"

He was perhaps as confused by the duration of this game, by his stamina, as she. Consented, strained but still irredeemably calm, "I don't know."

Once, months ago, she'd asked him the same thing; he'd been hurting her at the time. "Could you take this? Would you let me see you this way? Would you?" And he, safe behind his belt or his candle or his ice cubes or his cock, flippant: "It's true I'm not prone to loud noises. But a body's response is not a matter of choice. And if I'd ever scream for anyone, it'd be you."

He did not scream now. Did not cry, though his eyes teared, and she had to conclude that he did not know how to offer more. If she persisted long enough, his body would wear down so he'd moan more consistently, then sink right out of consciousness if she did not stop. In the absence of screams or tears, she knew no precedent of how to end. She was already panicked that maybe she had scarred him—multiple times. He couldn't, after all, see the blood running down his legs, though he must have felt it. Must have, but he had not commented.

She did not know what to do. Hit him with the board faster, and it was true: his moans increased, body losing energy. Perhaps this was all it took. She had been too ambling, too unfocused with her rotation of torturous techniques. If she beat him long and quick enough, he'd figure out how to bawl the way she did, to be weak the way she was. It *must* be the case. When he whipped her, she tried so hard, with everything in her, not to give him what he wanted. Not to shed a tear or make a sound. But she did—deep down she wanted to. She needed the explosion to quell a ticking bomb inside her. Needed force, needed *this*. What if he just did not?

Rhythmic, steady pounding. Enveloped by the shudders of his breath, uneven, so shaky that if she kept on he might lose oxygen altogether. Her arm wielding the board began to tremble. His breath, so weak, so close to what she was, disgusted her. What was the matter with him, letting her do this? Was he out of his mind? What kind of person would let somebody—?

She dared not look at his face. Had not dared for some time, but saw, unmistakably wedged between his hips and the desk, his hard on. The erection he had been unable to produce over the grave of her father. But there it was now, when she might have left scars scattering his back like a deadly outbreak of chicken pox. When his ass might be striped with zebra scar tissue. There it was, as though this were nothing to him, bore no life-or-death implications despite his watering eyes, his hoarse moans. His dick pushed against the dispassionate wood of the desk—some reminder of what she would get when this was through. He would never break for her. It was only *pain*. If she beat him long enough, he'd either pass out or ask her (politely) to please stop. She had achieved nothing. Reversed nothing . . .

His dick pulsed against the desk. The desk that had been her father's before sick leave, and Michael, who'd come to the firm a few months after Henry, claimed the space because it was bigger, had a better view. Michael's dick rubbed into her father's desk—some joke of mahogany and semen and power between men. A king did not weep at the revolution of his peasants, everybody knew. Even if they beheaded him, he went calmly to the guillotine, his blood still superior to theirs. Nothing she could do.

Groping without looking until it was in her hand. The flashlight she'd used to navigate the black, windowless halls to his office. The circularity of it in her palm, fingers wrapped around, felt right. The instrument was innocuous switched off. She held it by the would-be glowing end—bigger there, too wide. The face did not make a perfect handle. But it would have to do.

In the absence of her blows, her lover fell silent. He couldn't see her behind him. Could not witness her intent. She was sorry in that moment that he would not read the purpose on her face. She laughed—voice surprisingly strong. Rolled the flashlight along his ass, watched blood coat its sides. Nothing. No words. But recognition. His leg muscles throbbed with desire for movement. Futile desire. She ran a hand down the back of his thigh.

303

"Exactly how afraid are you to become a woman? I can use your pants to tie your legs to the chair, then you can't kick me if you panic. Tell me if you need me to do that. Your choice."

Between her own legs, the Kleenex had grown saturated. She was a woman, despite everything. A body could wait for years, and blood would still catch up to claim it. Kendra had waited one month, two, then a year, but her own blood hadn't come, and Kirby's did not return either. Kendra checked wastebaskets, in Bee's drawers and under her bed for pads. Nothing. Only Kirby growing chubbier and more silent by the day, developing crippling stomachaches, leaving bed sheets wet with piss so their mother hollered, then apologized and kissed Bee's forehead before another Valium was downed. Only Kirby's slipping grades and growing disinterest in their friends and in ballet until Kendra had inherited both for her own—a hollow victory. Only the sound of footsteps, at two in the morning, at four, until one day their father ceased drinking, never announced it but it was clear immediately to them all. Then the noise on the stairs just stopped. Still Kendra waited. Month after month, a year and then two, before the blood caught up with her, and with Kirby the very same week. They were genetically identical; it made sense, though their mother told everybody like it was a curiosity anyway. Fifteen by then— oldish—but they were small, with breasts that developed late too. Women suddenly, both of them; their father dry, mother active at a new church, but something that had once been the same, one set of genes communing through two bodies, was irrevocably shattered. Two separate bodies, suddenly; two separate women. That blood in the bathroom two years earlier had ripped them apart—

The man she was ripping was crying out. He might at one point have said something logical, pointed out the anatomical obscenity of her task. The untapered end of the flashlight; the switch protruding unwieldy from its side; the sticky, fast-drying, nonlubricant nature of blood. He might have said, *I do not agree to this, it is irresponsible and dangerous, if you want to play you buy the proper equipment and do it right.* Or maybe he'd never said any of those things. Groans clogged with mucusy rawness, he certainly now regretted the refusal to speak which led her to bind his legs to his heavy, expensive, swivel chair. He could move not at all. His pelvis stretched tight between desk and chair, suspended in midair, dick exposed.

304

His noises did not contain language anymore. Were not loud anymore if they ever had been. She could not recall. Was not sure whether, by the standards she'd fashioned earlier, she had even won. He was not pleading. (Did she want him to plead? Would she listen if he tried?) In the space between the desk and chair that bookended his body, his cock—purplish, veiny, painful looking—still pulsed hard. She was mesmerized by its audacity, its coked-up, dangling foolishness. Its total separation from the soul of the man who emitted low animal noises of torn-up agony. She could stick her hand straight up through to his heart, swish her fingers around in his emotions, his pain receptors. His cock stared back—inviting, unrepentant—just the same.

She dropped to her knees.

"An . . . ironic finale."

How much time had passed? Enough so she had forgotten the very possibility of language. His voice pricked down her spine: panting, contorted, but followed, unbelievably, by laughter. A start-stop kind, betraying pain; breath like wheezing. He managed to choke, "Can't make my anatomy your destiny, huh?"

She did not stop sucking. Could not.

"Untie me," he said, a bit steadier, "so I can come as near as possible to killing you."

It was not a threat; she did not feel threatened. It is important to clarify this. Her impulse had nothing to do with fear, with self-defense. He was telling her to untie him so he could hurt and fuck her the way he wanted to, the way she wanted him to. A simple, inexpressibly appealing command. One she wanted badly to obey but she could not move. Could not loosen her mouth from around him. He said nothing else, resigned enough to let her blow him to orgasm while he was still bound—perhaps, now that he was not being burned and whipped and anally probed, being restrained and sucked at once was not even such a bad shake. His moan, unbelievably, was one of pleasure. Chilling.

She grasped around his legs. Clung onto them tight, fingers swishing in the wetness on the backs of his thighs. His muscles relaxed into her despite what she *knew* to be blinding discomfort. The smell of the substance that leaked down his leg, that dried on her fingers as she clutched his thighs in desperation, constricted her throat. A dead, shameful smell, one she could not reconcile with the man she knew. He did not seem to care. Was no more squeamish about his own body than about hers; she knew it was part of their deal that she feel the same. But his body was not part of this equation anymore. Instead he offered up her *own* essence: filthy and soiled. Reflected back in all her ugliness right through his skin.

She could not let go, could not move her hands. Could not turn to leave despite *fingers too tight, digging in my shoulders. When he shook me, my neck flopped like in a car collision. His face was a collision of indignation, confusion—no desire. He said, You are on drugs. Like it was nothing we shared. I was furious the way teenagers are when accused of truths. Furious he dared treat me as his child when I was a warrior—a righter of wrongs. I'd ridden that elevator so sure of my mission, the vodka bottle I'd stolen from his filing cabinet stuck in my dance bag, righteousness tight in my chest. I'd marched into his office and said straight off, Take me. Heroically. No, bullshit—more like an amputee seeking my missing limb, willing to follow it into darkness if that was what it took. Will honed from years of ballet, body bending to commands, I begged, Kirby can't handle it anymore but it doesn't matter to me—I've done it before.*

Biting down as the last few spasms wracked him. Not yet hard enough to taste blood mingling with the hot, salt-liquid, but enough to make his stomach jerk, desperate to pull away.

First, nothing but the noise of his hand exploding across my face. Then his arms dragging me to the door. Yelling the whole time. Stuff like, Get out! and, I will not be spoken to this way! and, You're out of your mind! I'm pretty sure I was calm. I said, I know you love me more anyway, it was an accident, you didn't mean it to be her over me, I was too close, right down the hall. He clamped his hand over my mouth. Dragged me down the corridor past gaping secretaries and interns before dumping me in the hall like trash. Before he threatened, If you talk like this again I'll have you committed.

Tighter, harder. A thrill of piercing meat between her teeth. He ceased even breathing.

For a moment, I actually believed I was wrong. This drizzle of shame fell over me. Then he said, If you say anything about this to your mother I will kill you. And grief flooded me, worse than if I'd been imagining the whole thing, than if I'd come and thrown myself at him like some filthy insane whore without reason. No, worse— way worse to know I'd been right all along.

Oh God, Michael, naked, folding his duvet mornings. Massaging her feet on the couch, quoting *This is My Beloved*, source of his favorite pick-up lines in college. "Compliments become you/as tinsel becomes a tall snow covered cedar in a mountain cedar wood." Her greedy pleasure in his fingers, purring, "Yes, that's good, I like that one." His smell at 3:00 AM, ripe with sex. Then, just out of the shower, papaya shampoo and mint toothpaste, oatmeal soap Rachel had given him for Father's Day. Spicy cedar from his underwear drawer . . .

A rush of tremors shook her jaw. Kendra Braun let the man she had loved for a decade go, fell back against his desk and onto the carpet, sobbing. Teeth marks lay imprinted into her lover's shaft like a cock ring. The marks were not *exactly* bleeding. His penis hung soft at last, but decidedly still among the living.

Nothing left to do but untie him and face whatever was coming her way.

*   *   *

February 1994

Kendra held the note like an addendum to those magazines found years earlier, a delayed postscript. M in New York, Rachel at a sleepover, you may come—if you like? *Mrs. Kelsey, a woman beautiful in a way that, at seventeen, Kendra already knew she would never be, was inviting her father to imitate the bodies in those pictures. Mrs. Kelsey, beautiful in a way so powerful that any man who had her should never need another. Yet upstairs in the attic room, Kirby hid, proof men acted on desires that lurked somewhere uglier than need.* M in New York, come—if you like? *The illusion of questioning made Kendra's stomach twist with the games people played. As though there were any chance her father would refuse, would not move stealthily through the night to take his place in another woman's bed.* Wife unwilling to accommodate your desires, daughter unable to bear them any longer, you may come—if you like? *In the attic room when they were only thirteen, had Kirby been a sacrifice to nothing but libidinous excess—a body incinerated on the pyre for no grateful god? How was it possible that her sister's life could have been ruined on sheer impulse alone? Daughters in their fear, wife in her church, rather than to the comfort of the bottle,* you may come—if you like? *Kendra did not intend her proposition to be any more a question than was his married lover's. She would*

307

permit no more loopholes. No possibilities for escape. An offering of force, the last-ditch strategy of a warrior, not the clamoring of a daughter seeking to please. Her body felt ancient. And him. Was what passed between her father and Mr. Kelsey's wife only a respectable taboo, simulation of the true desire he had spilled in the attic? Or had Bee been a consolation prize before he found a real woman to give what their mother would not? Now that he was drinking again, could Mrs. Kelsey prevent his turning to Bee too? No guarantees. In the attic, Bee wept. Kendra heard her, awake or asleep, every night since the night of bloody sheets. She knew what she had to do: the only way. She was not afraid.

*   *   *

The key knocked farther out of reach. She'd slid the coat hanger too fast along the floor, manic, heard the key slide off to the side someplace. Now she'd need a hook. She pulled the hanger back from its exploratory mission inside the kitchen. Reshaped it so the hanging part was at the fore and re-slid her divining rod under the kitchen door. Lay on her belly, chin against floor, straining to see. Fast, back and forth. No, better to slow down, get her head together. This kind of frantic bullshit had slid the key farther away a minute ago. Again, with precision.

Her hook wasn't even touching the floor. She had to angle it, pull up on the body of the hanger 'til she heard the hook scrape against linoleum. Serious now. Off to the left; the key had veered to the left. Couldn't be that far out of reach, she hadn't belted it like a fucking hockey puck. Just outside the hanger's radius, just that one—shit, she needed something longer than this hanger—fraction of an inch. Why couldn't she have left the kitchen light on, her parents paid the bill anyway, maybe then she'd be able to see.

The lock—it might work to pick the lock. Kendra pushed herself off the floor with her hands. Her back had hurt earlier; she couldn't feel it anymore. One foot rested on an empty bag of Sun Chips—food wrappings from a post-Michael trip to the Mini Mart lay strewn like a minefield all around. Maybe something was left inside the Sara Lee cake box. Some goop of frosting stuck to the top. The part she and Kirby'd eaten first when they were small.

She needed a bobby pin, lost them like precious gems that fell into the hands of beggars from her hair. Left with six

308

holding up a French twist; came home with four. Did they fall into the same black hole as Rachel's socks and bungies? Did the girl steal them from Michael's bed so they wouldn't litter his carpet the way these convenience-store food wrappings did hers now?

Inside the kitchen was real food to be found. Some would be spoiled; it'd been awhile since Michael bought it—a few weeks ago? She couldn't remember. Frozen yogurt and whole wheat toaster pastries and boxes of cereal because it was her favorite thing and frozen flatbread pizza she could pass off as dinner in case they ever wanted to stay in and flour tortillas that might be okay since they'd never been opened and refried beans and salsa to go with a bag of real nacho chips not the flimsy Tostados kind and the turkey lunchmeat would be bad but she remembered a plastic-wrapped bulb of Gouda. She never ate cheese, way too fattening. Michael must have been planning to make her down it to force that weight gain . . .

Moving slow. In the bathroom cabinet were enough hairpins to hold her unmanageable hair. Enough to keep up some illusion of pristine elegance until Michael tore it down and she returned with fewer bobby pins than before. She did not let herself run. Was not an animal but a ballerina who could control her need to feed long enough to walk back to the kitchen door at a normal pace. Long enough to drop to her knees at a normal pace, jam the pin—fucking plastic coating, she hadn't considered the plastic coating, bit it off, no problem, that wasn't so hard. In.

The pin slid through the keyhole. She had tried to pick a lock before. Failed then, so she'd stolen the key off her father's ring in plain view. A tiny key to a filing cabinet in his study, locked 'cause it held the booze she was snooping for—also notes from his lover. Those she hadn't expected. But this was no flimsy filing cabinet from Target or where-fucking-ever, this was an antique door in an older-than-her-father building where he once used keys to uncover a Mistress Veronica pretending to shut him out. Mistresses were like that. *She* was not a mistress because her lover wasn't married and she didn't weigh enough to be one—Michael said that once. "Literally," he'd specified. "Figuratively you are nothing if not heavy." Ha fucking ha.

Pin ready, she had no idea what to do. Pushing, jiggling. The door did not respond. The door could not feel her efforts.

She was a flea on a great stallion: not even an annoyance. Like an inanimate object up a man's ass: only a momentary annoyance. Large enough to hurt but not large enough to kill. Michael must have trusted that or he'd have beaten her when she let him go instead of surveying her bawling on the floor and saying flat and impatient, "Oh stop it, this guilt bullshit doesn't become you." Then staggering to the bathroom to clean up and change into the extra suit. On the drive home blood still seeped—board and burns. "What is the poor doorman going to think this time?" Michael quipped. "Should we tell him I've been shot?" But she still couldn't quit. Said, *We* aren't telling him anything—I'm going home. Inconceivable that he was planning to walk into his building in the first place. He could hardly stand after what she'd done. He'd managed though. Not like she had killed him. Only raped him, although she wasn't sure he realized even that. What was a little rape between friends? Not like murder, though he'd started to say (before she shut him up) that he *knew*, that there were no mysteries . . .

Yes, of course! Leigh must be sick too. Why else would a sophisticated, urban woman flee to the mountains, if not to die without scrutiny? Why else abandon her daughter, throw an adolescent girl to the wolf, if not to spare her having to witness—wait, but Leigh had fucked Michael. Did she hate him so much, would she do that to her own daughter's father? Would any sane person take the risk Kendra had gladly run, oh God, this transferred revenge—

Shit shit shit. She did not know what to do with the pin. Why, *why* had Michael let her shut him up? Why couldn't he have dumped what he knew out in the open so she could have spilled her soul instead of his blood? Why had he sacrificed his body? A pitiful cop-out. Stuck now—she'd jammed too deep—the would-be key wouldn't come out. She pulled to extract it but her fingers were bleeding. Or maybe that was still his blood. Girls were stupid—so simple—she had been wasting her time. The door was old; she needed only to break it down. But girls never thought of force and look what happened when they did. She had betrayed the one person who had offered her a home, a body, a language, if only temporarily. The one who'd looked at all her twisted demons and hadn't turned away . . .

Necessary to have a running start. She cleared the aisle of Baked Lay's and Snickers and cinnamon raisin bagel wrappings. Sara-Lee'd, Sun-Chipped, Dove-Barred aisle. A ballerina flying the way they'd taught her grand jetés: legs splitting in air. Then body colliding into door on her forceful landing. The wood gave nothing still. She did not weigh enough to be a mistress. This apartment was for a mistress, but she did not weigh enough for her lover to even want to hurt her anymore now that she was something he wanted to keep. She could have given her body over to him, said, *Take me feed me don't let me go.* Maybe he would have even tried. She could have been like Kirby after all, lolling in blissful denial, truth fucked out of her pores by another paternal, well-meaning man. They could have gone out for a big family meal that would nourish and keep them alive. She and Michael and Rachel and Kirby and Aris and Henry and Gail. Aris could have said to Henry: *I will be you, I will make your daughter into her mother.* Michael could have said: *I already am you, I have my daughter and your daughter too.* But whom did that make Rachel? Nevermind, Kendra had gone and ruined it. Bitterness was so unbecoming in a girl.

The door gave. Under her shoulder, wood crunched its surrender. She could not feel her shoulder or the right-hand side of her jaw anymore. Who cared if the key belonged to her father? If you knocked your body hard enough against anything, you could tear it down. If you were willing to overlook the damage, to overlook the taste of tin flowing from the lip you'd bitten through. Inside awaited food Michael had bought to own her or save her: no difference. Inside was what she needed to become heavy enough to live with him inside a world where there was nothing—no one—that could not be broken down *I am broken down. Leigh slept with him that same year, first. If she's infected, what are my chances? Michael's? If I die—kill?—will I finally feel what you felt? But no, I forced our father—I was not his victim. Instead your sickly body and denial turn my choice into a joke. Leave my heart so hard, this close to bursting—*

Something from all her banging burst. The door, or her worn-down skeletal frame? Her body moved numb but intact through the entrance of the last room she ever planned to see. Inside was everything she required. Food, then booze, knives, gas. Soon her mother and sister would mourn a man they loved without reservation. Mourning lovely and uncomplicated, nothing like her shame. Who, though, could predict how far the Braun pox would reach? She would begin it here. Somebody had to pave the way.

In the kitchen's bright light, Kendra sat at the table catching her breath. Emptiness clawed just beneath her surface, demanding to be sated. A last meal—Michael's parting gift. With cool, clinical detachment, she surveyed all the choices her lover had so thoughtfully supplied in these, her final hours, wondering where she should begin.

Third Dream

My sister is dead. She died of a failure of
analysis.

—E. L. Doctorow,
Book of Daniel

Thanatos Can Kill You

I GOT MY PERIOD when I was fifteen. Kendra and I got it together. Our mother was thrilled; such oddities were among the few joys of having twins, generally only an unsettling pair of allies against maternal forces. We didn't tell our father. We were embarrassed—not that he'd think it was gross but that he wouldn't care. He worked a lot that year. He seemed busy and remote: a foreign entity so much taller and stronger and more important than we that it was mildly shameful for us to force him to enter our sphere.

There are memories from that time, you understand. My teenage years are not a blank. My parents making love in their room below us; Kendra masturbating in the bed across from mine. Fear, a sharp vise tightening on my throat, trying hard to hear neither. Mornings I'd have wet the bed, and my mother would scream, then feel sorry, then threaten to make me wear a diaper, then give me something sweet to eat. At fourteen: Kendra smoking with the older dancers at Ruth Page when she began her scholarship, her hip at a jutting, insouciant angle. Sixteen: Otto strumming his guitar while I sat in his basement and tried to love him, tried to feel anything but distance when he inched my jeans down around my knees. The smell of fresh flowers in the kitchen the summer Kendra went to Europe and left me with my parents gloriously all to myself, nerves fluttering just under my skin since I too would soon leave them for the adult world of college. And Aris. Aris, the proverbial jock from a good family, a dreamer who told me about buildings that had more history than I, whose kisses and declarations gave me material to write my glamorous ballerina sister about. I'd dated him for her, the bitch. I realize that now.

I know my own life. Possibly, she was plagued by incestuous fantasies and couldn't justify them any other way. Or maybe she needed some causality as to why I was having such a rough time—I'd become a pissing, weepy, expanding mass of a girl, incapable of the closeness she and I had once shared. That differentiation was painful for me too. I never suspected, years later, that she was still searching for an explanation. But apparently she searched for meaning in the same way she did everything: danced, fought, fucked. Much, much too hard.

Shadisha confirmed the restraint fiasco. When I called Northwestern Hospital and asked to speak to her, she came to the phone asking, "Is Kendra all right?" as though it had been weeks, not years since my sister had been under her care. She remembered the wrist welts Michael Kelsey spoke of, muttered, "Night staff," as though that indeed explained everything. I was weirdly crushed that this nurse I barely knew had withheld such vital information on the day of Kendra's release, when I'd called looking for her. Only irrational feelings of betrayal prevented my asking Shadisha, whose hands had coaxed my sister from the brink of death, out on a date.

Also corroborating Michael Kelsey's story, Kendra's journals place the locus of her pain on my father and me. I remain unconvinced she'd have met the same end had she never entered into such a destructive affair. Yet the language she used to write of him is not language of victimization but of art: of ballet's rigor and dedication, pain with a payoff, surrendering her body to a choreographer in whom she had the utmost confidence to create something beautiful. Any guilt ascribed to him is rooted solely in his failure to air what he knew in time. In his not admitting what he believed happened between her and our father, she read confirmation that the truth was unutterable even by him—her life too repugnant to be spoken. Maybe she is right. If he had not succumbed to fear (or the erotic lure of an incest fantasy that'd be spoiled by articulation of ugly facts), she might be with us still. But can his responsibility truly end there?

At every turn, my sister and her lover provide a united front. When he surrendered the final journal, written entirely in the hospital, he said, "She said to give this to you only if you sought me out, if you proved a genuine desire to know the truth. For years, she judged your denial, but in the end she respected your right to forget. She didn't want you to end up like she was."

I remembered them then, that morning outside my window: her utter, trusting certainty as she'd leaned all her weight against a force she knew could absorb her. She believed I would crumble. My own weakness forced her to turn to him instead.

"For the record," he held the notebook out loosely, as though if I did not snatch it immediately, he'd let it drop to the floor, too much to carry anymore, "I told her she was wrong. Trying to protect you was her same old mistake. Your right is to know."

"Then why have you waited nearly two years to give this to me?"

His eyes darkened, inexpressive as if electricity had abruptly gone out. I saw for the first time the hardness in him, a facet besides my parents' sardonic dinner guest, my sister's grieving lover. Instantly the image of him beating her seemed not abstract or inconceivable; I backed up, shoulder blades against the door. I had been a fool to hope, even for an instant, that sleeping with him could ever be a route to understanding. He was—a fact I was proud of—beyond me.

"Because Kendra asked me to."

Her journals, you have gathered by now, were all written to me. As such, they were surprisingly coherent—even in the absence of our father's, or my, counterpoint—convincingly logical. The one glaring exception hints, ironically, at a more sinister parallel to my own fixation on our father's former mistress. That an affluent woman who worked so hard, adapted so many personae to acquire her status, should advertise her success by sending her daughter to boarding school hardly, in reality, seems suspicious. That an artist who thrived on self-invention should desire a new canvas—or simply that an only child would choose to live near her aging mother—seems no outrageous indicator of terminal illness. Leigh Kelsey swore to my mother, to me, that she was healthy. But would Kendra, the ceaseless whispering devil on my shoulder, have taken the random circumstances of her death as all the confirmation she needed—a desperate suicide?

Maybe nothing is as it seems. Here, though, is one hard fact: with Leigh gone, Kendra could have been the one to watch over Rachel. Instead she left her—just as she accused Leigh in her journals of doing—to the wolf.

You'll be glad to know my bowels are tip-top these days. If anything, I suffer from constipation—a low-fat diet can do that. The toxic diarrhea of my engagement year is a powerless memory now. I remember it hurt, but I cannot—don't wish to—feel that pain.

My father's doing peachy too. Do you still keep in touch? I guess not—nobody wants their former psychiatrist around to remind them of the time when they were nuts. Besides, it's against the rules. Patients—sorry, *clients*—aren't friends. I've come far enough to accept that you hid what you knew about my family not out of any greater affection for my father but simply out of adherence to the tools of your trade—tools, after all, crafted to protect the privacy of men. My father, like I, was not entirely human to you, but a giant brain stretched out bare, over whom you held all power. Had you chosen *not* to believe his claims of Kendra's delusions, your obligation would have been to contact the authorities, to put on record that my sister's and my safety was in danger. That choice would have played havoc in another way—imagine social services' probing!—who can say you would not have ruined our lives still? I hate you, yes, but I am no longer so naïve as to believe I'd assuredly hate you less had you chosen that other path.

I know you thought you knew me. I know you sought to heal me. But there is more to me than the boundaries of my own skin. It was her we allowed to slip through my cracks.

So what would you have me do with this phantom pain, Doctor? They say a missing limb can bug you for the rest of your life. No way to scratch the itch or salve the burn. Thanks to you, I amputated Kendra of my own free will. Being a twin is like having body parts wander off at will. Like knowing my head is lost somewhere, hoarding knowledge hot enough to kill. That my legs are spread somewhere, ass in the air somewhere, throat raw somewhere, so each time I walk down a street dressed in her skin, my soul is subject to indignities I cannot see.

After reading so much dreary psychoanalysis for school, I have taken up new interests in my free time. Guitarist (who likes me better now that we can compare notes on girls) lent me a book on quantum physics because he thought, as a twin, I might be into Schroedinger's Cat. Do you know the thought experiment? A cat is put in a closed box in which there is a fifty percent chance of it being gassed to death within an hour. At the end of the hour, the scientist goes to open the box to see if the cat's still alive. But before he opens the box, since he can't know if the cat is living or dead, what we think of as one truth is fragmented into two parallel realities: one with a live cat happy to see the lid flipped back, the other with a dead, poisoned kitty that will prompt animal rights activists to march. Both exist simultaneously—only knowledge can determine one outcome over another. Without knowledge, both possibilities are true. The trick is, the source of knowledge must be absolute. If the observer is unreliable, even observation can't determine certainty, and ambiguity reigns.

The implications for twins are endless. We are, after all, already an everyday enactment of parallel realities— contradictory truths. But even one body can serve as the closed box of Schroedinger. Try this thought experiment: My sister may or may not have been raped by our father. If she was, she may or may not have HIV. If she has never been tested, never been observed, perhaps she is both sick and well simultaneously. If I am the observer, but can no longer flip back the lid of my own skin to see her, perhaps she is both living and dead at once. If she is a reliable observer, perhaps I was raped at age thirteen by a drunken man meant to love me—perhaps my life was predetermined by a truth only *she* could see. Perhaps she was a savior, a martyr who offered her own body on the block for mine. If, on the other hand, she is an unreliable observer, perhaps she left me with false nightmares, with a craving for bogus flashbacks that would only shatter me, with an empty void in lieu of repressed memories, and a father I'm ashamed to love but will never confront. Without observing her, all truths exist simultaneously in my body and always will. Oh, but I forgot to mention: the longer the box remains unopened, the more certain it becomes that the cat inside is dead. It has been more than two years since I saw my sister alive within the cells we share. As proof of her continued breath, I have only mine, only the fading belief that were she to succumb to blackness, I also would fall in the same instant to meet her there. (But that's another thought experiment entirely: see Einstein.)

She is gone. I weave our story, despite uncertainties. I refuse to translate her into the language of our father. Neither will I leave my sister a buried secret of scarred stomach, welted wrists, bruised ass. I will not see her slip into the reductive crack of history, into that mass, unknown-woman's grave. I came to you wrapped in the fancy paper of individuality; I came with shit and a shitty engagement and a self-image in the toilet and I called it all my own. I tossed projections off your blank-slate body, tried to make you into the mother/lover/ sister I lacked. And you. You held your silence. Though you are a woman, you did not tell me the one thing that could have offered what I needed most: my sister back. You chose one truth: his. I offer instead the messy parallel reality in which we dwell, the never-ending phantom pain of my missing limb. Our words. This.

And one final memory, for posterity. It was I, that winter we were seventeen. Motive I can no longer access, only my action: foggy, covert. I, her silent saboteur as she propped combat boots, awaited the consequences of her spurned proposition, her forever irrevocable mistake.

I gave him the key.

Gina Frangello is the Executive Editor of the award-winning literary magazine *Other Voices* and its new fiction imprint *OV Books*. Her short fiction has been published in many literary journals, including *Swink, Story Quarterly, Prairie Schooner, two girls review, Blithe House Quarterly* and *Fish Stories*. She guest-edited the anthology *Falling Backwards: Stories of Fathers and Daughters* (Hourglass Books) and has been a freelance journalist for the *Chicago Tribune* and the *Chicago Reader*. A graduate of the Program for Writers at the University of Illinois-Chicago, she has taught literature and creative writing at several Chicago universities and is the recipient of an Illinois Arts Council literary award and individual fellowship. She lives with her husband and their twin daughters.

Printed in the United States
57281LVS00002B/43-69